Mireille

Mireille

MOLLY COCHRAN

LAKE UNION
PUBLISHING

Published by Lake Union Publishing, Seattle

www.apub.com

Amazon, the Amazon logo, and Lake Union Publishing are trademarks of Amazon.com, Inc., or its affiliates.

ISBN-13: 9781477828571
ISBN-10: 1477828575

Cover design by Paul Barrett

Library of Congress Control Number: 2014919198

Printed in the United States of America

For Devin, as ever

Prologue

1961

The fans were moaning with disappointment even before Oliver Jordan stepped out of the limousine. They had come to see a star, not a producer. They had come to watch Mireille win the Oscar. They had come to show her their love.

And the bitch was ruining everything.

Jordan walked past the crowd without a glance, past the dozens of long-haired platinum-blonde women and the ever-faithful knot of handsome young men who had adopted Mireille as their goddess, between the rows of overly cultivated hibiscus that lined the VIP walkway into the Santa Monica Civic Auditorium.

At least the columnists weren't lurking, he thought with some relief. It was almost eight o'clock. Most of the journalists had gone into the theater long ago to pick up their quota of lies from the stars who insisted, if they didn't expect to win, that an Academy Award was of no importance to them in their personal quests for artistic integrity.

Nevertheless, a few flashbulbs popped in Jordan's direction. The producer of *Josephine* was worth a picture or two in the trade publications, especially since the movie was expected to make a sweep of the awards that evening. But the fans hadn't waited outside for hours to catch a glimpse of him.

"Where's Mireille?" someone shouted. Despite his frustration and annoyance, Jordan felt some small satisfaction at finally not hearing the name mangled by the masses. It had taken a colossal public relations effort, he remembered, to get Americans to pronounce it Ma-*ray*—not correct, but at least passable. It had occurred to him more than once that he should have changed it at the beginning of her career, back when he was inventing her, but that was all water under the bridge now.

Just as Jordan had almost cleared the obstacle course of Mireille's disheartened following, the person he wanted to see least of all God's creatures on earth stepped away from the crowd and onto the red-carpeted entranceway, touching a delicate hand to the brim of an outrageous orchid-sprouting hat. With her unerring sense of impending catastrophe, Hedda Hopper had waited for him.

"Oliver, dear," she gushed, seizing his arm. "You seem to be all by yourself tonight."

"Where's Ma-*ray*?" one of the platinum blondes demanded in a shriek.

Hedda laughed like a tinkling little bell. "Now, that does seem to be the question around these parts." She ground to a halt, braking Jordan with her. "Oliver, a lot of people in Hollywood think Mireille is going to win another Oscar for her stunning performance in *Josephine*."

Amazing, Jordan thought, how loud Hedda could be when she wanted people to hear her. At the moment, she was playing the crowd. They burst into cheers, as if on cue.

Jordan forced himself to acknowledge them, then gave Hedda a private and deadly look.

It didn't affect her in the least. "But the ceremonies are about to begin," she said, all wide-eyed innocence, "and we haven't seen a sign of the most beautiful woman in the world. As the lucky man who discovered Mireille, can you tell us where she is?"

Jordan made a mechanical motion with his lips that resembled a smile. "It's a woman's prerogative to be late," he said, moving inexorably away from the columnist.

"But wasn't she supposed to come with you?" Hedda asked in a lilting voice that carried to the suburbs as she followed him doggedly to the entrance. "Could there be some truth to the rumor about a split between Henry Higgins and his Eliza? Is that why Mireille's staying away?" She smiled sweetly.

Jordan resisted the impulse to strangle her. "All right," he said with a sigh. Hedda poised her pencil over her pad. "The truth is, Mireille came down with some sort of stomach virus this afternoon. She's very sick, and her doctor has told her to stay in bed." Hedda stopped writing. Her eyes traveled up to his own with murderous coldness. "But if I know Mireille," he went on, "she'll make every effort not to disappoint all the wonderful people who are standing behind her on this thrilling occasion." He gave a little wave to the fans.

Tight-lipped, Hedda leaned toward him. "Do you expect anyone to believe that crap?" she whispered.

He kissed her cheek. "You look lovely, darling," he said, and went inside.

The lobby was nearly empty. One of the few individuals remaining was Jordan's assistant, Adam Wells, who was shouting into a telephone along the far wall. Jordan strode over to him just as Wells slammed down the receiver.

"Did you find her?"

The young man shook his head. "I've tried everywhere. She's just disappeared."

"Don't be an ass," Jordan said. "She hasn't just *disappeared*."

Wells's eyes bulged with anger. "Look, Oliver, I've been searching for her for five hours. If you think you could do better—"

There was applause from inside the theater. "Christ," Jordan said. "I've got to go in. Wait here. If she comes, bring her inside."

"How long should I wait?" Wells pouted.

"All goddamned night, if you have to!" Jordan snatched a program from a smiling blonde usherette and followed her to his seat near the stage.

"I hope you win, Mr. Jordan," she whispered, brushing her ample bosom against his arm. "Your films always have such wonderful parts for women."

He glanced back at her. She had too many teeth, but she looked as if she'd be good in bed. When she stopped at the aisle seats reserved for Jordan and Mireille, he slipped his card into her hand, and she made him a promise with her eyes.

Loose-limbed and salty, he thought. Then he saw Otto Preminger glaring at him across the empty seat between them, and all thought of the toothy usherette evaporated. Jordan managed a weak smile. Preminger turned his noble bald head away in disdain.

It had been Preminger who made the now-famous statement that Oliver Jordan was too handsome to need any scruples. Even though that had clearly been a case of sour grapes—Jordan had refused to let Mireille work for Preminger—the phrase had caught on. "Too handsome for scruples" had become a commonplace expression, just as a phrase Mireille had blurted out while accepting her first Oscar had swept the country five years before.

Stumbling in her still-broken English, she had told the Academy that they had touched her with their hearts. It had made no sense, but the expression became a catchphrase for songwriters, greeting card companies, florists, and everyone else who made their living selling romance.

Mireille . . .

Jordan looked at the empty seat beside him. *The slut.* An actress did not snub the Academy Awards, not when she was sure to win. If she didn't show up tonight, she would never even be considered for another Oscar. Not unless Jordan could somehow stem the tide of bad publicity that was bound to follow a blatant no-show.

His brain was already gearing up for damage control. It could be done. He drummed on the arm of his chair, thinking. Mireille would have to stay in a hospital for at least a month to give credence to the too-sick-to-attend story he'd given Hedda. Then a lot of publicity, charitable stuff. He'd get some disease foundation or other to name Mireille as chairwoman. Adam Wells could research which foundation would elicit the most sympathy from the public. His PR staff would see to it that her name was on the wire services at least once a week.

Dimly he heard the announcement of each award and the endlessly thankful acceptance speeches. *Josephine* for best sound direction. *Josephine* for best cinematography. Each time the name of his picture was announced as winner, Jordan smiled graciously for the benefit of the television cameras and the celebrities seated near him.

The success of *Josephine* was enough to keep Jordan and his production company, Continental Studios, afloat for another year, but Jordan had to look beyond that. Television had already destroyed the big studios; if it hadn't, Jordan would never have been hailed as a genius for his revolutionary one-star, one-picture policy. Among the Hollywood hierarchy, Oliver Jordan was king.

But how long would that last without Mireille?

She was more than a movie star. Monroe was a movie star. Taylor. Gardner. Loren. But Mireille possessed something—an intangible quality that smoldered just beneath her flawless surface—that even those world-famous beauties didn't have. After only five films, the phenomenon known by only one name had become a legend.

Hedda Hopper was the first to call her "the most beautiful woman in the world." The phrase was as overused in Hollywood as most of the women it referred to, but in Mireille's case it was probably true. The first time Jordan saw her, he had been struck dumb by the sheer glory of those green eyes so full of love and hurt, the swan's neck, the white-gold hair, the ramrod-straight spine that spoke of boarding schools and debutante balls.

The press said she was a descendant of the Bourbon kings; an expert horsewoman; an adventurer who had hunted big game in Africa; the secret lover of a European prince. They were wrong, of course. The stories about Mireille's background had been carefully fabricated, piece by piece. Oliver Jordan was a master. He had created Mireille from the whole cloth.

And she'd wanted it that way. Mireille never talked about her real past. She guarded it as if it were Pandora's box, filled with demons that would destroy her if she exposed them to the light. Even Oliver Jordan didn't know all her secrets.

But he knew enough.

A hand on his shoulder startled Jordan back to the endless awards ceremony. It was John Wayne, smiling and giving him the thumbs-up sign as the actor on stage read the nominations for best actress. Jordan clenched his teeth, trying not to think about the empty seat next to him.

If Mireille left him, there would be no more Continental Studios. Jordan had earned his reputation from her stardom. Yet she *had* left him; he was certain of that. She had told him that very afternoon that she would never sign another contract with him, and then she had run—literally run—away from him.

No, that sequence wasn't quite right. She had refused to sign, and she had run, but something had happened between those two events. It had been something to do with the new painting hanging in his office, although for the life of him he couldn't imagine what about it had set Mireille off. She had gone crazy when she saw it.

The thing was perfectly wretched from a technical point of view, but he thought that she would nevertheless be pleased with it, since she was its subject and she looked stunning. Still, for whatever reason, Mireille had bolted.

But he would get her back. Not even Mireille herself understood how well he knew her. He possessed the key to Pandora's box. If he opened it, the demons inside would destroy more than Mireille. Much more.

"The winner is Mireille, for *Josephine!*" the presenter shouted exultantly. There was wild applause as Jordan stood up. "Accepting for Mireille is the executive producer of *Josephine*, Mr. Oliver Jordan."

He walked, smiling, toward the stage. Mireille would come back. He was sure of it.

Because Oliver Jordan always got what he wanted.

BOOK I

Paris

1945–1950

Chapter One

It was spring, and the Germans were singing. They sang every evening in the tavern next to the old hotel they had commandeered as their headquarters, filling the cobblestone streets of Champs de Blé with their Nazi marching music.

To an outsider they would have seemed incongruous there, black-jacketed soldiers goose-stepping past the shrine of the Virgin Mary in the village square, or swooping into the tavern like a flock of crows, but the French villagers were used to them. Whenever the Nazis appeared, the locals vanished. Outside the tavern was a row of military motorcycles. Beyond them, the streets were empty.

On the other side of the square, in the big house that had once belonged to her father, Mireille Orlande de Jouarre knelt on the plank floor of the kitchen with a scrub brush and a bucket of water. Through the open window wafted the sweet fragrance of the flower fields.

Champs de Blé, like the nearby city of Grasse, existed by providing flowers for the perfume industry. In the days before the first spring harvest, the scent of jasmine and lavender infused the air with an almost mystical sweetness.

Mireille closed her eyes, the scrub brush poised and dripping above the wood floor. The scent brought back her childhood, when life was warm and safe and full of wonder. She remembered the dashing legionnaire who was her father, showering her with beads from Morocco or sweets from Tunisia while telling her stories of the exotic far-off lands he'd visited; and she remembered her mother, beautifully elegant even in her threadbare clothes from before the war, comforting her gangling towheaded daughter after a merciless teasing.

"*Chouchou*, you will be a lovely woman one day," she said in her clear, bell-like voice. "To be tall is a gift, not a curse."

"But the other girls make fun of me," Mireille wailed. "I'm so tall and skinny, and my hair's so white." She hung her head. "They call me 'Dandelion.'"

"Shhh." She dried the child's tear-stained face and stroked her long blonde hair. "Only a fool would listen to the opinion of a gaggle of schoolgirls. Are you a fool?"

Mireille shook her head emphatically.

"Then you are not a dandelion, either."

She remembered her mother's laughter. The jasmine had been in bloom then, too, that day when she was eleven years old.

That had been only five years before. *Such long years,* Mireille thought. She felt the cold, dirty water from the scrub brush drip between her fingers.

So much had happened in those five years. Since the German soldiers began to sing their songs in the tavern across from the statue of the Virgin, Mireille's life had changed irrevocably. Everything of any importance to her had vanished somewhere in the rhythm of that music.

First, her mother, who had never possessed a hardy constitution, simply wasted away under the yoke of the Nazi occupation. After she died, Mireille's father remarried quickly in order to provide a new mother for his only child. Scheduled to rejoin his regiment within a week, Capitaine de Jouarre did not have time to be overly particular about his bride-to-be, and rashly chose a shrewish, vulgar woman whose greatest skill lay in her ability to lie convincingly. Three months after he left, the capitaine was killed in action. Mireille's stepmother, Giselle, had taken other men to her bed almost as soon as she heard the news. Her favorite seemed to be old Valois, the tavern owner. He was by far the ugliest of her lovers, but Giselle's practical-minded ambition was not for romance. Armand Valois, to her reckoning, seemed to be the only man in Champs de Blé who knew on which side his bread was buttered.

He supplied liquor by the case to the German officers, often going to great lengths to acquire products from their native land. He also brought them women when requested and provided the use of the tavern's back room for their pleasure, from which he earned a good profit. Sometimes, when the girls were unwilling or the soldiers too demanding, the whole village could hear the screams behind the singing in the tavern, but no one spoke of them.

Valois grew rich, and Giselle wasted no time. She married the Nazi collaborator as soon as she had officially inherited Capitaine de Jouarre's estate, and Valois moved from his rooms above the tavern into the large old house on the town square. It was there that he began to notice Mireille.

The girl had fulfilled her mother's prophecy. Mireille grew quickly into a beauty. Her platinum hair, once her bane, now spilled over her shoulders in a glowing cascade. Her bottle-green eyes, always startling, now glowed with a soft fire against her white skin. By thirteen, her breasts had begun to bud; at fourteen, her lanky five-foot-ten-inch stick figure had filled out with sensuous curves. Even in her prim blue school uniform, it was apparent that Mireille de Jouarre was already a woman.

She first noticed the change in the way Valois looked at her during an ordinary dinner at home. As usual, he had been drinking heavily, but this evening he was staring at her with the vacant curiosity of a beast, his mouth slack as he lazily chewed a piece of bread. Mireille lowered her eyes and tried to slink as far beneath the table as possible, but Valois only continued to stare.

"What are you gawking at?" Giselle shrilled, slapping his hand with the back of her fork.

He swatted her away like a fly. "Who are you fucking?" he blurted at Mireille. A soggy crumb spewed out of his mouth and plastered itself on his chin. "I asked you a question, girl."

Giselle laughed nervously. Her husband rose. He didn't bother to pull his chair away from the table, and the dishes clattered. Wine spilled onto the linen cloth.

Mireille's fingers gripped the table edge until they turned white. She felt her breath coming in short, hissing bursts. Inside her school uniform, her new breasts trembled and her legs began to twitch in fear.

"Don't put on your haughty airs with me," Valois roared.

"Armand, please," Giselle pleaded. "She's only a child."

He ignored her, shouting directly at Mireille. "It's that gypsy who hangs around here, isn't it?"

"Don't be silly," Giselle piped. "Stefan helps with the errands. He's been working here for years."

Valois's head swiveled to face his wife in accusation.

"Besides," Giselle went on, her voice beginning to crack, "he's a cripple."

"I'm talking to her, not you," Valois shouted. He hoisted the wine bottle to his lips and drained its contents. "A cripple," he muttered. "I'll bet he's not a cripple where it counts."

"Armand—"

"Shut up, slut!" He swung the bottle at her.

Giselle gave a little gasp of indignation and ran upstairs. Valois followed her, staggering and cursing. There were shouts, a hard crack or two, a few loud sobs, and then the rhythmic creaking of bedsprings and Giselle's moans of pleasure from behind the open bedroom door.

Mireille sighed with relief. Valois had been distracted, and he would forget the incident by tomorrow. But how long would it take for him to look at his stepdaughter that way again, dim and glassy-eyed, like an animal smelling sex?

Apparently, Giselle shared her worry. The next day when Mireille returned from school, her stepmother was waiting for her with a pair of scissors.

"Sit down," she ordered.

Before Mireille could protest, Giselle was hacking off her hair near the roots. "Giselle," she squealed. "Please . . ."

"I'll not have you flaunting yourself in front of my husband!" She yanked at the blonde tresses, attacking them with the scissors. "Things are going to be different from now on."

When she was done, she handed the girl a broom. "Here. Your parents may have turned you into a spoiled, lazy girl, but I'll put you right." She stormed upstairs, then came down a few minutes later with Mireille's old party dresses draped over her arm. "It's no wonder men look at you," she grumbled. "Clothes like a duchess. Take that off."

Mireille looked down at her school uniform.

"Now." Giselle wiggled her fingers impatiently.

"But what will I wear to school?" Mireille asked.

"You won't be going to school anymore. Girls don't need it. I never went a day in my life, myself," she said proudly as she pulled a shapeless black rag from a hook behind the kitchen door. "Put this on."

Then she stepped outside with Mireille's lace and silk dresses, her blouses of hand-stitched linen, the flowing robes her father had brought her from the corners of the world, and set fire to them in the backyard.

When she came inside, clapping the soot off her hands, she stopped in the doorway to look the girl over. The old black dress hung on Mireille's shoulders like a shroud, and smelled of someone else's sweat.

"That's better," Giselle snapped, and turned away. "By the way, you won't be having dinner with us anymore, either."

Stefan, the gypsy errand boy, was dismissed, and seemed to disappear entirely from Champs de Blé. After two years, he still hadn't returned.

Nothing else had changed much, either. Mireille's hair had grown in; she wore it pulled back like a widow's. She was thinner than she had been. And the black dress was two years older.

Now the Nazis' singing in the tavern across the way grew louder. "Stop it!" she shouted, dropping her scrub brush. She clapped her hands over her ears. Dirty water ran down her face.

But she could still hear the music.

Scrambling to her feet, she slammed the window closed with a crash. As she did, her hand brushed against a water glass filled with lavender. It went flying above the sink, exploded on the thin porcelain edge, and fell in a shower of glass at her feet.

"Oh, *merde*," she groaned, slapping the edge of the sink.

She felt the pain a moment later, when she saw the gush of blood. A triangular wedge of glass more than two inches wide was sticking out of her palm.

She removed the glass shard and ran her hand under the faucet, flooding the basin with blood. The towel she used to staunch the flow soaked through within seconds. Mireille was no stranger to household injuries and knew the cut was not serious, but she needed more than a towel for the bleeding.

Fortunately, Valois was well stocked with German military field bandages, huge antiseptic pads the size and shape of chalkboard erasers. Clutching the blood-soaked towel, Mireille ran to the bathroom up the stairs and tied on one of the bandages. She was pulling the knot taut with her teeth when she caught a glimpse of herself in the mirror.

She stared at her reflection for a moment, as if she'd forgotten what her own face looked like. Dirt ran in streaks down her cheeks. The hollows beneath her eyes were deep and purple-tinged. Greasy strands of white hair spilled out from under the rag she wore on her head.

"What have they done to me?" she whispered. Her vision blurred with tears.

She was sixteen years old.

After she stopped the bleeding in her palm, she headed back to the kitchen to clean up the broken glass. On the way, she stopped in her bedroom for a glove that might protect her injured hand while she finished her chores.

She didn't remember where she'd put them, the thin cotton gloves that she'd worn to church back when Giselle had permitted Mireille to attend. Now, of course, it wouldn't do for the girl to be seen in her threadbare black dress, her one garment.

She looked everywhere for the gloves without success but found, at the back of the bottom bureau drawer, a small silver-framed photograph of herself as a baby with her parents. Her father was in uniform, her mother dressed in rustling stiff taffeta and wearing the set of glittering diamonds that had been passed down through her family for three hundred years.

Giselle wears those diamonds now, she thought. *Only they don't look like diamonds anymore.*

Mireille had kept the picture hidden from Giselle and Valois. It was the last shred of her old self that she had left. She traced the outlines of the two beloved faces with her finger, as if the contact could somehow pass through time and death and bring them back.

Pressing the photograph to her chest, Mireille crawled to her narrow bed and wept for the lost years.

Footsteps woke her. It was full dark outside, starless and moonless. The singing from the tavern had stopped.

Mireille sat up abruptly in bed. The framed photograph of her parents clattered onto the floor.

Armand Valois picked it up and studied it.

He was drunk. He weaved unsteadily, his rank breath filling the room. "Kitchen's a bloody mess."

Mireille straightened her dress hurriedly and stood up. "I'll tend to it."

Without looking at her, he shoved her back onto the bed. "You're not going anywhere."

"Giselle?" She had meant to cry for help, but her voice came out no louder than a squeak.

Valois looked at her then and smiled, a gap-toothed grin that made her shiver. "She's out." He dropped the photograph. His heel broke the glass on his way toward Mireille.

"Get away . . . Get away from me," she said, feeling the heat rising in her cheeks.

"Don't be afraid, princess." Spittle sprayed from between the brown stubs of his teeth. "I won't make you do anything you haven't done plenty of times before."

"Please . . ." She heard the fear in her voice. "Let me get you some dinner."

"I've been watching you grow up, blondie."

"Some coffee . . ."

"Giselle likes to keep you ugly. But you're not ugly, are you?" He reached for the tattered scarf around her head. His odor was even stronger now. "Not with your clothes off." He grabbed the front of her dress.

Panicking, she elbowed the side of his head and slid off the bed. Valois bellowed and came lurching after her, but he was too drunk to maintain his balance. He thudded in a heap on the far side of the room.

Mireille ran for the doorway and flew down the stairs to the front door. *God, get me out of here,* she prayed fervently as she pulled at the old-fashioned handle.

It wouldn't give. She tried again, propping her foot against the door frame, until she heard Valois's laughter from the top of the stairs.

A big iron key dangled from his thumb. "Ready for Daddy?" he asked, grinning.

She sprinted for the back door. Behind her, Valois was thundering down the stairs, three at a time.

Please fall, she begged silently as she threw herself into the now-darkened kitchen and felt the first stab of pain on her bare feet.

She had forgotten about the broken glass. With a shriek, she fell backward on top of it with the full force of her body. She heard it crack against the muscles of her back, felt the sharp slivers pierce her arms and legs. Then the light came on in a blinding flash, and Valois stood over her, panting with the exertion of the chase.

"I'm hurt," she said, trying to get upright.

Valois bent down, extending both arms toward her. But when she reached for them, he clasped his hands tight around her wrists and forced her down again onto the broken glass. She screamed.

She kept screaming as he pulled up her dress roughly, then unbuttoned his filthy trousers. She screamed until Valois drew back his fleshy hand and slapped her across her mouth, again and again, until she could taste her own blood.

"Snotty bitch," he grunted. "I'll show you what I think of you and your high-handed ways!" Using the hand he'd struck her with, he spread her legs.

In that same moment, seized with fear, Mireille spotted a triangular wedge of glass twinkling on the edge of the sink above her. It was the same piece that she had cut her hand on earlier. Dried blood still darkened the tip.

Quickly, as Valois tried to lower himself onto her, she thrust herself upward. The big military bandage on her hand was bulky, and she had to take care not to knock the glimmering shard off its narrow perch, but Mireille somehow managed to snatch the glass wedge with her fingertips and anchor the broad side into the thick bandage.

Now, she told herself. *Don't think about it. Do it now.*

While Valois struggled to enter her, she lowered the shard to the level of his jaw, then jammed it up into his throat.

His eyes popped open in surprise. A hiss escaped from his neck, while his tongue seemed to grow inside his mouth. His big hands raised up into the air and hesitated, trembling, for a moment above Mireille. He still had the strength, she knew, to kill her. And he would if he were given the chance.

Mireille squeezed her eyes shut and, with a sob, forced the glass across the width of Valois's throat. He convulsed. A spray of red shot into her face.

Choking, tasting his salty, warm blood mixed with her own, she rolled his lifeless body off her, then stood up slowly, shaking with cold terror.

She backed up through the scattered broken glass to the door and opened it. Outside, the lavender fields were soughing in the darkness. Their scent was thick and sweet.

Dreamily, feeling as if she were walking through molasses, Mireille noticed that she was still clutching the piece of broken glass she had used to kill her stepfather. With an effort she opened her hand, and it tumbled to the floor.

"God help me," she whispered, and went out.

Chapter Two

Still floating in the dreamlike emptiness of shock, devoid of emotion or pain, Mireille walked until the rain started. She moved neither quickly nor slowly, and without direction. Only when the first cold drops washed over her face did she have any sense of where she had been. Through the fields, past the lake on the far side of the village, through a section of forest, into the foothills near the stone mountains . . . She'd gone miles.

Now she was climbing up an outcropping of limestone in a place far removed from any town. She could smell lavender somewhere in the distance. The night was quiet except for the gentle rustling of the summer rain.

No music. Exhausted, Mireille closed her eyes and listened. *No Nazi music.*

She collapsed.

When she came to, her entire body was throbbing with pain from the pieces of broken glass still embedded in her back and legs, but it was the searing, burning agony of the pain in her bare feet that was unbearable. The soles felt as if they had been pierced by spears that extended up to her knees.

Even though her eyes had grown accustomed to the darkness, Mireille had to rely on her sense of touch to locate the spiky ends of glass. There weren't many; most of the splinters had been driven deep into her flesh. Those she did manage to dig out shot arrows of pain with every movement and sliced the fingertips protruding from the sodden bandage on her hand.

The rain was coming down harder now. She shivered despite the warmth of the evening. Her face was hot with fever. She was lost, and there was nowhere to go.

It occurred to her that she might have been walking in an enormous circle. What if the lavender she smelled was part of Monsieur Forleau's lands? If it was, then the foothills she'd been traversing would eventually bring her to Forleau's windmill, and past that would be a view of the back of the tavern, and the sounds of women screaming to the background music of German songs . . .

She was gasping for breath. *No, no,* she reassured herself. The hills were wrong. If she were near the windmill, the hills would have been on the other side of her.

She had to keep moving. The sky was already beginning to take on the deep-blue hue that signaled the last hours before dawn. Not that she had any hope of escaping. It was inevitable that she would be caught. If the civil authorities captured her, she would be sent to prison, and perhaps executed.

That would be the easiest fate she could expect.

Another possibility was more likely. Her stepmother would surely be home by now, but she wouldn't bother with the police. Giselle knew that she and Valois were hated in Champs de Blé, but the Germans were their friends. The Germans would listen to her. The Germans would find Valois's killer. And when they did, Mireille knew, the pain she was feeling now would seem like a slap on the wrist.

And so she forced herself to walk, one agonizing step after another, away from the home she knew she would never see again.

Ahead, she could make out the silhouette of a scraggly scrub pine. At least she would be out of the rain there. She could think, and decide which direction to take.

Suddenly, she lifted her head, listening. In the distance she heard the buzz of motorcycles.

She looked around frantically. Not more than fifty yards away was a road. *A road,* she thought, groaning. She had been wandering for hours within a stone's throw of it.

The sound was moving nearer.

Motorcycles. Only German soldiers had the fuel to ride the roads after dark. Had they found Valois already? She lay flat in the tall, wet grass, trying to control the shaking of her limbs, not daring to open her eyes as they approached.

The sound grew louder, unbearably loud, filling the night with noise. Then, out of nowhere, there was an explosion so powerful that Mireille felt the earth shake beneath her. On the horizon, a huge corona of yellow flame shot skyward.

One of the motorcycles skidded off the road. Its rider jumped clear before the bike toppled onto its side, its rear wheel spinning only a short distance from Mireille's face.

The other motorcyclist stopped. *"Das Hauptquartier ist getroffen worden!"* he shouted, pointing toward the blazing sky.

Rubbing his leg, the fallen man stood up and waved his partner on. *"Geht aus! Jetzt!"* he called. *"Ich hole dich wieder ein."*

He limped to his bike. He was close enough to have spotted Mireille, but his attention was riveted to the fire in the distance as he righted the machine and mounted it. For a moment his silhouette wavered against the bright glow of the flames. Then he was gone.

Mireille stood up shakily, watching the eerie light in the distance. Champs de Blé was on fire, she realized with astonishment.

The soldier had said *Hauptquartier,* "headquarters." The Nazis had been using the Bellefleur Hotel as their command post in the area. It must have been the Bellefleur that had blown into the sky in a ball of flame.

How had that happened? There had been no air raid, no Allied planes overhead. Just an explosion.

As the rain dimmed the color of the fire, Mireille wondered if the rest of Champs de Blé were gone as well. Her house . . . Giselle's house.

She turned away from it and walked slowly toward the big tree in the field. Fire or not, she would never go back.

Above, the first gray streaks of dawn were appearing in the sky. The fire behind her would be extinguished by the rain, leaving a low pall of smoke in its wake. Slowed by the excruciating pain in her feet, Mireille finally fell on her hands and knees, unable to walk any farther.

The big tree that had appeared to be nearby in the darkness now seemed a hundred miles away. But dawn was coming, and even with the aftermath of the explosion to distract the Germans, there was no time to lose. The soldiers would soon be looking for her.

Struggling for every inch of ground she covered, Mireille crawled through the pelting rain toward the black shadow of the tree. Her dress, soaked and already in rags, tore at the waist. Her knees, practically the only part of her body that had been unhurt, were now as bruised and cut, from the small stones on the ground, as the rest of her.

At last she reached the tree and the small shelter of its leaves. She lay flat on her stomach beneath it, but she still dared not rest. Where would she go now? How much farther could she crawl? How much longer would she live? Despair settled over her like a net, heavy and immobilizing. She was too exhausted to move anymore. She laid her head on the wet ground, hearing the drone of the rain and smelling the scent of far-off lavender like a false promise.

She had almost fallen asleep when she heard a swishing in the grass. It was a new sound, arrhythmic but steady.

Someone was moving toward her.

Mireille gasped, her bowels quaking. Against the cobalt sky she could see the faceless dark figure of a man moving past the tree. He hadn't noticed her. His steps were awkward but quick, the gait of someone accustomed to walking with a limp. Something swung from his shoulder.

A fishing pole? It was possible. Just some old man out before dawn to try his luck at the lake, perhaps. Someone who might never notice her here, stretched out flat in the dark beneath the tree in the rain. She would lie still; she would force her whistling breath into silence.

Suddenly, as if sensing her fear, the man stopped. Now Mireille saw clearly what he carried over his shoulder: not a fishing pole, but a rifle. Smoothly, he snapped the butt into position under his armpit.

"No!" Mireille cried out involuntarily, drawing her knees in toward her chest while she waited for the bullet.

But there was no report from the rifle.

Why didn't he shoot? She peered up over her arms. Maybe he wasn't looking for her. Maybe he was a poacher who had thought she was a deer or a raccoon before he heard her.

The rifle lowered. The man walked silently forward.

And maybe he's just like Valois.

She scrambled to her feet and ran, careening crazily over the stones in the hilly meadow. The man followed, gaining on her quickly. Mireille could hear his strange, uneven footfalls and the slap of the rifle on his back.

The pain of the run made her nauseous, but she pistoned her legs, willing herself not to give in, moving toward the mountains even though she knew she would never reach them.

This time he'll have to kill me first.

He was close enough that Mireille could hear the whoosh of his breath and the thump of his lame leg behind her.

"Shoot me!" she screamed. "Kill me now, you bastard, because you won't have me any other way!"

Then something grabbed at her waist and she was yanked backward, skidding and kicking, arms flailing, sobbing, damning her captor to hell.

"Hold it," the man said. His voice was young.

She twisted far enough around in his grasp to stab blindly at his face with her fingers, but didn't take into account the thick bandage wrapped around her hand. It bounced off his nose like a fluffy ball, and he grabbed it.

"Will you stop, you wildcat?" he said, laughing. "I'm not going to hurt you."

She blinked, forcing out the tears that were blurring her vision. She knew him. "Oh God." It was Stefan.

He stared back at her for a moment. Then a smile of recognition spread across his dark, handsome features. "Is that you, Dandelion?" He touched her hair, straggly and wet. "What's happened to you?"

She wanted to speak, to tell him everything, but all she could do was hang onto his neck and sob into the sweet warmth of her old friend's chest.

"Relax," he said quietly. He lifted her chin. "Whatever it is, I'll help you, okay?"

Mireille nodded. "Th-thank you," she managed.

"I've got a place not far from here."

He felt her tense in his arms. "In town?" she asked with alarm. "Or near a . . . a camp?"

Stefan smiled. "Neither. It's all by itself. Mireille, are you running away?"

She stared at the ground.

"That's all right," he said. "You don't have to tell me. Let's go." He set her down.

Mireille hobbled a few steps, then fell with a cry of pain.

Stefan knelt down beside her. "What's the matter?"

She showed him her feet. They were swollen to twice their normal size. Dirt embedded in the deep cuts gave the soles the appearance of a crazy quilt.

"Mother of God," he said. "What happened?"

"Glass," was all she said.

"How long have you been walking?"

"I don't know. From the house." She clutched his shoulder. "Stefan, the village. There was an explosion—"

"Hush. We'll talk later." He touched one of her feet. She winced. "This doesn't look good," he said. "You'll be lucky if these cuts aren't already infected. I'll get you to a doctor."

"No doctor!"

He stared at her wild eyes, her expression of panic.

"No doctor," she repeated. "Please."

"All right," Stefan said.

She tried to stand, but Stefan scooped her up in his arms. "You've walked far enough, little Dandelion," he said, and carried her through the rain toward the lavender-scented hills.

His curly black hair smelled of flowers, and his arms were strong. The rocking motion of Stefan's limping walk made Mireille feel like a baby in a cradle. *Yes, that's it,* she thought drowsily. *Like a baby.* For the first time since the lost years of her childhood, she felt safe.

Chapter Three

Toward dawn they reached Stefan's house, an abandoned shack near the ruins of a farm. The farmhouse and barn had burned long ago. Among the charred pieces of wood and stone, only the dilapidated outbuilding where Stefan lived remained standing. It was no more than a makeshift structure with missing slats that let in daylight and rain, but it was clean and Stefan had furnished it with two old chairs, a cot for sleeping, and a small woodstove that made the place livable.

"How long have you been here?" Mireille asked while Stefan brought a basin of heated water.

"A few months." He smiled. "Gypsies never stay in one place very long." He set her feet in the basin. Thin streams of blood snaked out into the warm water.

"Are you really a gypsy, Stefan?"

He shook his head. "Not much of one. My mother was supposed to have gypsy blood, but I never knew her. To be honest, I think I got most of my tramp ways from my French father, but that doesn't make nearly such good gossip. Here, let me take a look."

He frowned as he examined the cuts on the soles of her feet. "These are bad," he said. "It's going to hurt to take out the glass."

She shrugged.

"You're a good actress." He took a small metal box from behind the stove. Inside were bandages, antiseptic, and an assortment of surgical instruments. "Now, you don't have to be brave for me. Yell bloody murder if you feel like it." He held her foot tightly and dug at the first shard with a long razor-thin pair of tweezers.

Mireille blanched. "It's like a hospital here," she said, forcing her words against the pain. "Do you have a lot of accidents or something?"

"Hold still." He pulled out an inch-long sliver.

Blood poured out of the wound. He went to work immediately on another. "No, not too many accidents. But when they happen, they can be pretty bad. That's why I've got a good first-aid kit." He pulled out another piece of glass, then gently touched her hand, bone white from gripping the wooden arm of the chair. "Are you sure you don't want a doctor?"

"Why don't you go to a doctor when *you're* hurt?" she countered.

He bent back over her foot. "You ask too many questions."

Stefan worked quickly. He bandaged both feet with heavy gauze, then washed up and put a kettle on the primitive woodstove.

"Stefan," Mireille said, rising.

"Yes?"

"There's more." She turned her back and pulled off her dress.

Stefan dropped the matches he was striking.

"Can you help me?"

He came over without a word and set to work again.

When he was finished, he clasped her by both shoulders and turned her gently to face him. "Mireille, tell me what happened," he said, and she knew that she could tell him the truth.

After she finished her story, Stefan held her in his arms until the patter of rain on the shack's tin roof stopped and the sun shone through the oilcloth-covered windows.

"Will I be sent to the guillotine?" she asked, swallowing.

"For killing that pig? They ought to give you a medal." His hands tightened on her. "I only wish I'd gotten rid of him first."

"Giselle will get the Germans to come looking for me."

"The Germans? What do they have to do with anything?"

"They're her friends. Valois was on their side."

Stefan lowered his eyes. "I really don't think the Germans are going to have the time," he said.

"The explosion! It was the Bellefleur, wasn't it? The Nazi command post was blown up."

Stefan shrugged. "How would I know?"

"You were out there. You must have seen the fire. It was a bomb—I'm sure of it."

"I saw no such thing."

"Stefan!"

He put his finger to her lips. "Now, that's enough about Nazis and bombs and wars. I want you to put those things out of your head, all right?"

"But there *is* a war."

"Not for long, Dandelion. It's going to end soon. Any day now, the German troops are going to pull out of Champs de Blé."

"How can you be so sure?"

"That's not important. Just take my word for it. All we've got to do is to keep you away from the police, and that won't be hard. They hated Valois as much as everyone else in town."

"Is there still a town? Maybe the rest of Champs de Blé was blown up with the Bellefleur."

"The town is fine," Stefan said. He took the big military bandage off her hand and absently cleaned the cut beneath it. "We were lucky to have the rain. No footprints."

Mireille looked at him through narrowed eyes. "You did see the explosion," she said. "You were in Champs de Blé. That's where you were coming from when you found me."

He looked up from his work, and for a moment it seemed as if he were going to admit she was right. In the end, though, he only chucked her under her chin. "Quit imagining things," he said. "I was out hunting."

He opened the door. Outside, the sunlight sparkled on the wet hills of lavender. Mireille followed him, hobbling on her bandaged feet.

Stefan watched her come. "I missed you," he said, putting his arm around her. "How long has it been? A year? Two?"

She shook her head. She didn't want to think about those years. "I missed you, too," she said.

The days passed quickly. In the mornings Stefan would leave for one village or another in search of whatever odd jobs might be available. He always returned before dark with some fresh vegetables or a skinned hare or even, sometimes, a few francs.

In time, Mireille healed. Stefan's medical treatment had been good, and he brought her spirit back to life as well.

In the evenings he would tell her about his small adventures, or read to her from one of the books he had stacked neatly inside a wooden box against the wall. They were old books, well used, and covered more subjects than Mireille had even heard of.

"Blow winds, and crack your cheeks!" he recited from an untranslated version of *King Lear*.

"Crack your . . . What was 'cracked'?" She shook her head, laughing. "English is too hard, Stefan."

"Everything worth knowing is hard at first."

She made a dismissive gesture. "But why English? I've never even met anyone who spoke English."

"Because the Americans are going to win this war, Mireille. They won't occupy our cities the way the Germans have, but they'll influence what happens here. And everywhere else, too. You'd do well to study it."

Mireille crossed her arms stubbornly. "You talk as if you were my father," she said. "You're only nineteen yourself."

"Twenty," he said.

"That's practically the same thing. Besides, you never went to school."

"That's why I have to read. To catch up."

She looked at him across the dancing candlelight. "Why didn't you, Stefan?" she asked shyly. "Didn't you want to go?"

He smiled and put down his book. "Oh, I wanted to. It wasn't my choice. My mother died when I was still a baby, and my father didn't like settling down. We moved around from one place to another until I was ten years old."

"And then?"

"And then he left. I woke up one morning, and he was gone. There was some money on the bed. That's how I knew he wasn't coming back."

There was a long silence as Stefan stared at the flickering candle. "I can't blame him, really. Papa was a tinker. In his heart, he was a gypsy, even though he didn't look like one. Having a little kid around slowed him down. Especially one with a clubfoot."

Mireille's eyes strayed down to his shoes. Stefan always wore shoes, she remembered. Even when he worked in the garden after the spring rains, he wouldn't wear the dry wooden sabots that had been set out for him, preferring to get his tattered leather shoes soaked through with mud.

Mireille's mother had understood. The Easter after he started working for the de Jouarres, she gave him a new pair of sturdy boots. Shortly afterward, she invited Stefan to move into the house.

Those were good times, when the garden bloomed with flowers and tomatoes and green snap beans. They celebrated the harvest of the first white asparagus in spring, and the last pumpkins of autumn. They lived together in a land of plenty, and they had everything they wanted.

While Mireille's father was away, Stefan would entertain her with stories and, when she begged him, with his drawings. He was a natural artist. Whenever he picked up a lump of coal or a piece of chalk, he would hold it in his hands, frowning, his fingers exploring its curves and planes until he knew exactly what it could create. He drew pictures of fairies and imaginary beasts for her, or caricatures of Mireille and her school friends that bore such startling likeness that they would all shriek with laughter.

On Mireille's tenth birthday, he had surprised her with a miniature zoo in the rose garden behind the house. The tiny buildings were made from stones and shell and pieces of wood, glued together and painted with pigment he had made himself, but it was the animals that were truly wonderful. He had carved them from stone: a delicate spotted giraffe, a whimsical bear, a horse that seemed to move of its own accord. Each was perfectly proportioned, and each was small enough to fit into a child's hand.

"Oh, Stefan," she'd whispered when he gave it to her, "it's the most beautiful thing I've ever seen."

Later, she gave him a sketchbook filled with thick blank pages and a box of charcoals. "Maman bought it," she'd said. "But I chose the book. Do you like it?"

Stefan could only nod, silent. He had been moved nearly to tears by his friend's kindness. But there was something else he desired even more.

He wanted to learn to read. Day after day, when Mireille came home from school, he made sure to be near the house so that he would be invited inside to share a cup of chocolate with her. But he rarely drank the chocolate. Instead, he bullied her into doing her schoolwork, peering over her shoulder as she read from her textbooks, asking questions, making her repeat everything she'd learned during the day.

"Stefan, I've done all my homework," she protested. "I don't want to study anymore."

He'd looked at her silently, then down at the open book on the table, and touched the precious, unknown words with his artist's fingertips.

With that gesture, Mireille understood completely Stefan's terrible hunger to learn, and made up her mind to help him. Secretly, to guard his pride, she taught him the alphabet and went over the letters with him, writing until their arms were sore from the effort. Then she brought him children's books from the public library. His appetite was voracious. Many times, when Mireille woke in the morning, the light in Stefan's room would still be lit as he struggled through the adventures of Babar and the fairy tales of Charles Perrault and, later, the works of Hugo and Zola.

Mireille became the best student in school. She rushed home in the evenings to share what she had learned with Stefan, as if the second ice age or the geography of Brazil were matters of great urgency. He always listened to her with rapt attention, eager to share her knowledge.

Then the war reached France and changed everything.

Madame de Jouarre developed the tuberculosis that was to kill her six months later. During the final agonizing months of her life, Stefan ran the house for her, quietly and efficiently, and distracted Mireille from the coughing and the smell of sickness until her mother was gone.

Giselle appeared soon after. At first she was friendly toward Stefan—too friendly, Mireille thought, making a point of hanging around Stefan while he worked and cooing to him in a voice like syrup. Mireille hated her from the beginning, and the distaste seemed to be mutual.

Once, when she slapped Mireille for spying on her, Stefan had pushed Giselle away. He was banished from living in the house after that. And after Valois's accusation that Stefan had seduced Mireille, he was sent away for good.

"They're worse than Jews," Mireille heard Valois say after Stefan left. "That boy ought to be sent to one of those camps I hear about before he gets a chance to taint the blood of true Europeans."

Mireille cried all that night, and the next. Then there were other things to cry about, and she accepted the loss of Stefan as she had the deaths of her mother and father, and the end of her dreams.

"It's rude to stare," Stefan said.

Mireille felt herself blushing. "I . . . I'm sorry. I was just thinking . . ."

He laughed. "Well, that's an improvement over the old days, at least."

"About you . . ."

Their eyes met and held, as if each of them had suddenly found the answers to all the questions of their lives.

Then Stefan turned away from her. "You ought to get some sleep," he said brusquely, throwing some sticks into the small fire in the woodstove. "Don't take too long. I'm tired."

As he had every night since she arrived, Stefan left while Mireille washed and got ready for bed. She slept on the cot Stefan had been using before her arrival. For himself, he'd brought in some straw pilfered from a barn some distance away and covered it with a blanket. He always made sure she was asleep before going to bed himself.

It's so I won't see his clubfoot, Mireille thought as she bent over the basin. But behind his shame, there had been something else.

What was that electric, intangible thing that had passed between them? It had also felt like shame, only good. Had he felt that, too?

No, he couldn't have. To Stefan, Mireille was still a child. He had cut her off so abruptly because he had seen the longing in her, and it had offended him. She dried her face. *Well, why should he want me?* she reasoned. She was a killer, after all, no better than the scheming, self-serving Valois or the blank-faced Nazis, who murdered without a trace of regret.

It was hours before Stefan returned.

Mireille pretended to be asleep, half covering her face with the thin blanket. She watched through half-closed eyes as he picked up a lit candle, but instead of blowing it out, he walked slowly over to the cot where she lay.

She closed her eyes. A light passed back and forth across her face. *He's looking at me,* she thought. But why? Was he just making sure she was asleep? Was he so afraid that she might see his deformity?

After a moment, Stefan snuffed out the candle, then went over to the stove to bank the fire. Its glowing embers shed the only light in the room, and when he began to undress, the firelight played on the muscles of his shoulders and back.

Mireille felt guilty. She knew that she was spying on something very personal, but she couldn't stop looking at him. With his back to the fire, he stepped out of his worn trousers. His leg, to Mireille's surprise, was not twisted and shrunken as she'd expected, but indistinguishable from the other; both were long and heavily muscled up to his buttocks, the sight of which was shocking to her. She wanted to turn away, but the sheen of sweat on his body made him seem to glow in the flickering light, and she was mesmerized, frozen in place.

Mireille had never thought a man could be so beautiful.

Chapter Four

A week later, Stefan came back from work carrying a bottle of red wine and a basket stuffed with food. "You're free," he said, beaming.

"What?"

"I was in Champs de Blé today. The Germans are pulling out." He winked. "Didn't I tell you they would?"

Mireille's mouth fell open in disbelief. "Is the war over?"

He smiled. "Not yet, Dandelion. They've just gone over to Toumiens. There's no place for them to stay in Champs de Blé now that the Bellefleur's gone. But they won't hold out long against the Americans. It's just a matter of time."

He took her hand. "Come on. We'll eat down by the flower fields. Madame Courbevoie paid me well for fixing her roof." He hefted the big basket and pulled Mireille outside.

"What about Valois?" she panted, running to keep up with his long strides up the flower-dotted hillside.

"Didn't you hear? Some heroic French patriot killed him." He laughed. "The police have closed the tavern, and everybody's celebrating. They're pulling out the stores of food that Valois and Giselle were hoarding." He took a thick sausage from the basket and held it aloft. "How long has it been since you've seen such a piece of meat, eh?"

"They don't know about me?"

"Oh, you've got nothing to do with it. The story going around is that you were abducted by the same people who killed your stepfather. The police spent a few days searching for your body, but they've given it up now."

"And Giselle?"

"She got her just deserts. They shaved her head and drove her out of town, naked as the day she was born. Then . . ." His exuberance faded and died. He became suddenly silent.

"Yes?" She caught up with him and tugged at his arm. "Then what, Stefan? What did they do?"

His eyes were pained. "They think you're dead, Mireille."

"What happened?"

"The villagers looted the house, then set fire to it."

She took a step backward, as if she had been struck.

"I'm sorry."

Her eyes were stinging with tears. "Even though I knew I'd never go back there, I never thought . . ." Her face crumpled. "I don't even have a picture of my parents."

Stefan wrapped his arms around her. The hillside where they were standing was covered with tall shoots of lavender, escapees from the formal cultivated fields that stretched for miles below. The scent of the flowers, carried by the soft breeze, was intoxicating. "It's hard for you, I know," he said. "But it's over now. Everything that's hurt you is over. You can start over, too. A new life. Just think of it, a fresh start with no mistakes to haunt you. Why, it's almost as if you were born today, this minute . . ."

"Oh, Stefan!" She hugged him fiercely and sobbed. "Please don't ever leave me!"

He stroked her hair. "Stop talking crazy. You're just afraid now."

"I'm not afraid with you!" She wept in great jagged bursts. "And I do love you, even if you think I'm ugly and evil. I'll never love anyone else, never!" She pulled him close to her, kissed him roughly, as if it were a punishment, then ran away.

He came after her. She was as fast as a deer, her hair shining like a halo in the sunlight, leaving a wake of sweet perfume from the crushed lavender.

Then she stopped, of her own will. Her shoulders were stooped and shaking. She covered her face.

"Mireille." Stefan touched her.

She turned away from him with a jerk. "I'm so ashamed," she whispered. "I know you couldn't love me. Not after what happened with Valois."

Gently, he forced her hands down. Her lips were trembling. Stefan wiped the tears off her face. "Of course I love you," he said softly. "I've loved you since the night you first came to me."

He kissed her. It was light, the touch of his mouth on hers, barely more than the caress of the scented breeze.

Mireille felt his muscles tense, and remembered the silky, animal sheen of his naked body in the firelight. She had never thought of herself as a woman before, but the feelings that were coursing through her body now were unlike anything she'd felt before.

"Kiss me again, Stefan," she whispered.

"I . . ." He closed his eyes as he brushed his lips against hers. "I can't." He held her away from him as he tried to steady his breathing.

Mireille's heart thudded inside her until she thought it would burst. "Why not?" she cried. "You said . . . You said you loved me."

"I do," Stefan said, not looking at her. "More than I can say. But it's too soon. We can wait."

"For what?"

He touched her face. "For it to be right," he said. Then he wrapped her in his arms.

The air was still, and the scent of lavender enveloped them like a blanket. Stefan held her—held her as if she were his very life, precious and wonderful.

Ages passed between them. Then, finally, Mireille spoke. "Do you think I'm not clean, Stefan?" Her tender mouth was quivering. "Valois didn't . . . He wanted to, but he didn't . . ."

"Shhh. Of course you're clean." His voice caught. "You had to kill Valois. It's nothing against you."

"Then why—"

"I want you to be sure of me."

"I am, Stefan. Why wouldn't I be?"

His gaze on her was steady. "I'll never be a normal man, Mireille."

"What—?"

"I want you to remember me with kindness, not as a monster who took your virginity from you."

"That's not how it is at all! How can I show you that doesn't matter?"

"You can't," he said.

He looked up at the sky. His eyes were sad.

"What are you thinking?" Mireille asked.

He smiled kindly. "Just about how beautiful you are." He drew his finger along her cheekbone. "So many men will love you for this face. I almost wish you were ugly."

"Stefan! How can you say that? There won't be any other men. I'll stay with you forever. We'll get married and start a farm, and live in a house with a white fence and a red door—"

"Hold it," he said, laughing. "I thought the man was supposed to do the proposing."

Her cheeks reddened.

He kissed her forehead. "Let's just see what happens."

"With us?"

He picked a sprig of lavender and twirled it between his fingers. "Yes." He seemed far away now, absorbed in his own thoughts. "And with the war."

His words crashed down on her. "The war? What can we do about the stupid war? We're not soldiers."

"We're French," he said. "And we're going to stay French."

"I thought you said the Americans were going to win the war."

"They're not going to win it alone."

"But the Nazis are gone!"

"They're gone from Champs de Blé, Mireille," he said. "Not from France." He tossed the flower away and kissed her. "Let's find Madame Courbevoie's picnic basket."

They ran together across the hillside, and when he reached the basket of food, he turned abruptly and caught her. They rolled down the hill together, laughing, until they finally came to a stop in a soft bed of fragrant lavender. Mireille's hair was strewn with leaves and grass and bits of purple flowers, and her shapeless black shroud of a dress had fallen off her shoulders.

She reached for it to cover herself, but Stefan stopped her. "Let me look at you," he said.

She lowered her gaze, embarrassed, but he lifted her chin, forcing her to meet his eyes. "You're too pretty to be real," he said. Then he leaped to his feet. "Don't move. Please."

He ran up the hill. In the sunlight, Mireille could see the keen definition of his flanks as he moved in his strange loping way. His back was perfectly straight, and every part of his body was in proportion to every other part. He had a thick neck and the sinuous, well-developed limbs of a laborer, yet his overall appearance was boyish, even ethereal. His face was that of an Arabian prince, dark and exotic. The near perfection of his large deep-set eyes, the straight nose and sensuous lips and the curly black hair framing his face like a soft cap accentuated the imperfection of his walk even more pointedly. Mireille felt her heart spilling over with love.

"You moved," he said, setting down the basket with a thud.

"I wanted to look at you."

"Well, your turn's over. I'm going to look at you now." Carefully, with delicate hands, he pulled the black dress up over her body, leaving her naked.

"What are you doing?" she asked, squirming with embarrassment.

"This rag ought to be burned," he said, tossing the garment aside. "Just sit."

He took a white sketchpad and a narrow tin of watercolors from the basket. "I spent a few francs on myself today," he said as he measured out small squiggles of paint onto the lid of the tin and mixed them with water.

"Oh, Stefan! You still paint!" Mireille sat up, her self-consciousness about her nakedness fading. She had always felt comfortable around Stefan, as she did now, clothed or not.

"Not much," he said, "and not very well, I'm afraid. Humor me." He pushed her back down. "Pretend you're asleep."

"Why?"

"It's the only time you stop talking."

"Can I keep my eyes open?"

"What for?"

"To look at you," she said, reaching over to touch his face.

He kissed the palm of her hand. "All right. For a while."

Quickly he began to make strokes on the paper, his eyes sparkling in his still face. He worked until the sun hung full and yellow above the horizon, then set his brush down with a sigh. "I didn't get a good likeness," he said.

Mireille looked at the painting in wonderment. The nude was herself, only more so. In the soft brushstrokes Stefan had captured a quality of freedom, of energy straining to be released. A Mireille was on the paper, but not the Mireille who had spent her youth scrubbing floors and eating alone in the kitchen. Not the Mireille who had been attacked by her stepfather on a bed of glass. Not the Mireille who had killed a man. The girl in the drawing was the essence of joy.

"This is who I always wanted to be," she said.

Stefan smiled, shy and pleased. "It's who you are." He painted a blue dot on the end of her nose.

"You didn't sign it," she said.

"It isn't a big enough nose."

"Not my nose, silly. The painting. You didn't sign the painting."

"It's not good enough."

"It is too. It's wonderful. Everything you do—"

"Is wonderful, yes." He laughed, but the laughter in his eyes soon dimmed into sorrow. "You won't always feel that way, Mireille."

"Why . . . why not?"

"Because you're the one who's special, not me." He dipped the end of his brush into a drop of black paint and wrote something in English across the bottom of the painting.

"*Fortune's Child*?" Mireille asked. "Why did you call it that?"

"Because you're going to have a wonderful life. The world is going to belong to you."

"And you," she said.

He shook his head. "One day you'll see me for what I am, an uneducated cripple who has nothing to offer you."

She took his hands. "You could offer me your love," she said.

"That won't be enough. You'll want it to be, but it won't be nearly enough."

She sat up abruptly and shook the flowers out of her hair. "Honestly, Stefan, sometimes I don't understand a word you're saying."

He gave her a noisy peck on the forehead. "Neither do I," he said, uncorking the bottle of wine. "I forgot to bring glasses."

"No matter. I don't have any clothes to spill anything on, anyway."

"That's the spirit. From now on, we'll always dine in the nude."

"Hear, hear." She cocked her head sideways. "Does that mean you'll be getting undressed, too?"

"No," he said.

"You can keep your shoes on, if you like."

He ignored her. "Toast?" He held the bottle up between them.

"To us," she said.

"No." His eyes softened. "To you, Mireille de Jouarre. To the rest of your life." They drank. They ate. They laughed and cried, and their eyes held a long wordless conversation until the sun went down.

Chapter Five

The day the police stopped looking for the remains of Mireille Orlande de Jouarre was truly the beginning of her life. There was purpose in it now that Stefan was part of it.

While he was away during the day, Mireille set about reorganizing the small shack with the zeal of a born housewife. She cleaned and scrubbed the worn, unpainted wood of the floor until it shone. She stuffed the open spaces between the slats of the wall with woven grass. Using some scraps of cloth Stefan was able to pick up, she sewed cushions for the rickety furniture. She hung bunches of dried lavender from the ceiling so that their fragrance permeated the room. She collected kindling for the fire, dusted his books, baked their bread. It was as if touching Stefan's things brought her somehow closer to him.

Still, some things bothered her. "That night when you found me in the field . . ." she began as they ate supper together.

"Yes?"

"You were carrying a gun. A rifle."

"I told you, I was hunting."

"I know that's what you told me," she said stubbornly. "Since then I've cleaned everything in this place, and I've never seen that gun again."

"I leave it in a hollow tree near where I hunt."

"You leave a gun outside? What about the rain?"

"It's all right there," he said testily.

She sat back, silent.

"Your flowers smell nice," he said.

Mireille spoke almost to herself. "You brought the gun in with you that first night. It was gone the next day."

"Leave it, will you?" He got up and took out one of his books.

Mireille didn't mention it again.

There was another mystery about Stefan. He still insisted that she be asleep before he would consider retiring himself.

"This is crazy," she said one night. "Why do you have to wait for me to go to sleep?"

"I just want to make sure you're safe."

"What if I don't feel like sleeping?"

"I don't see why you wouldn't," he said, looking uncomfortable.

"Is it your feet?"

"What about my feet?"

"Are you afraid I'll peek under the covers and look at your bum foot? If that's what the problem is, you're dumb, because I don't care. You could have warts all over your nose and carrots growing out of it, for all I care."

"That'll be my next trick."

"Please go to bed. By yourself, or with me. Your choice."

"No."

"Please."

He lit the candle and sat down with one of his books beside it. "Go to sleep."

Mireille knew it was no use arguing with him. It was just another thing Stefan wouldn't talk about.

Like the gun.

There was nothing she could do. She went to sleep while he remained awake, standing sentinel.

Hours later she was awakened by a sound. She half opened her eyes to see Stefan crouching in the dark in the middle of the room.

His back was to her, and his head was craned over his shoulder. Clearly, he was looking to see if she was awake.

He's hiding something, she thought. Groaning as if her sleep had only been temporarily disturbed, she rolled over on her side.

Stefan remained motionless for a moment. Then, probably convinced she hadn't seen anything, he turned away from her again.

Slowly, with infinite patience, he removed a floorboard. From it he pulled out something long and shiny.

It was the rifle. Why did he keep it hidden there? And why had he lied about where it was? Silently, Stefan replaced the board, then left the house.

Mireille sat up in bed. It was four thirty in the morning.

If he was hunting, there was little sign of it. They rarely ate meat, and when they did, it came from the places where Stefan worked. Anyway, she thought, who went hunting when it was pitch dark outside?

She tiptoed over to the floorboard and held the candle to it. There was a knothole on the side big enough for a man's thumb to lift it out. The board was heavy as she moved it aside. Dropping it with a clunk, she held the candle down inside the hole.

What she saw set her mind reeling. Beside the space where the rifle had been were several handguns; boxes of ammunition; a collection of grenades, wires, timers, and powders; some unidentifiable puttylike substance; and a dozen or more sticks of dynamite.

Shocked, she squatted near the open cache. There was one other item, a small crockery pot filled with money.

There's got to be an explanation for this, she told herself over and over as she replaced the floorboard and returned to bed. She pulled up her knees, wound her arms around them, and waited.

Near dawn he returned. He was carrying the rifle. "I know what you've got under the floor," she said without preamble.

He stuck the rifle in the corner and sighed. "All right. I suppose it's for the best." He limped over slowly to sit beside her. "Where do you want me to begin?"

"Just tell me what you do, Stefan. At night."

Weary with fatigue, he rubbed his hands over his face. "Do you know why the Germans took over Champs de Blé?"

Mireille shook her head. "I never thought about it. They occupied Paris, so . . ."

"Paris has somewhat more to offer the Third Reich than a provincial village that grows flowers," he said. "They came here because their supply routes meet in this area." His eyes met hers. "They need our roads and bridges. The Germans first set up headquarters in Grasse, but it was bombed. Twice. The bridge at Toumiens, which used to be their principal supply route, has been destroyed. When they tried to rebuild it, a number of their men were blown up by hand grenades."

She stared at him, almost afraid to speak.

"Who did those things to them?"

"I did," Stefan said evenly.

Mireille held her breath. "And the Bellefleur Hotel?"

He nodded. "They're rebuilding the bridge, of course, despite the work of the Resistance—"

"Stop!" She clapped her hands over her ears. "I don't want to hear any more!"

"I didn't think you would," Stefan said, "but it's the truth. That's why you can't plan a future with me."

She dropped her hands. "Because you expect to die?"

"I don't expect anything," he said. "But anything can happen."

She turned to him, her green eyes flashing with anger. "You weren't even going to tell me."

He was silent.

In the morning when she awoke, he was lying next to her.

Stefan didn't go to work the next day. He slept until the early afternoon. He ate little. He rarely spoke. There was an almost palpable
tension in all his movements. Toward evening, he cleaned his rifle.

"You're leaving tonight," Mireille said flatly. It was not a
question.

Stefan gave her an apologetic look. "I have to."

"Will it be dangerous?"

"No." "I don't believe you."

He said nothing more. He finished cleaning the rifle, then
propped it in the corner. When he turned back, Mireille was
unbuttoning the man's shirt she now wore. She stepped out of a
pair of baggy trousers, then dropped the shirt from her shoulders
and stood naked before him.

"Love me, Stefan," she said. "No questions, no arguments. Just
come to me."

He nodded once, slowly, and walked toward her. This time
when they kissed, his tongue probed deeply into her mouth and
she felt his sex pressing against her belly.

"Let me undress you," she said, unbuttoning Stefan's shirt.
Beneath it his smooth tan skin shone. With a soft moan, she kissed
his chest, tasting his salt.

His hands glided over her, tracing the curve of her buttocks,
the two dimples at the base of her spine, and her breasts, full and
round as melons. He played her pink nipples with his tongue,
sucking them to hardness until she shivered with pleasure.

They made love as if the act were a sacred ritual binding them
together for all time. Every touch of his hands on her body seemed
to burn into her with indelible permanence; every kiss was tinged
with the bittersweet taste of unshed tears. Mireille wanted to possess him completely. She kissed every inch of his smooth skin,
finally taking him inside her as she cried out with pleasure and
pain.

He pulled away from her. "I'm hurting you," he said.

"No," she breathed, throwing her arms around his neck. "Don't stop."

"But it must hurt. You're crying."

She blinked the tears out of her eyes. "That doesn't matter. I want this, Stefan. I want to be yours."

"You are." He kissed her wet cheeks. "And I'm yours. Forever."

Then slowly, languidly, as if their time together were infinite, they moved together until there was no longer any distinction between them, their bodies rocking together as if they shared a single beating heart. She held him, waves of joy and sadness spreading over her as she crested and climaxed and felt him pour his life into her.

"I'll come back to you, Mireille," he said as she lay spent in his arms. "If I can," he added in a whisper.

The sun set in a huge red smear, tinting the dried flowers on the ceiling the same crimson color as the spot on the sheets they lay on, stained with her virginal blood.

In time, Stefan got dressed. He took out the floorboard and removed its contents. One by one, he placed the weapons into a large gunnysack.

"How many others will be with you?" she asked.

He shrugged. "Enough." He took out the small crockery pot. "Mireille, listen to me," he said. He stuffed the bills into her hand. "I want you to sleep in your clothes tonight, and keep this money on you."

Suddenly, her languor soured into fear. "Why, Stefan? You're coming back, aren't you? You said you'd come back!"

"I will, Mireille," he said. "At least I'll try. If I can't, if something goes wrong—"

"No!" she shouted, raising her arms like a shield in front of her.

He grabbed her wrists and forced them down. "*Yes*," he said. "You have to hear this. If I'm not back here by dawn, it means the worst has happened and the Germans will come here. In that case, you must be gone by morning."

"How . . . how long . . . ?"

"Don't stay past first light." He scribbled something on a piece of paper and gave it to her. "This is the address of some people I know in Paris. They'll take you in. Listen to them. They'll tell you what to do next."

"Paris?"

"You'll be able to get lost there. But don't use the main roads on your way. There's a map inside the box where I keep my books."

"Stefan, please don't talk like this."

He smiled. "This is just a precaution, that's all. Everything will be fine." He kissed her forehead, but she clasped him tightly and covered his lips with her own.

"I'll never stop loving you," she said.

Two hours later, Mireille heard the sound of an explosion. She sat on Stefan's chair near the candle and waited.

By dawn the candle had burned out. Still, she waited.

A few minutes later, there was a pounding on the shack's door. Mireille froze, expecting a Nazi soldier to crash through with a rifle pointed at her, but the man on the other side was only a French civilian—a boy, really, not much older than Mireille herself.

"Miss," he began, taking off his cap. "I'm sorry, I've forgotten your name."

Mireille stood up quickly. "What do you want?" she demanded.

"I have news. Bad news. From Stefan."

"Tell me!" Mireille closed the door behind him.

The young man shifted from one foot to the other. "He's been shot," he said finally. "He sent me to tell you to leave this place as soon as you can."

"But . . . where is he? Why didn't you bring him back here?"

He shook his head, and Mireille knew that her questions were just a way for her to hang onto hope for a moment or two longer. "Is he dead?"

The boy burst into sobs. "He was hurt too bad to move. His leg was gone, and the Germans were coming after us . . . He sent me here to say good-bye. He . . . he said . . ."

A gunshot rang out in the distance. Then another. The boy turned his head toward the window.

"What's that?" Mireille asked as another shot sounded.

He hung his head. "They're shooting the wounded," he said, wiping his nose with his sleeve.

A fourth shot. "Stefan," Mireille whispered.

"It was important to him that you get away from here," the boy said, unable to stop his own tears. "He sent me here to help you." He peered out the window. "But we'll have to be quick."

"Go ahead," she said. "I'll be fine."

The boy hesitated a moment. Then Mireille opened the door and pushed him out. "Go."

"He . . . Stefan . . . He said—"

"I know what he said." It was what Mireille would have said in his place. She didn't have to hear the words secondhand. "Thank you."

He nodded once, then ran toward the hills.

She stood in the open doorway for what seemed like a long time, forcing herself to breathe. Then, numbly, she gathered some things together: food, the map, a pair of shoes Stefan had brought her. She put them in a bag and slung it over her shoulder.

Stefan was dead.

His last thought had been of her, of her safety. He hadn't known that her life without him would mean nothing, but she would obey him anyway.

To keep faith.

She closed the door to the shack behind her and never looked back.

Chapter Six

Mireille reached Paris on May 8, 1945, the day the Allies declared victory in Europe. The streets were filled with cheering crowds, drunk with relief and wine. The tall gray buildings of the city sported French flags hanging from every window. The outdoor loudspeakers that had been installed to broadcast Nazi edicts to the civilian population now blared "La Marseillaise" as the free French, openly weeping, sang the words.

Mireille hadn't slept in a bed for more than a month. She had traveled most of the distance from Champs de Blé on foot, trudging through the grass and mud beside the back roads, sleeping wherever she could find shelter.

Now that she was in the city, the festive atmosphere struck her like a slap in the face. Only hours before, Paris, and everyone in it, had been the property of the Nazis; now it was a riot of color and sound, a celebration. Delicious aromas poured from the open doors of restaurants, where conversations were loud and punctuated with laughter. Mireille bought a half loaf of bread and ate it as she walked, zombielike, toward the Left Bank across the Pont Neuf, with its carved gargoyles. She moved more slowly than the city folk around her, and they jostled her as they passed, spilling around her like sand over a rock.

On the Boulevard Saint-Michel, she stared open-mouthed at the colorful cafés and open-air tables, where waiters dressed in black and white carried trays filled with bottles of wine above their heads.

It's as if there had never been a war, she thought.

There were no bombed-out buildings in Paris as there were in villages she'd seen along the way; no pits filled with rubble; no scorched tracts of land; no piles of boulders marked by a black cross to signify that the bodies of the dead had not been found.

Here were shops of every conceivable variety, bookstores specializing in rare volumes, *oiselleries*, where birds—rare creatures after the depredations of war, when even the pigeons were eaten—sang in cages. Along the street were musicians and performers of all sorts, from jugglers in clown makeup to violinists playing sonatas by Paganini and Saint-Saëns. And everywhere, enterprising men carrying armloads of balloons and small French flags wove among the celebrants.

It was not a city. It was a carnival. *Stefan had gone out alone in the night to die for this,* she thought. The obscenity of it sickened her.

"Hey, beautiful!" a man in a French army uniform shouted in her ear.

He was drunk. The moth-eaten uniform, obviously not worn since the early days of the war before France's surrender to Germany, was clearly just for show. "*Vive la France!*" he called, saluting. He lunged forward and grabbed her around the waist. "Come on, baby. A kiss to celebrate the victory."

She fought him off, scratching at his face, biting and kicking in a fury until a group of strangers pulled her off the hapless soldier.

"Crazy bitch," he said, wiping the blood off his lip as the others helped him up off the ground.

"Don't mind her," one of the strangers said, dusting off the soldier's uniform. "Trash. She doesn't even know a hero when she sees one."

Mireille wiped her mouth with the back of her hand.

At the corner of the boulevard, she checked the address in her pocket. *Jacques and Beatrice Messaline, 13 Rue Bujas.* She had arrived.

They'll take you in, Stefan had said. *They'll tell you what to do next.*

Her heart began to skip a little faster as she approached number thirteen. It was a clean-looking two-story building, recessed from the street, with an iron fence around the small yard. Timidly, Mireille knocked at the door, then tried to pat down her hair and straighten her clothes. Her efforts did little good. In the small window beside the doorway, she caught sight of her reflection.

I look like one of those gargoyles they decorate their bridges with, she thought. *And smell like one, too.* But the Messalines would understand. They would give her a meal, a bath, perhaps a bed with clean sheets. She would be safe with them.

A sweet-faced middle-aged woman came to the door. "Madame Messaline?" Mireille asked.

A flicker of something—concern, or perhaps annoyance—passed over the woman's features.

Mireille straightened up, trying to look more respectable. "Stefan Giroux sent me." She added hurriedly, "I've come from Champs de Blé, near Grasse. I guess I look frightful—"

"I'm sorry, child," the woman said. "The Messalines were arrested by the Germans long ago."

Mireille felt as if the earth had fallen from under her feet.

"I've rented their apartment to someone else."

When the girl on her doorstep said nothing, the woman muttered another apology and closed the door.

Mireille looked down at the scrap of paper in her hand. The Messalines had been her only possible link to the world outside Champs de Blé.

She could never return to her village. Despite Stefan's assurances, the police might still be looking for Valois's murderer.

Besides, without her mother or father—and without Stefan—there was nothing in Champs de Blé for her any longer.

She looked around. Somewhere in this vast, frightening city she would have to make a life for herself alone.

She crumpled up the address and let it fall.

Farther down Rue Bujas she saw a sign reading "*Chambres* à *Louer*" hanging over the door of a seedy, crumbling building. A boardinghouse.

At least it didn't look very expensive, she told herself. She might be able to take a room there.

As she walked in the door, two thin Arabs slid past her, ogling her openly. One of them spoke in a garbled tongue Mireille had never heard before, and both men laughed.

"What do you want?" grumbled a scowling woman from behind a small counter near a stairway strewn with litter. Behind the counter was a door standing ajar. Beyond that, Mireille could see a cluttered living room from which emanated the smell of cooking cabbage.

"I need a room, please."

"Forty francs a week, no meals, no cooking in the rooms, bath and towel extra," the woman said without looking at her.

Mireille took her money out of her pocket and counted it.

"A week in advance, and two weeks' deposit," the woman added quickly.

Carefully straightening out the bills, Mireille handed them to her. "Do you know where I could get a job?" she asked.

"Hah! You'll have to look far and wide for that. The men are coming home." She squinted at the girl. "And don't you get any ideas about having men in your room, either. I run a clean house." She wagged a finger at Mireille. "I've never had any trouble with the police, and I want to keep it that way. Got that?"

"Yes, madame," Mireille said.

"Fifth floor, on the left." She handed her a key. "My name is Loquin. Madame Loquin, to you."

"How do you do. I'm Mireille—"

The woman waved her away. "Go, go. I haven't got time to chat."

Mireille started up the creaking stairs, then turned back.

"I'd like a bath, too, please."

"Twelve francs." Madame Loquin held out her hand, palm up. She took the money, then pointed to a door. "In there. Pick up your towel when you're ready, and turn it in when you're done."

"Thank you," Mireille said.

Twelve francs for a bath! Paris must be the most expensive city in the world, she thought. On her way to her room, she opened a door marked *"Toilette"* on the third-floor landing. Inside was nothing more than a filthy dung-spattered hole in the floor that stank so badly it made her retch. A rat scurried out of the darkness past her and vanished up the stairs.

Her room was low and dingy, its walls marked with a thick band of grime where countless hands had touched it over the years. A single dim electric bulb hung from the ceiling. There was a bed with sheets of dubious freshness, a dresser with a small cracked mirror hanging above it, and a hook in one corner to hang her few clothes.

At least it was a place to sleep. Tomorrow she would find a job somewhere. *Tomorrow will be better*, she told herself. She sat down on the bed and removed one of her shoes.

She fell asleep still wearing the other.

Mireille did find a job the next day, washing dishes in the Dôme Café. She got her meals there, and was able to use a clean toilet. She also discovered a public swimming pool nearby that offered a hot shower for three francs.

She worked as many hours as the manager permitted, saving her money, buying only the absolute necessities so that she would be able to move out of Madame Loquin's boardinghouse and into a real apartment. She even looked at a place, a bright, airy room with a small stove and two windows.

Then she began to be sick in the mornings.

She passed it off at first as the flu, then as fatigue from over-work; but she knew. There would be no apartment now. Not with a baby to care for.

Stefan's baby. The realization struck her like lightning. He wasn't dead, not really. He had left his child inside her.

Slowly, her hands moved over her still-flat belly. "This is ours," she whispered.

That evening she walked to the Cathedral of Notre-Dame and lit a candle for Stefan. "My darling," she said, looking up at the great rose window that seemed to lead straight to God. "Can you hear me? Can you see you're still alive, after all?"

She found pictures of babies in magazines and put them up on her walls. She scrubbed the grimy room where she lived as she had scrubbed Stefan's house, until it sparkled and smelled of strong soap. With some of her savings, she bought some wool and a pair of knitting needles and made a blanket decorated with sprigs of purple lavender. She converted one of the drawers in her dresser into a bed for her baby.

And she worked harder than ever, not minding the suffocating heat of the kitchen at the café or the long hours she spent on her feet. She was working for Stefan's baby, for a new life. "One day we'll have a home of our own," she said, stroking her swelling belly as she lay in bed at night. It gave her comfort to talk to the unborn child, even if it meant losing precious hours of sleep.

She had no time for friends. The baby was her only reason to climb down the steep stairway of the boardinghouse before dawn every morning and walk the fifteen blocks to her job. The baby was all there was for Mireille. Most of the time, that was enough.

"Our house will be in the country, with a white fence and a red door and a garden like the one my mother used to keep . . ."

She felt the baby move inside her. "Did I tell you about the stone-animal zoo your father made for me when I was a little girl?" She could say no more, because the baby would have felt her crying if she did.

As her pregnancy progressed, it became harder for her to stand all day and then climb the five flights of stairs to her room. Often she became so out of breath that she had to stop and rest on one of the stairway landings, where the stench from the toilet nearly sickened her.

The stairway was lit by means of a *minuterie*, a timer that could be switched on only at the base of the stairs. The dim light would come on with a droning, buzzing sound for exactly one minute, then automatically turn off. The most gifted athlete would have had trouble making it to the top floor in one minute; for a woman in the latter stages of pregnancy, it was impossible.

While stumbling up the stairs in the darkness one evening, Mireille tripped over a bag of garbage left outside a tenant's door. She slipped and fell, screaming, down to the landing.

Several doors opened, and wary, suspicious faces peered out. The *minuterie* buzzed on. Madame Loquin leaned out her doorway, scowling, her hair curled up in bits of cloth.

"What's wrong with you?" she demanded.

"I . . . I fell." Mireille pulled herself up by the railing. "But I think I'm all right."

"Well, you woke everyone up. We have to work in the morning."

"So do I, madame—"

"You'd better make arrangements to have someone look after you when you have that baby," the woman warned. "This isn't a hospital, you know. I'm not running a charity."

Then the buzzing stopped and the lights went out.

Madame Loquin's door slammed shut first. One by one, as Mireille passed in the darkness, the other doors closed, too.

In her eighth month, in the freezing rains of winter, Mireille collapsed at work and lost her job.

Her ankles and hands had swollen to twice their normal size. The skin around them was cracked and bleeding. She spent her days in delirium, her nights wracked with fever.

Dimly, she noticed the figure of Madame Loquin standing beside her, holding a glass of water to her lips.

"Thank you," she croaked, gratefully accepting the drink.

"Where's your money?" the woman demanded. "Your rent is past due. I've been nursing you for days. I told you this wasn't a hospital."

"In the dresser drawer," Mireille said weakly. "The top drawer."

"You'll have to pay for my time."

The landlady continued to bring her water and later, when the fever began to abate, some broth.

She has some kindness, after all, Mireille thought.

But Madame Loquin's care was minimal. When Mireille was well enough to sit up, she saw that her bed linens were filthy with her own waste, and her body was covered with sores. Perspiring with the effort, she dragged the sheets off the bed.

There was a sharp rap at her door. The landlady came in, using her own key. "It's about time you got out of bed," she said.

"My sheets are dirty," Mireille said, her ears ringing from hunger and sickness.

"Oh, so I'm supposed to be your laundress, too, am I?" She walked around the room, tearing Mireille's baby pictures off the wall. "You smell like a sewer."

"I'm sorry . . ."

"And you're overdue with your rent again. You won't be able to stay here for free."

"Don't do that," Mireille said, picking up the discarded pictures. "I can pay you." She opened the dresser drawer where she kept her money. It was empty. "I had two hundred francs here," she said. "It's gone."

The landlady went on ripping the pictures. "It was mine by right. A hospital would have charged more."

"You stole my money," Mireille said incredulously.

Madame Loquin walked over to her and slapped her across her face. "I'll not have some cheap whore calling me a thief in my own house. Get out." She shoved her toward the door. "Get out before I kick you down the stairs."

Hurriedly, Mireille grabbed the baby blanket she'd made.

"Take this, too," the woman said. She tossed her the thin coat Mireille had bought secondhand. "Everything else in here belongs to me until you've paid me what you owe. Go on." She backed Mireille to the stairs, then stood at the top with her hands on her hips like a colossus until Mireille went down. "Common slut," she called after her.

Chapter Seven

It was December, and the shop windows were already decorated with colored lights. Mireille walked aimlessly around the city, clutching the baby blanket with its embroidered bunches of lavender, trying not to think about what the future would bring.

Toward evening, her stomach aching with hunger, she stopped to rest on a cement bench in a small park between the Seine and the exclusive residential district of the Île de la Cité. The winter wind was strong. Piles of litter swirled in pinwheels in front of the shuttered gray buildings on the other side of the park's winding road. Mireille spread the blanket against her belly underneath her thin coat.

The traffic on the stone bridge nearby was sparse. It was Sunday, she remembered; she had seen the date on a calendar in the window of a children's store, with Christmas marked in a big red circle.

Beneath the bridge, some hobos had built a small fire for warmth. Its flame shot out in jagged angles in the wind.

The clochards, Mireille thought. These were the homeless, the lost people, the quaint folk whose presence, like that of the roosting pigeons outside the Louvre, lent a picturesque character to the city. Parisians were fond of writing romantic songs about them, so long as they didn't have to smell their stink or look into their hungry faces.

Will I be one of them? she wondered. *When my pride gives out, when I can't walk any longer, will I huddle with them under the bridges and flap my arms together for warmth?*

A page of a newspaper kited toward her and plastered itself against her legs. She stuffed it into her coat.

Will my baby?

It began to snow. The air took on the insulated quiet of a cave. With the low sky and the fog from the river, the buildings on the other side of the park slowly vanished into a miasma of cloudy darkness. There was only the low whistle of the wind and the spiky orange flame from the clochards' fire under the bridge to connect Mireille with reality. Without them, she might have been a character in a play, sitting alone on a prop bench in the middle of an empty stage.

A chestnut vendor appeared out of the fog to break the eerie mood. The wheels on his cart squealed loudly as he pushed it past her at top speed, anxious to get home.

"Maman, Maman!" A small boy in a bright-red jacket tugged on the sleeve of a woman carrying a net bag filled with groceries in one hand and a sleeping baby in the other. "Look, chestnuts!"

"He's not selling," the mother said irritably.

The boy ran up to the vendor's cart and banged on the metal bins with delight. "Please, mister? I have my own money."

"Get away from there," the mother said, trying to juggle her groceries to snatch his hand. The baby woke up and started wailing.

"Mister! Just one bag, all right?"

The vendor stopped with a sigh and shoveled out a white paper cone of chestnuts from the steaming bin while the boy dug a coin from his pocket.

Mireille watched the scene with amusement. *That will be my own child someday,* she thought. *If I'm lucky.*

She smiled at the boy's mother, but the woman only glared at her. She pulled her baby closer to her breast, as if she were afraid Mireille would contaminate the child.

"Hurry up," she said to the boy. "The storm's going to be bad."

He skipped toward her as the chestnut vendor squeaked away into the snow. "Yuck, I got a rotten one."

"Spit it out. And for God's sake, keep up with me or we'll all catch our deaths."

The boy popped the nut out of his mouth and took aim at a wastebasket near Mireille. He hit her square on her face.

"Sorry," he called out, giggling.

The mother hushed him. "Don't talk to her," she said, bustling away.

The boy dawdled behind her. When they were almost out of sight, he turned back and threw another chestnut at Mireille.

She went after it greedily, rolling the warm ball in her hands, cracking it open with her teeth to get at the sweet nugget inside.

The small nourishment made her ravenous. She went over to the trash bin and dug through the rubbish, looking for food. There was a hard butt-end of bread there, smeared with cigarette ashes. She stuffed it into her mouth and swallowed it, not caring about the taste, and went on rummaging until she reached the bottom.

Then a bus drove by, and through the wooden slats of the garbage bin, Mireille saw the faces of the passengers watching her.

Slowly, she placed both her hands on the rim. She stayed there for some time, bent over the empty trash container, a pile of garbage strewn at her feet, while the snowfall turned into a blizzard.

It was time to join the clochards.

The people under the bridge moved slowly in the deep shadows of the fire, like figures in a dream. They neither welcomed Mireille nor forced her away as she inched beneath the shelter of the embankment.

The damp ground, permeated by the cold of the river and the blowing snow, was covered with the detritus of the homeless: empty bottles; old newspapers; bits of rags, earth-colored and wet from the river; the charred and scattered bones of some small animal. There were women here, gray-faced and lean, and men who had lost their real ages beneath the hard lines of their faces. They all looked old.

Mireille did not venture near the fire. She squatted down instead in the farthest corner she could find, where the wind still blew snow on her cheeks, and rested her head on her crossed arms.

"What's the matter? Don't want to be friendly?" a man's scratchy voice called from another point in the darkness.

Mireille jolted awake, her head jerking in every direction like a bird's.

"Nervous little thing, so you are." The man moved closer to her, crouching as he walked under the low ceiling. He was grinning through long tombstone-shaped teeth mottled with decay. "Down here you'll need a protector, pretty girl like you." He stroked her face with his dirt-blackened fingers.

His fingernails were more than an inch long, and jagged at the tips. "I'll make sure you eat, little girl." He laughed, a dry, empty chuckle that crescendoed to a raucous roar.

Mireille glanced desperately at the others for help, but no one under the bridge paid any attention to either of them. A woman in a knit hat gnawed on a large bone like a dog, smacking her lips noisily as the clochard pawed Mireille's face.

"Yeah, I'm going to take real good care of you." His hands moved more slowly, then stopped, poised in midair. He cocked his head to one side as his smile disappeared and his eyes gleamed with lust.

When he brought his hands down again, they cupped her breasts.

Mireille leaned backward until she lost her balance and fell over, too terrified to scream. The man bent over her, leering, his threadbare jacket flapping open to release the putrid stench of his body.

"Come on, come on," he whispered, beckoning impatiently to her with twitching fingers.

She drew her knees in as far as possible over her bulging belly. Then, bracing herself on her elbows, she shot out both her legs as hard and fast as she could into his stomach.

He staggered backward with a long wheeze, stumbling over the woman with the bone. She never looked at him, but only raised her elbows protectively to cover her food while she continued to eat. The man crashed on the ground behind her.

Her heart hammering, Mireille scrambled to her feet and ran from the bridge, clawing her way up the steep snow-covered embankment on all fours.

Halfway up the hill she felt a pain, as if someone had kicked her, and then felt herself urinating. The water poured out of her by what seemed like gallons, and she was helpless to stop it. Still, she forced herself to keep climbing, until the next pain sent her rolling back down the hill.

She dug in her fingers to stop her fall, then started up again. Panic raced through her. *The baby is coming,* she thought.

But it couldn't be the baby. It was too early. She couldn't have it now. Not here.

The third pain was worse than the other two. Several seconds passed after it subsided before she could rally the strength to try the hill again. Early or not, she knew her child—Stefan's child—was going to be born very soon. Nothing she did could change that.

At the onset of the next pain, she gripped some tall weeds and hung on while she stole a glance behind her. To her relief, the clochard had not followed her out into the storm.

A searing contraction coursed through her body. She ground her teeth together to keep from screaming. If the man under the bridge knew exactly where she was, he might brave the weather to reach her. This time, Mireille knew, she would not be able to defend herself.

With a small sigh of victory, she reached the top of the hill. There was not a soul in sight. The tracks on the sidewalk made by the chestnut vendor and his customers were completely covered with thick, wet snow. Overhead, a streetlamp illuminated the empty road. There was nothing visible beyond.

She managed to drag herself almost to the curb before the next pain shot through her. Doubling over, she looked up as if expecting to see the face of God.

The streetlamp was ringed with a rainbow. The wind sang its lonely song in her ears, and the snow no longer felt cold. She knew then that her baby would never be born, because she would not be alive to bring it into the world.

"Stefan," she cried, but her voice was too weak to carry beyond her own lips.

She laid her face against the snow. It would all be over soon.

Chapter Eight

The taxi had to swerve up over the far curb to avoid hitting the girl. Rapping his head smartly on the steering wheel, the driver cursed as he got out and ran over to the still body covered with snow.

Hit and run, he thought. The poor creature on the road was probably dead and frozen stiff. He had seen them before. "Always on my shift," he muttered as he bent over the girl. He sighed and turned her over.

Mireille's glazed eyes opened wide, and she screamed. The sound echoed through the empty park.

"Take it easy, lady," the man said, visibly shaken. "Look, I got no radio in my car. I'm going to have to take you to the hospital myself. Where'd you get hit? Can you talk?"

She grabbed his jacket with hands as strong as steel clamps. "Help me. Please. My baby . . ."

"I'm trying, lady. Now I just got to get my arms under you, see, and I'm going to carry you to the car. Okay, that's good."

He was a big man, but the road was so slippery that he fell, over and over again, under her weight while trying to get to his feet. When he was finally able to stand upright, he staggered toward the curb with the young woman in his arms, thinking that he would have to push the car back onto the street. Then Mireille screamed again, writhing in pain. The cabdriver lost his footing and fell to one knee, but he never dropped her.

"Hang on, mama, that's right," he said, wobbling to his feet again. A bright spot of blood was stamped into the snow where his knee had struck. He slid her onto the backseat, talking all the while. "It'll just be a few minutes. The car's stuck, see, and I—"

"No time," she groaned, and opened her coat. Her swollen belly was rolling with another contraction. Between her splayed legs, the crown of the baby's head was already showing.

"Merde de la Vierge," the driver said. Mireille took his hand. Tears were spilling down her face. "Hey, it's all right," he said kindly. "I got five kids of my own. I'm an expert at this."

She squeezed him harder, the fear still shining brightly in her eyes.

"It's no sweat, I tell you. Hey, you got to let go of my two fingers there, on account of you're breaking them, okay?"

The contraction passed, and Mireille shuddered. "Sorry," she whispered.

He washed his hands in the snow, then piled some inside a rag and dabbed her sweat-covered face with it.

"One thing's for sure," he said, leaning into the taxi's open door to help shelter the young pregnant girl from the wind. "We're not going to make it to no hospital."

Mireille moaned again.

"Don't worry, it'll be fine. This is going to be over one-two-three, you'll see. And then it won't hurt no more. That's what my wife says, and she ought to know, right? Five times, all of them big as elephants."

Mireille gasped. Her hand flung out to the top of the seat. She gripped it so hard that her fingers tore through the upholstery.

The driver checked the baby's head. "It's coming good," he said. "The next time you get a pain, you'll want to push, understand?"

She nodded. The cords in her neck stood out like ropes.

"Hey, relax," he said gently, smoothing down her hair. "You're going to come out of this just fine. You both are." He took her hand

and rubbed it between his own. "And what's the idea of wrecking my seat, huh? I'll have you know that's genuine burlap the company equips these cabs with." He laughed uncertainly. "That was just a joke, miss. It's no skin off my nose if—"

He felt her stiffen, and the smile on his face vanished. Immediately, he dropped her hand and pushed her skirt over her hips. "Okay, now push hard." He brushed his face against his shoulder to wipe off the sweat.

The top of the baby's head was throbbing between her legs.

"Do it again, honey. Suck in your breath and push. Push!"

With a groan and a spill of blood, the baby's head emerged.

"One more time," the driver commanded.

Mireille pushed again, and a pair of chalky shoulders wriggled out. The baby slid onto the man's arms, wailing loudly. "Perfect," he said.

"What . . . what is it?"

"A beautiful little girl. Here, see for yourself." He handed the baby to her and took off his jacket to cover the wrinkled little body, then he closed the door.

The baby cried, rooting instinctively for her mother's comfort. Mireille offered her breast, and the tiny mouth took it eagerly.

Within ten minutes the taxi driver had pushed the car back onto the street. He got in, brushing snow from his hair and blowing on his hands. "Hell of a night," he said. "I can't remember it snowing this hard in Paris in the past ten years. But we had a baby, so who cares what the weather's like, huh?" He smiled into the rearview mirror. "Hey, what's the matter?" he asked when he saw Mireille's tear-stained face. "You ought to be jumping for joy. I'll have you in the hospital inside of five minutes, guaranteed."

"I can't go to a hospital." She squeezed her eyes shut, trying to remain conscious. "I don't have any money. I can't even pay you for your trouble." Her head fell back against the seat. "I'm sorry. I wish I could."

"Look, lady," he said gently. "I don't want your money, all right? I just want you to come out of this okay. Somebody's got to cut that belly-button cord, and it ain't going to be me."

"I can't go to the hospital," she repeated, thinking of the explanations she would have to offer the authorities. Word about her might get back to Champs de Blé, to the police who might still be searching for Valois's murderer. "I'm . . . I'm in trouble."

"With the police?"

She didn't answer.

The cabbie took a deep breath. "How old are you?" he asked.

She remained silent.

"Never mind. I know you're too young to be going through this alone." He rubbed his stubbly chin. "Got no husband, I suppose."

She shook her head.

"I didn't think so. Where are your folks?"

"Both dead."

"And the cops are after you. For what, stealing?"

She hid her face behind her hand and wept silently.

"Okay, okay." He reached behind him and pulled her hand away. "Listen, I don't know much, but I know what it's like to be broke. During the war I had to lift a few things myself so's my kids wouldn't starve. I'm not going to turn you in."

He ran his fingers through his hair. The baby made small sucking noises. "I got it," the cabbie said suddenly, starting up the car. "Leave this to me."

He drove to Le Marais, the old Jewish quarter of the city, with its twisting, narrow cobblestone streets, and stopped in front of a large white house. Another "*Chambres à Louer*" sign hung over the door.

Mireille looked up at it in despair. "I told you, I have no money," she said.

"Quiet." He got out and went inside. After a few minutes, he came back to the car. "It's okay. This lady's going to take you in till you get back on your feet. No charge. She's a midwife, too. Delivered all my kids. You'll be okay with her."

"But—"

"Her name's Racine. Augustine Racine. And the old girl's my godmother, so if you steal anything from her, I'm personally going to come back and box your ears."

Mireille shook her head in wonder. "Why are you doing this for me?"

"Because my wife's kept dinner waiting for me for two hours, and I can't spend the rest of the night listening to you sing the blues," he said. "Here." He opened his fare box, pulled out all the bills, and handed them to her. "There isn't much. It was a slow night. Get yourself some food."

She held the money in her cupped hands as if it were a living thing, a bird about to fly away. The man closed his fist over hers. "Go on," he said. "I'll tell the company I got robbed." He shrugged. "It happens."

"I don't even know your name. How will I pay you back?"

"You won't, and that's the way I want to keep it," he said. "Look, no offense, okay? I think you're a sweet kid, but if I give you my name, my address, the next thing you got maybe a boyfriend come knocking at my door causing trouble for my family. I got to think about things like that. Like I said, no offense, but this is a one-shot thing. No more handouts—I can't afford it. And when Augustine tells you to clear out, you got to go. Deal?"

She nodded slowly.

"Good. Here she comes now. You're in good hands with her, believe me."

An old woman with a knot of white hair on top of her head came waddling out, carrying a sheet.

Madame Racine and her godson wrapped Mireille and the baby in the sheet and carried them into the house, where a bed was waiting. The warmth of the room felt welcoming. The linens were crisp and white and smelled of homemade soap.

As the old woman prepared to cut the umbilical cord, Mireille gave the taxi driver his jacket. "Thank you," she said, her eyes filling. "For everything. Thank you so much."

The man winked at her. "Have a good life, mama," he said.

Chapter Nine

The baby was healthy, but Mireille's condition worsened. The delivery of the afterbirth was irregular, and the bleeding that had begun in the taxicab grew progressively heavier. Madame Racine ministered to her into the night, but by midnight the hemorrhaging was too serious for the old woman to handle alone.

"I've got to call a doctor," she said.

"No," Mireille rasped. "No hospital. Please!"

"Not a hospital," Madame Racine reassured her. "Just a doctor. A friend."

The doctor gave Mireille a shot to put her to sleep, then set to work. "This woman has been ill for some time," he said gravely. Mireille heard him through a swirl of distorted sound and light as she fought the effects of the tranquilizer. "Eclampsia. A pernicious condition in pregnancy. It probably accounts for the premature delivery. Has she had convulsions?"

"Not since she's been here." Mireille recognized Madame Racine's powdery voice, now cracking with concern and fatigue. "Will she be all right?"

"Well, she's young. Except for some signs of malnutrition, she seems to be in reasonably good health. I doubt that she'll ever have another child, though."

Another child, Mireille thought bitterly as the voices faded into the whirlpool of her waning consciousness. *Where would I raise it?*

By the river where I'll keep this one? Around the garbage cans where
I'll eat my food?

She sank into oblivion.

In the morning Mireille awoke to a flood of sunlight falling through
clean white curtains. Madame Racine was standing over a wicker
laundry basket, making cooing sounds. A tray with a glass of milk
and some gruel was on the night table beside the bed.

Mireille sat up in a panic, for a moment not certain where she
was. "My baby," she said.

"She's right here." The old woman picked up the infant from
the basket with strong, experienced hands and sat with her in a big
white rocking chair. In the sunlight, her snow-white hair looked
like a dollop of whipped cream. "And she's fine, just fine. You eat
your breakfast while it's hot." Slowly, Mireille reached for the bowl
and ate. The porridge was delicious, smooth and sweet. She gulped
down the cold milk.

"Hungry?" the old lady teased.

"Yes, ma'am," Mireille said, embarrassed. She touched her lips
with the small napkin, resisting the urge to scrape the bowl with
her fingers.

Madame Racine laughed. "That's a good sign. You've been
asleep since the day before yesterday. Don't worry, your baby's
been well fed." She stood up, bouncing the child gently in her arms.
"My own formula. A hundred babies have used it. Still, I'm sure
she'd rather have your milk." She handed the infant to Mireille. "I'll
go fetch you some more breakfast."

"No, really, that's not necessary," Mireille said politely.

"Nonsense. You'll need your strength. Your daughter was
lucky you're so young and strong. You lost a lot of blood. What's
her name?"

The little girl squirmed and clamped her mouth over Mireille's breast. At least she still had milk, Mireille thought. "I haven't given her one."

The old woman clucked. "She really must have a name, you know." She picked up the tray and went out.

Mireille touched the soft pink cheek nestled against her. "What shall I name her, Stefan?" she asked aloud. "She has your dark hair, and your stubborn chin, too." Then she knew.

When Madame Racine came back with more food, Mireille smiled at her. "I'm going to name her Stephanie," she announced proudly.

The old lady beamed. "Stephanie. That's a lovely name."

The baby belched in agreement.

Within a week Mireille was on her feet and helping Madame Racine with the housework.

"You do too much," the old woman chided one day when she came home from her shopping to find a Christmas tree decorated with red ribbons in the parlor. Mireille had used the last of the money the cabdriver had given her to buy it. The rest had gone to pay for the expensive medication the doctor had prescribed.

"I've cooked the dinner," she said, removing the lid from a steaming lamb stew on the stove. "I don't know if it's any good, though."

Madame Racine bent over the pot, fanning the steam toward her face. "Ah, *magnifique*," she said, kissing her fingers. "Although unfortunately, I doubt if either Monsieur Brévard or Mademoiselle Joelle will notice."

She was referring to the two other boarders in the house, both octogenarians. "Mademoiselle Joelle has started taking showers in the middle of the night again." Madame Racine shook her head as she put the groceries away. "Poor creature, she never knows what time it is anymore. I believe she thinks she's getting ready to teach school at that hour. That was her profession, you know. A shame, a shame."

She closed the cupboard with a click. "Well, at least we've got you and little Stephanie to keep this place from turning into an old-age home." She clapped her hands together. "Come, let's have a cup of tea and admire our lovely tree."

"You go ahead. I want to clean the oven before Stephanie wakes up."

"You'll do no such thing," Madame Racine insisted, pulling her bodily into the sitting room. "Enough is enough. You do the work of ten people, when you ought to be lying in bed and putting some meat on those skinny bones of yours." She sat her down. As she took down the cups and saucers from a kitchen cabinet, Mireille picked up some knitting.

"What are you making, dear?" the old woman asked when she came back with the tray.

"A blanket, of sorts, sewn closed." She lifted the garment for Madame Racine to see. It was pink, made of the softest lambswool. "I'm afraid I've hardly done justice to your beautiful yarn."

"Pah," the woman said, blowing on her tea. "That old wool's been lying around here for years."

"Madame Racine . . ." Mireille set the knitting needles down in her lap. "You've done so much for me already. I hate to ask for another favor, but I have to."

"What is it, dear?"

Mireille took a deep breath. "I'm well enough to work," she said, "but I'll need someone to look after Stephanie. I'll pay you, of course, once I find a job—"

"I'd be delighted!" the old woman said, patting her hand. "Nothing would please me more. Er . . . what is your line of work, child?"

Mireille flushed with embarrassment. "I used to wash dishes at the Dôme Café. Maybe they would take me back."

The old woman made a face. "Such disagreeable work."

"I don't mind," Mireille said.

"I know, dear. But there must be something else for a well-spoken, attractive young lady like you." She stood up. "We'll look in the newspaper. I've got today's *France-soir* here."

She snapped open the page to the "Female Help Wanted" section and sat down with a pencil. "Ah. What did I tell you? Here's just the thing." Holding the paper at arm's length, she read, "'Reception clerk, must be poised and well mannered,' etcetera, etcetera. 'Hôtel du Lac, Rue du Faubourg Saint-Honoré.' Very chichi address, *non*?" She circled the ad, then set down her pencil with a snap. "That's settled, then."

Mireille didn't answer. She was looking at her hands, spread over her lap.

"Is that the only dress you have?" the old woman asked.

Mireille nodded.

"Oh, what's the matter with me," Madame Racine exclaimed, popping up onto her feet in exasperation. "I should never have let you pay for those medicines. And this tree! You're a foolish sentimentalist, Mireille. And now . . . Oh!" She darted out of the room, her whipped-cream hair bobbing.

She bustled back in just as rapidly, holding an enormous rustling pile of tissue. "Clear these away," she ordered, flicking her fingers over the tea things. When the table was empty, she laid down the bundle with great care and opened the folds of age-yellowed paper.

Inside was a floor-length dress of dark-green velvet trimmed with handmade lace. The woman's gnarled hands caressed it lovingly. "I wore this on my honeymoon in 1902," she said, her eyes twinkling. "We went to London. Oh, it was all very grand on the boat going over, with banners and a band playing. Not like today.

And of course I wanted to show all the English women that we Parisians were the last word in fashion."

She laughed, high and lilting as a girl. "So I had this made especially for me. My father was furious with the bill." She ran her hands over the exquisite lacework. "You know, it was so lovely that I never wore it again. Isn't that silly? I was saving it—for what, I couldn't tell you."

She lifted it up. The thick velvet poured to the floor like a cascade of liquid.

"It's beautiful," Mireille said.

"It would have to be updated, of course." She swung it around to show a small bustle in the back, and they both chuckled. "Fix the sleeves, lop off the skirt to show your legs—"

"Oh, I couldn't do that," Mireille protested. "It should be saved."

"It's been saved for more than forty years! It's time we got some use out of it. Can you sew?"

"Yes," Mireille said, touching the lush fabric. It was a dress from a fairy tale, with its silk piping and dozens of tiny buttons down the back, the most beautiful dress Mireille had ever seen.

When they were finished with the alterations, Mireille stood mesmerized before her image in the mirror. She was no longer the gawky, scraggly-haired girl who had scrubbed her stepmother's floor on her hands and knees; no longer the starving waif looking through the slats of a public trash barrel at the world passing by. She had been transformed into a princess cloaked in velvet, willowy and beautiful.

"I'll never be able to repay you for this," she said.

"Oh, yes, you will." The old woman hugged her. "Make a good life for yourself and your daughter. Pass on some kindness when you can. And light a candle for me at Notre-Dame when I die. That will repay me a hundred times over."

Mireille kissed the top of Madame Racine's head tenderly. "I will," she said. "I promise I will."

Chapter Ten

She arrived at the Hôtel du Lac at eight in the morning. In the lobby she discreetly removed her thin, baggy coat and draped it over her arm. Then, trying to force some saliva into her dry throat, she walked past the sumptuous furnishings and the huge Christmas tree covered with tiny gold balls to the front desk.

A well-dressed brunette almost as tall as Mireille gave her a withering glance and raised her eyebrows in inquiry.

"I'd like a job, please," Mireille said timidly, producing the newspaper ad. "The reception clerk's job?"

Without deigning to speak to her, the woman picked up a telephone. "An applicant," she said, her cold eyes traveling from Mireille's hair, which was braided and pinned to the top of her head, to her shoes. She exhaled with a sneer. "Oh, you'll have to see this one for yourself." She put down the phone and gestured to the hallway to the right of the desk, away from the lobby. "Third door on the right."

The third door was marked "M. Saint-Georges, Personnel." Monsieur Saint-Georges was a thin man in his forties with darting eyes and the manner of someone perpetually on the brink of a nervous breakdown. He snatched Mireille's application from her and settled behind his desk to read it with a sigh, indicating that he had more pressing business to attend to.

"No, no," he said, thumping his fist on the paper.

"I beg your pardon?" Mireille asked.

The man picked up the telephone and dialed one number. "Is this your idea of a joke?" he said loudly into the mouthpiece. "Don't you think I have anything better to do with my time than talk to every misfit who sneaks past the doorman? I'm warning you—"

Mireille heard a loud bang on the other end. Monsieur Saint-Georges gnashed his teeth while he struggled to compose himself before turning his attention vaguely to the tall, thin girl in front of him. "It's out of the question. I'm sorry." He handed the application form back to her.

She stood there in silence, not knowing whether she had been dismissed or not. "I'll work hard," she ventured. "Whatever has to be done, I'll do it. I won't miss a day of work unless I'm too sick to stand up, and I'll do my best to make a good impression on your customers."

The man sighed. "Guests. We do not entertain *customers* at the Hôtel du Lac. They are guests."

"Yes, sir. Guests."

"Mademoiselle, I don't doubt your good intentions, but you are definitely not suitable for the position we have available." He shook his head rapidly and emphatically, setting his sagging jowls quivering. "And that trollop at the front desk knew it," he added under his breath.

Mireille felt a sting of anger. "How am I not suitable?" she asked, thinking how strident her own voice sounded.

Monsieur Saint-Georges flapped his mouth open, then shut it.

Mireille persisted. "You said I was definitely not suitable. On the telephone you were yelling about misfits sneaking past the doorman, and I guess you meant me. Well, I've walked the whole way across the city to see you, and I'd like to know what you think is wrong with me."

He folded his hands, prayer-like, and spoke with quietly contained fury. "All right," he said, narrowing his eyes. "In the first place, you look ridiculous." He waved his hand toward her in a dismissive gesture. "That dress is right out of a Gilbert and Sullivan musical. Secondly, your speech is as uncultivated as your manicure. The Hôtel du Lac does not wish for its guests to be greeted by a provincial bumpkin with little education and a résumé consisting of one job washing dishes."

He enunciated each word with careful precision. "This is why you are not suitable. Have I made myself clear?" He gave her a frozen smirk and blinked exaggeratedly.

Mireille seethed inside. In her seventeen years, she knew, she had been through more than Monsieur Saint-Georges would ever understand in his entire bow-tied life.

"You've made one thing clear," she said, feeling her face redden. "Of all the fools I've ever met, you're the biggest." She snatched her job application out of his hands, crushed it into a ball, and then threw it in his face before stomping out.

She was halfway through the lobby before her knees started wobbling and she felt her heart racing as if she had just engaged in physical battle. *I can't believe I did that,* she thought.

She cast around for a place to sit down and pull herself together. There was a grouping of chairs around a potted palm, where a man was sitting alone reading a newspaper. He was slight and harmless-looking. A pair of pince-nez glasses perched on the bridge of his long, pointed nose. His fingernails were polished.

A guest, no doubt, Mireille thought with contempt.

He possessed the effete air of someone who would come to an overpriced place like the Hôtel du Lac in order to be fawned upon by the likes of Monsieur Saint-Georges. *Well, if he minds having a provincial bumpkin in a ridiculous dress sitting near him, he can lump it,* Mireille told herself defiantly. *Whatever a "bumpkin" is.* She plopped down on one of the overstuffed chairs across from him.

Her confrontation with the personnel manager kept coming back to her in alternating waves of dismay and triumph. She hadn't managed to say anything witty or memorable, but the fact that she had answered him back at all, however crudely, continued to amaze her. In all her life, it had been the first time she had dared to speak up for herself. It felt good, she decided. It felt very good.

Her self-satisfied reverie was broken by the presence of a large pair of gray trousers beside her. She looked up to see a towering man with a nose that obviously had been broken more than once.

"I'm sorry, miss. Security," he said by way of introduction. "You'll have to leave now."

Beyond him, at the reception desk, the tall brunette woman stood with her arms crossed, watching her.

Mireille looked from one to the other. "I'm only sitting," she said.

"Sorry." He bent over with a grunt to take her arm.

Then, strangely, the man wearing the pince-nez snapped his newspaper into his lap and barked, "Stop that at once!"

The security guard halted, his big ham hand still spread open in preparation for the grab, and looked to the desk clerk for guidance.

She waved her arms in a small, ladylike way, as if sending a message to abort the mission, then strode over toward them wearing her most winning smile.

"Monsieur le Comte, I extend my most sincere apologies for your inconvenience," she said in a charming tone utterly unlike the rude drawl she had used earlier with Mireille. "We were under the impression that this individual was disturbing you."

"This individual, as you call the Baroness Clothilde Francoise Honoré de Bercy, is a personal friend of mine," the man snapped. "Since you are not, I shall not bother to introduce you. Please leave us."

Mireille gazed at the little man in wonder as the desk clerk backed away, murmuring apologies while discreetly shoving the security guard out of her path.

The man she had called "Monsieur le Comte" was dainty, and the pince-nez, which had given his voice a silly nasal quality, made him look very much like a little dark-feathered bird. Yet when he spoke, it was with complete authority. Mireille only hoped he wouldn't be angry when he found out he'd defended the wrong person.

"That was kind of you," she said once the desk clerk was out of earshot. "But I'm really not the Baroness Clothilde, or whoever it was."

"What?" he exclaimed. "You're not?" He slapped his face. The pince-nez fell off his nose.

She was so taken aback that she started to laugh. He joined her with a shrug.

"Of course you're not," he said, wiping his eyes with a handkerchief of such fine linen that it was almost transparent. "That's my aunt, and she's at least a hundred years old. I just couldn't bear to see them bullying you so." He looked at her with twinkling eyes, holding her gaze a few seconds longer than necessary.

She stood up. "Well, thank you."

"Why the hurry?" he asked.

"I've got to look for another job." She smiled. "I don't think they're going to hire me here."

"Five hundred francs," he said quietly.

"Excuse me?"

His lips curved in a slight smile. "I offered you five hundred francs."

"What for?"

His brow furrowed in an expression of exquisite pain. Then he burst out laughing.

She blushed, confused. "I guess I really am a bumpkin."

"Darling, you're an angel." He took her hand and kissed it. "An absolutely ravishing, perfect angel. I must have you. Please come to my rooms and let me make love to you."

"*What?*" She withdrew her hand as if it were on fire. "You mean that's what you were offering? I've got to go." She walked away briskly, but he caught up with her.

"Please stop," he panted, huffing to catch his breath as if the few steps he'd taken had done him in. "This is a charming drama, but I'm an asthmatic, and I haven't the stamina for it."

He reached up to grasp her shoulders and gently led her back to the chair. "Five hundred is more than fair, and we both know it. After all, I'm not some sweating, smelly beast who's going to tie you up in chains."

Mireille brushed him away from her. "I am not a prostitute," she said haughtily.

"And I am not looking for one." He mimicked her indignation, tossing his head righteously. "Mademoiselle, I am Anatole Jean-Claude de Balfours, fifty-third Comte de Vevray, and I do not make love to streetwalkers."

"But—"

He held up a hand to cut her off. "It is simply that I have just found the most beautiful woman in Paris and, as such, I do not expect her to accompany me to my rooms without adequate compensation for her time. Now, I could go through the charade of having honorable intentions toward you, but that would be untrue, and perhaps cruel as well. Whatever else I may be, I am neither a cruel man nor a liar."

He placed a cigarette into a tortoiseshell holder and lit it. "So the question is not whether or not you are a prostitute," he said, blowing out a long thin stream of blue smoke, "but whether or not you will accept a rather large sum of money in exchange for passing the time with a lonely and rather sweet fellow." He smiled.

She watched him for a moment, terrified of her thoughts. *He's crazy. Just leave. Get out before you start believing him.* In the back of her mind, she saw the clochard under the bridge, stroking her face with his dirty fingernails.

Where will I raise my child? In the garbage cans, where I find our food?

The Comte de Vevray was offering her more money for one afternoon than she had earned in a month of washing dishes at the Dôme Café.

"Well, will you come loll the afternoon away with me, or are you saving yourself for the man you love?" the Comte asked dryly.

The man you love. The words cut her like a knife. But Stefan was dead. Nothing would bring him back now.

Nothing she did would change anything.

After a moment, she met the small man's eyes. "I'll come with you." The words nearly choked in her throat.

"A wise decision," he said, extending his hand.

She took it.

They walked together toward the elevator. "What shall I call you?" the Comte mused.

"My name is—"

"No, no. I'll choose it, if you don't mind." In the elevator he studied her face. "L'Ange, I think," he said softly. "The Angel." He smiled. "Yes, that will do."

Chapter Eleven

The rooms occupied by the Comte de Vevray resembled an elaborate stage set. The decor was entirely art nouveau, from the Tiffany lamps to the Egyptian pattern on the rugs. A grand piano swelled out of one corner. A six-foot-tall oil painting signed by Toulouse-Lautrec commanded one rose-colored wall.

"Do you like it?" Vevray asked as he knocked on an adjoining door.

"I've never seen anything like this place," Mireille said. "Are all the rooms in this hotel the same?"

"*Dieu, non,*" he laughed. "I own these rooms. They're where I prefer to stay when I'm in Paris."

The door opened, and a tall man in formal attire appeared standing at attention.

"Please see to it that breakfast is brought up," Vevray told him. "A soufflé with herbs, caviar, some small brioches . . ." He waved him away. "Whatever you think, Jean. And two bottles of Dom Pérignon 'twenty-nine."

The tall man nodded solemnly and shut the door.

"My manservant," Vevray said. "Now, what were we talking about?" He took Mireille's coat from her and hung it up.

"You said you stayed here when you were in Paris," Mireille said, trying not to sound nervous. "Isn't the city your home?"

He shrugged. "I don't suppose I have a home, really," he said. "My parents live nearby, but they don't particularly care for me to stay with them. Actually, I rather enjoy being a nomad. I've got several places to hang my hat."

He took off his jacket and lit another cigarette. "There's a rambling old *Schloss* still standing in Berlin, all gingerbread and bric-a-brac; a Bauhaus monstrosity in Vienna, with silver walls and a swimming pool in the living room, from my younger days; and a houseboat in Marseilles, much too worldly for me to describe to you." He wiggled his eyebrows suggestively. "And there's a Victorian town house in London, too. I suppose that's where I spend most of my time. Terribly fussy and embroidered, but naughty in secret ways, like the English are."

He threw his head back. "Oh, what a bore I must be, blathering on so. Would you like to tell me about yourself?"

"No," Mireille whispered.

Vevray burst out laughing. "Good! You shall always be a mystery, then. A beautiful enigma. Come with me." He led her through a black-and-white dining room and down a short corridor into a large dressing area filled with dozens of men's suits and at least fifty pairs of shoes.

"I'd like you to wear something for me," he said.

Mireille felt a moment of panic as he opened a carved armoire. "What is it?"

"Nothing objectionable, I assure you." He pulled out a magnificent robe. It was emerald green and covered with tiny glass beads arranged in elaborate patterns.

"Yes," he said softly. "This matches your eyes." He handed the garment to her and opened a door on the far side of the dressing room. "I'll be in here when you're ready."

Mireille stood immobile long after he left. "Oh, Stefan," she whispered.

Stefan is dead. Madame Loquin and Giselle and all the people like them are still left in the world, but not Stefan.

Stefan couldn't protect her anymore.

She unbuttoned her dress.

The bedroom on the other side of the door was draped with fabric, forming a tent, with the middle of the ceiling as its apex. Lights were positioned behind the fabric, suffusing the room with soft, warm color. A cart loaded with silver serving trays stood against the draping. The bed, covered in peach-colored satin, was round.

Vevray waited on it, nude, sipping from a glass of champagne. "Unfasten the clasp," he said.

She did, trying not to tremble as the robe fell open over her breasts, exposing the creamy skin of her belly and the mound of soft hair between her legs.

He came over to her and ran his hands softly over her body. "L'Ange," he whispered, and sank to his knees. "Let me worship you, my angel."

He kissed her thighs, cajoling them open. Then, holding her buttocks, he flicked his tongue over the button of flesh beneath the light dusting of her blonde pubic hair.

Mireille's breath caught. His mouth was soft and expert, caressing her first with long, smooth strokes that made her juices run, then harder and faster, his tongue dancing wildly on her, his lips enclosing until her knees spread wide and she felt herself thrusting into his welcoming mouth.

She touched his face as he bobbed frantically, smearing her slick juice over his lips, then cupped her hands over her breasts. Her nipples were hard, and droplets of her milk stood on the tips.

He was using his tongue like a penis now, pushing inside her, slurping noisily as he took himself in his hand, pumping his erection with heavy strokes.

"I need to fuck you now," he said. His voice was quivering. He slid onto the satin bed and pulled her on top of him. She rode him then, bucking on his stiff rod, bending low to fill his open mouth with a jiggling breast.

He looked into her eyes for a moment as he tasted her milk. Then his fingers dug into the hot flesh of her backside and he sucked out the liquid greedily, moaning as he felt her body clench around him in climax and he shot his cream into her.

She gasped for air. It was the first time since her final day with Stefan that Mireille had been touched by a man.

"You're full of surprises," Vevray said languidly, touching her hair. "Mother's milk. How delightfully unexpected."

"I have—" She was going to say "a child," but her confession was cut short.

"Yes, yes," the Comte said impatiently. "Now tell me." He leaned forward and kissed the end of her nose. "Did you enjoy making love with me?"

"I . . . Well, yes. That is, I didn't expect to . . ."

"But you did? I'm flattered." He kissed her, and she kissed him back.

"I loved someone once," she said haltingly. "I didn't think I could ever . . ."

He held a champagne glass to her lips. "Now, now," he said. "It's been lovely. Let's please not spoil it with a lot of talk."

Mireille was stunned. "You said you adored me. You said all sorts of things."

"And then we negotiated a price, darling. To my recollection, it included neither my heart nor yours. Caviar?" He offered her a silver tray.

When she was dressing to leave, Vevray slipped a bill into her hand. She almost refused it, then thought better of it. *I've earned it,* she told herself bitterly.

It was a thousand-franc note. "The extra is for the milk," he said with a smile. "By the way, I won't be in the hotel for a while. I'm leaving Paris tomorrow."

Mireille hesitated while putting on her coat. She bit her lips, smiled, and shook her head. "Since you're my only client, I guess that makes my career as a femme fatale just about the shortest in history." Her shoulders heaved.

Vevray put his arm around her. She was crying.

"Darling, I thought everything was clear from the beginning," he said, his face full of distress. "Now I feel like a cad of the worst sort."

"I'm sure there must be worse," Mireille said, sniffling. She opened the door.

"Wait." He held her arm. "I want to give you something. An address."

Vevray walked quickly to his desk and scribbled something on the back of one of his calling cards, then blew on the ink to dry it. "Please don't be offended," he said, handing it to her. "I'm trying to help. Take it in the right spirit."

She read the name and address he'd written. "Who is Madame Renée?"

Vevray smiled. "You really are a country girl, aren't you? Madame Renée runs the most exclusive . . . shall we say, escort service in the world. She's quite nearby. I thought perhaps you might want to pay her a visit. She would certainly be interested in seeing you."

Mireille felt herself reddening. "You're telling me to look for work in a brothel?"

"Darling, I really don't care where you work. You can go to her or not. Just please . . ." He rubbed his forehead, impatient for her to leave. "Look, I'll be back in three weeks. You can come back then." He forced a weary smile.

Mireille put the card in her pocketbook. "No, thank you," she said coldly as she walked out.

After dinner, Augustine Racine and her two elderly boarders sat in the parlor eating the small frosted cakes Mireille had bought. "Imagine the Hôtel du Lac giving our Mireille an advance on her salary," Madame Racine chattered excitedly. "Didn't I tell you they would hire you, dear? Didn't I say you'd be perfect?"

Monsieur Brévard began to sing "Silent Night." Mademoiselle Joelle joined him in her high, quavering voice.

"Are you feeling all right, Mireille?" Madame Racine asked.

"I'm fine." They were almost the first words she'd spoken all evening.

"Well, I would think you'd be more excited. Don't you realize what a wonderful opportunity this is for you?"

"A wonderful opportunity," Mireille echoed flatly.

"Now, something is wrong, dear, I just know it. Tell me what's bothering you."

"Nothing is bothering me!"

Monsieur Brévard and Mademoiselle Joelle were startled into silence by Mireille's outburst. In the distance, the baby began to cry. "I'm sorry," she said. "I'm just tired. Excuse me."

She ran to her room and picked up the infant, holding her as if she were a life buoy in an ocean in which Mireille was drowning. "Stephanie, Stephanie," she sobbed, rocking the little girl until her cries subsided.

You are all the good left in me, she thought as she watched the innocent sleeping face nestled against her arms.

What small measure of pride she possessed had vanished this afternoon. At seventeen, when she should have been beginning her life, Mireille had nothing more to live for.

"Except you," she whispered to the tiny pink face. "It's your life that matters now."

The thought filled her with a fear greater than her despair. What sort of life would Stephanie have? A duplicate of Mireille's current life, struggling for every morsel of food until the day she sold her body to a stranger, as her mother had?

"Never," she vowed, hearing the rasp of her own breathing. "You'll never have to live my life over. You'll never be hungry and homeless and at the mercy of every passing stranger. I promise you that, Stephanie."

She, reached into her pocketbook and pulled out the wad of currency remaining after she'd changed the large bill the Comte had given her. There was already enough there to feed her and her baby for months.

Her thoughts were racing. The arrogant personnel manager at the hotel had been right. A girl her age with no education and no family was unsuitable for any decent job. Yet Vevray had paid her a thousand francs to spend an hour in his bed.

It hadn't even really been her, that body in the bed with the Comte, not really. He hadn't cared a whit who she was. He hadn't even wanted to know her name. For that hour, she had been no more than the little man's fantasy, an angel, the embodiment of a dream that was his alone.

Could she not be that for other men, as well? Could she not, for the time it took for those men to live out their fantasies, become someone other than herself, an anonymous woman who had nothing to do with Mireille de Jouarre? Did any of them have to be any more real to her than she was to them?

In exchange for this pretense, her daughter would eat well and go to school. Stephanie would never have to put on someone else's filthy cast-off black dress. She would never know the fear of sickness without a doctor or medicine. She would never have to go barefoot because she had no shoes.

"Ah, yes, little one," she whispered to her sleeping baby. "It will be a game, nothing more. None of it will be real. And nothing of this game will ever touch you. Ever."

Mireille set the baby down and spread the money on her bed. *This is mine,* she thought. *Mine and Stephanie's.* Whatever Mireille had done, or would do, whatever she was or would become, this money belonged to her.

In the middle of the bills was Vevray's calling card with Madame Renée's address on the back. She picked it up.

"L'Ange," she said aloud.

Chapter Twelve

Madame Renée's library was elegant and somber, with a leather-covered desk and books lining the walls. Whatever Mireille had expected—red flocked wallpaper, perhaps, or lurid paintings of nude women hanging over an upright piano—it wasn't this. The building itself was on the Rue le Sueur in Paris's fashionable sixteenth *arrondissement*, where even the rich had difficulty finding apartments, let alone town houses the size of Madame Renée's.

A uniformed maid had led Mireille through an immaculate marble-floored foyer where two staircases curved on either side of the entrance to meet below the vaulted twenty-foot ceiling. Tall glass vases filled with gladiolas were tastefully arranged to add touches of color. It hardly seemed possible that this place could be a bordello.

"I am Madame Renée Auvergne," a woman in a cream-colored Chanel suit and pearls said as she closed the heavy double doors behind her. She looked to be in her forties, with a swirl of upswept red hair and the perfect posture of an army general. "You wished to see me?"

"Yes," Mireille said, standing up. "My name is Mireille de Jouarre. I'd like to work for you."

The older woman crossed her arms and circled around her, eyeing her suspiciously. When she came around to face her again, she held out her palm. "Your hand," she said.

Mireille lifted her hands uncertainly, as if she were holding an invisible soccer ball.

"No. Here." She tapped her palm with her finger.

"Oh," Mireille said, smiling with embarrassment as she extended her hand to shake.

"*Sacré coeur,*" the madam muttered. She grabbed Mireille's fingers and examined them. "No nails, but clean, at least," she pronounced after her inspection. "How long is your hair? Take it down."

Mireille removed the pins that had held her hair in a tight knot at the top of her head. Madame Renée rubbed a few strands between her fingers. "This platinum color," she said. "It's real?"

"Yes, ma'am," Mireille answered sheepishly.

"I thought so. Very unusual."

She went to her desk and sat down, pointing with a gold-plated pencil toward a chair for Mireille. "Now," she said. "What makes you come here?"

Mireille took Vevray's card from her pocketbook and gave it to her. "A . . . a friend gave me your address."

"Ah, yes. We know the Comte de Vevray quite well here. He is your friend?"

"Well, not exactly . . ."

"How much did he pay you?"

Mireille blushed. "A thousand francs."

Renée raised one eyebrow. "That's impressive. You're a professional, then?"

Mireille felt an almost uncontrollable urge to cover her face. "No," she said, shaking her head. "Just the one time, yesterday."

"Come, come, girl," Renée snapped. "Sit up straight. Pull your neck back. Speak so that you can be heard."

"I said no," Mireille pronounced carefully.

"That's better." The woman smiled. "And it's good that you're not very experienced. I don't accept pros. They tend to have bad habits. How old are you?"

Mireille hesitated.

"Tell the truth. I'm not the police."

"I'm seventeen."

Renée threw up her hands. "A child. How can I accept you?"

"I'll be eighteen next month," she lied.

Renée squinted at her. "You do look older," she said finally. "Your height gives you a certain maturity. And your body . . . Unbutton your blouse, please."

"Excuse me?"

Renée waved her hand in an impatient gesture. Mireille obeyed, undoing the buttons of her plain cotton shirt.

"*Bon*, no padding," the madam said, making another swift movement with her hand to indicate that the scrutiny of Mireille's breasts was over. "Also, your voice makes you seem older. It's rather deep for a young girl. When you speak up, that is. You'll have to learn to speak up. You aren't married, of course?"

"No." She almost told her about Stephanie, but decided against it. Stephanie would have nothing to do with this part of her life.

"Then you live with your parents?"

"My parents are both dead. I have no family."

Renée tapped the desk with her gold pencil. "Good," she said abstractedly. "Still, you're too young. If you're arrested—"

"I won't be."

Their eyes met. "I hope I can believe you. I want you to know I won't tolerate any trouble here. If you're ever picked up by the police, if there's even the hint of scandal about you, you'll regret it. Do you understand?"

"Yes, ma'am," Mireille said.

Renée leaned back in her chair. "Then I might take you on. As an apprentice, of course, and on a trial basis."

Mireille smiled despite herself. "An apprentice?"

The madam prickled. "Do you find that amusing?"

"No. I mean yes." Mireille faltered. "I don't know. It just seemed—"

"My clients pay between twelve hundred and twenty-five hundred francs for an evening with one of my girls," she said.

Mireille blinked. Those figures were staggering. "Half a year's wages," she said softly.

"That's one evening. Do you think anyone is willing to pay that kind of money for nothing more than an hour of sex?"

"What else do they do?" Mireille asked, open-mouthed.

"That is what you will be expected to learn as an apprentice," Renée said. "You have the raw materials. The face, the figure, the possibility of a speaking voice. Perhaps even a passable mind. But that is all they are, raw materials. They must be shaped, cultivated."

She went to the bookcase and pulled out three large volumes, which she plopped into Mireille's arms. One was a book on etiquette. One was an English-language textbook. The third was a study of social customs around the world.

"There will be more for you to read when you've finished with those," the woman said. "It is especially important to learn to speak English. These days it is the language of power."

Mireille remembered Stefan reading Shakespeare by the fire.

"Someone else told me that once," she said softly.

"Speak up!"

"I'll study them," she said.

"You'd better, if you expect me to trust you with one of my clients."

She touched the bottom of Mireille's chin with her long fingernail, examining the beautiful face in the sunlight.

"Your manners must be impeccable. Your provincial accent will have to disappear. You must learn to make intelligent conversation with the most sophisticated people, because my girls are taken to functions completely out of the reach of others in the Life."

"The Life?"

"The Life, my dear. Our life. This is not a job, Mireille. It is a world. And Madame Renée's girls are the reigning queens of that world. That is why my standards are so high." She leaned toward Mireille. "One of my girls married a baron, you know."

"Really?"

Renée nodded imperiously. "It is well known." She rose. "Come upstairs. I will introduce you to someone."

"These are some of the rooms." Renée flung open a few of the doors on the second floor as they walked past. They were all bedrooms, and each was large and exquisitely furnished.

One room was a study in red, from the velvet bedspread and matching divan to the heavy draperies. The brilliant color was balanced by a crystal chandelier, a white fur rug, and the paintings on the ivory-flax walls.

"Older men tend to like this setting," Renée said.

Another was a replica of the royal bedchamber at Versailles, with a canopy of blue watered silk over the bed. Still another resembled the bedroom of an English country manor, filled with pillows and floral prints. And the sumptuous Persian room at the end of the hall, studded with brass incense burners, came complete with Arabian music supplied by a hidden gramophone.

"Not all our clients come here, of course, but those who do can expect every amenity. Meals of every cuisine in the world are served in the rooms, and each has its own bar. The baths are quite luxurious, too."

She led Mireille up the stairs. "The third floor is for those with more exotic tastes."

There were fewer rooms here, and each was more bizarre than the last. One had been designed to look like a Roman fantasy. Painted statuary and fruit-bearing trees in enormous clay pots lined the white stucco walls. Several one-armed settees were clustered on one side of a shallow reflecting pool; on the other stretched a bed big enough to sleep ten, tented by a hundred yards of gossamer netting.

Another room was literally covered—floor, walls, ceiling—with black rubber. There was no bed here, only an austere rubber-covered pallet on steel legs. The lights were neon strips running along the moldings of the ceiling.

Madame Renée knocked at one door before opening it. Inside, the room was bare of furniture except for some green gymnasium-style tumbling mats covering the floor and a dozen vats stuffed with yellow roses, but the place was abuzz with activity.

Three maids in frilly aprons were kneeling beside the huge vats, systematically plucking the petals off the flowers and stuffing them into burlap bags.

"Goddamn it," someone shouted from the bathroom. "This frigging thing's got a nail sticking out of it!" Something that looked like a flat pillow covered with yellow satin and lace flew out and landed with a thud in the middle of the room. Close behind it, a woman hopped out on one bare foot. The other was sloppily bandaged with white gauze. "I'll probably get frigging tetanus!"

"Good afternoon, Barbara," Madame Renée said icily.

Barbara turned, her blue eyes still ablaze. She was the most beautiful woman Mireille had ever seen. Her skin was the color of alabaster, and her hair, as red as Madame Renée's, floated down to her waist in a cloud of curls.

"I'd like you to meet Mireille," Renée said.

Barbara hobbled a couple of steps, then steeled herself and walked over to them with the grace of a cat.

"Do you see the kind of discipline she has?" Renée asked, her tone warming as she watched. "Apparently, Barbara has stepped on a nail. But if she had to, she could spend the evening dancing in high heels."

"Sure," Barbara said. "And if I didn't, Madame Renée would have me murdered in my sleep. Hello." She extended her hand to Mireille. "I guess you're new to the stable."

Madame Renée snapped her fingers irritably. "Barbara, I've warned you about your language."

"Right. I keep forgetting." She leaned toward Mireille. "We're not supposed to use words like 'stable,' 'trick,' or 'john.'"

The madam cleared her throat. "Mireille is starting out with us," she said imperiously. "I'd like you to help me with her instruction."

"Give me a break," Barbara said, pained. "I'm booked up through next July, and this kid's barely out of diapers."

"This is not a subject for discussion," Renée said frostily. "Excuse me for a moment." Sedately she walked over to the maids and proceeded to shriek at them.

"These stems you're throwing away are full of petals!" she screamed. "Do you know what roses cost? How would you like to pay for them out of your salaries?"

While the tirade was going on, Barbara took a cigarette from a pack on the windowsill and lit it. Then she sauntered back, looking Mireille over. "Oh, all right, what the hell," she said, exhaling a long stream of smoke. "What's your name again?"

"Mireille."

She nodded. "That's nice. Elegant. Where'd you get it?"

"I beg your pardon?"

"It's not your real name, is it?"

"Why . . . yes."

"Take my advice, honey," Barbara said. "Change it."

"Change my name?"

Barbara sneaked a glance at Madame Renée, who was still scolding the maids. "I suppose she told you that you'll marry a baron."

"She said one of her . . . employees had," Mireille said.

"Right. And her dog shits gold turds. Don't believe it, sweetie. Just do your job and take the money, understand? There's nothing else."

Mireille nodded uncertainly.

Barbara squinted her eyes and inhaled deeply. "Minette," she said. "No, that's too cute. You need something more ladylike."

"Someone called me 'l'Ange' once," Mireille offered, blushing.

"L'Ange." Barbara expelled the name in a cloud of white smoke. "I like that."

"But why can't I just be Mireille?"

"Honey, if you're going to stay in this business, you aren't going to want everyone to know your name."

"What's yours?"

"Barbara. I got it from Barbara Stanwyck. She's an American actress."

"I mean your real name."

"Oh, that. Létitia." She stuck out her tongue in distaste. "Létitia Pauchon. It's too hard for foreigners to pronounce. I haven't used it for years—since the last time I got picked up by the cops." She took another deep drag from her cigarette. "Renée never knew. See how a fake name comes in handy?"

The madam came back. "I'll look after her," Barbara said, giving Mireille a wink. "She's going to be a knockout when she grows up."

Renée glared at her, then gave Mireille a businesslike smile. "All right, then. Barbara will look after you for the next several weeks and report to me on your progress. Ask her any questions you may have. Meanwhile, I expect to see you once a week. Tuesdays are good for me, say at two in the afternoon. Agreed?"

"Yes, ma'am."

"Read those books by then. And stand up straight." She pressed Mireille's collarbone. "For God's sake, Barbara, teach her how to stand."

"What for? She'll spend most of her time on her back, anyway."

Renée made a hissing sound from between gritted teeth, then strode away without a backward glance.

"You'd think the old floozy was running a finishing school," Barbara said.

"'Scuse me, miss," a workman said, handing her the yellow satin plank. "Is that better?"

She turned it over. "Great. There's a hole in the satin, and hammer marks all over it. Jesus." She gave it to one of the maids, who rushed out with it cradled in her arms.

"What is that?" Mireille asked. Her gaze moved up the ladder the workman was climbing. Two long white satin ropes now hung from a pair of eye hooks in the ceiling. "And that?"

"It's going to be a swing," Barbara said, exhaling two streams of smoke from her nose. "My client's a real wacko. An Arab, lives out in the desert. So when he comes here he wants roses. Millions of yellow roses. The floor has to be knee-deep in petals. It takes three days to get rid of them all. Can you believe that?"

She flicked an ash into the flower vat. "And a swing, with the whitest ass money can buy sitting on it."

"Just roses?" Mireille asked, raising her voice to be heard above the hammering and the mounting chatter of the maids. "Nothing else? No bed?"

Barbara shook her head. "Just frigging petals. And hedges." She turned toward the women on the floor. "Where are the goddamned hedges?"

"They're on the way," one of them said.

Two burly men huffed and panted as they carried in a white plaster fountain with a cupid standing in the middle of it.

"Oh, yes, and that," Barbara said with disgust. "Water squirts out of his dick. Lots of class. In the corner, boys."

She waved toward the far end of the room. "The first time, I set it up in the middle of the floor. Then Hamid had me jump off the swing into his arms. Only he missed, and I got knocked out on the goddamn fountain."

She took a final deep drag off the cigarette, then tossed it out the window. "Welcome to the Life, kid."

Chapter Thirteen

Barbara sent Mireille home before her rendezvous with the nature-loving Arab. They met for breakfast the next morning at the Hôtel de Crillon, surrounded by hanging plants and a magnificent array of silver that the management had somehow kept out of the hands of the Nazis.

"How did it go?" Mireille asked.

"Yesterday? Oh, fine. Hamid was dead asleep on his rose petals by eleven. He likes to drink." She made a face. "Out of a goatskin. What a mess."

Mireille laughed. "Maybe you should have used the rubber room."

"You saw that? I'm surprised. Renée likes to keep those johns a secret. Sonja's the only girl who'll go near them."

"Why?"

"They're the real bad ones," Barbara whispered. "Whips, handcuffs, that kind of thing. Piss, lots of pissers."

Mireille put down her toast. "I guess Madame Renée doesn't like Sonja very much," she said.

"Are you kidding? She loves her. Sonja brings in more money than any two girls combined. Renée's no dummy." Barbara rubbed her finger and thumb together. "She makes those guys pay hard for their fun. Besides, Sonja's really a head-turner. A six-foot-tall Viking who likes to wear leather. For years, Renée was just falling all over her. She even used to wear her hair like Sonja's, black

and cut straight across like an Egyptian's. Christ." She shook her
head. "The old broad looked demented. Nobody could keep a
straight face. Once Sonja got a guy to chase Renée all over town,
pretending he had the hots for her. Then, when they were in bed,
he pissed all over her." She laughed wildly. "The next day Renée
came in with hair the color of mine. I guess she thought I was a
safer type."

"Are you all *types*?" Mireille asked. "I mean, do all of Renée's
girls have to be different from each other?"

"Different from everyone, honey. That's the key to the big
bucks. We're one of a kind, every one of us. Sonja's the Black
Widow, and no one can play it better. Then there's Nicole, with a
face like an angel and this soft, feathery voice. All the big, tall guys
want her. And Denise, who looks like jailbait and makes all her
money off of pedophiles, even though she's pushing thirty. And
Annelise—she's a real vamp. You know, smoky eyes and terribly
mysterious. She calls herself Ankha these days."

"Why?"

"Who knows?" Barbara shrugged. "I think she's beginning
to believe her own image. She drinks absinthe. God only knows
where she gets it, but if you work for Renée, you can make enough
contacts to satisfy whatever vice you'd care to cultivate."

"What about you, Barbara?" Mireille asked.

"Me? I have no vices." She filled the room with one of her belly
laughs.

"No, I mean your type. Do you have one, too?"

"Oh, sure. It's nothing like the way I really am. You'll see for
yourself. We'll probably be sent out together before long. Just
promise not to retch."

"How do you act?" Mireille asked, fascinated.

"I'm wholesome. You know, all sparkle and gung ho." She
framed her face with her two open palms and wiggled her head

coquettishly. "It's stupid, but men love it. There's an Italian film director who wants me to star in a movie."

She shook her head the way fashion models do, so that her extravagant red hair billowed about her shoulders. The gesture was so proudly adolescent that Mireille had to smile.

"Really, he asks me all the time. We just have to find the right vehicle. That's what Gino calls movies—'vehicles.'" She lit a cigarette. "Anyway, he thinks my type has box-office potential, even though it's a pain in the ass. I mean, I have to play tennis all the time and go around wearing sneakers. I hate tennis."

"Barbara," Mireille interrupted, "do you think I could be . . . I mean, could I pretend to be . . . someone special, too?"

"Sure. Renée wouldn't have hired you if you didn't have something besides a gorgeous face." She rested her chin on her hands. "Now let's see," she said, narrowing her eyes. "She wouldn't want you to look like Little Bo Peep. Nicole has had that market cornered for nine years. You're not the party girl type, either. Too much class."

She clapped her hands. "Class. That's it. We're going to groom you to be a lady, a real ice princess."

"Me?"

"Why not?" She grabbed the check. "Baby, we're going to turn you into royalty. Get your coat."

Outside, she hustled Mireille into a taxi. "Maison de Coty, please," she told the driver.

"Where are we going?"

"To the beauty parlor. Relax. You're going to love it."

"Barbara, I can't. I don't have any money."

"Of course you don't. This is going on Madame Renée's account."

Mireille gulped. "Does she know?"

"Wait till you get your first fee," she said. "Everything you spend will be deducted, to the penny. Renée's so tight she squeaks.

But she wants you to look good. That's part of the investment. So we're going to make the investment pay off, okay?"

Mireille smiled. "Okay."

She was seated in the middle of an army of white-smocked hairdressers, manicurists, and cosmeticians who poked and rubbed her as if she were a doll in a toy store.

"Beautiful hair," a man with a pencil-line mustache said as he ran his fingers through Mireille's shoulder-length tresses.

"Not an inch off the length," Barbara commanded while she chain-smoked. "Honey, no matter what they tell you is in style, keep your hair long. Men like long hair on a woman, and they always will."

"What am I supposed to do with these?" the manicurist moaned in despair as she picked up Mireille's rough, hangnail-studded hands. "*Chérie*, you don't do housework, do you?"

Mireille looked at her in surprise. Who didn't do housework?

"Not anymore," Barbara said, laughing. "Let's just see some false nails for the time being. And not too much makeup. Keep it subtle—grays and peaches."

"*Oui*, mademoiselle," the cosmetician said. "This face should not be covered." She drew her fingers along Mireille's cheek. "A few eyebrow hairs removed, a little color . . . Trust us, *ma belle*." She touched Mireille on the end of her chin. "When we are finished, you will love this face."

Mireille could hardly believe the result. Her glossy blonde hair had been smoothed flat around her head, blossoming into an intricately braided chignon at the back of her neck. Her eyebrows were shaped to give prominence to her eyes, made larger now by a rim of smoky-gray shadow, and on her lips and cheeks was a hint of color that brought out the sensual curve of her mouth.

"Not bad, country girl," Barbara said with approval as they left. "But this is just the beginning. Do you feel like walking?"

Mireille looked up at the dark winter clouds and drew her coat around her. "I guess so," she said. "Why?"

Barbara laughed. "I don't mean walking *here*," she said. "We'll take a cab to my place."

They went to Barbara's spacious apartment on the Île de la Cité. It was on the twelfth floor, overlooking the Seine. Almost all the furniture was white, its pristine blankness broken only by the pastel lamps and vases of bright flowers.

"Your home is beautiful," Mireille said, looking around in wonder.

"It's a long way from Pigalle."

"Is that where you're from?" Mireille had once accidentally taken a train to Pigalle at night. It had been like a carnival sideshow, she remembered, its narrow sidewalks teeming with sailors and American GIs, painted prostitutes and seedy young men who wandered about dead-eyed and indifferent.

Fast-talking men in shiny suits had stood in front of the *boîtes* and burlesque houses, shouting above the loud music spilling onto the street, urging passersby to come in past the flashing lights and the entranceways littered with empty bottles and cigarette butts to see the beauties inside and sample their wares.

"Born and raised," Barbara said grimly. "Actually, I come from a long line of whores. I'm the first to make any money at it, though. Here, see if these fit."

She brought out a pair of shoes with four-inch heels and tossed them into the middle of the room. Mireille put them on, teetering uncertainly.

"Well, go ahead," Barbara prodded. "Just walk."

"I . . . I don't know if I can." Mireille wobbled, lurched forward, then crashed face-first onto the sofa with a shriek.

Barbara helped her up. "Jesus! What the hell happened? Are you hurt?"

Mireille rubbed her ankle. "I guess I just wasn't used to them. I've never worn high heels before."

"Ever?"

She shook her head.

"What did you wear back on the farm, or wherever you're from?"

"Sabots," Mireille said. "Wooden shoes."

Barbara rolled her eyes. "Terrific. Maybe we can dress you up like a little Dutch girl and set you up in a windmill."

"I'll practice, Barbara. Really I will." She stood up again and dived immediately into an end table.

Barbara took a deep breath. "Gimme," she said, wiggling her fingers. Mireille gave her the shoes. Barbara slipped them on and walked for Mireille.

"Cheerful, nonthreatening party girl," she said as she bounced across the room. Then her walk changed to a sensual glide, catlike and predatory. "Sexy," she said. "Oh la la, the lady's a tramp." On the third lap, she used yet another walk, stately and elegant. "If I'm going to the opera," she said. "Which I hate. All those screaming fat women." She plopped down on the chair that Mireille was still draped over after her collision with it, and took off the shoes. "Here," she said, handing them to Mireille. "Your turn."

"You . . . you want me to do *that*?"

Barbara snorted. "For starters." She picked up her martini and the latest issue of *Vogue* and pushed Mireille off the chair. "Get moving."

"But . . . but I . . ."

"Shut up and walk," Barbara said, flipping through the pages of the magazine.

By Tuesday, when she presented herself to Madame Renée for inspection, Mireille's feet were nearly as blistered and raw as they had been after her escape from Champs de Blé, except this time her wounds were covered by a pair of expensive pumps.

The madam gestured to a spot on the middle of the floor where Mireille was to station herself, then began her vulture-like circling ritual. "An improvement," she said, tapping her fingers on her crossed arms. "The look is right." She touched the stylish white wool Dior suit Mireille was wearing.

"Barbara's?"

"Yes, madame," Mireille said quietly.

"Be patient, dear. You'll soon have your own. Sit down." She pulled out a chair in front of a small table piled randomly with china, glasses, and silverware. "Arrange these, please."

Mireille moved the place settings around, with the wineglasses in their proper place and the silver in order, down to the oyster fork.

"I see you've opened the books," Madame Renée said with approval.

Mireille had known how to set a proper table since she was a child, but she agreed without protest. The woman took two other books from the shelves and handed them to her. "A compendium of wine and *Who's Who*," she explained. "Have you been practicing your English?"

"Yes, madame."

"Look at me when you speak. Give me a sample of your handwriting." She tossed a card and a fountain pen in front of her. "All right," she said, watching as Mireille wrote. "Good. Not too fancy." She smiled perfunctorily at her. "You've made good progress. I'm pleased."

"Thank you, madame." Remembering Renée's admonition, she looked up and tried a smile.

The woman shook her head. "If only you had more personality," she said with a sigh. "Well, one can't have everything. Just try to appear well bred and aloof. With your figure, maybe no one will notice."

She picked up the phone and spoke into it briefly. When she hung up, she gave Mireille a businesslike nod. "Have Barbara take you to Balenciaga," she said. "I want you to be fitted for a dress."

The dress was a strapless black taffeta gown. A model whisked around the elegant silver-gray showroom wearing it as a white-haired gentleman led Mireille and Barbara to the fitting rooms. While Barbara sipped café au lait on a silk love seat, two seamstresses took Mireille's measurements.

"Please come back in a week for the first fitting," the gentleman said as they left. "And do give our sincere regards to Madame Renée."

The door closed softly behind them.

"She's going to send you out," Barbara said.

"When?"

"A week, maybe two. Don't worry. It'll be an easy one, probably a freebie for the guy."

"What should I do?" Mireille blurted in a panic.

Barbara laughed. "If you don't know that by now, honey, you've definitely chosen the wrong line of work."

"I mean, what should I say?"

"Say?" Barbara asked archly.

"Yes."

"You got it," she said, pointing at Mireille's breasts. "'Yes' usually does the trick. As it were."

"I'm serious," Mireille said miserably. "Madame Renée thinks I'm dull. She says I've got no personality."

Barbara shrugged. "Considering she's the tackiest woman on the planet, that's not so bad." She put her arm around Mireille and whispered in her ear. "Besides, dazzling conversation never gave anybody a boner."

"I don't think that's what she meant," Mireille said.

"Okay, okay. Look, if it really worries you, there's a trick to seeming smart."

"There is?"

"Mind you, I said *seeming*. If you were really smart, you wouldn't be peddling your ass in the first place."

"What is it?" Mireille insisted. "The trick."

"Simple. Just keep your face close to your date's when you talk, like this." She insinuated herself near Mireille. "Now speak quietly, as if you're telling a big secret, and look deep into the guy's eyes. Then give him the old lollapalooza."

"The lollapalooza?"

Barbara demonstrated. She smiled. It was a dance of a smile, always changing, always interesting. In the span of ten seconds, her face took on a dozen subtly different expressions, from mystery to humor to desire. Then she took it further, to sweetness and then to hilarity, when the two of them broke up laughing on the street.

"See?" she said finally, pulling herself together. "An old pro taught me that when I was ten years old. It was good for a lot of candy."

"That was wonderful," Mireille said breathlessly. "What were you thinking about during all that?"

"That's the point, fool. I wasn't thinking about anything. You don't have to think. You just have to smile."

Mireille struggled to keep a straight face while trying it herself.

"A natural," Barbara said. "Feel better?"

Mireille hugged her.

"Hey, save that for the paying customers," Barbara said, prying her away. "Gratitude gives me a headache."

Chapter Fourteen

Mireille heard her baby crying before she entered the rooming house, and knew instinctively that something was wrong.

Inside, in the parlor, were two people she had never seen before. A man, in his early thirties with the blunt features of a brute, paced, smoking, near the door. An overweight woman with frizzy hair and too much makeup sat on the sofa, drinking from a tumbler of whiskey.

Ignored by them both, the senile Mademoiselle Joelle waited vacant-eyed on a straight-backed chair, her feet primly together. She was wearing her best flowered dress and a hat. Beside her was a single suitcase. Everyone except the elderly woman looked up as Mireille entered the room.

"Who're you?" the man demanded sullenly.

"I live here," Mireille said, looking at Mademoiselle Joelle. "What's going on? Where's Madame Racine?"

The baby wailed. "Shit," the woman on the divan muttered. "If that's your brat in there, you better shut it up. I can't take much more of that screaming."

Mireille ran to her room. Stephanie was lying in her bassinette, soaked and cold in a dirty diaper. On the floor lay a full bottle of formula. Beside it was one of Madame Racine's decorative hair combs.

After feeding and quieting the baby, Mireille came into the parlor again. Another couple was there now, carrying Mademoiselle Joelle's suitcase and escorting the old lady out the door.

Noticing Mireille for the first time, Mademoiselle Joelle turned to her and smiled. "You're Stephanie's mother," she said. "I'll teach her in school one day."

"Mademoiselle Joelle," Mireille called, rushing to take her arm. "Please tell me what's happened. Where is Madame Racine?"

The old woman's eyes filled with tears.

"What is it? Please tell me."

"She's dead," the frowsy woman on the divan said between gulps of liquor. "Stroke, looks like."

The woman with Mademoiselle Joelle cleared her throat. "My aunt—Mademoiselle Joelle—found the body," she whispered, straightening the old woman's hat.

The lady on the divan snorted. "Screamed like a maniac, to hear the police tell it. The old kook went running around outside dressed in nothing but her underwear. The neighbors called the cops to come after *her*, not the corpse."

Mademoiselle Joelle lowered her eyes in shame. Her hands trembled. Mireille took them. "Now they say we all have to move out," the old lady said in a quavering voice. "Monsieur Brévard is already gone."

"Who says that?" Mireille asked.

Mademoiselle Joelle gave an accusatory look to the woman on the sofa, and then to the man who stood in front of the window with his hands in his pockets. "Them," she said bitterly. "Madame Racine's poor relations."

"Just clear out, you old bat," the woman on the sofa said.

Mademoiselle Joelle's niece stiffened. "Come along, Aunt." She tugged on the old lady's arm.

Mireille kissed her good-bye. "I'm sorry," she said as Mademoiselle Joelle shuffled outside, her small hat trembling in the winter wind. She watched her go until the man in the room walked over and shut the door in front of her. "Coal costs money," he said, and resumed his position by the window.

"Who are you?" Mireille asked.

"Well, ain't we high and mighty," the woman said, polishing off the dregs of her glass. "For your information, missy, my husband is Augustine Racine's next of kin. Which means this house belongs to us now, and we're not about to let you or anybody else stay here and loot the place before we sell it." She tossed her chin at Mireille.

"But I haven't got anywhere else to go," Mireille said. "I don't have any money, and—"

"Hey, do you think I want to hear your troubles? Go sleep in the street, for all I care. Just take that squalling kid with you."

Mireille swallowed the anger that was bursting inside her. "Where will Madame Racine be buried?"

The woman stood up with difficulty and poured herself another glass from the bottle of whiskey on the dining room table.

"Vincennes," she said. "Where we're from. I'll be damned if we're going to pay an arm and a leg for a plot at Père-Lachaise Cemetery. Everything costs too much in Paris, even dying." She took a gulp from the glass, spilling some of the whiskey over the side. "So what are you waiting for? Get your stuff packed. We've been hanging around here all day as it is, waiting for you to get back."

Mireille looked at the man, hoping to make one final appeal to him, but he was still turned toward the window, his hands in his pockets.

"I won't be long," Mireille said quietly.

The winter wind was high outside as she entered the Cathedral of Notre-Dame. With Stephanie in her arms, she knelt at the altar and tried to pray, but her thoughts were a confusion of memories and regrets. First her parents. Then Stefan. And now Augustine Racine. She felt as if, one by one, pieces of her past were being chipped off her like limbs from ancient statues, until in the end what remained would not be her at all, but another person altogether, a stranger.

Soon, she thought, everything about Mireille Orlande de Jouarre could be summed up in one word: "prostitute." There would be nothing else left.

"Forgive me," she prayed, clasping her hands together. "Forgive me for betraying the memories of everyone who loved me."

The baby sucked on her ear, making small mewling sounds. The gorgeous hues of the rose window melted together through the tears in her eyes. "Don't you see, I have no choice!" Other supplicants at the altar turned to stare at her.

She covered her face. She knew that her prayer, the prayer of a woman who trades her body for money, would not be heard. Still, she could not pretend to be repentant. She had found the only way to provide for her baby. And, sinner that she was, her baby was more important to her than her soul.

Cradling Stephanie against her breast, she stood up slowly and moved toward the back of the cathedral, where she lit a candle for Augustine Racine, as she had promised. But she would not presume to speak with God again. She would not desecrate Madame Racine's funeral with her presence.

When she left Notre-Dame, rain was pouring off the roof in sheets that exploded onto the sidewalk in white bursts. Mireille took off her thin coat and wrapped it around the baby, then picked up the bundle containing most of her possessions and stood at the great arched door.

"Where to now, Stephanie?" she whispered, stepping outside. With the rain slapping at her face and Stephanie's cries of fear, Mireille's worry about where to go turned to panic.

The storm worsened within minutes. On the sidewalks, people walked hunched into the wind, holding their black umbrellas
like bayonets. Mireille arranged the folds of her coat more tightly
around her baby as she made her way toward the fluttering awning
of a café.

The place was packed to bursting with grumbling Parisians
seeking shelter from the weather. Mireille carefully counted out all
the money she had. There wasn't much, not even enough to rent a
cheap hotel room for the night. If she'd been in possession of the
Balenciaga gown Madame Renée had ordered, she might have sold
that, but it wasn't completed yet.

She had given almost all of the thousand francs she'd made
from her afternoon with the Comte de Vevray to Madame Racine.
The old woman hadn't wanted it, but Mireille had insisted. Now
the silent man from Vincennes and his drunken wife were going to
have it all, after giving the kind old lady a pauper's funeral.

Through the rain-streaked window, Mireille could see the river
in the distance and the Pont Neuf, the bridge where the clochard
had tried to rape her in the snow. A shudder ran through her. He
was probably still there. They were all still there, the vagrants who
blew on their hands in the cold, who peered out at the rain with
despair in their eyes.

She clutched her baby tightly to her. *With God's help or without
it, my daughter will never see that place,* she thought bitterly. *No
matter what I have to do.*

"Your order, please?" the waiter asked. He had red hair, the
same shade as Barbara's.

Barbara. Barbara would help.

Mireille looked at Stephanie, and a knot formed in her stomach.
If she went to Barbara, she would have to tell her about Stephanie.
It would mean the end of Mireille's employment. Madame Renée
didn't even want married women working for her. She certainly
wouldn't accept one with a child.

Barbara owed Mireille nothing. She couldn't be expected to cover for her.

Still, Barbara might lend her enough money to keep her baby alive. Nothing else mattered.

"Your order?" the waiter repeated, looking around the busy café impatiently.

"Excuse me," Mireille said, picking up Stephanie and brushing past him toward the doors.

It was a long walk to Barbara's apartment building. By the time the doorman announced her, Mireille was soaked through.

"Good God, you look like a drowned rat," the redhead said. She was leaning against her doorway, smoking. "And what the hell is that?" She gestured with the cigarette toward the bundle in Mireille's arms.

Mireille pulled back the black coat to reveal the baby's sleeping face. "She's mine," Mireille said softly.

Barbara blinked. She tossed the cigarette onto the hallway floor and crushed it with her shoe, then flung open the door and pulled Mireille inside. "Well, don't just stand there while the poor thing freezes!" she shouted. She scooped Stephanie into her arms. "Christ, her lips are blue." She stripped off the baby's clothing and covered her with her own sweater. "Your mommy must be crazy, taking you out on a day like this."

"I'm sorry to bother you, Barbara—"

"You just shut up and get those wet clothes off." She waved toward the bedroom. "There are robes and things in there. Have you got diapers for her in this ragbag of yours? I'll change her."

While Mireille got out of her sodden white suit, she could hear Barbara singing to the baby. Stephanie gurgled and squealed with joy. "See? She likes me," she said as Mireille reappeared with a soggy armload of clothing.

"I'll pay you back for these as soon as I can," Mireille said.

"For what?"

She held up the Dior jacket. It was soaked and flecked with mud.

Barbara shook her head. "Honey, I knew you were a disaster the minute I set eyes on you."

"I'm sorry, Barbara."

"Yeah, yeah. Go put on a pot of coffee."

Mireille hesitated, then sat down next to her. "I've been thrown out of my room. I need to borrow some money for a week's rent someplace. Fifty francs will be enough."

"Fifty francs? Where are you planning to live, in the men's room at the bus station? And what happens at the end of the week?"

"I'll get a job. A regular job. I can wash dishes, like I used to."

"It's going to take a lot of dishes to pay off that taffeta Balenciaga," Barbara said.

Mireille covered her mouth with her hand. "You mean I'd still have to pay for it? Even if I never wear it?"

"What do you think?" Barbara asked sarcastically.

"Then could they . . . could they take it back? Would Madame Renée—?"

"Take it easy," Barbara said, rocking the baby until she slept. "You're talking crazy. So you got kicked out. All of us do sometime or other. You and the baby can stay here." She gestured vaguely. "There are three bedrooms, anyway. I used to have roommates, back when I was working for myself. How about it?"

Mireille could hardly believe what she was hearing. "You . . . You don't mind Stephanie?"

"Is that her name?" She kissed the baby's forehead. "I always wanted to have a baby."

"What about Madame Renée?" Mireille asked tentatively.

Barbara looked up at her. "What about her? It doesn't seem like any of her business to me."

Mireille sighed with relief. It was more than she had ever expected. "Thank you." At Barbara's reaction, she held up her hands defensively. "I know. Gratitude gives you a headache."

"Well, coffee doesn't, so how about getting a move on?" While Mireille scrambled to find the coffeepot, Barbara nuzzled the baby's nose. "Good times ahead, little girl."

Mireille heard her from the kitchen. More than anything, she wanted to believe her.

Chapter Fifteen

She was called within the week for her first job. The client, Madame Renée warned her, was an important man with exacting tastes.

"Don't let her scare you," Barbara said as Mireille slipped into her new dress. "Men are men. They pop their cookies, they're happy. Still, he'll report every move you make to Renée, so don't stick your elbows into your soup." She zipped up the taffeta gown. "Hurry up, now. Your limo will be here any minute."

"I've never been in a limousine before," Mireille said. Nervously, she patted her hair into place.

Barbara studied Mireille critically in the mirror. "It needs something," she said. "Wait a sec."

She dashed out of the room, then came back a few minutes later with a pair of earrings. They were glittering and large, fashioned into the shape of two perfect roses. Each petal was a dazzling half-carat diamond.

"Hamid gave me these," Barbara said.

"Who?"

"The Arab with the yellow rose petals." She held one of the earrings up to the light. "They're my old-age pension."

"Barbara, I couldn't."

"Go on. They're insured." She put them on Mireille and smiled. "There. You look fabulous. If I didn't like you so much, I'd hate you." The intercom rang. "That's the car."

Mireille looked out the window. On the street below was a long black Peugeot. A rising wave of nausea passed through her body.

Barbara was holding up a white mink stole to put over Mireille's shoulders. "Come on. What are you waiting for?"

Mireille stood frozen, staring at the black car below. "I'm going to go to bed with him," she said. "And I don't even know what he looks like."

"Oh, brother," Barbara muttered in exasperation. "Look, you knew from the beginning what this was all about."

Mireille nodded numbly. "He's expecting a whore."

Barbara threw the stole on the bed. "You're damned right he is. And if you don't want to go, there are plenty of pretty girls who'd step into that car in a minute in exchange for a crust of bread to eat."

"I know, I know . . ."

"You don't know anything!" Barbara spat. "You, with your fine manners. You don't know what it's like to grow up wearing rags and sleeping on a cold floor with a stick in your hand to fight off the rats when they come at you in your sleep. You've never had to steal food to stop the ache in your belly."

"Actually, I have," Mireille said quietly.

Barbara cocked her head and stared at her for a long moment. "Then you should know better," she said at last. "For your baby's sake, throw away your pride. Okay, so you're a whore. So what? At least be a good whore."

With a sob, Mireille rushed past her into the hall toward Stephanie's bedroom. She stopped short at the door, remembering the nanny Barbara had hired for the baby, and knocked diffidently.

A plain woman, her hair already braided for the night, opened the door. "Stephanie is asleep, madame," she said coldly.

"I just want to look at her."

The woman looked annoyed but let her in. The sleeping child lay in a crib of ruffles and satin, her innocent face untroubled.

"How can I tell you what I am?" she whispered. And she knew that she couldn't, not ever. Stephanie would never know her mother as anything except the woman who raised her and loved her, no matter what steps Mireille would have to take to ensure her daughter's ignorance.

"None of it will be real," she said, choking on her words. "I promise you that."

"*Pardon*, madame?" the nanny asked. "You are feeling ill, madame?"

"No. No, I'm fine." She touched Stephanie's little fingers, balled into fists.

"Madame will be late?" the woman asked with a trace of malice.

Mireille turned and walked out of the room. Then she picked up the white stole.

"That's better," Barbara said.

Mireille put on a brittle smile. "There are worse things than mink."

Barbara winked at her. "Don't forget it, baby."

Jacques Bourlier was a man in his early forties, with the soft, petulant face of a pampered child. The thought of having sex with him repelled Mireille.

He looked at his watch pointedly as the chauffeur closed the door of the Peugeot behind her. "You've kept me waiting," he said.

Mireille flushed with anger. *Don't talk back,* she told herself. *Who do you think you are?*

Then, looking at the man's arrogant face, she answered herself. *I am whoever I choose to be.*

She blinked at the thought. Whoever she chose to be . . .

She saw a reflection of her face in the half-open glass partition between the front and rear seats of the limousine.

I am the most desirable woman in Paris, then. Because I choose to be. Who does this fat little fool think he *is?* "Perhaps I should leave," she said coldly, reaching for the door.

Bourlier slammed the partition shut and grabbed Mireille's shoulder. "Mademoiselle, this display is hardly necessary. May I remind you—"

"I beg your pardon?" she snapped. Her gaze traveled from his hand to his eyes with aristocratic disdain.

He withdrew his hand. There was a moment when the tension between them threatened to explode. Then, her eyes as green and hard as emeralds, Mireille spoke. "I assure you, monsieur, you need not remind me of anything. I am l'Ange." Her chin lifted a fraction of an inch, allowing the man to feel the full measure of her majesty. "If you have been kept waiting, that is because I am worth the wait."

Mireille had decided on no more than a whim to play the role of a haughty courtesan and, amazingly, Bourlier believed it. More surprisingly yet, he seemed to actually like it. He was looking at her now with a mixture of admiration and meekness. The power he had exuded was gone. He had given it—willingly—to her.

For Mireille, it was difficult to keep from laughing aloud. This is a play, she realized. That's what the Life was all about. The costumes were elegant and the props were expensive but, at bottom, her exchange with this forgettable man amounted to nothing more than an evening of make-believe.

Can it be? she wondered. *Does he really want this person I'm pretending to be?* She touched his thigh lightly with a gloved finger, then trailed it up his chest. "Do you find me insufferable?" she teased.

His breath quickened. "I find you beautiful."

"Oh, I am much more than that," she purred, meeting his eyes, moving her face close to his. "Much . . . much . . . more . . ."

She smiled for him then, the studied, changing smile Barbara had taught her, and she knew he was hers.

"I'll stay," she said languidly.

Trembling, Bourlier slid open the partition and barked an address to the driver.

Mireille sat back. The Life wouldn't hurt her, she knew, because none of it was real. Nothing that happened with all the nameless, faceless men whom she was obliged to accept with her body would be real. She was l'Ange, "the Angel," the most desirable *poule* money could buy.

Chapter Sixteen

From that moment, Mireille's invention of herself took on a life of its own, and that life was splendid.

In the opinion of many connoisseurs of female flesh, she was the epitome of the Parisian *demoiselle*—beautiful, pampered, available yet strangely unattainable. Madame Renée's appointment calendar was crowded with requests for l'Ange, the blonde beauty with the bearing of a queen and the sexual skill of an eighteenth-century courtesan.

When a reporter from *L'Oeil*, an underground magazine for devotees of Parisian nightlife, tried to take a photograph of her at a glitzy after-hours club, she covered her face with the collar of her black sable coat so that only her eyes showed. She told the reporter, "L'Ange is not an image. She is an experience."

The photograph—the only one of her in existence, since she was clever about dodging cameras, and club owners were careful about protecting their clientele—was picked up by *Elle* and *Vogue*. The quote traveled throughout Europe.

By the time she was twenty, she knew how to please any man of any taste without ever relinquishing her sleek reserve, so that none of her clients doubted for a moment that the Angel was granting them a huge favor by honoring them with her company.

"I really don't know what you have," Madame Renée trilled gleefully as she leafed through her calendar, "but every man in the civilized world seems to want it." The madam had taken recently to bleaching her hair blonde and wearing it pulled back in a chignon like Mireille's. "Just remember that too much publicity is poison for those of us in the Life. The clients certainly don't want to see their pictures in national magazines, and the police . . ." She gave a little shudder. "Well, we don't even want to think about them."

"I've never permitted photographs after the one in *L'Oeil*," Mireille said.

"Quite so. And a wise decision it was. The photograph has become famous, in its way. Rumor has it that the son of an English duke offered five thousand pounds for the original and the negative, but was turned down. Everyone who looks at it wants to see the rest of that face."

Mireille laughed. "If that was all they wanted to see, I wouldn't be working for you."

Renée narrowed her eyes over her gold-rimmed bifocals. "You've been living with Barbara too long," she snapped. "Speaking of whom, the two of you, along with some of the other girls, have been invited to a party in London next weekend. Won't that be fun?"

Mireille's face fell. "Not the weekend," she moaned. "Not again."

She hated weekend assignments. When she first began with Madame Renée, she had only worked on single-evening dates. The plum weekends, usually in distant locales, were reserved for the top girls, and were much sought after. Mireille had never requested a weekend. She preferred to spend them with Stephanie, finger painting in the apartment or picnicking in the country. But as her reputation grew, more and more men insisted on l'Ange and l'Ange alone, and were willing to pay exorbitant sums for a two-day stay in her company. She was a prize flaunted by the very rich, who often battled to outbid one another for her as if she were a champion racehorse for sale.

"The big fees are not earned on Tuesday evening, dear," Renée said, tapping her pencil.

"Yes, but a party? Any one of us could go."

"The client has specifically requested you."

"And has paid in advance, of course," Mireille added sardonically.

"Of course." Renée raised her eyebrows. "You should be thankful, dear. You aren't going to be commanding these fees forever, you know."

"I know." She sighed. Her fees, and the expensive gifts her clients brought her so that she would remember them, were paying for Stephanie's future.

"Then you'll go?"

"Fine. Whatever you say."

"Good. Your plane tickets have been arranged. Frankly, I think you'll enjoy this party. The host is your old friend the Comte de Vevray. He's restored his mansion in Belgravia, and always gives fabulous parties. He was most insistent on your presence."

Mireille blinked. "Really?" she asked. "I'm surprised that he even remembered my name. He gave it to me, actually."

Renée laughed. "I doubt he recalls doing any such thing," she said. "He's probably never given a second thought to that encounter. After all, you were a nothing back then. He wants the girl whose picture was in the magazine."

"Oh," she said. "I should have known."

"The party's for an American friend of his," Renée chattered amiably. "Very rich. The Americans always like Barbara. You're for the Count. That is, unless he prefers one of the others, naturally."

"Naturally. Who is the American? Have I read about him? Maybe Barbara should know."

"*Sacré Dieu*, no. The man's a film producer. His name is Oliver Jordan. Whatever you do, don't tell Barbara. She's always hoping to be discovered, and I won't have her behaving even more obnoxiously than usual."

"Oliver Jordan," Barbara shouted over the noise of the airplane. "He's the head of Continental Studios. His films won nearly all of the awards at Cannes last year!"

Mireille laughed. "How do you know all that stuff?" she asked. "Anyway, why do you care?"

Barbara sniffed. "Honey, you might be willing to shake your tired old ass for the boys in the old folks' home twenty years from now, but I'm not." She primped her hair.

Mireille smiled. Even though Barbara was the older of the two of them, she was still a child in many ways, and Mireille loved her for it. In a profession as devoted to deception and fantasy as the Life, Barbara's bluntness was like a beacon in a murky sea.

It was Barbara who finally fired Stephanie's sour-faced nanny after a thinly veiled remark about women of low morals. "If your bony butt's not out of here by the count of three, I'm going to smash a cream cake into your ugly kisser," Barbara had threatened. Within three hours she'd hired a sweet old grandmother to replace her.

It was the best gift Barbara ever gave Stephanie or her mother. Suzanne, the new nanny, seemed not to have an inkling about Mireille's profession, and apparently did not care to know. Her only concern was the child, whom she loved like her own kin.

Suzanne and Stephanie were together now in Bretagne for a three-week visit with Suzanne's grown children. That had been Barbara's suggestion, too.

"I hope Stephanie doesn't miss me too much," Mireille said.

Barbara smiled. "Are you kidding? She doesn't know you exist. Now, do you think you'll be able to relax a little?" She reapplied her lipstick for the fifth time.

"Maybe you ought to take your own advice," Mireille said.

"About what?" She separated her eyelashes with a fingernail.

"Relaxing. This is only a party, Barbara, not an introduction to the Queen."

"Hah! The Queen I could handle. We're talking about a Hollywood producer!"

Mireille laughed. "Madame Renée warned me against mentioning Jordan's name. She said you wanted to be a movie star."

"Well, why not? I'm sure not going to end up some old pimp like her. Let me tell you, there are only two ways out of the Life: marriage or the movies. Judging from the married women I know, I'd rather be in movies." She lit a cigarette and thoughtfully exhaled a smoke ring. "Oliver Jordan," she said, savoring the name. "What a coup!"

"I thought you had a moviemaker in your pocket."

"Oh, Gino," Barbara said dismissively. "He makes promises in bed, then forgets all about them as soon as he's got his pants on. Besides, he only makes dumb Italian cowboy movies. And he isn't a producer, just a director. He's got nothing going for him."

"I see. On the other hand, Americans always keep their promises."

"Mireille, Oliver Jordan's not just any American. He owns a studio. He can give out a contract at the drop of a hat. He's even supposed to be good-looking. Mark my words, girl. By this time next week, I'll be on my way to California."

"This sounds serious. I hope you're packed."

"Make fun if you like. You'll see." She took out a nail file and worked on her manicure.

Mireille sat back and closed her eyes. She was going to perform in another play, nothing more. She would play the role of l'Ange.

It was how she kept her sanity. She was not the woman who sold her body to the highest bidder, the bejeweled prostitute the magazines referred to as the twentieth century's answer to Madame de Pompadour and La Belle Otero; that was the actress in the play. Someday the play would end, and Mireille would walk off the stage, clean and whole again, and Stefan would be by her side, and their daughter, the proof of their love, would hold onto them both . . .

But a small voice inside her always called out to spoil the image, a voice saying, *Stefan is dead.* There was only the Life now.

Chapter Seventeen

The residents of Belgrave Square had never seen anything like the exotic passengers who stepped from the convoy of limousines in front of the Comte de Vevray's Georgian mansion.

First there was Sonja, all six feet of her, stunning by anyone's standards, in black satin and rubies. She had left her skin-tight leather skirts in Paris, but brought along a nondescript black satchel containing the tools of her trade.

"You're too much," Barbara had teased her at the airport. "Do you really think someone's going to ask you to tie him up and spank him before dinner?"

"This is England," Sonja answered in her deep voice. "Someone always does."

She was followed by Nicole, fragile and porcelain-pretty, and the mysterious Ankha, whose languid walk and glazed kohl-rimmed eyes betrayed her absinthe habit.

"Help me keep her off the stuff tonight," Barbara whispered to Mireille. "She'll be dead soon enough, without Renée firing her."

Mireille nodded as the front door opened and a butler admitted the stream of gorgeous women to the strains of a swing band. Denise, at thirty-two, was the oldest among them, even though she was often mistaken for a teenager. She wore a tiered white gown that made her look like an antebellum bride, a stark contrast to Barbara's formfitting sheath of royal-blue sequins.

Mireille entered the oak-floored ballroom last, vastly under-stated in a gray silk Chanel dress.

"Coo, will you look at that," a pretty blonde English girl said. She was standing near the door, next to a tall, overly made-up woman whose eyes followed the newcomers as they made their way into the crowd.

"Who are they?"

"Hookers," the blonde whispered. "The Count always hires them for his parties. I hear these are from Paris."

"Well, if that isn't cheek," the tall woman said. "But I suppose that if all a man wants is sex, anything will do."

"Oh, some of them are quite smashing," the blonde said knowl-edgeably. She lowered her voice. "Like that one in the gray."

"Shush! She's not one of them."

"She is, I tell you. The Count's got a picture of her in his bed-room. She's famous."

The tall woman folded her arms and narrowed her eyes at Mireille. "She's got her nerve, queening it up in front of us. You'd think she'd have the decency at least to be embarrassed."

"Bea, you're talking about a French whore." The two of them broke up laughing.

Mireille had heard enough. She had stood quietly as the women talked about her within hearing distance. Now, her impas-sive face betraying nothing, she walked over to them.

"Love a duck, she's coming here," the blonde squeaked, tug-ging at her friend's sleeve.

Mireille stopped directly in front of the smaller woman and looked levelly into her eyes. "Yes, I am a French whore," she said.

The woman gave her companion a triumphant look.

"And you are an English sow."

She moved on, unruffled as a nun, toward the bar.

The Count had set up a massive bowl of champagne punch with ice swans floating on its surface. Mireille accepted a drink from the server. She had the uncomfortable feeling that she was being watched. The two English women were undoubtedly staring daggers at her back.

She put down her glass and looked around the room. Barbara had already homed in on the Comte de Vevray, and the two of them were dancing a lively jitterbug in front of the band. The rest of Madame Renée's girls mingled among the guests, picking out the unescorted males with practiced ease.

Sonja was surrounded, as she always was, by sweet-faced young men drawn to her imposing presence, although Mireille knew that Sonja was only biding her time. Sooner or later, a special guest would seek her out. He would be older, most likely, fastidious in appearance, and probably would occupy a position of importance in politics. That type was Sonja's bread and butter.

The man, whoever he turned out to be, would approach Sonja hesitantly, circuitously, until he was certain that he could trust her with his shameful secret. Then Sonja would disappear with him for the evening, and the next morning her little black satchel would have a hefty roll of banknotes she had earned to keep her silence.

What a strange world I've chosen to live in, Mireille thought.

Or did it choose her?

Then she saw a face across the room watching her, and she knew that somehow, in a way she could not hope to understand, her life had changed forever.

She did not know his name. She had never seen him before. Yet when their eyes met, the crowd of people between them seemed to vanish into the air.

He was tall, with hair the color of antique gold coins, and the easy elegance of a man accustomed to having his way without asking for it. Over the rim of his champagne glass, his piercing blue eyes met hers and, for an instant that seemed like eternity, nothing else existed for Mireille except those eyes, quick with intelligence inside the tanned face, eyes that seemed to look into her most secret places, to caress them and know them. And there was something dangerous in them, too, something that frightened Mireille even as it drew her inexorably closer to him.

"Angel!" someone shrieked beside her, shattering the moment. "Hey, where have you been?" Barbara asked as the music blared once more and the mob of party guests crowded in front of Mireille so that she could no longer see the golden, perfect man who had appeared to her like a god out of nowhere.

"Anatole, darling, I'd like you to meet l'Ange," Barbara said, hanging onto the arm of the Comte de Vevray. Barbara was always careful not to use Mireille's real name in public.

"Mademoiselle," the Comte said, breathless, as he clicked his heels together and bent at the waist to kiss Mireille's hand. He still reminded her of a little fluttering bird. "Forgive me for not coming to greet you sooner, but my old friend Barbara always forces me to dance with her until I am on the verge of collapse. I assure you, it is my very great pleasure to meet you." Suddenly, he frowned and fumbled in the pocket of his tuxedo. "Good heavens," he said, perching his pince-nez on his nose. "I know you!"

"How kind of you to remember, Monsieur le Comte," Mireille said coolly. "It was a long time ago."

"I daresay it was. You were no more than a child. But now . . ." He turned to Barbara with a great agitation of his hands. "She's magnificent. Wouldn't you say, darling? Truly magnificent."

"That she is," Barbara agreed, winking at Mireille. "Now, if you two will excuse me, there's someone I really must meet."

Mireille's breath caught in her throat. The man who had been watching her was walking toward them, his eyes still fixed on her.

"You mean Oliver?" the Comte asked. "But of course, my dear. How insanely neglectful of me. He's the reason I invited you here. That is to say . . ."

Barbara gasped. "Oliver Jordan! Merciful Lord, he's an Adonis." She looked at Mireille. "He's even more handsome than his pictures," she whispered.

Mireille barely heard her. She was lost, transfixed by the stranger's sensual animal aura.

"Can it, baby, he's mine," Barbara growled with a discreet jab to Mireille's ribs as she trotted toward Jordan, her lollapalooza smile ablaze.

"How do you do, Mr. Jordan," she said in English. "My name is Barbara. Bar-ba-ra." With each syllable, she drummed her perfect fingernails against his chest for emphasis.

Jordan seemed to look right through her. His eyes were transfixed on Mireille.

Only one thought entered Mireille's mind. It glowed there, burning, until it burst: *This is not part of the play.*

"Er . . . Oliver . . ." the Comte said uncertainly, looking from Jordan to Barbara's frozen smile. "I'm sure you'd like to meet . . ."

Jordan extended a long, bronzed hand toward Mireille.

Silently, she took it, and the two of them moved to the dance floor, where they held one another as if they had been lovers for a lifetime.

"Shit," Barbara muttered.

"Shit," the Comte de Vevray said at precisely the same moment. They turned to each other, dissolving in laughter.

"I don't suppose you'd care to dance," he offered.

She gave him her hand. "My dear Count," she said in an imitation of an English aristocrat, "I'd be delighted."

Neither Mireille nor Jordan spoke a word while they danced. There was no need. Their bodies understood one another perfectly.

By the time the music ended, Mireille was flushed, confused by her surprising feelings about this man who had suddenly made her make-believe world a little too real. *Don't be insane,* she thought. *You can't have feelings like this. Not with him. Not with anyone.* "I'd better go," she said, pulling away from him reluctantly.

He held her even more tightly. "Don't." His blue eyes were urgent. "Please stay."

She bit her lip. Clearly, he didn't know about her. There was no other explanation for his interest. For a wild instant, Mireille considered not telling him her profession. Perhaps, for a few hours, at least, l'Ange would die, the play would end.

No, that was out of the question. One didn't leave the Life that easily.

"Mr. Jordan," she said, so embarrassed that her words were barely audible, "there's something about me you should know."

He smiled. "Tell me. I intend to know everything about you."

He was making it so much more difficult. There was no way to tell the truth now without blurting it out.

Mireille closed her eyes and spoke. "I'm not a guest at this party. I've been paid to attend."

Jordan traced the plane of her profile with his finger. "Do you think I didn't know that?"

She blinked.

"It's too loud in here," he said. "Come with me." He guided her gently through the high French doors of the ballroom into the garden, where the moon shone full overhead and the scent of roses surrounded them. He lifted her chin.

"I want you to listen very carefully to me," he said softly. "You are, without question, the most beautiful woman I've ever seen in my life, and I'm not going to let you go. Do you understand, Mireille?"

"You know my name," she said, surprised.

"Naturally. The moment you arrived, I made a point of finding out who—and what—you are."

"And you don't care?"

Jordan laughed. "How old are you?"

"I'm twenty."

He looked up at the moon. "God, I'm glad I'm not young anymore. Everything is of such importance when you're twenty."

"I don't understand," she said.

"You will when you're forty," he said. "And that day will come soon enough, believe me." He took her in his arms. "It's this moment that will never come again."

He kissed her eyelids lightly, chastely. "Ah, Mireille," he whispered. "How I wish . . ."

"Yes?" Mireille asked, faintly ashamed of her growing emotions. Though she earned her living by having sex, she took a strangely perverse pride in her invulnerability to the men who used her body. To love again would be to break the last frail tie that connected her with Stefan.

But this man was too strong, his power undeniable. Just being near him almost caused her to forget her vow to love Stefan forever. To forget every vow she'd ever made. In Oliver Jordan's presence, the field of lavender where Mireille had felt the first stirrings of love was far, far away.

"How I wish you were real," Jordan said.

She felt as if a bolt of lightning had shot through her. Real? *Real?* But she *was* real, couldn't he see that? This was not part of the play. This man, this strange and magical lover whose kiss on her eyelids had left her wet and quivering with pleasure, had, more than any man since Stefan, seen into Mireille's true heart.

Then, with an expression almost of pain, Jordan stepped back until he stood at arm's length away from her. "It feels like sacrilege to touch anything so perfect," he said.

She lowered her gaze. "I see."

"No, you don't. You think I only want your body, but you're wrong. I need to know everything about you. I need everything you are."

From inside the house, sounding as if it came from a great distance, they could hear the brassy music and the muffled laughter of the guests.

"Leave with me," he said.

"Now?"

"Right away."

She smiled, having come back to her senses. At least they were back on level ground again. Hooker. John. Trick. No melting heart. No *coup de foudre*. "Your room or mine?" she asked.

"Sardinia," he said.

"*What?*"

"I've got a house on the Costa Smeralda. We could be there in six hours."

"Are you serious? I can't—"

"You can," he said. He touched her hair. "Please, Mireille. I'm begging."

"Mr. Jordan . . . Oliver . . ."

"Come with me," he whispered into her ear. The night breeze sang around them, stirring the rose-scented air. She turned her back to him. He came up behind her and kissed her neck. "Let me love you in a place as perfect as you are. Come for a day, if that's all you'll give me. I promise you'll get back whenever you want to leave."

"A day?"

He nodded. "Or a lifetime. It's up to you."

A lifetime.

She had not given a thought to any future except her daughter's since her last night with Stefan. When he died, all of her dreams had died with him. But Oliver Jordan had sparked something inside her that made her want to live again, something wilder and darker than anything she had known with Stefan. Something very nearly uncontrollable.

And even as she shuddered with the touch of his lips on her neck, even as every nerve in her body longed to go away with him, a terrible, mocking voice inside her asked, *Is it you who's falling in love with him, or is it l'Ange?*

She banished the thought from her mind. She knew the difference between who she was and who she pretended to be.

Didn't she?

"I can't," she said finally. "Madame Renée—"

"I've already spoken with her."

"You . . . you what?"

"How do you think I learned your name?" He gave her a mischievous grin. "The Count will understand. No one else need know you've even left London, if you're back in a day."

"Or a lifetime?" Mireille asked, smiling.

"We'll worry about that later." He pressed his hands against both sides of her face, as if she were a statue still soft in the clay. "For now, the world is only you and me."

Then he kissed her, tenderly, exquisitely. "Only you and me."

"Only . . . you . . ." Mireille said. She never finished the sentence as his mouth found hers again.

BOOK II

1950–1960

Chapter Eighteen

Oliver Jordan was ecstatic. Not only had he kissed the most beautiful creature he had ever seen, in a fairy-tale garden with music playing, but afterward, he still wanted to be with her.

Good God, he had to get her away quickly. To Sardinia, where the salt air might preserve his lust for a day or two. Or more, with this fabulous woman. Perhaps as much as four more days.

Four days was Jordan's limit. His boredom threshold was low.

Oh, there had been exceptions here and there, of course. There was a Nigerian princess once, six feet two, with a neck like a swan and a thick tangle of pubic hair that smelled like wild game, who had enthralled him for a full week. And Jordan had probably kept her around longer than he should have. Toward the end, he had begun to see her long neck as something vaguely reptilian, or interplanetary.

He had always been easily bored. At five, he had set fire to his mother's monogrammed D. Porthault towels in order to have something to do. At fourteen, he ran away from home, having stolen the keys to his father's Bentley and the servants' payroll cash. He made it from Portland almost as far as the California state line before crashing into a tree. An empty bottle of Moët & Chandon was found next to his unconscious body.

The following year he was sent away to school in England, where he was dismissed within six months for fornicating with one of the local girls beneath a pew in the school chapel. The incident made him a kind of legend among the underclassmen, and on Sunday mornings for years afterward, students would vie for the honor of sitting above the spot where the famous "Jordan Porking" had taken place.

After that he moved from one school to another, leaving a trail of rumors behind him, but he accepted it all with good grace, having learned the two things that he knew instinctively would be most important to him in later years: he was impeccably groomed, and he had charming manners. Combined with his naturally dazzling good looks, these two things opened countless doors to him.

When he smiled, with his beautiful even teeth and his cherub's mop of curly golden hair, no one could believe that this boy would cause any trouble. When he sulked, his sensuous deep-pink lips pouting, the brilliant blue of his eyes smoldering to gray, people thought that this boy had been mishandled somewhere along the line and that with a little love, a little careful discipline, he would emerge a great leader. This boy had promise.

And then one of their daughters would turn up pregnant, or an orgy would be discovered in the boys' dorm, and Jordan would move on, smiling, ready to make new friends.

"Quantity," "quality," and "variety" were his watchwords. QQV.

By 1925, when he was seventeen, sex was virtually the only thing that held Oliver Jordan's interest. After all, the act suited his personality perfectly. It was exciting, endlessly stimulating, easily obtained, and relatively quick.

But by the time he entered Princeton (by an act of providence, his admissions interview was conducted by a woman), he had come to a dismaying realization: that the most lusty, randy, desirable, and attractive females of his acquaintance were beginning to look for more than a hot evening in Manhattan or the occasional weekend at the shore. Obeying some ancient nesting instinct, these ripe and perfect beauties now wanted not thrills, but "relationships." They not only wanted to liberate their passions with Oliver Jordan;

they wanted to marry him. More than the freedom they professed to desire, these wild young things with their soft breasts and red lips wanted the old gold ring on the third finger of their left hand, and were prepared to do battle for it.

Oh, they would give it up for free once, twice, maybe a few times more. After that, the noose would tighten. The free spirit who delighted in romping naked with Jordan in a hotel room a month before would suddenly shoot darts through narrowed eyes while speaking through tight, wormlike lips about how a man ought to grow *up*, take some *responsibility* for his life, look to the *future*.

To add to Jordan's dismay, he discovered also that his tastes had become so refined that fewer and fewer women appealed to him physically, thus narrowing the field even further. The young girls, the innocents, still fell over themselves around his practiced charm, yet only occasionally could he be transported to ecstasy by the milky naïveté of a teenager.

There were some, he knew, who considered green fruit the most succulent, but Jordan was not one of these. He wanted perfection. He liked women in the ten-year range between nineteen and twenty-nine, old enough to know how to behave in public and how to show off their skills in bed, yet far below the age of jodhpur thighs.

By the end of his sophomore year, though, Jordan had become almost impossibly particular. He didn't want a woman, even in the correct age range, who walked with her toes stuck out like a duck. He didn't like girls with thin hair, small eyes, or gums that showed. Women who required makeup to look beautiful were out. He did not tolerate slumpers; good posture was a must. No nail-biters. No excessive perspirers. No one with bad breath or marked skin. Flat chests were in vogue during the thirties, but they revolted him, as did pockets of fat in the upper hips, abdomen, or inner thighs. He also despised giggling, garrulousness, stridency, sentimentality, and above all, predictability.

Jordan despaired. There was no way, he realized, that he could fulfill his QQV quotient without radically lowering his standards. And to make matters worse, he was flunking out of school. Women, it seemed, required his full attention.

He dropped out and moved back to his family's lumber empire in Portland, where he was soon named as co-respondent in a divorce case involving a judge—a friend of his father's—and the judge's young wife, who had been discovered performing oral sex on Jordan in her husband's chambers. The woman had been wearing an abbreviated version of a French maid's uniform. Jordan had donned the judge's robe for the occasion.

By this time, he knew that his time in the Northwest was up. But where would he go? What would he do? He liked Europe, but the Depression was even worse abroad than it was in the States. It was 1932, and the nation's long postwar party was now definitely over. Even in Oregon, where the money had remained in land and resources, and stock market speculation had not been commonplace during the boom years, the economy was pinched. Money was scarce. Pleasure was considered even more sinful than it had been. Only in the movies did people lead lives of gaiety and abandon.

Only in the movies . . .

Then he had it, one of those once-in-a-lifetime ideas that crashes into the head like a thunderbolt.

There *was* a place where the supply of perfect women was endless, where none of them used sex as leverage for marriage, and where he could actually make a living.

"I'm going to Hollywood," he told his parents over dinner.

"Excuse me," his mother said, leaving the table in an admirable display of self-control.

His father wrote him a check for five thousand dollars and told him that when that well ran dry, Oliver had better go fishing in other waters. "By the way," his father added, "do you know what you're going to do down there?"

Oliver was, of course, planning to roll around in pussy until it oozed out his ears; however, he felt that might not be an appropriate explanation under the circumstances.

"I'll become a film producer," he said, smiling with his beautiful cherubic grin to which no woman could ever deny anything.

"That's a pile of horseshit," his father said. "This is the last of the tit money."

Jordan agreed and packed his bags for California. Before he left, three of the household maids gave him a good-bye to remember.

And he did remember, although only for sentimental reasons. None of them met his standards by a long shot.

Chapter Nineteen

In 1932, five thousand dollars went a long way. It was enough for a family of four to live in moderate comfort for a year. It was enough to buy a home, a farm, or a tract of land. It was enough to start a business or sail around the world.

Five thousand dollars supported Oliver Jordan in Hollywood for less than three weeks. Fortunately, he'd had the foresight to seduce his father's bookkeeper before leaving Oregon. She gave him a half dozen blank checks from the back of the family's personal bankbook, complete with rubber-stamp signatures, in exchange for Jordan's solemn promise to return the money before the missing checks were noticed.

They bought him nearly two more months of the lushest, hottest, loosest, wildest poontang west of the Mississippi. There were dozens of starlets, some singers and dancers, a pair of twins who were both married to dentists, a visiting countess from Italy, and Anne Rutledge.

Anne was older than Jordan—so much older, in fact, that she was out of the optimal age range. She walked with her toes out. She had stringy brown hair that showed her scalp. Her posture was that of the class weakling, slumped into a turtle shape to hide from the big girls. Her nails were short and ragged. Her complexion was spotty. She wore no makeup. She was almost perfectly flat-chested.

This was the woman Oliver Jordan married.

Alas, even though she'd fallen short in nearly all of Jordan's prerequisites, her family owned most of the real estate in Beverly Hills. Her inheritance amounted to just over twenty million dollars. Given that Jordan's father had hung up on him when Oliver had called asking for more money (the missing checks had been noticed, as it turned out, and the ex-bookkeeper brought up on charges of embezzlement), Anne Rutledge soon became the object of Oliver's sudden and irresistible infatuation.

They were wed in a ceremony that could best be described as "smallish," since no one from either Anne's or Oliver's family attended. Afterward, in a bungalow of The Beverly Hills Hotel, Jordan forced himself to make love to Anne, while mentally composing the speech he would make later that evening that would get him out of this place and into some more interesting company.

Ignorant of his lack of interest in her, Anne nuzzled against his chest. "Now that you're a married man," she asked sleepily, "what are you going to do with your life?"

"Well . . ." He thought of all those grasping, husband-hunting coeds. "It's time for me to grow up," he said stoutly, hoping to sound earnest. "Take some responsibility for my life. Er, our lives. Look to the future. All that."

Anne laughed. She laughed so hard that she had to sit up in bed, the expensive silk nightgown shimmying against the tiny dugs of her breasts. She laughed until tears ran down her pockmarked little face.

"Oh, Oliver," she said, still laughing. "Don't you think I know anything?"

"What are you talking about?" Jordan asked with some annoyance. He wasn't used to women laughing at him in bed.

"You don't really think I believed for a minute that you married me for anything other than my money, do you?"

"Anne!" Shock and dismay carefully registered on his face.

She laughed even harder. "Ollie, dear, you keep forgetting that you're twenty-four years old. I'm thirty."

"So? What does that mean?"

"It means I'm six years smarter than you." She stopped laughing. "At least. And I know everything there is to know about you and your kind. All my life I've been chased after by charming young men who wouldn't have given me the time of day if I weren't one of the richest women in California, and early on I realized that I would probably marry one of them. So I have."

"That's not true . . ." he began, then realized that there was no point in dissembling. "Well, then, why did you marry *me*?" he asked with a twinge of irritation.

Anne smiled, and her plain face softened into near beauty. "Because I love you," she said.

"And I love you," Jordan answered. He had responded to the cue automatically, without thinking.

"Don't insult me, Oliver. You've never felt an emotion stronger than mild amusement in your life."

"Oh, really," he said dryly. "What a shame you're wasting your great love on me, then, shallow gold digger that I am."

She shrugged. "It's my choice. Besides, you're the best of the breed. You come from money, so you won't embarrass me by not knowing how to handle it. My friends won't accuse me of marrying the pool cleaner. Who knows? We may grow to like each other."

"Marvelous," Jordan said wanly, thinking that women over thirty always claimed that what they wanted most from him was "friendship," whatever that was. "We'll be great friends."

"You're too cynical for your own good." She switched on the bedside lamp. "But anyway, here's the deal."

"The deal?"

She took a sheet of hotel stationery and a pen from the night-stand, and wrote as she talked.

"You'll get a weekly allowance of a thousand dollars, whether you have any other income or not. Any expenses you incur beyond that will have to be signed for, in the form of a loan, and handled by my bank. You'll have to pay the interest on it, of course, but I won't insist that the capital be repaid unless the marriage fails, that is to say if you humiliate me publicly, fail to escort me to a function where I deem your presence necessary, or deny me the personal satisfaction due a wife."

"Are you talking about sex?"

"'Denial of bed,' it used to be called."

"You've got this all worked out, haven't you?" he asked hotly. "You and the lawyers and the accountants."

"It won't be so bad, really. My wants are small. We will have no children."

"I see," Jordan said, blinking away his irritation. "What if I want children?" he asked, though they had never figured even marginally in his plans.

"The point is not negotiable," she said. "Shall I go on?"

Jordan rolled his eyes.

"Any money you make on your own is yours to keep, unless you owe me part of it. Naturally, any debts to me will take priority."

"Naturally."

"On the bright side, I won't expect anything like fidelity from you, as long as it isn't done under my nose or in my house."

"Your house," Jordan repeated.

"Most certainly my house." She looked at him levelly. "If you take a separate residence, I will consider that grounds for divorce, at which time all money owed me comes due."

"Are you so sure I'll be in your debt?"

She switched off the light. "I just face facts," she said. "It's about time you did, too." She slid under the covers and reached for him. "Come here," she said sweetly. "You're mine now."

Jordan huffed once in anger, then smiled and drew his wife close to him. He was not entirely sorry to be married to this woman, after all. Because Anne Rutledge Jordan, he realized, fulfilled another of his prerequisites.

She was not stupid.

In time, Jordan became accustomed to his wife's rules. After all, he had access to virtually anything he wanted, including women.

Of course, there were never enough women. It was not that the ladies of their social circle were above casual dalliances; on the contrary, Jordan was assailed by a constant stream of secret invitations. The problem was that the high-bred girls from old-money families rarely had much more to offer than Anne herself. He had to break into Hollywood's inner sanctum, that stratum of the California elite where rules did not exist, and anything was possible.

But how? He certainly wasn't about to become an actor, spending five years or more playing bit characters in grade-B whodunits while the studios looked him over. And it would be much too boring to begin as an assistant to another producer, even if anyone would hire him as one.

"Don't be naive," Anne told him over brandy after an unusual dinner à deux. "You want to learn about movies? Make one."

Make one. But of course! Why not? Jordan—or, rather, Jordan's wife—possessed the one thing necessary to become a producer: money. Why bother with the studios at all? He would make a movie of his own.

Taking an enormous loan from Anne, he hired Albert Neumeyer, a director who had cut his teeth in the silents and had matured in such stunning vehicles as *My Ántonia* and *Stardust*. He was on leave now from Metro-Goldwyn-Mayer, vacationing in the South of France. Jordan sailed over, offered the man a tidy fortune in salary, and persuaded him to pull strings with MGM so that he might be permitted to work on an unnamed film with an inexperienced producer.

Neumeyer, whose reputation was so big that he could afford to gamble, suggested a property. It was *The Rock*, a sprawling novel about the Pilgrims' settling in America, written by the most popular author of the day. Several studios had been bidding for rights to the book. Jordan went straight to the author, offered him twice as much as the next-highest bidder for the property and an additional ten thousand dollars to write the screenplay, and walked out with a deal.

The actors cast in the movie were among the most famous in Hollywood. The sets were glorious, the costumes magnificent. Jordan hired three press agents to make sure that word about the new picture and its independent producer got out, although the press agents were hardly necessary. Everyone in the movie industry, particularly the heads of the major studios, was intensely interested in every move that the brazen twenty-four-year-old golden boy from the north woods did. Although it was impossible to find out exactly how much money the young upstart had thrown away on *The Rock*, they knew it must have been a king's ransom.

But it took more than money to have a box-office smash, they told themselves smugly, sitting back in their leather swivel chairs and lighting their cigars. Louis B. Mayer was particularly interested in witnessing what he thought would be Jordan's inevitable demise. The little snotnose had grabbed a property that by rights should have gone to Mayer himself. Produced by MGM, *The Rock* might have become the benchmark film of the talkies; now it was going to turn to dreck in the hands of a baby-faced patzer from the sticks.

"We'll just see how much rope this Oliver Jordan gives himself," Mayer told Louella Parsons in an unofficial interview that he later denied. "Then we'll watch him swing from it."

Surprisingly, while Jordan discovered that it took more than money to make a motion picture, he found also that he actually had a talent for producing. He had wells of organization and discipline that he hadn't even known existed before. When the script came in nearly as long as the novel on which it was based, Jordan edited it himself, with Neumeyer's approval, and the result was good. To avoid having to buy the expensive camera equipment, he leased it from another independent. Then he hired a cameraman from France and a lighting designer from Italy, and allowed them to work out the shots with the director during an uninterrupted weekend in Capri.

He kept the stars in line by fining them a hundred dollars for every five minutes they arrived late, and rewarding good work with lavish gifts and the prize of his good grace. The intimate parties he held for "his people" at the fabulous Rutledge (now Jordan) mansion ranked among the most talked-about events of the Hollywood social calendar, featuring entertainment ranging from Josephine Baker's *Revue Nègre* from Paris to an all-nude team of acrobats that left his guests more gasping and flushed than the performers.

For those privileged enough to be invited to the Jordan soirees, their attendance meant instant acceptance into the innermost circle of discreet decadence. Even before *The Rock* was completed, stars Jordan had never met were calling, hinting that they might be persuaded to make an appearance at one of his parties. He used them to his best advantage. Only the most important, most beautiful, most useful people received invitations, and they were never disappointed.

To his delight, Jordan also found time, despite the long hours at work and the endless entertaining, to stretch out with at least four or five women a week.

And such women! They were all his childhood dreams come true at once. They came from small towns and cities, from the open spaces of Montana and across the oceans. They were models, showgirls, preachers' daughters, ex–department store clerks, rich girls, comediennes, dancers, stage actresses, singers, and more than an ample share of hookers—all leggy, buxom, long-nailed, low-voiced, all come to Hollywood with dreams of stardom.

Ah, yes. Oliver Jordan was in heaven.

"You know, you owe me more than a million dollars," Anne told him in passing after he came to bed. The laughter and music of the party still going on downstairs wafted up to the bedroom.

"You'll get it back," Jordan said testily. "*The Rock* is going to break every box-office record in existence."

"If anyone gets to see it," Anne murmured.

"What's that supposed to mean? Of course people will see it."

"Really? Where?"

"Why, in the theaters, of course. Tell me, Anne, is this tiresome train of thought leading somewhere?"

"I've been reading about this business of yours. It seems that most of the theaters in the country are owned by the big studios. One of them has to agree to show your movie in their theaters, or you have no audience. And from what I've seen in the newspapers, the studio heads hate you, Oliver."

Jordan swallowed and felt his entrails turn to ice. In his naive arrogance, he had not even considered the problem of distribution. There was only one solution: he would have to cut a deal with one of the studios to show *The Rock* in its theaters in exchange for a percentage of the film's earnings.

Unfortunately, no one would speak to him. Warner Brothers, RKO, Paramount . . . Every door in town, it seemed, was suddenly closed to him. There was no question who was behind the conspiracy of silence. Louis Mayer had succeeded in turning the entire distribution industry against Oliver Jordan.

So to Louis Mayer he went.

"What do you want to show my picture in your theaters?" he asked.

Mayer lit a cigar. "Maybe nothing. Maybe I just want to teach you a lesson."

"A lesson that costs you money? I doubt that, Mr. Mayer."

"I heard you had balls. With the ladies, anyway. You got balls enough to play this game, kid?"

"Time will tell," Jordan said.

Mayer chuckled.

"I'll give you thirty percent of the gross," Jordan offered. "It's a lot, but I imagine you know how much I need this."

"Seventy-five."

Jordan took a deep breath. "I might be in a position to help you one day, Mr. Mayer."

"Is that a threat?"

"No, sir. But seventy-five percent is."

"I'll cut you a break. Sixty-five."

"Forty."

"Fifty. And that's only because you're a kid."

"At fifty, I won't make any profit."

Mayer raised his eyebrows. "But I will." He grinned. "And I didn't even make the picture." He stuck out his hand. "Welcome to the big leagues, son."

The Rock, publicized like no other film in history, grossed a staggering three million dollars in its first two weeks of play, half of which went to Louis B. Mayer. The remainder was enough for Jordan to pay back his wife's loan, and to convince him of the necessity of running his own studio.

Three months later, he opened Continental Studios. Its distribution was taken care of by a long-term lease with Warner Brothers, anxious now to get even with Louis B. Mayer for breaking his own boycott against Jordan and profiting handsomely by it.

Continental soon established itself as a small but quality studio. And its head, Oliver Jordan, quickly became one of the most powerful men in Hollywood.

Sixteen years later, at the age of forty, he had everything he had ever wanted in life: money of his own, access to a great fortune, satisfying work, and an endless supply of the most beautiful women in the world.

But he was still easily bored.

Chapter Twenty

By the time the Comte de Vevray held his hooker-studded party in Belgravia, in fact, Oliver Jordan's boredom had reached a new plateau. Now even the most extravagantly beautiful women failed to hold his attention for longer than the span of a single sexual encounter. He began to think of himself as a sort of latter-day Marquis de Sade, endlessly seeking out newer and ever more twisted ways of satisfying himself.

One woman, whom he saw once a month or so, always showed up wearing a floor-length gingham dress and a gray wig styled into an *American Gothic* bun. She would lie in wait for Jordan in his office after hours and, at the appointed time, rise like the ghost of his grandmother to harangue him about his infidelity and per-versions. When he showed himself to be adequately penitent, the woman would turn on a record player and strip down to her high-button shoes—she was otherwise naked, except for two shiny fringed tassels over her nipples and the gray wig—and perform a steamy dance on the conference table.

Others came with props—whips, costumes, music. One even had a snake. These and the gray-haired lady were, of course, paid for their efforts. Jordan no longer felt anything more than the most casual curiosity for women who were not prostitutes. The mere thought of having to woo a starlet again, of listening politely to another recital of the vaulting ambitions of a nineteen-year-old, created a hideous sense of weariness in him. Hookers were infinitely

less trouble. They were reliable hired help who didn't require anything except Jordan's money and his presence.

And even his presence was only minimally necessary. Lately,
he'd pared down the sex act itself to merely watching while the
ladies feigned sweaty ecstasy with one another. Most of the time
he didn't even remove his clothing. Sometimes he read. It was
abstract sex, beyond laziness, the stone-dead end of the erotic
urges he had once harbored in such abundance. It was the nadir of
Oliver Jordan's existence.

On his way to London, anticipating the stultifying weekend
ahead of him, he had briefly entertained the bizarre notion of
going into retreat at a monastery. Temporarily, of course, just long
enough to work up an edge and rid himself of the feeling of surfeit.

Sex had become to Jordan what a greasy sausage was to a
man who had just eaten so much that he could no longer sit up.
He needed to grow hungry again, to appreciate the small gifts a
woman gave. How long had it been, he wondered, since the sight
of a woman's tongue running along her lips excited him? Or the
slick, bouncy double curve of buttocks beneath a skirt?

And so, understandably, it came as a huge surprise to him
when he had felt stirrings of lust as the pale-haired woman in the
gray dress entered the room.

It was not just her beauty, although she had beauty to spare.
Nor was it the sense of an almost childlike vulnerability that
emanated from those perfect features. Clara Bow had possessed
that quality and had exploited it in a little-girl-lost-in-all-the-
champagne image. The new girl, Marilyn Monroe, had it too,
although she wrapped it in a showy, brainless vulgarity that
Jordan found personally unappealing. But this one . . .

She had walked over to a couple of shopgirl types—Vevray's
regular standbys—and said a few words that sent them scurrying
away, blushing and furious, while she herself remained as polished
as a diamond.

Yes, that was it, he decided. The blonde had an aura of art-less mastery about her. Not bitchiness—he had known plenty of bitches—but the kind of real authority one was either born with or wasn't. She was Garbo with a body. She was Helen of Troy. She was . . .

"Who the hell is she?" he had whispered to the Comte.

Vevray had pulled on his pince-nez. "Which?" He'd squinted, then laughed delightedly and pulled off his glasses. "Oh, that's l'Ange. From Madame Renée, and a pretty penny I've paid for her, too." He kissed his fingertips. "*Formidable*, I hear, one of the great *poules* of history."

"I have to have her," Jordan said.

"Ah-ah-ah!" The Comte raised a warning finger. "Be careful, my friend. You fall in love too easily. But I suspect what you fall in love with is your own reflection."

Jordan made a face. "How much have you had to drink, Anatole?"

The Comte laughed. "So much for my deep existential thoughts, eh? Come along, I'll introduce you."

Just then the Frenchman was not so much greeted as engulfed by a firebrand redhead who would have sent Jordan reeling in his younger years. Count Vevray immediately forgot his promise and swirled away with her to the dance floor.

L'Ange, Jordan had thought. The Angel, come to deliver him.

And she had. He had actually kissed her. He had not kissed a woman for more than a year. Kissing, with its chaste overtones of love, seemed somehow too intimate for a man of Oliver Jordan's experience. Yet he had kissed the Angel, one perfect kiss, and he had not felt at all like a fat man confronting the last greasy sausage on the plate. On the contrary, he'd wanted more. And more.

And when he'd invited her to Sardinia—Good God, had he really done that?—he had felt like a lust-crazed schoolboy, pant-ing and sweating and begging. Yes, oh, yes. Kissing the back of

Mireille's neck had been better than getting into Betsy O'Donnell's pants under the pew in Saint Andrew's.

Angel of mercy!

He knew then that he had to have this woman for a night, for two, for whatever measure of passion his jaded old senses would afford him.

Chapter Twenty-One

They were ferried down the Costa Smeralda in a rickety skiff manned by an ancient Sardinian boatman who navigated through the choppy waters of the Tyrrhenian Sea without moving more than a foot in any direction from his place at the helm. It had taken some time for Jordan to arrange for a private plane and pilot, and he had only been able to take them as far as Olbia, the northernmost airfield in Sardinia. From there they would have to travel by boat to Jordan's villa near Porto Cervo, but by then it was nearly four in the morning, and the beach was deserted. They had to wait another hour before the first fishermen ventured on shore. Jordan paid one of them the equivalent of the day's catch to fetch the ferryman.

Through it all, Jordan had been strangely silent, his randy charm discarded like a pair of boots one leaves at the door. On the plane he'd suggested that Mireille take a row of seats for herself to sleep while he busied himself redlining contracts. He'd loosened his tie and put on glasses.

It had amused Mireille to think of Oliver Jordan as a sober and serious businessman, so at odds with his reputation. Which was he, really? Barbara had described him as a man of insatiable appetites whose conquests had included some of the world's greatest beauties, but then Barbara believed a lot of things that weren't true. Now, bleary-eyed and exhausted as they finally reached their destination, Mireille thought that the famous Hollywood producer seemed reticent, almost shy.

Jordan's house was a rambling villa that stood on a low cliff above the sea. At low tide, a flight of moss-covered steps led from the boat slip to a stone-paved path that surrounded the villa, passing through a grove of orange trees whose blossoms suffused the air with their fragrance.

Mireille stopped before she entered, to breathe in the scent.

"What is it?" Jordan asked, taking her elbow.

"Nothing. The air . . ." She smiled at him. "It's lovely here."

"I know," he answered softly. "Sometimes I feel like a fool for living in Los Angeles when I could be here."

Inside, the villa, with its high ceilings and marble floors, had the cold, sparse look of many expensive Italian homes built at the turn of the century to resemble the residences of patricians from the Roman Empire. A middle-aged couple greeted them, and Jordan responded in rapid and fluent Italian. The woman nodded, then took Mireille's overnight bag to a spacious room with mosquito netting covering the bed.

"*Ecco*," the woman said as she opened a set of double doors that looked out onto the ocean. The breeze brought with it the intoxicating fragrance of orange blossoms, which made Mireille think of another time, with another man. With an effort, she shook the memory from her mind and heard running water being drawn for a bath.

She had brought only one change of clothing, having anticipated no more than a single night's stay in London, but the servant, whose name Mireille learned was Claudia, brought her an elaborately embroidered caftan and a pair of sandals, then bowed slightly before departing.

But where was Oliver? "Signor Jordan?" Mireille inquired.

Claudia performed a series of gestures that seemed to indicate that her employer was elsewhere in the house but that this should be of no concern to Mireille. *"La vostra,"* she said, her arms spread. *"Solamente la vostra."* She pointed to Mireille.

This, then, Mireille realized, was to be *her* room, hers alone. She was not being squeezed into Oliver's bed and expected to cater to his desires, but was being treated instead like an honored guest. Likewise, she'd expected her host to insist on having sex as soon as they unpacked, yet Oliver didn't distract her solitude until it was time for lunch, when he appeared outside her patio doors wearing a white shirt and white trousers. His blond hair, still damp from washing, curled at the ends like a schoolboy's.

"Hungry?" he asked.

"Famished."

He smiled as she walked toward him. "How lovely you are," he said. "Did you sleep?"

She nodded. "And you?"

"A little." Again, he seemed almost shy as he led her to a table on the patio, set with two green salads, a platter of sliced tomatoes, some black olives, thick slices of white cheese, a trencher of crusty bread, a bowl of tiny marinated octopi, and a bottle of delicious red wine from a local vineyard.

"So do you think you could love it here as much as I do?" he asked, tearing off a piece of the bread. "I want you to."

"It's heaven." She sighed. "The air is so clean, it reminds me of . . ." She swallowed. She hadn't meant to talk about her past. That was the first lesson she'd learned in the Life, made clear by the Comte de Vevray. He'd told her not to ruin things between them with a lot of talk. After that, she had never forgotten: do not mistake a man's lust for love, or friendship, or anything else. No one wanted to know who l'Ange really was.

"Of what?" Oliver asked. "What does this place remind you of?"

"Monte Carlo," she lied smoothly.

What does he want with me? she wondered. There was no question that she would sleep with him—or do anything else he demanded of her. That was how she made her living, by satisfying the urges of rich men. But she wasn't just a guest in his house, either. She didn't really know why she was with him, why he had invited her, or why she had come.

As if reading her mind, Oliver's eyes crinkled in a smile. "So much consternation," he said. "Over what? Are you afraid I'll fall in love with you?"

She frowned, thinking that with her imperfect grasp of English, she'd misheard him. "What do you mean?"

He took her hand across the table. "Because I want to, Mireille. From the moment I saw you, I knew that you belonged in my life." He released her hand. "The harder I look at you, the more I want to see." From a box on the chair beside him, he took a framed photograph and propped it on the table between them.

"*Dieu,*" she whispered. It was the photograph of her that had appeared in *L'Oeil.* "So you are the one who bought it."

"No, that was Vevray. I bought it from him." He stood up. "Walk with me," he said, extending his hand. She took it, and the two of them followed one of the lesser-traveled footpaths that led into the hilly scrub beyond the villa's manicured environs. With each step, Mireille felt herself slipping further into the past, into a field of lavender where a boy with a clubfoot found her, wounded and covered with broken glass. She cried out at the memory, unaware that she had uttered a sound.

"Are you all right?" Oliver asked.

"I . . . yes, of course. I must have . . . stepped on a rock."

His eyes on her were steady. "Let me in," he said, touching her forehead with his fingers.

"I don't know how," she answered.

They veered off the path through a short expanse of brush to a clearing dominated by a low, smooth rock. "We can rest here,"

Oliver said. Near one end of the rock stood a gnarled fig tree laden with pendulous green fruit. Jordan plucked a fig and offered it to her. "Dessert," he said.

He didn't feed it to me, she thought with a part of her mind that she normally didn't use when she was with men. That would have been the expected thing, for him to have slipped the fig into her mouth so that she would suck his fingers. She would have gone along with him, of course, if things had played out that way; it would have been an elegant, if rehearsed, beginning of the physical seduction.

Was that what he wanted, a seduction? That in itself was charming, in its way. Was Oliver Jordan pretending to woo her, as if she were a girl raised in a convent? Was this a new script in which she was to act out a role written by him?

A part of her longed to believe the impossible, that, for once, someone could truly love her. That notion, embarrassing as it was for her to admit, was probably part of what had prompted her to leave the Belgravia party with him in the first place. Since arriving in Sardinia, she had tried to rid herself of that foolish idea. Mireille was French; she was practical. Above all, she was a *poule,* whose favors were for hire—to Oliver Jordan or anyone else with the price of admission. Men didn't fall in love with women like her. They used them, enjoying them like expensive cars until it was time to discard them. Yet there was something in his eyes that called to her like a kindred soul.

For a day . . . or a lifetime, he had said.

Had he meant that? Had he seen beyond the photograph to the woman behind it? The real woman?

"Go on," Oliver said softly. She looked at him, puzzled, and he laughed. "The fig."

It was still in her hand. "Oh." She took a bite, feeling the fruit's warm, creamy seeds in her mouth.

"You were so far away," Oliver said. "What were you thinking?"

She shook her head. "Nothing important."

He touched her hair, which was blowing across her face, and tucked it behind her ear. "Have you ever been in love?" he asked, his eyes gray and serious in the yellow afternoon light.

"Once," she said simply.

"And?"

"He died."

"Is that all you're going to tell me?"

There was a long silence between them. Finally, she spoke. "Yes," she said.

He nodded in resignation. "You keep too many secrets."

"Perhaps you do, too."

He kissed her then, his tongue gliding over the smooth seeds still in her mouth. "We all need our lies," he said, his lips touching hers. "The trouble is, after a while we start to believe them. Then we're lost."

"Are you lost?"

"That happened long ago, I'm afraid." He put his arms around her. "What do they say about the Sphinx—a riddle wrapped around an enigma? Is that you?"

She laughed lightly. "What do you want to know about me?"

"If I ask, will you tell me the truth?"

She smiled. "If I say yes, will you believe me?"

He was making everything so *difficult*, she thought. As a whore, she was a receptacle for whatever attributes a man chose to give her. She was not asked to trust, explain, connect, or love. He sighed. "All right. I won't force you."

"What do you want me to be, Oliver?" she asked plainly.

"I want you to be mine." The look in his eyes was naked and filled with rekindled hope.

She kissed him then, tenderly at first and then urgently. *Yes, yes, yes,* she thought. *Let me love you, if just for this moment. Let me love you truly, totally, believing it will be forever.* And he responded with such passion and purity that she felt she was safe at last, safe in his arms. Safe. And though she had never believed it would happen again, she felt loved.

He lifted the caftan over her head, so that Mireille stood naked and shining in the dappled light. Then he laid the garment over the rock as she helped him undress. He lifted her gently onto the makeshift bed and eased onto it beside her.

"I've never brought anyone else here, in case you're wondering," Oliver said.

She shifted her weight over the hard surface. "I wasn't."

"No, I don't suppose you were," he said with a smile. "But I'll bet people have been making love on this rock since the time of the Etruscans."

"That would account for its extreme discomfort," Mireille said.

"Ah. Forgive me." With that, he lay on his back and pulled her on top of him. "Is that better?"

She spread her legs to straddle him, but he stopped her before she could take him inside her.

"Kiss me first," he said, pulling her down to meet his lips again.

She closed her eyes. His touch was almost more than she could bear, but what she felt wasn't just about sex. The kiss was more intimate and loving than she could have imagined. It felt like a promise.

"Just a kiss?" she whispered. "Don't you want me?"

"More than anything." He touched her cheek. "But I need you to want me, too."

She stroked his hard shaft with her juice. "Why?" She would not meet his eyes. "What does it matter what I want?"

He gasped, on the brink of giving in to her expert manipulations. "It's the only thing that does matter." Gently, he pushed her away, though her naked legs were still hot against his flesh. "I think I love you, Mireille," he said, his voice raspy with desire. "Oh, I know you don't believe me, and I know I can't convince you so soon after we've met, but I do. And I want you to love me. Let me into the secret place where you live. Then maybe, for once, we can both let down our guards and allow ourselves to be happy."

She breathed in deeply, raggedly. "I . . . I don't know if I can," she said.

"You don't know if you can love me?"

"I don't know if I can be happy," she said.

"You can." He kissed her neck. "I want to see to it that you are," he breathed. "For God's sake, I've waited for you all my life."

With that, he allowed her to guide him inside her, and their bodies began the slow dance of love, their limbs entwined, their flesh pulsing as he pressed into her and she accepted him into her wet darkness. They moved together on that low rock, gasping with pleasure as their lovemaking ignited into frenzy. She cried out, clasping him to her as he thrust deeper, deeper, until they both exploded in a flood of wild sensation.

Mireille wasn't quite sure what had happened. How much time had elapsed—a second or an hour? All she knew was that her ear was pressed against Oliver's chest, and inside it his heart was beating like thunder.

Slowly, she opened her eyes. All around her were dwarf trees and wildflowers, the scent of the sea, the heady perfume of orange blossoms, and the sun warming everything. It was so much like Champs de Blé that she wondered for a moment where she was.

Then her reason took over, and she knew that this was not France, that she was not with Stefan. Those were just memories, pictures carried over from a time in her life when things made sense and she knew who she was. What she had now, what was real, was this man, Oliver Jordan, with his golden hair and eyes the color of a summer sky, lying beside her in the hills of Sardinia. A new memory. Perhaps a new life.

"I could stay with you forever," he said that night, "if you'd let me."

"We shouldn't think about that now," she answered.

"Too intimate?"

"Too frightening."

They were in Jordan's bedroom, lying naked in front of a fire that danced with the breeze from the ocean. He propped himself up on one elbow, causing his skin to shimmer with a hundred different colors. "All right, then," he said. "What's your favorite food?"

She laughed. "What sort of question is that?"

"It's just the beginning. I want to know everything about you."

She sat up. "Fine. Let me think. White asparagus."

"Asparagus?"

"In my village there was a festival in early spring when the new asparagus was brought into the town square in carts. Everyone bought some. That evening, every house and restaurant cooked the asparagus in their special way, and we all went from place to place trying every dish."

"Just asparagus?"

She laughed. "You don't eat that way in your country, do you?"

"Hell, no, ma'am," Oliver said in his best lumberjack's accent. "We like slabs of meat. Forget the veg."

"The Germans, too," Mireille added. "When they came . . ." The sound of gunfire exploded in her memory. *They're shooting the wounded.*

She cleared her throat. "So. Asparagus. Next question."

"Your favorite color."

She rolled her eyes. "Blue. Like your eyes."

"Green. Like yours."

"Like money."

"I've never been in love with money," Oliver said. "Does that surprise you?"

She shrugged. "What are you in love with?"

He pressed his lips together. "You," he said finally. "Is that too frightening as well?"

She felt her eyes welling.

"You don't have to answer," he said. Then he kissed her, softly, lingering. "Don't tell anyone else about the asparagus. Please. I want that to be a part of you that no one else knows."

They looked at each other for a long moment.

"I wish—"

He touched her lips with the tip of his finger. "No," he said. "No wishes. Everything between us will be real."

"Yes," she whispered.

By the light of the fire, he kissed her eyelids. She touched his neck. Their lips explored one another as Jordan cupped her white breasts in his hands and lowered his face to suck them. Each nipple filled his mouth in turn and throbbed with her desire. She arched her back, her breath catching as she stroked the bare skin of his chest, still as smooth and hairless as a boy's. They were on their knees now. His buttocks were hard, rounded hills, cleft in soft shadow, that prickled at her touch. His sex jutted against her. It pressed between her pliant legs, kissing her with its own sweet moisture.

Their tongues flicked lazily. Mireille lolled her head, and her hair cascaded over his chest. Then slowly, tasting every inch of him, she trailed her tongue down his neck, over his erect nipples, down to his rippled belly, around his pulsing shaft.

He moaned when she took him full in her mouth. Her lips sought to pleasure him wholly, while her tongue licked greedily at the small opening, to drink and fill herself. He caressed her, his hands gliding over the curve of her back and haunches as she sucked him with a wild abandon, squeezing his cock with her lips, flicking the glans with the tip of her tongue. Her legs spread of their own accord; he touched her slick wetness and felt her breath coming fast.

"Mireille," he said. His voice was thick. He pulled her up and kissed her hard, tasting himself. He touched her lips with his fingers, still hot with her juice.

"Now, Oliver, now," she whispered.

Gently, holding her in his arms, he lowered her to the carpet. They both cried out when he entered her. They were blind and deaf, immersed and drowning, aware only of the pulsating rhythm of their love. Their bodies poured sweat; he sucked her lower lip between his teeth. They clutched, holding back, willing themselves away from the edge where they were inexorably drawn until they could wait no longer and they leaped free, moaning as they climaxed together.

Afterward, spent and sweating, they stood up and ran naked, hand in hand, out of the villa and into the foaming surf of the sea.

This is real, Mireille thought. No matter what they said in the Life, some things, some people, some feelings, were real. It had been a long time coming, but her chance at love had come at last, hers and Oliver's both, and they would hold onto it with both hands.

Chapter Twenty-Two

And so he had her in the wild hills of Sardinia, with its sultry sun and the smell of goats. He had kissed her and held her and sucked her till she screamed. He took her standing up and kneeling and lying on her belly in the sand and floating in the sea with her legs wrapped around him, all the while making his confessions of love to her, and still the passion did not ebb. They made love on a huge white feather bed, in the pontoon on the man-made lake near the villa, on the white sparkling shore of the Mediterranean, in the wine cellar, in the flower beds . . . and still he loved her.

He did love her, he realized with astonishment. How many days had it been, four, five . . . seven? And not a moment of boredom, not so much as an unconscious yawn. This woman, this fabulous creature, this perfection, had given him back his youth.

"I'll love you forever," he had said as the warm breeze sang them both to sleep.

Mireille smiled and touched his hand, then closed her eyes again.

"Forever," he repeated in a whisper.

And he had meant it, truly, until the morning when the houseman knocked discreetly on the bedroom door at dawn and informed him that "La Signora" was calling and had insisted on speaking with her husband immediately.

At the sound of Anne's voice, the creamy passion in which Jordan had wallowed for a week suddenly curdled.

"I expect you home by tomorrow evening," she said pleasantly. "Otherwise, my lawyers and I will consider you to be residing in a separate domicile. Have a pleasant trip, Oliver." The phone clicked off. There was no need for further elaboration on her part.

Jordan sat down, the phone still in his hand, and felt the buoyancy that had filled his chest turn to lead. He sighed, then walked back into the bedroom, took a last look at Mireille lying in the folds of the eyelet sheets, shook his head to rid it of whatever hopeful dreams remained there, and got dressed.

Before he left, he scribbled a note:

Sorry, darling, business!
Love you madly,
Oliver

Then he placed five thousand American dollars on the foot of the bed, where she was sure to find it. She was, after all, a professional, and her work had been flawless.

Mireille sat up, rubbing her eyes. A sudden breeze had billowed the gauze curtains and sent up a whirlwind of paper from the bed. It fell around her. It was money, she realized, a storm of hundred-dollar bills.

"Oliver?" she called. When he didn't answer, she dressed hurriedly in the fisherman's clothes she'd picked up with Jordan at the local market and ran out into the terrazzo-floored hallway barefoot.

In the living room, the maid was sweeping with a straw broom. "Signor Jordan?" Mireille asked.

"*Momento.*" The woman held up her index finger. "Giorgio!" she shouted, summoning her husband. "*Parla alla* signorina *in inglese!*"

The houseman dashed inside. "*Scusi*, signorina," he said, panting to catch his breath. "I was out of doors, feeding the animals."

"Never mind that," the maid shrilled in Italian. "Just tell her Loverboy's wife is onto him."

He glared at her, then turned fawningly to Mireille. "*Ah*, signorina," Giorgio dissembled, trying to ignore his wife, who was cackling while she swept. "Signor Jordan, he have to go away, very sudden."

"Have you told her this is how he always leaves?" Claudia swept furiously. "Pfft, gone in a cloud of dust. Next, please. Take a number. Line forms to the rear."

"Claudia, *prego*. Excuse, signorina. Mr. Jordan . . . uh, he have to take his plane. I will arrange a boat for take you to Napoli, *si*? Okay?"

Mireille stood for a moment, staring at her bare feet. "Did he say when he would come back?"

The houseman shook his head. "No, signorina. He say nothing."

"Tell her to check under the pillow for her money," Claudia said. "He always leaves them something. One of them told me, a *napoletana*. A hundred dollars American, he gave her. For one night! She had no complaints, believe me."

Giorgio spread his hands in a gesture of helplessness. "Perhaps in the bedroom . . . Perhaps there is a gift," he said, smiling.

Beside him, his wife leaned on her broom. "Doesn't this one understand anything?"

Mireille burned with shame. *They've seen this all a hundred times before,* she thought. *He just leaves us behind like bundles of wastepaper.*

"I get the boatman now, okay, signorina?" the houseman asked helpfully, smiling and nodding his head.

"Thank you," Mireille answered in a whisper. "I'll be ready when he comes."

As the launch pulled away from the stone harbor, her shame had grown so deep that she was afraid she would choke on it.

It had been so easy for him to leave her.

So easy.

"I should fire you immediately!" shrieked Madame Renée. She fairly leaped out of her chair. "Do you know what you've put me through? The cancellations, the apologies . . . At least two good clients will never come again. One was a Saudi prince. He'd come thousands of miles . . . Oh, *merde alors*, look at you! Sunburn! And you have dark circles under your eyes."

"I've spent fifteen hours on a train." Mireille blinked wearily. She was dead tired. After the grueling journey, her bed had looked almost overwhelmingly inviting, but she had only remained in her apartment long enough to wash and change into a plain white dress. Her hair was wet and pulled back into a braid. She wore no makeup.

"Well, you're of no use to me looking like that," Renée shrilled.

"I didn't think you'd want me back."

"I don't! Believe me, you're more trouble than you're worth. Gone for eight days without a word."

"Madame, I'm sorry . . ."

"The contract was for only one night, not eight solid days!"

"One night?" Mireille asked. *Or a lifetime. It's up to you.* "He only wanted one night?"

"Yes, the scoundrel! He's cheated me out of thousands!" Renée spoke with machine-gun rapidity, gesticulating and occasionally pulling her hair for added drama. "How could you be so idiotic? Eight days! Eight days of your time—for free!"

This last appeared to be more than the madam could bear. She jabbed upward into the air with all ten red fingernails, then sat down in a heap.

Mireille felt her eyes stinging. "It wasn't free," she said hoarsely. She reached into her purse and took out the five thousand dollars. "He left this."

"Ah." Renée's attitude changed instantly. She was up like a shot, expertly counting the bills. "Well, at least he wasn't cheap about it." She gave half of the money back to Mireille, thought about it for a split second, then snatched away two more bills. "That's for the grief you've caused me. Not that any of this can begin to make up for—"

The money slid from Mireille's hands to the floor. Her shoulders heaved, and she covered her face in shame.

"Oh, stop that," Renée said, trying to sound harsh.

She put an arm around Mireille. "Do you think I don't know what you're going through?" She led her to the sofa and sat down beside her. "You thought he loved you." She gave Mireille a lace-edged handkerchief and patted her hair. "It happens to all of us once. Now look at me."

She lifted Mireille's face and looked directly into her red-rimmed eyes. "You are l'Ange," the madam said softly. "Men from all over the world want you. But you have made the mistake of believing you can expect more from a man than his money."

Mireille turned away, but Renée pulled her face back to her. "This is a hard thing for you to hear, I know, but you must hear it. You must understand, Mireille. Loving a man will only hurt you, because he cannot love you in return. No matter what he says— even if he believes it himself at the time—a man will not give his heart to a whore. And that, even with all our money and glamour, is what we are. The sooner you accept that fact, the easier things will be for you." Renée released her hand from Mireille's chin. "I'm sorry."

Mireille shook her head. "Don't be," she said. "It's the truth. I just didn't want to face it."

Renée smiled gently and patted her hand. "Yes. Now go home and have yourself a good cry." She picked up the money and folded Mireille's fingers around it. "And when you're finished, dry your eyes and wash your face, and send l'Ange back to me tomorrow."

"Taxi, miss?"

Mireille gave the driver her address and then sat back wordlessly.

"Nice day, isn't it?" the driver said.

"It's fi—" She caught a glimpse of his face in the rearview mirror.

The driver noticed his passenger staring at him and turned around. "Is everything all right, miss?" he asked politely.

He had not recognized her.

It had been less than five years since the night this man had delivered Mireille's child in the backseat of his taxi. But then, Mireille thought, she had changed considerably since then. Inside and out. Nothing about her was the same anymore.

Mireille de Jouarre was dead, as dead as her childhood dreams. She was l'Ange now.

The driver pulled over to the curb in front of her apartment building. "That'll be twenty francs, six centimes, miss," he said.

She took the roll of American bills out of her pocketbook— two thousand three hundred dollars—and placed it in his hand. "For your kindness," she said.

While the driver stared, dumbfounded, at the money, she disappeared into the building.

Chapter Twenty-Three

At twenty-two, Mireille had already become a legend of sorts. "L'Ange" was unquestionably the most famous prostitute in Europe, frequently compared by the press with the likes of Marie Duplessis, La Belle Otero, and other famous courtesans throughout history.

Madame Renée's early fears about too much publicity being bad for business were radically allayed when the elegant brothel on the Rue le Sueur became the subject of several books, from gossipy novels to scholarly tomes. L'Ange had put Madame Renée's exclusive house of joy on the map, and there was hardly a tour bus passing through Paris that didn't at least have some men make an attempt to register in Renée's now-burgeoning black book.

By 1952, Mireille herself had been covered so much by the press that she was known more as a celebrity than a call girl. Every day, bottles of champagne arrived at Madame Renée's for her, often accompanied by florid declarations of love. Couturiers vied with one another for the privilege of designing gowns for her. They knew that their creations would be seen and talked about for months among respectable dowagers who would never have invited Mireille to their homes, but who would gladly give a year of their lives to look like her.

A prominent French publisher approached Mireille by mail with a hefty offer to print her autobiography. A ghostwriter would be supplied, he enthused, and the book would be published simultaneously in English and French. Her only responsibility in the project would be to pose for some photographs.

She refused. She always refused pictures. Not a single photograph of her had ever been published in which all of her face could be seen clearly. So rare were images of l'Ange, in fact, that one enterprising modern artist created a vogue by collecting every available copy of the famous *L'Oeil* magazine cover and coloring the black-and-white photo with garish poster paints. The transfigured prints, titled *Green-Eyed Angel*, sold for hundreds of francs each.

Mireille's reticence delighted Madame Renée. L'Ange had become a rarity, a being so sought-after that men paid astronomical sums just to see her and be with her. Once a group of gay men paid handsomely for an evening with her. They took her to a swanky transvestite club where fully a quarter of the clientele were dressed to resemble l'Ange.

"I don't think you know how famous you are," Barbara said as she looked through a pile of invitations. Mireille never attended parties on her own time.

"Yes, I do," Mireille said, deadpan. "After all, I'm in *L'Etoile* nearly every day."

"Oh, that." Barbara dismissed it with a wave of disgust. *L'Etoile* was a tabloid of the worst sort, feeding on misfortune and scandal for its stories. Its usual practice was to find the skeletons in the closets of prominent Parisians and expose them to the public in high-toned, moralistic prose. More often than not, the paper's allegations were completely false and based only on the flimsiest evidence, but the public continued to read it anyway.

L'Etoile's latest crusade was against l'Ange. *The toy of the rich*, it repeatedly called her in a series of vicious stories designed to play off Mireille's fame. They accused her of everything from perversion to spying.

"That rag's nothing," Barbara said. "A bunch of communists looking for a freebie. Every magazine in Europe wants an interview with you. Do you know what they call you in England? 'The Angel of Night.' You can't buy publicity like that."

"Good grief, haven't I had enough publicity?"

"But you could make a fortune. And it would be legitimate money."

Mireille laughed bitterly. "Oh, yes. 'Here is a picture of the great French whore. See the whore talk. Next week, the whore will tap-dance on television.' *L'Etoile* would have a field day." She leafed through a catalogue of country homes.

Barbara sighed. "I just think you're missing the opportunity of a lifetime. And what are you reading? I suppose you're going to be a farmer next."

"Maybe. I don't want to live in Paris forever."

"Honestly," Barbara said, shaking her head. "If I could look like you for one minute . . ."

Mireille looked up. "Yes? What would you do?"

"I'd cash in. I'd go for the big money while the offers were still coming in. I sure as hell wouldn't still be making my living on my back."

"Yes, you would." There was an unexpected harshness in Mireille's voice, and her eyes were cold. "Once you're in the Life, there's nothing else. It always comes back. No matter how much money you have or how famous you are, they'll still laugh at you behind your back."

"You're paranoid," Barbara said hotly. "And who's *they*, anyway? Those horny moralizers at *L'Etoile*?"

"*They* are the people who keep *L'Etoile* in business! The people who invite us to their parties but won't let us move into their buildings, the clients whose sons you'd never be permitted to meet unless it was in one of Madame Renée's bedrooms, the movie directors who forget their promises as soon as they put their pants on . . ."

Barbara looked down at her hands.

"I'm sorry, Barbara," Mireille stammered. "I'm just . . ."

"Forget it." The redhead shrugged. "You're just wrong, that's all. Gino loves me."

"Oh, Barbara!"

"He does! He's not anything like Oliver Jordan, Mireille. It's been seven years, and we're still together."

"He lives in another country," Mireille shouted.

"That can't be helped," Barbara countered primly. "Gino just hasn't advanced at the studio the way he hoped he would. But he's going to make it, I know. And when he does, I'm going to be a star. And you'll be . . ." She bit her lip. Her eyes were shiny with angry tears.

Three months later, Barbara had good news.

"I'm in a movie!" she cried, clutching the telegram to her breast. "Gino's put me in a movie! I start at Cinecittà Studios in Rome in two weeks!"

Mireille read the telegram excitedly and hugged her.

"This is wonderful," she said. "What's the movie?"

"Who knows? Who cares? Didn't I always say I was going to be a star? Even when certain people scoffed at me?" She cast a triumphant glance at Mireille.

"Okay, you've made your point." Mireille laughed.

The two of them celebrated in grand style that night, and Barbara told Madame Renée the next day. The girls on the Rue le Sueur gave a party for her and presented Barbara with a necklace on which was suspended a tiny gold dildo.

"We know you won't wear it," frail Denise said, sitting instinctively in the shadows. The tiny lines around her eyes were beginning to give the lie to the little-girl clothes she wore. Denise was already scheduled at a clinic in Sweden for a facelift, although the doctor had told her that, at thirty-three, she would probably require another within ten years. She'd answered that in ten years, if she was lucky, she might not need to look seventeen anymore.

"Of course she'll wear it," Sonja boomed. She dangled the pendant from between her scarlet-tipped hands. "She'll wear it when she picks up her award at the Cannes Film Festival. And we'll all be there to say we knew her when!" They all cheered then, all except for Ankha, who sat staring, glassy-eyed, at whatever images danced inside her absinthe-clouded mind.

Ankha was so thin now, Mireille noticed, and her skin was so pale that the small veins in her jaw showed. She would be gone from the Rue le Sueur long before Denise.

Mireille looked from one face to the next, all those beautiful faces aging slowly, falling imperceptibly into decay.

Mine too, she thought. Will I end up like Denise, going under the knife for the chance at a few more years at Madame Renée's before I take to the streets, offering myself to sailors for a meal? Or will I go quietly, like Ankha, dying by inches?

Her eyes welled with tears. Suddenly, she hugged Barbara fiercely. "Go to Rome and don't ever look back, understand?"

"Mireille," Barbara said, laughing.

"No! Don't write to us. Don't call. Just forget you were ever one of us. You're getting out, Barbara. Close the door between us and keep it closed."

There was a long silence, finally broken by Denise's faint sob. Then all the women closed in around Barbara, pressing against each other as if they were sheltering in a windstorm.

Ankha died less than six months later. She was found by her land-lady, fully made up, hanging from the light fixture in her bedroom by a silken cord. The light fixture was not particularly strong, but Ankha had weighed less than ninety pounds at the time of her suicide. There was an empty bottle of absinthe on the nightstand beside her bed, and a beautiful art deco glass of green crystal trimmed with gold.

At the funeral, the women who had celebrated Barbara's going-away party stood apart from the younger ones, who gossiped excitedly about the star of Madame Renée's stable in their midst. The brothel had grown immensely since Mireille had first come to work for her. Most of the women did not even know one another's names. But they all knew of l'Ange.

"She's still just a hooker," a buxom eighteen-year-old whispered.

"How old is she?" a slender brunette asked, peering above dark sunglasses.

"Twenty-three. I read it in a magazine."

The brunette sniffed. "I'll bet she's older than that."

"I guess she could be," the young one conceded. "She still looks pretty good, though."

"Well, I'm not going to be turning tricks when I'm her age, whatever her real age is. Besides, if she's so great, why isn't she married? Did you know, one of Madame Renée's girls married a baron?"

"Sure. Everybody knows that. But I'm going to open a business. A store or something. I figure I can save plenty in the next few years. Then I'm going to kiss the Life good-bye."

"Me too. Before I turn into . . . that." She was staring at the casket resting at the bottom of the grave.

Her friend shuddered. "Who was she?"

"I don't know. Hung herself."

"Must have been a mental case."

"Yeah."

"She was really old."

"Shhh!" Madame Renée poked them both between their shoulder blades.

On the other side of the grave, the older women were silent. Sonja, clutching her black mink coat around her like a shield; Nicole, chain-smoking, tossing the smoldering butts absently into the open grave, oblivious to the black stares of the minister; Denise, her new face shiny and stretched to the small scars at her hairline . . . They huddled close to one another as they had when Barbara left them for movies and Rome. Another one of their own had gone away, and they averted their faces, sheltering together again.

Only Mireille stood alone. She stared vacantly at the open pit where Ankha's casket lay, but she was not thinking of Ankha. Ankha had died long before her wasted, shaking fingers had wrapped the silken cord around her neck. She had died when her name was still Annelise, at the moment when she had embraced the Life.

Mireille thought of Stephanie. The child was seven years old now. For the past year she had been enrolled in L'Académie Thomasienne, the best private school in the city.

Mireille could still recall the knowing look of the headmistress during the interview, the vague sense of distaste in the woman's patrician eyes. Mireille had tried to bolster her self-confidence by reminding herself that she was there to interview the school, but she knew it wasn't so. The question was not whether or not L'Académie Thomasienne was good enough for Stephanie, but whether or not the place was hard up enough to accept the illegitimate daughter of Europe's prize bedmate.

It had been, apparently. Stephanie was accepted. And there had been no incident, no talk about it.

Until today.

It had been the first thing Stephanie said in the morning. "Maman," she asked, her eyes glittering with excitement as she rubbed the sleep from them. "What's a 'whore'?"

Mireille felt her skin go cold. "What do you mean, Stephanie?" she stalled.

The girl shrugged elaborately. "I don't know. The big girls were saying it in the lavatory. They said it and pointed at me. And they laughed. Is a whore a funny thing, Maman, like a clown?"

"No, darling," Mireille said softly. "It's not a word you should use. It's a . . . a bad word."

Stephanie's face fell into a mask of injured pride. "They were calling me a bad thing?"

Mireille took a deep breath. "Don't be silly," she said breezily. "They weren't calling you anything at all. They were just being silly girls. Now get dressed. Suzanne has your breakfast ready for you in the kitchen." That had been the end of it.

That was just the beginning, Mireille thought. The children knew. Their parents read *L'Etoile,* though they pretended not to. And they sent their children, cruelest of creatures, to punish Stephanie for her mother's sins.

You knew she would find out one day, didn't you? taunted a niggling inner voice. *Soon she'll know everything . . . and she'll hate you forever . . .*

Something cold was pressed into her hands. It was a silver spade, flecked with dirt. Sonja was looking at her with some concern as she passed along the tool.

Mireille saw that the casket was mounded with clods of earth. It was her turn to bury Ankha, who had lived too long.

She dug up a scoop and tossed it on the coffin. Then, slowly, she walked over to Madame Renée. The young women surrounding the madam stepped respectfully to either side of Mireille as she moved through them.

She gave the spade to Renée. "Good-bye, madame," she said. "I won't be coming back." She walked away.

A low murmur went up among the young women as she left the cemetery. Madame Renée did not try to silence them. Her eyes followed Mireille. She would be back, Renée knew. They all came back eventually, and for the same reason.

They had nowhere else to go.

Chapter Twenty-Four

Mireille had no regrets about her decision and no fears, even though it had cost most of her savings to buy the house in Normandy. It was a large eighteenth-century stone-and-stucco farmhouse with a terra-cotta roof and a well-kept English-style garden that sprouted delphiniums and hollyhocks and roses.

"I want to show you something," she said as she walked Stephanie through the garden.

"I love this place," Stephanie said. "I hope you never work in Paris again."

Mireille colored. "I won't," she said. "Never again. That's a promise."

Stephanie whooped for joy. Mireille picked her up and danced around the garden with her, laughing. She had outrun the past. The Life, she hoped, was finally behind her.

"Are there models in Normandy?" the girl asked.

It was a lie Mireille had perpetrated since Stephanie first started questioning the peculiar hours her mother kept. She had told her that she was a *mannequin*, a term vague enough to encompass all sorts of occupations, from photographic and runway models to the frowsy ladies who showed off coats to department store buyers in the wholesaler showrooms. It explained her nightly absences neatly enough, as well as the high-profit weekends that had been unavoidable.

"I don't need to model anymore," she said. "We've got some savings, and . . . well, don't worry, we're quite fine here."

It was not going to be easy, she knew. There was not much in the way of savings. Before Barbara left for Rome, Mireille had bought the expensive apartment from her. She had paid cash for it, as she had for the Normandy house, to avoid any outside involvement. It had cost her to furnish the new house, too. And then, there had been the sculpture she had commissioned a year ago. Now that it was finally completed, she had to pay for it. The artist's fee for the piece had been astronomical, but she'd had to have it.

It was Stefan's memorial.

"This is what I wanted you to see," she said as she led the girl to the center of the garden, where a menagerie of tiny carved marble animals stood atop a large flat-topped pedestal. Mireille had commissioned a prominent Parisian artist to carve the pieces according to her detailed instructions. She had drawn each one for the artist from memory, hoping to re-create the hand-carved figures Stefan had given her as a child.

"Look at this," Stephanie cried in delight, picking up an exquisitely carved white horse. "Where did these come from?"

"They're for you," Mireille said, touching the girl's long hair. It shone blue-black against the alabaster whiteness of her face. "Your father once made a set of stone animals for me. I wish I could have saved it for you, but it was lost."

Stephanie examined the tiny hooves of the horse with her fingertips. She set it down. "Was my daddy very handsome?" she asked quietly.

Mireille smiled. "Yes, darling. Very handsome. You look like him."

And then, as always when she thought about Stefan, Mireille felt herself sinking back, remembering the weeks they had spent together.

Weeks! It had been such a short time. In all the years of hurt and shame and fear that had made up her life, she had only a few weeks of happiness to remember.

"What was his name again?" Stephanie asked. "I've forgotten it."

"Stefan," her mother answered, running her fingernail along the stone mane of the little horse. In the unbidden memory it brought, she could see hills covered with lavender where Stefan had lived with her. She saw his strong, sweat-glistening body as he ran, limping toward her like a wounded puppy too happy to realize he should have been in pain. She could smell the crushed flowers beneath their feet, hear once again the wild pounding of her heart.

She pulled her hand away from the sculpture. It had brought the past too close. "His name was Stefan." She kissed the child's sun-warmed hair.

Suddenly, she gasped. A man, a stranger, was in the garden with them, crouching behind the boxwood hedges, with only his head raised above them.

His head, and a camera with a telephoto lens.

"Maman, what—?"

"Get inside," Mireille ordered.

"But—"

"Don't ask questions, just get inside!"

She bolted for the man. He stood up and ran, his equipment bumping at his hip as he mowed down a path through the newly bloomed flowers.

"What do you want with me?" she screamed. The photographer didn't answer. He ran onto the lawn, turned once to snap a last picture of Mireille, then sprinted toward the road.

A few moments later there was the sound of a car door slamming shut and an engine revving. When the car came into view, she knew what the photographer had wanted. On the door was printed "*L'Etoile*—The News You Want."

Mireille watched the car race away, then she glanced back at the house, sunny and vine-covered. It had been foolish to think she could escape the Life so easily, she thought. It was a living beast that would follow her forever, reaching its tentacles into every corner where she tried to hide, reaching now to wind around her daughter.

No, she told herself, trying to be rational. *It's not as bad as it looks. A photograph of a prostitute on the back page of a tabloid . . . would that be so terribly important to anyone?* She would stay in Normandy for a few days until whatever publicity the picture generated died down.

"This is nothing," she said out loud. Nothing. Nothing.

She had underestimated her own notoriety. By the time she brought Stephanie back to Paris, the *L'Etoile* story had spawned a dozen other prurient pieces about the secret life of the most mysterious woman in the city. Reporters loitering outside her apartment building leaped to their feet and thronged around her as she got out of her car and led Stephanie by the hand toward the door. Everyone seemed to be shouting at once.

"It is true that you slept with the president?"

"How much do you get for a trick, honey?"

"Any truth to the rumor that you passed secrets to the Russians in the bedroom?"

Stephanie moved close to her mother, the small marble horse clutched in her hand. "What are they saying, Maman?" she asked, her voice high and frightened. "What do they want?"

"What's the kid's name?" someone shouted.

One reporter, a thin woman with a bright slash of orange lipstick across her mouth, grabbed Stephanie's arm roughly. "What do you think about what your mommy does, little girl?"

Mireille lunged at the woman and slapped her backhanded across her face. "Don't you touch her!" she shrieked.

A dozen flashbulbs popped to capture the moment. The reporter toppled backward onto the sidewalk.

"You're not going to get away with this, bitch!" the reporter screamed. "My paper's going to turn you inside out, do you hear me? You won't have a *sou* left when I'm through with you!"

Two orange streaks smeared the back of Mireille's hand. She wiped them off, picked up Stephanie, and carried her inside.

"Who are those people, Maman?" the girl wailed, burying her face in Mireille's shoulder.

"Shhh. They're not important."

When the elevator doors closed, shutting out the sight of the mob that the doorman managed to hold at bay outside, Mireille was shaking violently.

"But why were they talking like that?" Stephanie's voice cracked. "That lady . . ." She touched her arm where the reporter had held her. Red finger marks were still imprinted on it.

"That was no lady," Mireille said weakly.

The elevator opened, and she ran to her apartment, but her hands were shaking so badly she could barely get the key in the lock. At last the door opened.

"Suzanne," Stephanie said. "There are so many people outside . . ."

"Hush, sweetheart," the nanny said, lifting the girl into her arms. The woman's hair was disheveled and her lips were trembling as she looked past Stephanie to Mireille. "I went out for the groceries," she said, obviously on the brink of hysteria. "They were already waiting. Some of them followed me. The groceries . . . they all spilled . . ."

"We'll talk later," Mireille said. "Please take Stephanie to her room."

"Yes, ma'am."

"And . . . thank you for staying."

The woman bit her lip. "I can't," she said. "Not after today. Madame, I am too old for this. I cannot—"

"For a while, then. Please. Just until I can get organized."

The old woman shook her head. "I'm sorry. My daughter is coming for me soon. She's in Paris visiting, and she saw the newspaper, and . . . well . . ."

"I understand," Mireille said quietly.

"This pains me more than you know, madame. I love Stephanie like she was my own, but . . ." She looked reproachfully from under her shaggy gray brows.

"I'll draw a check for you."

The nanny lowered her head. "Thank you." She put her arm around Stephanie's shoulders and led the girl toward her room.

"Did you get the newspapers?" Mireille asked.

"Beg your pardon?"

"*L'Etoile*," Mireille said thickly.

"Yes, ma'am. It's in there." She gestured toward the kitchen.

Stephanie stopped in front of her bedroom door and turned around, her face showing confusion and bewilderment.

Mireille smiled at her, standing rigid, her hands clasped in front of her, as if her tightly locked fingers were all that kept her from dispersing into particles.

"I love you, Maman," the girl said.

Mireille only nodded. She did not trust herself to speak. When the door closed behind her daughter, she walked slowly to the kitchen and sat down with the tabloid spread in front of her on the table.

L'Etoile's circulation was over two million, despite the fact that most of its stories could not even be construed as news. The edition in front of Mireille contained an account of someone who had been taken on a ride in a flying saucer over Peru; a story about a little girl who had been dismembered by bees; and a testimonial from a man who claimed that standing on his head had turned him into a financial genius. These were the inside stories. On the front page was the headline:

LOVE GODDESS UNMASKED
SCHOOLGIRL DAUGHTER WITH CALL GIRL MOM

Below the scant paragraph of text were five fuzzy photographs. Mireille examined the first two with an odd sort of detachment, as if they were about some stranger she had never heard of. There was a two-shot of Mireille and an English duke. Another showed her walking outside Maxim's with a German industrialist. Both of those photos were grainy and dim, obviously taken with a tele-photo lens. They had no doubt been in the paper's files for months, previously rejected for print because of their poor quality.

The remaining three had been taken in the garden in Normandy. One showed Mireille standing alone, angrily shouting at the photographer, with the house in the background. That alone was enough to guarantee that she would never be able to live in that house.

The second showed Mireille leaning close to Stephanie while the child held the little stone horse from the menagerie. Mireille was in profile, but Stephanie was facing the camera. The caption read "L'Ange teaching youngster about the birds and bees?"

The last picture nauseated her. It was a blurry blowup of Stephanie's face. Beneath it were three smaller photographs— of the king of Norway, the French singer Yves Montand, and an American movie star named Peter Rockwell. Mireille had never met any of them. Beneath the pictures were the words "Who does she call Daddy?"

Mireille stared at the page, trembling uncontrollably. Then, with a sound from deep in the back of her throat, she tore the newspaper to ribbons.

"Maman?" she heard Stephanie call from behind the closed door of her room. "I want to see my *maman!*"

"No, child," the nanny said. "Your mother is all right. She just needs to be alone now, that's all."

Mireille stuck her fist in her mouth and bit down hard on her knuckle to keep from screaming. *What have they done to you, Stephanie?* she wanted to cry out. *What have they done?*

Finally, she was able to pull herself together. She picked up the torn pieces of the newspaper and carried them to the wastebasket. On the top piece, wrinkled and torn, was the name Oliver Jordan.

. . . been visiting the Comte de Vevray in the Comte's Schloss near Berlin. Insiders reveal that the naughty aristocrat likes young girls—very young. Tsk-tsk.

Mireille heard a brittle sound, hollow as the call of a dying man, come out of her own throat. She laughed and laughed, swallowing the bile that threatened to spill out of her. She laughed until she was hoarse and the very air tasted bitter.

Chapter Twenty-Five

Five hours later Mireille was arrested on charges of assault and battery, the result of slapping the reporter.

Two young male officers and a uniformed woman built like a bull surrounded her in the apartment. The policewoman took Stephanie's hand as one of the men shoved Mireille roughly away.

"What are you doing with my daughter?" Mireille demanded, still unable to believe that she was being taken to jail.

"We're just going to get some of her things together, ma'am."

"Why? Where are you taking her?"

"She'll be assigned to a temporary residence while you're in custody."

"A temporary . . . No, she won't! Not on your life!"

"Ma'am . . ."

Mireille pushed the two men aside and knelt beside Stephanie, holding her.

"I'm afraid you'll have to let her go, ma'am," the policewoman said flatly.

"Get away from us."

The officer yanked Mireille up by the collar of her blouse. "I've had about enough out of you, missy," she said between clenched teeth.

Stephanie screamed. "Stop it! You're hurting my *maman*!"

Mireille pushed the woman away. The officer staggered two steps backward, then ground into forward gear. Her fist felt like a speeding truck when it connected with Mireille's cheekbone.

The two male officers sprang into action then, grabbing Mireille's arms and handcuffing them behind her back as the policewoman picked Stephanie up bodily and carried her away. Stephanie was shrieking wildly.

Despite her throbbing cheekbone, Mireille felt numb. Stephanie had been snatched away from her like a stuffed toy. "My daughter," she whispered.

"She'll be all right," one of the male officers said as they led Mireille to the police cruiser outside.

A feeling of unreality settled around her like a shroud as she stared, unseeing, out the wire-reinforced window. Grinning photographers snapped her picture.

"Nice shiner, Angel," one of them said amiably.

After an hour in a cell with a dozen streetwalkers, a young, nervous-looking man introducing himself only as an attorney escorted her out.

"Where is my daughter?" she asked.

"I'll take you to her now," he said.

"But who . . . who are you? You're not my lawyer."

"Please, I've been instructed not to answer any questions. Just to set your mind at ease, your lawyer is aware that I'm with you now."

"Then why didn't he come himself?"

"I'm afraid he wouldn't be able to do much to help you."

"And you can?"

The man sighed. "Mademoiselle, I represent a law firm and a client who do not wish for their names to be connected to this matter. Everything has been taken care of, I assure you. Please follow me." He headed toward the police station's exit doors. A throng of reporters was waiting outside.

"The press—" Mireille began.

"Just stay close to me." The young man rushed her past the waiting journalists into a nondescript black automobile. Then, for more than an hour, they drove aimlessly around the city, changing cars and drivers twice before stopping finally at the elegant Hôtel de Crillon.

"Go to suite four-fifteen," the man said as the chauffeur opened the car door for her. "Don't stop for anyone." As soon as she ran up the steps into the entrance, the car sped away.

Stephanie greeted her at the door with a cry and a pair of outstretched arms. When Mireille picked her up, she saw Madame Renée standing behind the door.

"You," Mireille whispered, dumbfounded. "How did—?"

"Put the child to bed," Renée snapped. "She's had a dreadful day."

"Madame, how can I ever thank you?" Mireille mumbled miserably.

"You can't. I'm a fool to help you. Is your daughter asleep?"

"Yes," Mireille said. "She told me that you were very kind to her."

Briskly, Renée waved her away as she lit a cigarette, then picked up a newspaper from a small table.

"*Le Figaro!*" she declaimed, brandishing the paper above her head like a torch. Smoke shot out of her nostrils. "This is not some fourth-rate tabloid, Mireille. *Everyone* reads *Le Figaro.*"

"I'm sure they do." Mireille closed her eyes and rubbed her temples. "What does it say about me?"

"Only that you've taken to beating journalists with your fists. The story must have come in just in time for the evening edition." She slammed the paper back onto the table. "You look ghastly."

"A policewoman hit me."

"You should become a prizefighter. God knows, you're getting enough practice." She paced, rubbing her elbows as if they were covered with insects. "If only you hadn't hit that woman! It cost me the price of a mink coat to get that harridan to drop the charges against you."

Mireille could hardly believe what she was hearing. "She's dropped the charges?"

"Yes, yes," Renée said with disgust. "Not that you're getting off easy, oh, no no no." She shook her head frenetically. "The lawyers I've engaged are the most expensive in Europe. Needless to say, they charged me double their usual fee, the swine." She inhaled deeply on the cigarette. "Well, I'm not going to upset myself over that now. You'll pay for them, of course."

"Of course."

"And the payoff to the greedy *salope* at *L'Etoile*. Not to mention the tax bill you're going to be hit with. The thieving lawyers are fairly sure they can keep you out of jail, but you'll have to pay a mint in taxes and fines."

"I've always paid taxes," Mireille said.

"Trust me. The government will claim it wasn't enough. The papers have made you out to be a millionairess. You'll be lucky not to go to the poor farm after they're through with you."

"I'll find a way to pay them," Mireille said quietly. "I appreciate everything you've done."

"And the child!" Renée threw her hands up and rolled her eyes. "You might at least have told me about her. All these years, and not a word!"

"I was afraid—"

"Oh, shut up! Now every do-gooder fanatic in France will be on my back. It will take every cent I own just to keep *myself* out of jail."

"Have the papers mentioned you?"

"Not yet!" Renée screeched. "I haven't quite run out of money yet!"

Mireille hung her head. "I'm sorry," she said.

"*You're* sorry? I'm the one who's sorry, believe me. You've ruined me. You've . . ." She slapped her palms together and took a deep breath. "Well, what's done is done." She sat down on the overstuffed chair opposite Mireille and picked up the newspaper.

"*Le Figaro,*" she whispered.

"Madame?"

"What, what, what?" Renée said irritably.

Mireille frowned. "I haven't worked for you in months."

"So?"

"So why are you helping me now?"

Madame Renée was strangely silent for a moment. Then she sniffed disdainfully. "For business reasons, of course. It was in my best interest to stop this nonsense before it turned into a complete catastrophe for all of us."

"I see."

Renée ground out her cigarette. "What are you going to do?" she asked.

Mireille stood up and went to the large window. "I don't know."

"Frankly, I suggest you leave the city. For your own good. And the child's. The lawyers will contact you when they need you."

Mireille nodded.

"Does she go to school?"

"In Normandy," Mireille answered quietly. "I'll withdraw her tomorrow."

"Where will you go?"

"Does it matter?" Mireille's voice was like an automaton's.

The two women sat in silence for a few minutes. Then Renée stood up and picked up her handbag. She took out a piece of paper on which were listed a row of figures in her neat handwriting, with a circled total at the bottom.

"This is a list of debts you owe me, including the bribe to the woman and the cost of this hotel room," she said crisply.

"I'll have it to you in the morning."

"That will be fine. Good luck to you, dear." She began to walk away, but she hesitated before she reached the door. She stood there for a moment, her back to Mireille.

"What is it, Renée?"

When she turned around, the madam's expression had changed. It was softer, older.

"There's . . . there's something else I have for you," she said, her carefully made-up face suddenly blossoming into red splotches. Quickly, she walked back to the table, took a sheet of the hotel's stationery, and wrote down a name and address.

"Switzerland?" Mireille said, reading. "What's this?"

"La Voisine. It's a school for girls near Geneva."

Mireille set down the paper. "Are you suggesting that I send Stephanie away?" The idea felt like a frozen dagger in her stomach. "No, that's out of the question."

"Why?" Renée snapped. "Why is it out of the question?"

"Well . . . It's just . . . I've never even considered the possibility of . . . leaving her . . ."

"Then you should."

Mireille allowed the idea to roam around her mind for a moment, then swiftly discarded it. "She's going to stay with me," she said decisively.

"Oh, wonderful. I'm sure you'll be able to give her great happiness. She'll grow up with a reputation as the bastard child of a notorious harlot—"

"Stop it!"

"Just what a young girl needs, isn't it?"

Mireille turned away, trembling. "We'll go away together," she said, her voice no more than a breath.

"Where? This is nineteen fifty-two. You can't hide out in some quiet village somewhere. The press wants you. And if they can sell a few more copies of their rags by hanging you upside down in a public square, they will."

"I can survive that."

"You, yes. But not a seven-year-old girl. Think of her."

"I do think about her," Mireille rasped. "She's all I think about. All I care about."

"Then you know I'm right."

Mireille clenched her fists. "Yes," she said finally, hopelessly. "I know."

"La Voisine is quite a good school," Renée said, her voice cracking. She cleared her throat. "It's excellent academically, and it's run by nuns, so the children aren't exposed to a lot of bad influences and . . . newspapers . . ." She opened her pocketbook, took out a handkerchief, and blew her nose. "My daughter attended it years ago."

Mireille looked up at her.

"You see," Renée said quietly. "I do understand some things."

"Oh God, I'm sorry. I didn't know."

"No one does." She shrugged, dabbing at her nose. "I never raised her, of course. I paid a family to adopt her when she was born, but I've always taken care of her expenses."

"Then she doesn't know you're her mother?"

Renée shook her head. A deep frown creased the center of her forehead. "She's never seen me. I've seen her, of course. I've got a whole photo album filled with pictures of her. She's thirty-four now, with three children. All boys. Her husband is a big land developer in Lyon." Her eyes were glassy, but she smiled with pride. "She graduated from the Sorbonne, my daughter."

Mireille stood up and put her arms around Madame Renée, and for a moment she could feel the woman's unhealed pain.

"Enough of that," Renée said, pulling away from her. "What's done is done, eh? Like I said before."

"Renée . . ."

"Don't. You can't change anything, for me. Or for you. But you can give Stephanie a good life. A clean life." She snapped her handbag closed. "*Alors.* In a year or two, when *L'Etoile* has lost interest in the mysterious Angel of Night, you'll be able to pick up where you left off, yes?"

Mireille nodded. "Yes," she said.

"Good." Renée kissed her on the cheek. "Try to be happy, *ma belle.*"

Then, with her head held high, her carriage perfect, and her hair exquisitely in place, she left without a backward glance.

Chapter Twenty-Six

The school was a converted stone mansion along the western shore of Lake Geneva. It was a lovely old place with fanciful fairy-tale turrets, and it was surrounded by ancient chestnut trees and blooming rhododendron. In the distance, the white serrated peaks of the Dents du Midi rose above the morning mist.

"Look how beautiful this place is," Mireille said, trying to sound cheerful.

Stephanie took something out of her pocket and stared at it. It was the stone horse from the sculpted menagerie at the Normandy house.

"Please, darling." Mireille knelt down and hugged the girl. "This won't be for long. I promise."

"But why can't I stay with you, Maman?"

"I've tried to explain that. I've got to go away—"

"I can go, too! I'll be good, Maman, I promise. I'll never do anything bad, ever. Please don't leave me."

Mireille forced herself to speak calmly. "You haven't done anything wrong, Stephanie. Anything at all. And there's nothing I'd like more than for us to stay together every minute. But we can't. Not for a little while. Please try—"

Stephanie sobbed and threw her arms around her mother's neck.

How could she understand? Mireille asked herself. She had not been given any real explanation at all. She was a little girl being told to live in an institution in a foreign country, for no reason other than that her mother wished to move away.

"What about our house, Maman? Our new house with the stone animals?"

"I . . . we won't be able to keep that."

"Not the animals, either?"

Mireille stood up, her hands over her eyes. "They're gone. I went back to get them, but . . . they're gone." She didn't tell Stephanie that the garden had been trampled by uninvited visitors, and that someone had placed a sheet of paper with the single word *"putain"* scrawled across it inside her postbox. "I'm sorry," she said.

Stephanie bit her lip. "It's all right. I still have one of them." She opened her fist. The stone horse was damp with moisture from her palm.

Mireille held her close, while a nun in an enormous white wimple seemed to float over to them across the sloping lawn.

"Madame de Jouarre?" she asked cheerfully, extending a big work-reddened hand. "I am Sister Marie-Thérèse. And this must be Stephanie."

"Don't go," Stephanie said in a low voice harsh with fear. She squeezed Mireille's fingers so hard that her knuckles were white.

"Now, now," the Sister said, gently prying her away. She gestured for Mireille to remain where she was while she took Stephanie inside. "All new places are a little frightening at first, but I know you'll enjoy being here. All the girls do."

"No," Stephanie screamed. "Don't leave me, Maman! How will I find you? Don't leave me!"

Sister Marie-Thérèse resolutely led her away.

"Maman!" Stephanie whirled around, struggling to get away, but the nun held on to her. Then Stephanie quieted suddenly, as if realizing for the first time that the unthinkable had come to pass. She stared blankly at her mother for a long moment, then turned away. At the top of the lawn, near the granite portico, she vanished into the shadows.

Mireille stood watching the closed door for a long time. *She'll be safe here,* she told herself. *The Life won't touch her now.* Then she left, feeling a deep hollowness in her belly.

Stephanie sat on the edge of her bed, her face a blank.

"Ah, here's your valise," Sister Marie-Thérèse said as an old custodian lugged a big suitcase inside. "We don't have many girls staying with us during the summer, so it's all very cozy. I'm sure you'll make friends right away." She clasped her hands in front of her and peered coquettishly out of her outlandish headgear. "Would you like to meet some of your dorm mates now?"

"No, thank you," Stephanie said in a monotone.

The nun touched her shoulder. "Very well. I imagine you're quite tired. You've come all the way from Paris?"

"Yes."

"What a long drive! Well, perhaps you'd like to unpack your things and take a short nap before lunch. I'll introduce you to our little family then."

"I don't have a family," Stephanie said.

"Of course you do, dear. And I'm sure you'll feel much better after a nap. I'll be back for you at twelve noon. All right?"

"I don't want lunch."

The Sister laughed. "We'll see," she said, closing the door softly behind her.

Alone in the room, Stephanie stared at her suitcase blankly, her legs swinging in monotonous rhythm, her hands pressed tightly around the stone horse.

More than an hour passed before the doorknob turned with a squeak. Stephanie expected Sister Marie-Thérèse to bustle in, exhorting her to come to lunch with her new family of strangers, but the door only opened a crack.

Stephanie's legs stopped swinging. She held her breath as the door opened with almost imperceptible slowness.

Finally, one eye, half hidden behind one lens of a pair of glasses and a curtain of brown bangs, appeared from behind it. The person the eye belonged to made no move to come in farther, as if Stephanie were some exotic animal under intense but fearful observation.

"Why are you standing there?" Stephanie asked at last. "What do you want?"

Slowly, the entire shaggy head emerged, followed by a pair of bony shoulders. Long, scabby legs stuck out from beneath the skirt of a blue school uniform. The creature said something in a strange language. Stephanie stared at her dumbly.

"I asked you if you spoke English," the girl said with a sigh. "I'm Nora Stillwell. What's your name?" Her French was good, but she had an accent.

"Stephanie."

"Stephanie." Nora considered it for a moment. "That's okay, I guess. At least it isn't one of those silly French names like Yvette or Mimi. Stephanie is practically American."

"Are you an American?"

"The only one here. I keep looking for someone to talk sensibly to."

"I talk sensibly," Stephanie said.

"In French. French is a useless language now, you know. My father told me. It used to be the language of diplomacy, but it isn't anymore. Now everybody important speaks English. You can't be a scientist unless you speak English."

"I don't want to be a scientist."

"Oh." Nora loped into the room, banging into the corner of the dresser. The blow seemed not to affect her at all. "I don't, either. I'm going to be a great writer, or else a movie star." She went straight to Stephanie's suitcase and opened it. "Is this all you've got?"

Stephanie nodded.

"When I arrived here, I had ten trunks. They had to get a truck just to bring them from the airport. My father's very rich. He's a banker in New York. Our house on the Hudson has fifty rooms on four floors."

Stephanie went back to swinging her legs.

"What's that?" the tall girl asked, reaching for the stone horse.

Stephanie yanked it away, rolling over on the bed in a violent, protective movement.

"I wasn't going to break it or anything." She blinked behind her owlish glasses.

Slowly, Stephanie peered over her shoulder.

"You don't have to show it to me, really," Nora said. "I understand these things."

"You do?"

"Sure. It's a talisman."

"A what?"

"A talisman. Something special, like a lucky thing you wish on."

"Yes," Stephanie said in astonishment. "Sometimes I do wish on it." She looked down. "Only my wish doesn't come true."

"But you keep on wishing, right?"

Stephanie nodded.

"That's because you've got a neurotic attachment to it. My psychiatrist told me that before I got shipped off to this place. I used to have something like that. It was a dead frog."

"A dead . . . frog?" Stephanie found herself laughing despite herself.

Nora did, too. "It was neat. A car ran over it, and it was squashed flat. I used it for a bookmark." They howled with laughter.

"And you wished on it?"

"Not while it was a bookmark. But later, I made a special place for it in my bedroom and put candles all around it. That's when I wished."

"Did your wish come true?"

The girl shook her head. "My father told one of the maids to get rid of it."

Stephanie curled her fingers even more tightly around the little horse.

"So anyway, your statue is safe around me. If I took it away, you'd probably go off the deep end."

"Go off what?"

"Kill yourself. You know." She drew her finger across her neck with appropriately grisly sound effects.

"Is that what you did?"

The girl turned her hands palm-up and thrust them in front of Stephanie's face. Her wrists were gnarled with ugly red scars. "I tried to off myself two years ago. Razor blade."

Stephanie gaped at the horrifying marks. "Because . . . because of the dead frog?"

Nora shrugged. "Because I knew my wish wasn't going to come true."

Stephanie took a long breath through her open mouth.

"Dr. Holmes said it was the most determined effort he'd ever seen by a preteen," Nora said proudly. "The walls were covered with blood."

Aghast, Stephanie edged away, toward the corner of the bed.

"Want to touch my scars?"

"No! Well . . ."

"Go ahead. They feel weird."

Fascinated, Stephanie ventured to touch one of the ropy welts. "What did you wish for?" she whispered.

"Can't tell. Not yet. I might find another dead frog."

Stephanie nodded sagely.

"Want to see my room?" Nora asked. "It's nicer than yours."

"Okay."

Nora's room was actually identical to Stephanie's, except that every square inch of wall space was covered with pictures of faces cut from glossy magazines. Stephanie's first impression was of walking into an enormous party where no one moved or spoke. "Who are they?" she asked.

"They're stars, silly. Don't you go to movies?"

Stephanie shook her head. "Maman and I don't go out."

"You mean she doesn't take you out." She laughed cruelly.

Stephanie blushed, feeling the hotness rise in her cheeks. She turned to leave, but Nora grabbed her arm and hung on to it tightly. "Hey, don't get mad, okay? I'm just saying that grown-ups don't like to hang around kids. I mean, that's why we're here, right?"

Stephanie felt tears start in her eyes.

"Oh God," Nora moaned. "I can't stand crybabies. How old are you, anyway?"

"Se-seven," Stephanie said, brushing the unwanted tears from her face.

"That explains it. I'm ten. Okay, wait a second." She poured a glass of water from a big ceramic pitcher on the bureau. Then she rummaged in one of the drawers, tossing underpants and socks over her shoulder onto the floor, until she came up with a brown pharmacist's vial. She threw it to Stephanie.

"What's this?"

"Valium. It'll make you feel better."

Stephanie gave it back to her. "No, thanks," she said. "I hate medicine."

"But you'll stay? You're not mad?"

"You called me a crybaby." Stephanie gave her a dirty look. "But I guess I can stay," she said, relenting. She bent over to look at Nora's bookcase. It was large and crammed with volumes written in English. "You've got a lot of books."

"I'm the best reader in the school," Nora said. "I am, really. Even in French."

"What are these about?"

"They're psychology books, mostly. My dad's secretary sends them to me. She marks all the parts about crazy kids."

"Have you read them?"

"Most of them. They're pretty boring. I get tired of reading French all the time. She sends me magazines, too." She pulled out a few of the psychology tomes. Behind them were a stack of *Modern Screen* magazines from which all the color photographs had been cut.

"Hey, I've got something else," Nora said conspiratorially, reaching far back into the bookcase.

She brought out a rumpled pack of Gauloises. "Want a cigarette?"

Stephanie made an exasperated noise. "No!"

Nora shrugged. "Suit yourself." She lit one and exhaled languidly, posing with her hand on her hip.

"Stephanie?" came Sister Marie-Thérèse's voice from the hallway.

Nora crushed out the cigarette on one of her books and stashed the butt inside the cover.

"Nora, have you seen . . . ?" The nun knocked while opening the door. Nora was fanning smoke away from her face. "Ah! I see you've already made a friend, Stephanie." She paused, her eyes narrowing. She sniffed. "Nora, have you been smoking again?"

"Not me, Sister." She poked Stephanie's ribs. "Hey, did you see anyone smoking?"

Stephanie looked at Nora's face. Behind the big glasses, her eyes were dancing. "Not me," Stephanie said, and they both giggled uncontrollably.

"That will be enough," the Sister said. "One more warning, Nora, and your family will be notified in writing."

"I know. Tell me, Sister, did you ever get an answer the last time you wrote?"

Sister Marie-Thérèse ignored her. "Come along to lunch, Stephanie. Nora, you will be served in your room."

"Tell the chef to hold the Bordelaise," Nora said.

The two girls broke into new paroxysms of laughter as the nun escorted Stephanie away.

"Hey," Nora called after them.

The nun turned around sternly. "Nora, at La Voisine we do not say 'hey.'"

"Oh. Excuse me, Sister. Oats!"

Stephanie didn't understand the joke, but Nora's mirth set them both off on another laughing jag. When she managed to contain herself, Nora handed Stephanie the carved stone horse. "Here. You left this behind."

"Oh . . . thank you."

"I didn't wish on it or anything, because I knew it was special."

"You can wish on it if you like," Stephanie said.

Nora smiled, her plain face lighting up. "See you later, Steff?"

"Okay."

Nora waved to her.

"Hmmph," said Sister Marie-Thérèse, though her eyes were smiling.

Today had been the first time she had ever seen anyone, visitor or student, inside the lonely American girl's room.

Chapter Twenty-Seven

In Paris, the sidewalk in front of Mireille's apartment building was filled with circling picketers bearing placards announcing the end of the world. As she got out of the taxi, they besieged her with accusations of "Sinner!" and entreaties for her to repent and follow the Lord.

As usual, the reporters and photographers were present, greeting her with an almost jocular familiarity.

She was an ongoing story for them, and they were an annoyance she had grown used to, though in the two weeks since the first story had broken she had lost nearly fifteen pounds, and the dark circles around her eyes betrayed her almost total lack of sleep.

Ignoring them, she walked into the elevator of her building. An elderly couple inside stared at her, then turned to look at each other with raised eyebrows.

On her door was a petition signed by the other tenants of the building demanding that she leave her apartment.

Could anything else go wrong? she thought with a bitter smile. She tore off the paper, rolled it into a ball, and tossed it into the corner of the hallway before going in.

"Well, what are you going to do now?" she asked herself aloud.

She had lived in only two places in her life, Champs de Blé and Paris, and she wasn't welcome in either of them. She was dead broke, her daughter was hundreds of miles away, and she was a national figure of scorn. It was, in its way, quite an accomplishment for someone barely twenty-three years old.

She looked out the windows at the picketers. *Thanks to you, I couldn't even get back my dishwashing job at the Dôme Café now,* she thought, digging her fingernails into her palms until one of them snapped and broke.

There's only one job you're fit for, and you know it.

How many years did she have left? Five? Ten, if she counted the years she would spend on the skids. Then again, she might make a great success of herself. She could become another Madame Renée, operating a chic bordello and spending her mornings looking through photo albums filled with pictures of the daughter she'd abandoned.

Oh, yes, a wonderful future awaited her. She could go anywhere—London, New York, Rome. There was always a place for a great hooker . . .

Rome.

Her breath caught. "Rome," she whispered.

It had been more than a year since she'd seen Barbara.

A few months after she'd left, she sent Mireille a postcard with a picture of a nude Italian sculpture. On the back she had scrawled, *For a good time, call Roma 4152.*

Mireille hadn't called, but she'd kept the card. She took it now from the drawer of her telephone desk and hesitantly picked up the receiver.

While she waited for the operator to place the call, she almost hung up. It had been Mireille who had told Barbara to sever her ties with the past. That was why she had not answered the card. Now that Barbara was free of the Life, why should she burden herself with a ghost from a time gone by, a time that she would not even want to remember?

Mireille was beginning to set down the receiver when she heard the click of a distant connection and Barbara's bright voice.

"Pronto?"

Mireille hesitated.

"Sì? Chi parla?"

"Barbara, it's Mireille," she said quietly.

There was a shriek on the other end. "Honey! Where are you?"

"I'm in Paris," she answered. "And I've got to get out."

"What do you need, a vacation or a hideout?"

"A friend," she said.

"You got one, baby."

Barbara's new home was on the Via Sabrata in Rome, at the top of a steep hill lined with palm trees. The apartment building was small but elegant, with a black tiled floor in the lobby and a curving stairway in place of elevators.

"Get on your hiking boots, honey. You've got five flights to go!" a voice called out from the top of the stairs.

Mireille looked up through the curving rail to see a shock of long red hair.

"Jesus, girl, what happened to you?" Barbara said. "I can tell from here you need a plate of spaghetti. Come on in. I've got some champagne in the refrigerator."

"Champagne?" Mireille laughed. "It's ten o'clock in the morning." They embraced at the entrance to Barbara's tiny flat.

Barbara snapped her fingers. "Oh, damn, that's right. This is no time for champagne. I'll have a rum and Coke." She laughed. "It's an American drink."

"I think I'll stick to coffee. I never saw you drink before," she said as Barbara poured herself a generous glassful.

"Times change," Barbara said, gulping down the rum and Coke and pouring another. She looked up and smiled.

"Where's Gino?" Mireille asked.

Barbara took a deep drink. "Gino who?" She laughed a lot longer than was necessary, then came over to sit beside Mireille on the living room sofa.

The furniture, Mireille noticed, was becoming threadbare. The elegant white sofa was soiled in spots, stained by wine and food, and the Aubusson rugs were faded with ingrained dust.

"Gino's gone," Barbara said quietly. She lit a cigarette. "He decided that my looks—which are pushing thirty along with the rest of me—didn't outweigh my past."

Mireille looked away. "I'm sorry," she said. "I shouldn't have troubled you."

"Are you kidding?" Barbara's face broke into a wide grin, and she looked once again like a fresh-faced schoolgirl. "Seeing you is like a shot in the arm. So what's the most famous hooker in Paris doing these days?"

"You mean the most famous *ex*-hooker in Paris."

"You've left?"

Mireille shrugged. "I hope so."

"Now, that's cause to celebrate. It's time for the champagne."

She uncorked the bottle with great ceremony and, over Mireille's protestations, poured two glasses. Mireille took one polite sip, then watched Barbara finish the rest of the bottle.

"Did the movie fall through, too?"

Barbara laughed uproariously. "The movie! God. No, Gino kept that part of the bargain. In a way. Which is to say I wasn't the lead, but I was in the movie." She downed the last of the champagne. "I played a hooker."

"Oh, Barbara . . ."

"Hey, I got paid. Not as much as I would have for the real thing, but it's a buck, right?"

Mireille set down her cup. "You mean you're still acting in films?"

"Damn right. My ninth one's playing in the city now."

"Really? That's wonderful! You're a movie actress!"

Barbara laughed again, that deep, throaty, infectious laugh that Mireille had forgotten how much she missed.

"Damn straight. Hey, you look like you could use a laugh. There's a feature downtown in half an hour. We can make it if we hurry."

The two of them stood outside the theater, admiring the marquee.

"*Wrath of the Caesars*," Mireille said. "It looks like a big movie. Look at all the people waiting in line."

"Antonio Buonasera's a big director," Barbara said. "This movie will probably be translated into English and distributed in America."

"It's in Italian?"

"Don't worry," Barbara said with a smile. "You'll be able to understand my part perfectly."

After an hour and a half of ancient Rome in Technicolor, Barbara nudged Mireille's elbow. "I make my entrance soon," she said.

The scene switched to a filmmaker's approximation of a Roman bath, in which an orgy was taking place. Mireille strained to follow the camera as it panned over dancing girls, chained bears, bare-buttocked acrobats, and a midget pouring wine into a woman's navel near a centurion, dressed in full armor, who bobbed up and down to drink it. Interspersed through it all were a half dozen peacocks parading among the writhing bodies.

"Those birds were hilarious," Barbara shrilled merrily. "They kept shitting on everybody's costumes. The director got so mad he grabbed one of them by the tail, and all its feathers fell out."

The people in front of them turned to silence them with reproachful looks, which Barbara ignored. "Okay, now, look! Look!"

The camera had moved back to reveal the scene in all its glory, with the reveling figures in the foreground eating and drinking lustily as pink feathers fell on them from above. The leading man, playing Tiberius, cast his eyes heavenward with a smile of approval as the camera moved back to show a redheaded woman wearing an abbreviated toga, tossing feathers from a basket as she dangled from a swing.

"There I am!" Barbara shouted.

"You're still on a swing?" Mireille asked, and the two of them dissolved in wild laughter. The couple in front of them turned around to shush them sternly, which did no good.

"Well, we might as well go now," Barbara said finally, wiping tears of hilarity from her eyes. "The empire remains, despite my earthshaking performance. Come on. I know a nice little place nearby."

The two of them caught up on old times in a comfortable little restaurant specializing in veal steaks prepared in the manner of northern Italy. Mireille noticed that Barbara hardly touched her food but finished all of the wine they'd ordered.

"Aren't you eating?" she asked lightly.

"I'm fat enough, thank you. You're the one who needs some meat on your bones. Take this." She transferred her veal onto Mireille's platter. "Eat, darling, eat. You'll thank me for it later. Now tell me what you're doing in sunny Italy with the likes of me."

Mireille told her with as little sentiment as possible about the events that led to her departure from Paris.

"The bastards," Barbara said. "So now Stephanie's in Switzerland?"

Mireille nodded. "I had to get her as far away from me as I could. All this would have hurt her too much."

Barbara placed her hand on Mireille's. "We'll get her back, honey. How's your money holding up?"

"It's gone," Mireille said. "Taxes, lawyers . . . It's amazing how fast it went. I haven't even got enough to pay Stephanie's tuition at La Voisine past this year." She sighed. "I've got to find work. The problem is, I don't know how to do anything."

"I know a lot of men who'd disagree with that."

Mireille shook her head. "Not that. No more. Stephanie's not going to find out about me, ever. That means no stories, no books, no interviews, either. I need real work, even if it's scrubbing floors, until this mess clears away and I can bring Stephanie back. But I have to stay outside of France."

Barbara shrugged. "No problem."

"No?"

"Cinecittà's casting a new movie next week. A Western, with an American director. I know the guy who's casting the extras. He'll give you a job."

"Me? In a movie? Are you serious?"

Barbara laughed. "Hey, I'm not talking about playing Saint Joan. It'll be extra work. 'Atmosphere,' they call us. The money's nothing like the old days at Renée's, but it's a living, and it's not porn. Sound okay?"

Mireille grinned. "Sounds great."

"Just don't get any aspirations about becoming a movie star."

An image of Oliver Jordan flashed through Mireille's mind. Beautiful, charming, and utterly false, he had taught her how empty celebrity really was.

"Don't worry," she said.

Chapter Twenty-Eight

Mireille and Barbara showed up at six a.m. for what Barbara described as a "cattle call." The term, Mireille thought with dismay, was an accurate one. Hundreds of people of every conceivable description were already milling around a back lot of Cinecittà Studios by the time they arrived.

Most of them, she noticed, did not look like movie stars. There were old ladies knitting on portable lawn chairs, men who looked like laborers, several mothers dragging children dressed in garishly cute attire, and a great many pretty young women. Some of them were dressed in skin-tight evening dresses, their faces painted like low-class streetwalkers. Others made a point of looking severe, with wire-frame glasses and lace collars, their hair pulled back into tight knots.

"Are all these people actors?" Mireille asked, fascinated by the motley group.

"Not really. The war left almost everyone in Italy broke. A lot of people are still living hand to mouth, looking for any kind of work that'll put food on the table for a day. We get paid in cash. It's a big plus." She squeezed Mireille's hand. "Stop worrying, okay? Your name's on the list. I guarantee it."

"It's not that. It's just that . . . well, I don't feel right taking a job away from somebody who needs it just because you pulled strings."

"Oh, brother. Aren't you ever going to grow up? You're practically a beggar yourself." She took a compact out of her handbag and powdered her nose. "Look, if it makes you feel better, you'd probably get in anyway just because of your hair."

"My hair?"

"Sure. Take a look at the women. They all want to be blonde."

Barbara was right. Most of the younger women at the call were blonde, regardless of their skin coloring. At least half of them were obviously wearing wigs.

"That's the strangest thing I've ever seen," Mireille said. "Why are there so many blondes?"

"It's a Western," Barbara said. "They want people who look American. No swarthy Sicilians, unless there are Indians in the movie. See him?" She pointed to a tall, bony-faced man with jet-black hair. "He always plays Indians. He's even gotten some good parts. Hey, Marcello!"

She waved at the man. When he saw her, his stony exterior melted into a wide grin. He blew her a kiss.

"He's queer as the Queen of the May, but on-screen, he's a pure stud. He'll be picked today. This is just a formality for the old hands. And for you, believe me."

Within a half hour, a young man with a megaphone came out of one of the studio buildings and stood on a box in front of the throng.

"Okay, listen, everybody," he shouted into the megaphone. "The script calls for sixty extras."

There was a collective groan from the assembled crowd. The young man shrugged in commiseration, then said into the megaphone, "What can I do? It's a cheap movie." The crowd laughed good-naturedly.

He held up a sheet of paper. "These are the names of those of you who have already been selected."

A pretty girl with improbably golden hair who was standing beside Mireille smiled and stuck out her chest.

"She's sleeping with him," Barbara whispered.

"When you hear your name called, please move behind me, where my assistant will cross your name off the list."

A businesslike woman with a pencil behind her ear waved the sheet of paper in her hand so that the aspirants could see her.

"Then I'll ask the rest of you to walk by me in single file. Silence, please! Marcello Andalucci." The tall Sicilian ambled toward the woman.

"I guess there are going to be Indians," Barbara said.

"Angelica Vespari."

The young woman beside Mireille exhaled, as if she had been holding her breath for minutes, then walked through the crowd with such an exaggerated roll of her hips that some of the old-timers laughed out loud.

"She works in a butcher shop," Barbara said, cackling.

The girl turned her nose up and flipped her peroxided curls.

"Barbara Ponti."

"That's me," Barbara said, squeezing Mireille's hand.

"Ponti? I thought your last name was Pauchon."

"I changed it. We're in Italy now, sweetheart. See you over there."

"But . . . but I can't speak Italian," Mireille said in panic.

"Just listen for your name."

"Mir . . ." The man faltered. "Mireilla della Jouarre," he said, pronouncing it in the Italian manner.

"What did I tell you? Come on." Barbara dragged Mireille past the man with the megaphone, saluting him as they passed. He saluted back, raising his eyebrows at Mireille.

"He likes you," Barbara said. "But don't bother with him. He's only the extras casting director."

After all the chosen names had been called, the young man put down his megaphone and began the long and laborious process of "interviewing" the others, which consisted of looking at each one, sending some back to the growing group behind him, and passing over the others. When the sixty chosen ones were finally assembled, the woman with the pencil escorted them all into the studio to wait.

"Have a seat," she instructed them, gesturing toward rows of folding chairs. "The director will be coming in to meet all of you."

They were grateful for the chairs. It was more than an hour before the doors opened again. This time, the casting director and the woman were joined by two other men who walked to the front of the group. The actors immediately gave the two men their attention.

One was tall and attractive, dressed in pleated pants and a white shirt unbuttoned to show hair on his chest. The other was short and rumpled-looking, with a ferret-like face that seemed to be permanently embossed with a scowl. He spoke English in a low, nasal voice to the tall man, who translated his words into Italian.

The translation was lost on Mireille. "What's he saying?" she whispered.

"He's introducing the director."

"I thought he *was* the director."

"Don't we wish. That's Roberto, the director's assistant. I've worked with him before." She sighed. "He's married, with five kids, and doesn't fool around. A hell of an excuse for an Italian."

"You mean the other one . . . *him?*" She couldn't believe that the diminutive rodent-faced man in wrinkled clothes was in charge of something as important as a movie.

"Shhh. He's an American. His name is Victor Mohl. As in the animal, I guess."

Mireille stifled a laugh as the little man stepped in front of the crowd and thrust his hands into his pockets.

"Okay, everybody, I guess you know why you're here," he mumbled in English, not bothering to speak clearly to a group who didn't speak his language. "The name of the movie is *Lone Gun*. Rotten title. Anyway, if you've got any problems, take them to Roberto. I've got enough on my mind without worrying about extras." Then he took two steps backward, crossing his arms over his chest. His entire speech, which the extras had waited an hour to hear, had lasted less than thirty seconds.

Mireille blinked in astonishment and disgust as Roberto translated, obviously embellishing Mohl's curt speech considerably. She had picked up enough English through Madame Renée's books and her English clients to understand every word the unpleasant little director had said. It made her feel sick when the extras applauded his contemptuous little talk.

"I may not speak Italian, but I understood Mohl," Mireille said. "I don't think that was an exact translation."

Barbara laughed. "Like I said, it's a living." Everyone was getting up. "He wants us to line up at the front," Barbara said. "There are some small parts to be cast from among us."

"Oh God. They'll find out I don't know the language."

"So what? You're still the only natural blonde here."

Roberto shuffled the actors into six lines of ten. Then Mohl walked slowly among them like a general inspecting his troops. He was followed by Roberto, the casting director, and the woman with the pencil, who took notes on everything anyone said.

He passed most of the actors with an air of general disinterest, but he singled out one skinny old man. The old man fell to one knee and kissed Mohl's hand, which was withdrawn immediately.

"You get a little more money if you've got some business to do in a scene," Barbara said.

The girl from the butcher shop was at the front of the line in which Mireille and Barbara stood. She took a deep breath and batted her eyelashes shamelessly at the director as he approached her.

Mohl patted her on the shoulder. "Relax," he said with a smile as he walked on.

He stopped when he reached Mireille.

Barbara gave her a sidelong glance.

"Where'd you find her?" he asked in English.

Roberto translated for the casting director, who shrugged expressively.

Mohl studied Mireille, smiling occasionally in a pinched manner that suggested that smiling did not come easily to him. "I want her for Lily," he said. "Ask her if she can do a French accent."

The tall man began to translate, but Mireille stopped him with a gesture. "Please," she said. "I speak English better than I do Italian. In fact, I don't speak Italian at all."

Barbara pinched her.

"Where are you from?" Mohl asked.

Mireille lowered her eyes. "Paris," she said.

The little man beamed. "Perfect! I'm looking for a French dance-hall girl. The part's got one line. You can speak it in English."

Flustered, Mireille looked from Barbara to the director to the translator to the casting director. "But I'm not an actress," she blurted.

Barbara elbowed her in the ribs, but Mohl laughed. "Who is?" he said. "Schedule her for wardrobe."

The woman with the pencil scribbled a note.

"Call for six a.m. tomorrow, Studio B," the casting director called, and the crowd dispersed.

"Leave it to you," Barbara said with mock disgust as they walked toward the car. "You couldn't have interviewed worse if you'd tried. But you still get a part. A speaking part." She blew a lock of hair off her forehead. "I swear, I'll never understand your luck."

Chapter Twenty-Nine

"Ever'body, take a look at the deadest dadgum deadeye shot west of the Pecos," a grizzled American character actor said through a haystack of white whiskers. "Tom Handy's the name, and don't you fergit it, neither."

Lily, the dance-hall girl played by Mireille, winked at him. He tipped his hat to her before noticing the entrance of the movie's heroine, a purehearted virgin who had come to the saloon to solicit funds for the new chapel.

"Cut," Mohl said. "I want a close-up of the girl."

"I'm supposed to be running," the leading lady said.

She was an American model named Dallas Cole who had made her reputation by tossing her hair in shampoo commercials. *Lone Gun* was to mark her debut as an actress, although her acting seemed to consist of little more than her famous hair-tossing routine.

She tossed it now. "Maybe I can stop in the doorway." She stepped back, rested her arms on the swinging doors, and flung her hair back and forth with abandon.

"No, the other girl," Mohl mumbled. "The blonde." Dallas's arms slid off the doors as she leveled a murderous look at Mireille.

"I *am* a blonde," she said.

Mohl didn't answer.

From the bar, decked out in a satin dress and pink feather boa, Barbara laughed out loud.

"Ready here," the cameraman announced.

The scene was reshot, with Mireille winking slowly, teasingly, directly into the camera. The wizened old actor playing Tom Handy improvised a funny response by not only tipping his hat but placing it over his heart and then falling backward onto the bar with a beatific smile on his face.

"Good," Mohl said when the scene was finished. "Good work, all of you."

Dallas Cole stomped back to her dressing room, tossing her curls in a frenzy while the rest of the cast basked in the director's rare compliment.

"Guess Mohl's going to have to make peace with Miss Muffet now," the old American actor said with a grin directed at Mireille. "By the way, you were damn good. You could make a living at this if you wanted to."

"Really?" Mireille was genuinely surprised. She'd just been playing a role, the same way she'd played around her clients.

"Don't say you didn't enjoy it."

She smiled. "I did, I suppose," she said, blushing. "I enjoyed every minute."

Mohl made no move to placate the leading lady.

When Mireille looked over at him, he was staring at her.

Mireille's only other scene was shot the next day. In it Dallas Cole ran once again into the saloon to tell the leading man that Indians had burned down the new chapel.

"He's in the back room," Mireille said. It was her one and only line.

Mohl shot it four times.

"Cut!" he shouted, walking away agitated. "It's not going to work," he muttered. He turned to Roberto, then walked away.

"What was that about?" Mireille whispered to Barbara.

The redhead shrugged. "Some technical thing, probably."

"But he's acting so strangely around me. He shot yesterday's scene over and over again, too."

"And you ended up with a close-up. Hey, quit complaining, will you?"

Mireille rubbed her arms. "I can't help it. Something just doesn't feel right. Maybe Mr. Mohl doesn't like the way I look."

Barbara rolled her eyes with a chuckle. "Honey, the man who doesn't like the way you look hasn't been invented."

The assistant director clapped his hands.

"Everybody go home," he shouted.

"Or to La Taverna," Barbara called out. Her suggestion was met, as it always was, with a cheer.

With her antic, garrulous charm, fractured Italian, and an encyclopedic knowledge of inexpensive watering holes, Barbara had quickly become the film's unofficial social director. At the end of every shooting day, she arranged for everyone with enough money for a drink to meet in some out-of-the-way café or bar.

"Where are we, exactly?" Mireille asked as the two of them led an entourage from the studio on foot along the cypress-shaded street bordering the Tiber River.

"Exactly? Who knows? We'll get where we're going sooner or later."

Mireille smiled. She had missed Barbara more than she'd realized during her years alone in Paris. "You'll never change," she said.

"Hah! Tell that to my mirror." She jerked her head toward a ruin they were passing. "Feel like a five-cent tour?" She pointed to a building. "That's the Temple of the Vestal Virgins, poor things. Next door is the Temple of Manly Fortune. They go together."

"They're still so beautiful, after all this time," Mireille said, breathing in the scent of the umbrella pines that lined the temples. Even in the middle of the city, despite the wild honking traffic, the air smelled buoyant and green.

Rome, unlike Paris, had no sense of urgent frenzy about it. The pace of pedestrians was leisurely. People leaned out of windows, their arms folded over flowerpotted sills, chatting easily with the passersby below.

"If it weren't for the cars, I could almost believe we were in another century."

"That's the wonderful thing about Rome," Barbara said. "The old and the new—it's all mixed together. It's like . . . like there's no time. Like a person who gets older and older but never loses anything of his past. No regrets . . ." She winced.

"A city's made of stone and wood," Mireille said softly. "We're not." She touched Barbara's hand.

"Hell, I need a drink," Barbara said. "All this philosophizing is making me thirsty." She turned to the others walking behind them. "Are you coming?" she shouted.

They passed the Church of Santa Maria, where a crowd of tourists gathered around an odd fountain-like artifact.

"That's the Bocca della Verità," Barbara said. "The Mouth of Truth. Legend has it that if you put your hand inside while there's a lie on your conscience, the gods will bite it off." She laughed. "I wish I'd asked Gino to stick his pecker in it."

They turned into a narrow alleyway, where the vines from a rooftop garden hung nearly to the ground. Barbara parted them like a beaded curtain to reveal a set of chipped cement steps leading to a basement door.

"*Ecco vino,*" she said, waving to the stragglers behind them.

Inside, the place was smoky and poorly ventilated, permeated with the stench of spilled liquor and damp stone walls.

"Ugh," Mireille said.

"Isn't it wonderful? No matter where you go, a saloon smells the same."

"So does a sewer."

"Loosen up, girl. Neither one of us is going to see Maxim's again for a long, long time."

Then the movie people pulled the rickety tables together, the wine began to flow, and gradually Mireille was pulled into the easy camaraderie of the group.

The film people were a motley bunch, from makeup artists to studio technicians, but Mireille's fellow extras were the most interesting of the lot. A few of them were professional actors who supported themselves between stage roles with their anonymous work as film extras. The others were a wild assortment of eccentrics, street people, starving artists, unpublished writers, out-of-work carnival folk, inventors, retired laborers, failed politicians, and a few housewives earning some extra money before their children got home from school. A number of them spoke English to some degree, a few spoke French, and in just a few days, Mireille had picked up enough Italian to fit in with her odd new associates.

I belong, she thought with a sense of wonder. She was an actress now, no longer her stepparents' scrub-girl to beat and ridicule whenever they wished. She was no longer a penniless, pregnant woman searching through other people's trash for her food. And best of all, she was no longer l'Ange.

A few men on the set had asked her out on dates. When she turned them down, as she always did, there were no recriminations, no fines or lectures from a madam who controlled her life. Even the would-be suitors themselves did not seem angry. They continued to speak with her, laugh with her, work with her. Certainly none of them had ever entertained the idea of paying her to sleep with them.

She was part of a team, she realized. It felt almost like a family.

After the first three bottles had been emptied, one of the Italian extras leaped up onto the bar and performed a crude but funny impersonation of Victor Mohl on the toilet. Then Barbara, imitating Dallas Cole, tossed her hair and, muttering breathlessly about motivation, repeated the act.

The group cheered the performances, laughing and shouting lewd remarks until the door opened and Roberto, the assistant director, walked in. With him was Victor Mohl.

The conversation at the table ended abruptly. Both the Italian extra and Barbara slid off the bar and took their seats as unobtrusively as possible.

"Look who's slumming," Barbara said out of the side of her mouth.

Roberto's expression was one of helpless bewilderment. Nevertheless, he took it upon himself to break the ice.

"Mr. Mohl has expressed a desire to socialize with his cast," he explained in rather formal Italian. "Hope you don't mind if we join you."

"Charming," Barbara said, smiling brightly.

Mohl smiled back awkwardly as he pulled up a chair next to Mireille.

Slowly, cautiously, the conversation at the table resumed.

"Well, how do you like the movie business so far?" Mohl asked.

Mireille could see by his frozen smile and wet palms that the man was nervous. *Nervous to be talking to me,* she thought. "I'm enjoying it," she said, sounding false.

"You know, it's good to have someone to speak English with."

She laughed. "If you can call what I speak 'English.'"

"No, really. Most of the time I feel like I'm on another planet here. I'm paying dues, sort of. The big studios won't hire me as a director until I've got some films under my belt, so I'm turning out spaghetti Westerns."

"Spaghetti . . . ?"

"That's what they call Westerns shot in Italy. It saves money." He shrugged. "Not a lot of prestige, but it's a step up the ladder. All in all, I've done pretty well for a boy from Brooklyn."

"Brooklyn?"

"That's a place in America, in New York. Ever heard of New York?"

Mireille nodded. "I hear it is a beautiful place."

Mohl smiled and shook his head. "I've never heard it described that way before, at least not in Brooklyn. Say, we've got so much to talk about, why don't you have dinner with me sometime? I can take you to a really nice place, not like this dump." He set his hand on her arm. It was cold and clammy.

Mireille instantly thought of all the American businessmen she had been with over the past seven years. Intense, hurried men who fed on power and made love like rapists, men who insisted on the most beautiful women in Madame Renée's stable, then treated them like beasts. Mohl's touch made her shiver.

"I don't think so," she said, gently pushing the hand away. "I don't go out with men."

"What's the matter? You like girls?" he said with the instant aggressiveness of an insecure man who'd been rejected.

"Excuse me," Mireille said, and stood up.

"Hey, where are you going?" Barbara asked.

"I'm not feeling well," Mireille said, and left.

When Barbara came home, Mireille was waiting up for her. She hadn't been able to sleep. The memory of Mohl's clammy hand on her arm and the look in his eyes filled her with revulsion.

"I think you've got an admirer," Barbara said. "Roberto told me that Mohl's been asking about you since yesterday. When he found out you hung out with us, he insisted on coming along."

Mireille shuddered. "That awful little man," she said.

"Jesus, he's the *director*, Mireille."

"I don't want him to touch me."

Barbara rolled her eyes. "Hey, I don't know what Oliver Jordan did to you, but you can't let yourself go nuts every time somebody asks you out to dinner. Hell, you flew out of that place like you were on fire."

"I didn't like him," Mireille said.

"Why? Because he tried to make a little conversation with you? He didn't attack you. He didn't send someone over to bring you to him so he could work his wicked will on you."

"I know, but . . ."

"All in all, I'd say it was pretty nice of him to make the kind of effort he did." She lit a cigarette and blew the smoke out noisily. "Look, he's a bachelor, he's lonely, he's living in a country where he doesn't have any friends and can't speak the language. Give the guy a break."

Mireille listened in silence. Finally, she said, "You're right, Barbara. I'm being foolish. He didn't mean any harm."

"That's better. Hey, he can't help it if he has a face even his mother can't love."

Mireille laughed.

"Who knows? Maybe he'll give you a part in another movie."

Chapter Thirty

The unfinished scene was not reshot the next day. Instead Mireille, dressed in a brown wig and shawl and holding a doll that was supposed to pass for a baby, was ordered to mill around the street with the other extras while the principals performed.

"I guess I lost my big part," she told Barbara during a break.

"What'd you expect? You treat the director like poison, you think he's going to kiss your ass? Hey, maybe he'll give the line to me." She narrowed her eyes and pouted her lips. "He's een zee back room," she said in English, jerking her thumb over her shoulder.

Mireille laughed despite herself. "That's better than I could ever do it," she said.

The following week, Roberto handed her a thin sheaf of papers. "That's the rest of your part," he said with a smile.

She looked through the partial script in disbelief. There were three extra scenes, all of them prominently featuring Lily.

"Mr. Mohl thought you were too pretty for a walk-on. He's made you the second lead."

"What?" She couldn't believe her ears.

Roberto shrugged. "Don't complain. The leading lady will do enough of that for both of you."

He was right. Dallas Cole threatened to walk off the film when she learned about Mireille's expanded part. But there were few enough leading roles for former shampoo models, even in

low-budget Italian films, so when Mohl called her bluff, Dallas
backed down.

Mireille learned the part easily. To everyone's surprise, she
handled it well. She was reliable and punctual for every call, and
played the part of the dance-hall girl with a touching believability.
Her final scene with the leading man was one in which the cowboy
seeks her advice about the prim schoolmarm. Lily's response was
to treat him like a child so that he would go to the other woman.
When she delivered the lines, with a touch of moisture in her eyes,
everyone was left with the feeling that she had loved the cowboy
and was sending him away to help him. When the scene was finished, Mireille's friends gathered around her, patting her on the
back and pinching her cheeks.

"That was sensational!" Barbara shrieked. "I didn't know you
were such a good actress."

"Don't be silly," Mireille scoffed.

"But you did like it, didn't you?" Barbara teased. "Go on, admit
it."

They both burst into laughter.

Victor Mohl approached her. "Like having the spotlight on
you?"

Her laughter caught in her throat. "I did my best," Mireille
answered uncertainly.

The others drifted away, sensing the unease between them.

"I could do a lot for you," he said, piercing her with his gaze.

Mireille felt herself reddening. "Thank you, Mr. Mohl, but I've
never had ambitions to be an actress." She tried to leave gracefully,
but he took her arm.

"Look, I'm sorry. I'm always saying the wrong thing. I'm not a
bad guy, though, really." He scowled and wrung his hands. "Hey,
let me make it up to you. Have dinner with me tonight, okay?"

"I don't think—"

"There are some things about the movie I want to talk about. Seriously."

She smiled. "Mr. Mohl, you know there isn't anything about *Lone Gun* that you have to consult me about."

He smiled back. "Yeah, you read me like a book, don't you?" He shoved his hands into his pockets. "I guess I just wanted some company." He turned away, looking bent and small.

The sight of the defeated little man embarrassed Mireille. "I'll have dinner with you if you'd like," she said finally.

He turned back, suddenly beaming. "Great. I'll take you to a place like you've never seen. The best." He scurried off then, leaving Mireille with a vague sense of embarrassment.

It was a quiet dinner at Vecchia Florio, the most expensive restaurant in Rome. To impress her, Mohl had hired a limousine with a driver. During dinner, he filled the silences with nervous chatter.

Mohl was young, it turned out, much younger than he looked. He had come from a poor family and had worked in the film industry in all sorts of menial jobs since he was eighteen years old. He had only begun directing a year before, but he expected to make his first million before he was forty.

"I mean, I've done a lot of stuff for a guy my age." He leaned forward in his chair. "Did you see *The Last Stampede*?"

"I'm afraid not," she said.

"*Shoot-Out at Big Fork?*"

"No, I—"

"How about *The Hunted*?"

She shook her head.

"Sheesh. Well, nobody else has, either. That's why I'm working over here. What do I know about Westerns? I hate Westerns."

Mireille laughed. "You don't give yourself enough credit, Mr. Mohl."

"Victor."

"Victor," she said, feeling uncomfortable. "Besides, I am not a good judge of these things, because I'm not American."

"But you see movies, don't you?"

"Not many."

He cocked his head and smiled crookedly at her. "You're a strange girl, know that? What'd you do before you came to Cinecittà?"

Mireille put down her fork. "I . . . I was a model."

"Oh yeah? High fashion?"

She took a drink of water. "Sometimes."

"I'd like to see your book."

"My book?"

"Your portfolio."

"Oh. Most of my things are still in Paris."

"Paris." He smiled at her, moony-eyed. "Most of the guys I grew up with are still hauling ice or cutting meat back in Brooklyn, and I'm having dinner with a fashion model from Paris." He shook his head. "Life's something else, isn't it?"

Mireille agreed enthusiastically. She had no idea what else life was supposed to be, but she was grateful that the conversation had shifted from her.

Mohl snapped his fingers at the waiter and ordered two brandies. "You know, I'm going to be somebody one of these days," he said, leaning back expansively. "I've always known it. Somebody big."

Mireille stifled a yawn. She had been up since five o'clock in the morning and still had to write her daily letter to Stephanie.

"Right now, I go into El Morocco, the Brown Derby, the headwaiters act like I'm not there," he said bitterly. "But I'm going to change all that—you wait and see. All I need is a break, an opening at a big studio like MGM or Continental. Then bingo. Everybody in town's going to want to get close to Victor Mohl." He nodded for emphasis.

"I'm sure you'll get what you want," Mireille said blandly.

"I am, too," he said, placing his hand over her own. "Damn sure."

The next day three dozen roses arrived for Mireille, along with a note from Mohl asking her to accompany him to the premiere of Federico Fellini's *La Strada*. Again she refused, but he whined and wheedled until she agreed to go.

She saw him four more times during the course of filming, always with reservations, but Mohl made it clear that he only wanted her company. Despite his boorish manners, he always treated her with respect, asked few questions about her, and never even tried to kiss her.

She did not consider him a lover, surely, and not really a friend, but in time she grew more comfortable with him. Mireille had pretty well categorized Victor Mohl as a sort of relative, dull but needy, whose company was, at times, inevitable.

Besides, she reasoned, it would all be over soon.

Shooting for *Lone Gun* would end within a week. Mohl would go home to America to fulfill his dream of being a somebody, and she would make a drive to Switzerland to see Stephanie and pay another portion of her daughter's school tuition. This chapter of her life would close, and she would be one more step removed from her memories of Paris.

On the last day of shooting, Barbara arranged a party on the set. Mohl sat quietly through it, dictating notes to Roberto for postproduction work and shaking the hands of the actors as they left. But when he saw Mireille putting on her sweater, he rushed over to her.

"I have to see you tonight," he said.

"Is something wrong?"

"Yes. No. Hey, let's just go, all right?"

"I'm leaving for Switzerland in the morning," she said.

"That's tomorrow. Please, Mireille. It's important."

He took her to a small garden café in the Piazza Navona, where they drank creamy coffee and watched the waterworks of the Bernini fountain in virtual silence.

"You said you wanted to see me?" Mireille asked. She checked her watch. It was nearing ten.

"Yeah, yeah," Mohl answered. He looked agitated, toying with a vase of flowers. Suddenly, he slapped his hands on the table. "Look, I'll be going back to LA a week from Tuesday." He fell silent again.

"Yes?"

"So what are you going to do?"

"Me?" she asked with some surprise. "I have a seven-year-old daughter in school in Switzerland. I'm going to drive up tomorrow to see her. After that . . ." She shrugged and smiled.

"You've got a kid?" he asked. It sounded like an accusation.

"Yes, I do."

"And a husband, too, I suppose."

"No. He's . . . He was killed during the war."

"Yeah?" Mohl's face brightened visibly. "That's not so bad, then."

Mireille inhaled sharply.

"Sorry," he said, touching her hand. "Just saying the wrong thing again. Me and my big mouth." He tried a laugh. "I just meant . . . What I meant was . . ." He scowled. "Come on, let's get out of here. This place stinks."

He threw down some money and grabbed Mireille's arm.

"Where are we going?"

"I don't care. We'll walk around or something."

They headed toward the fountain. "Victor, I must pack some things for my trip—"

"Don't go." He held on to her tightly, almost desperately. "Not just yet. I have to tell you something."

Mireille waited patiently while he stuck his hands into his pockets, his face a mask of anguish. "Look, I'm not a good talker, okay? That's why I don't fit in with those polo-playing assholes in Hollywood. I don't play croquet with Sam Goldwyn." He snorted. "That guy's got no more education than I do, but he wouldn't be caught dead inviting me to his estate. That's only for those phony smooth-talking jerks like Zanuck and Oliver Jordan."

Mireille felt herself grow cold with the mention of Jordan's name, but she said nothing.

"Anyway, I know I don't sound like much. And I don't look like much—I know that, too. I come from a family of fishmongers in Brooklyn. There aren't any dukes or earls in my family tree, that's for sure." He turned to face her. "But I'm the hardest-working son of a bitch in the business, and I swear to you I'm going to make it big someday, Mireille."

She looked at him, puzzled. "I'm sure you will, Victor."

"What I'm trying to say is . . . Oh God, I love you." He pulled her close to him and kissed her suddenly, awkwardly.

Shocked, Mireille tried to pull away from him, but he held fast. "I've loved you ever since that first day when you showed up with the extras," he said breathlessly. "It's been killing me, eating me alive. I thought I could handle it, but I can't. And I can't go back without you. You've got to come to LA with me."

"Go to America?" she asked, stunned. "But that's impossible—"

"Oh, I know you don't love me. Hell, you're thinking you don't even know me, right? But I'll be good to you. I'll never look at another woman. And I'll take good care of you. I'm not rich, not by Hollywood standards, but I've got a house in a good part of town, and enough money to get by." He grimaced. "Jesus, if I had the time, I'd show you in a million ways how much you mean to me. But I've got to leave this place in a week and a half. Come with me."

"Victor, please . . ."

"I'm asking you to marry me, Mireille."

Chapter Thirty-One

"How many times do I have to tell him no?" Mireille fumed after the fourth bunch of roses came.

"Persistence is a good quality," Barbara said with Gallic practicality. "You could do worse than marry Victor Mohl."

"You can't be serious!" Mireille said. "I couldn't love him in a thousand years."

"Who said anything about love?" Barbara took out an emery board and began filing her nails. "Look, the movie's over. In two weeks I'm going to go to another cattle call. I don't know the casting director of that one, so I'll have to hang around like a piece of meat waiting to see if some pimply-faced kid thinks I look good enough to stand around in the background of some grade-Z movie. I'll do it. I've got no choice. But you . . . Is that really the way you want to spend the rest of your life?"

"Barbara . . ."

"Or do you think you're going to go on to become a famous actress here in Italy, where you can barely say your own name?"

Mireille sat down with a sigh.

"Mohl's a director, dummy. He gave you a good part in *Lone Gun*. If you're married to him, there'll be other parts for you. You can be somebody."

"*Merde alors*, you sound just like him!" Mireille exploded. "I *am* somebody! I'm a human being, not a dog who comes to anyone who calls it."

"Right. A while ago, you were crawling between the sheets with men whose names you didn't even know. Now suddenly, when it's completely inconvenient, you decide to be a queen."

"I'm not a queen. But I'm not a hooker anymore, either."

"Oh, no? You think like one."

"What are you talking about?"

"You're looking for the perfect date. What do you want, another Oliver Jordan? Or someone who'll be a father to Stephanie?"

Mireille blinked.

"Remember her?" Barbara said acidly. "That little girl's marking time with the nuns in Switzerland while you're cooling off your hot reputation. How many years is that going to take in Europe? Hell, you'll be a gray-haired old crone before the tabloids forget the scandals about l'Ange."

A moment passed. "In America, nobody's heard of l'Ange," Mireille said softly.

"No shit." Barbara blew on her nails.

"It wouldn't be fair to Victor. He . . . he doesn't know anything about me."

"Who says he has to? You're not running for president, for Christ's sake. You can keep house for him, or whatever it is wives do. Have sex with him once in a while. Close your eyes and pretend he's a john." She laughed wickedly.

Tears came to Mireille's eyes.

"Okay, okay. I'm sorry," Barbara said. She moved over to put her arm around Mireille. "All I'm saying is that you don't have a lot of choices anymore. So maybe you won't have the most romantic marriage in the world. Most people don't. But you can give Stephanie a new life. You can have your daughter back again." She dried Mireille's eyes with a tissue. "Don't be a dunce. Mohl's your way out."

"My way out," Mireille repeated.

"I'll marry you," she told Mohl.

He let out a whoop. "Oh, baby, you won't regret this. I'll make all the arrangements—"

"However," she said before he could go on, "I must bring my daughter to live with us."

His smile faded.

"Please, Victor. This means so much to me."

"Sure," he said with unconvincing enthusiasm. "Sure, no problem. She doesn't have to come this minute, does she?"

"I had hoped—"

"Look, things are going to be crazy over there, with postproduction work and all the publicity. This could be my big break, you know. Everybody knows Dallas's face, and . . . Man, what am I talking about? Dallas's face? *Your* face! Baby, with the two of you plastered all over the papers, *Lone Gun* is sure to have a shot at major release."

"My . . . my picture?" Mireille felt an icy chill run down her spine. "I don't want my picture in the newspapers, Victor."

He was dumbstruck. "Why not?"

"I just . . ." She cast around for the right lie. "I would rather keep my private life to myself."

"For crying out loud!" he sputtered. "A face like yours, everybody should see it. You're nuts." He ran his fingers through his wiry hair. "Okay, fine. I'll change your mind."

"I don't think so, Victor."

"Yeah, well, you just don't know how beautiful you are. That's your problem. Hollywood's stacked end to end with gorgeous girls, and believe me, you make them all look like shit."

"Victor, my daughter—"

"She's in school, isn't she?" he snapped crossly, then softened. "We can bring her over at Christmas. That's only a few months from now. How about it?"

Mireille wavered. "I suppose . . ."

"We'll have a house full of toys and baby dolls for her. Hell, if I get work with one of the big studios, we can even buy her a pony."

She nodded reluctantly. "All right," she said. "Christmas."

"Good. That's settled." He nestled his arm around her. "Hey, we're going to be newlyweds. It won't be so terrible with just me hanging around you, will it?"

She forced a smile. "Of course not," she said.

"Maybe we'll make some kids of our own," he whispered, nuzzling her neck.

Mireille bit her lip. She would not tell him that she could never conceive another child. That was only one of the many things she would never tell him. Victor Mohl might be a simple, coarse man, she thought with shame, but his heart was filled with trust and honest love for her. In exchange, she would give him nothing but lies.

She felt dirtier than she had in all her years at Madame Renée's.

"I'll try to be a good wife to you, Victor," she said. "I'll do everything I can to make you happy."

He kissed her. "Oh, baby, you already have."

They made love that night. Victor was brutal and quick, thrusting into her with wild, uncontrolled jabs. Afterward, he rolled onto his back and fell immediately into a sound, noisy sleep.

Mireille looked at him lying next to her in the bed of his hotel room. He had hair all over his chest and shoulders. She had slept with many men like him before—honest, hardworking men whose sexuality had been entirely channeled into their work. Victor Mohl had no sense of passion, and that could never be learned. Such men had paid so dearly for her services only to be seen with her; the sex act itself had meant almost nothing to them.

So this is the man I will marry, she thought, feeling a dull ache in the middle of her chest.

It wasn't supposed to be this way! She was supposed to marry Stefan. Stefan, with his fine hands and strong body, with the limp that made his every step seem so precious.

Only she wasn't marrying Stefan. She was doing what she had to do. And she was taking Stephanie with her.

She touched Victor's face while he slept. He woke momentarily, eyes bulging, his wiry hair standing on end. "What's the matter?" he mumbled.

"I'm sorry. I just wanted to touch you."

He flopped over in annoyance, then turned back and held her hand. "I love you, baby," he said.

He was a good man. He would give her a good life, a new life, and provide a home for her daughter.

Maybe she would learn to love him. She was certainly going to try.

But first, she would have to tell a seven-year-old girl that her mother was moving even farther away.

Chapter Thirty-Two

Stephanie crayoned in the finishing touches on the picture. It showed three figures, two large and one small.

One of the large ones sported a smile, a long veil of yellow-white hair, and a triangular skirt above two stick legs. Beneath it she wrote "Maman." The small figure, representing herself, had long black hair and gray dots for eyes. The largest of the three had no face and no hair. Its head was an unadorned circle.

She squinted at it, disapproving. She had never seen a photograph of her father. Oh, she could picture him easily enough—he must have been beautiful, like her mother, and as brave and strong as the gallant knights Sister Marie-Thérèse talked about in school.

Sister had read *Saint George and the Dragon* to Stephanie's class at the beginning of the week, and Stephanie had stared, awestruck, at the illustrations of the Red Cross Knight on his white steed. He had been breathtakingly handsome, with his blue eyes and golden hair curling above a suit of gleaming silver armor.

Saint George was the man Stephanie wanted her father to be. In her mind's eye she could see him clearly, doffing the heavy armor after slaying the dragon, then gathering his daughter up in his arms and covering her with kisses. He would never die, not this father. He would never leave her.

She picked up the silver crayon and coated the stick-figure body with it. Then she colored the knight's hair yellow and drew in two blue eyes.

It was finished. Carefully, she carried it to a painted cardboard box, set upside down in a corner of the room, on which she had set the stone horse and two candles, and placed the picture behind them. Then she ran down the hall to Nora's room and slammed open the door.

"It's ready!" she shouted. "My wishing place! Come look!"

"Can't you see I'm busy?" Nora scolded. She pushed her glasses up from the end of her nose with the tip of her finger.

She was pasting more magazine pictures on her wall. Because of the lack of available space, she was papering over a section previously devoted to Queen Elizabeth's coronation.

"You're covering up the Queen of England," Stephanie said, sensing that her friend was committing some sort of sacrilege.

Nora shrugged. "She's not very pretty, anyway," she said. "Besides, it's for a good cause." She waved some pictures in her hand. Stephanie took them from her and studied them. They all showed the same young man, clean-cut and boyish.

"Who's that?"

"Robert Walker. He's dead."

"Oh."

Nora's eyes lit up. "He killed himself with drugs and alcohol."

"Why would he do that?"

Nora shrugged. "Wanted to see what it was like, I guess." She pasted a picture of Walker seated in a restaurant onto the wall. "Maybe he just got sick of living," she added in a small voice.

Stephanie watched as the tall girl smeared blobs of glue onto the backs of the frail pieces of paper. "Who's he with?" she asked, peering at the newest addition to the wall.

"There? Natalie Wood. I love Natalie Wood. I mean, she was this disgusting-looking kid, you know? Ugly and skinny. Although she didn't wear glasses." Nora pushed her own back up to the bridge of her nose. "I don't think."

"You've got glue on your glasses."

The older girl crossed her eyes, identified the small iceberg straddling the nosepiece, and picked it off. It landed in her hair. She pulled at it, smearing it through her long bangs until they stood straight out from her forehead like a visor.

"Anyway," she said, abandoning the project, "Natalie Wood grew out of being ugly. Skinny's okay, as long as you've got boobs. You know what she orders when she goes to a restaurant?"

Stephanie shook her head, eyes wide.

"Mashed potatoes."

"Mashed potatoes? That's all?"

"That's it. She's trying to gain weight," Nora said with authority. "Personally, I don't think she needs to. She's already got boobs."

"What are 'boobs'?"

Nora sighed and rolled her eyes. "Never mind. You're too young."

Stephanie turned back to the picture to search for Natalie Wood's mysterious boobs, but her gaze fell instead on the other man in the picture.

Her breath caught at the sight of him. The man was perfect, down to the light eyes and curly golden hair. "That's him," she whispered.

"Who?"

Stephanie pointed. "Saint George. The Red Cross Knight."

Nora squinted and bent over, nearly touching her nose to the black-and-white photograph. "Dummy, he's not with the Red Cross." She tapped at the caption under the picture. "That's a movie producer."

Stephanie smiled. So Saint George had a job, after all.

"His name's Oliver Jordan. He's not important."

Stephanie ignored her friend's dismissal of the golden-haired man. While Nora constructed her shrine to the late Robert Walker, Stephanie drank in every feature of Oliver Jordan's face. He was the knight, brave and pure, who would belong to her forever. In her mind, he was the artist who had carved the stone horse. He was the father who would never leave her.

"Can I have it?" she asked, her face flushed.

"Have what?"

"This picture."

"The one with Natalie Wood? Are you crazy?"

"I don't want Natalie Wood. Or the boobs. Just him. Just his face."

"What, you think I'm going to cut a hole in the picture and just take out that guy's head?"

"Could you, Nora?"

"Get lost."

After a moment, Nora was again absorbed in her work, and Stephanie shambled back toward her own room.

Sister Marie-Thérèse was standing in the corridor, knocking on Stephanie's door. "Oh, there you are, child. I have wonderful news. Are your hands clean? Your mother is here."

"Maman?"

"She's in the parlor, dear."

With a squeal, Stephanie bolted toward the stairway.

"Walk! Walk!" the nun called futilely after her.

She leaped into Mireille's arms. "Maman! You've come back!" She buried her face in her mother's neck.

Mireille stroked the girl's back with trembling hands. "Of course I came back. I told you this wouldn't be for long."

"Can I go home with you now?"

"No, darling, not now. You've got this term at school to finish. But soon." She tried to keep her voice calm. "How does Christmas sound? Christmas . . . in America."

"America?" Stephanie looked puzzled. "Why are we going there?"

Mireille smiled. "Stephanie, a man—a good man, a kind man—has asked me to marry him. His home is in Los Angeles, California. He wants us all to live there together. Would you like that?"

"Oh, Maman, yes!"

"Good. That's settled, then." She tried to hug Stephanie, but the little girl wriggled out of her grasp, shouting, "Nora, Nora!"

Mireille looked up to see a tall, gangly girl in oversized glasses peering furtively into the parlor. At the mention of her name, Nora walked in awkwardly.

"Hello," she said, tripping over one shoe.

"Hello," Mireille answered with a smile. "Are you a friend of Stephanie's?"

"Nora's my best friend," Stephanie shouted. She ran over to her. "I'm going to America! I'm going to live in California with Maman and a new daddy!"

Nora's owlish eyes moved from Stephanie to the beautiful woman who was her mother, then back to Stephanie.

Then, without a word, she bolted from the room.

Stephanie stared after her.

"I think she's sorry to see you leave," Mireille said.

Stephanie turned back to her. "My wish came true," she said solemnly. "But I don't think Nora's did."

Mireille spent the weekend with Stephanie in a small hotel on Lake Geneva, where they went boating and rode horseback and made plans for their permanent reunion at Christmas. Victor, Mireille explained, made movies about cowboys and Indians. Stephanie listened raptly as her mother recounted the plot of *Lone Gun* as a bedtime story, playing each character's part in a different voice.

"Can I be in a movie?" Stephanie shrieked, clapping her hands together.

"Most certainly not. You have to go to school."

The girl's face fell. "Even in America?"

"I'm afraid so."

Stephanie thought for a moment about the injustice of it all, then smiled shyly. "I don't mind, Maman. As long as I'm with you."

Mireille hugged her. "Soon," she said, her voice thick with emotion.

"How far away is Christmas?"

"Not long. Just a few months."

"Then I can get my daddy back."

Mireille looked at her sadly. "No, Stephanie. Your daddy can't come back. But you'll have another daddy. And a home. And a real family."

"He will be my real daddy," Stephanie said. "That was part of my wish."

"What wish?"

"I wished on the stone horse. I wished that you and me and Daddy could be together." She yawned. "I drew a picture of us. So that the horse would know how to find all of us." She settled her head into the soft pillow. "And he did."

"Stephanie, your father isn't living," Mireille said firmly.

The little girl's eyes fluttered. "Yes, he is. He's been fighting dragons and making movies. He's the Red Cross Knight."

"Ah," Mireille said. The child would learn soon enough that Victor Mohl was a far, far cry from a fairy-tale knight.

When Stephanie returned to the school, Nora was waiting for her. "I've got something for you," the older girl said. Her eyes were red-rimmed and puffy. "For your wishing place."

She held out her hand. On the end of her index finger, smeared with white paste turned gray by newsprint, was a small flat circle picturing Oliver Jordan's face.

"The Red Cross Knight," Stephanie said in wonder, taking it reverently.

"I told you. He's just a movie producer."

"What about your wall . . . Is it ruined now?"

Nora shrugged. "Queen Elizabeth's face was underneath. It looks pretty funny, the Queen sitting next to Robert Walker. She's wearing a crown and a man's suit, and staring at Natalie Wood's mashed potatoes." She tried a laugh, but tears came instead.

"What's the matter, Nora?" Stephanie asked.

The older girl shook her head. "Here, stick this on your stupid picture." She snatched the tiny photograph of Oliver Jordan's disembodied head and placed it above the knight's silver armor. It fit perfectly. "He's going to be my father," Stephanie said.

Nora stood up and walked to the door.

"Nora?" Stephanie called.

"What?"

"Remember when you had the dead frog?"

"So what?"

"What did you wish for?"

Nora's shoulders slumped. She took off her glasses and wiped her eyes with her sleeve.

"The same thing you did," she said. "That I'd have a dad again."

Chapter Thirty-Three

Mohl hired a publicist to promote his return to America.

"There'll be a mob of photographers out there," he said excitedly as the plane taxied to a stop at LA International.

But there were no news photographers. Only the publicist herself showed up, gamely snapping pictures of Mohl and his bride-to-be.

"That's it?" he growled as the other passengers complained that he was blocking the exit stairs. "What do you think I'm paying you for?"

"It's all right, Victor, really," Mireille said. "I don't really like photographers, anyway."

"Well, you'd better get used to them, because you're going to be the wife of a famous man." He stomped down the stairs as the publicist looked at Mireille and shrugged.

The photographs were sent to all the daily and trade newspapers. None ran them. Even *Variety* failed to mention the engagement of the brilliant young director and his beautiful French fiancée.

"They think I'm not big enough for them to mention my name," Mohl grumbled inside his small house in Brentwood. He could have afforded a much larger place in a less prestigious neighborhood, he explained to Mireille, but one's address was important in Hollywood.

"I'll show them. We're going to have the biggest wedding this town has ever seen. They'll know who I am then, believe me," he said with a knowing laugh. "There's nothing the press likes better than a great party. They kill themselves to get invited to some of the parties around here. This one'll top them all. Just wait and see."

"Victor," Mireille said, putting her arms around him, "it doesn't matter to me if we have a big wedding."

"Well, it matters to me! If I'm going to make it with the studios, people have got to know my name. And you've got to help me, understand? If you're not with me, you're against me."

"Yes, Victor," she said, pulling away from him.

A week later, Victor ran into the house shouting exultantly.

"Peter Rockwell!"

"Who?"

"Peter Rockwell," he repeated with some annoyance. "Don't tell me you don't know who he is."

She blinked.

"Jesus, you really don't know, do you? Peter Rockwell happens to be one of the biggest stars in Hollywood. His last two pictures grossed over ten million apiece. What kind of a wife are you going to be if you don't even know who Peter Rockwell is?"

"I'm sorry," Mireille said. "I've tried to read—"

"Oh, forget it," he said, slapping her rear playfully. "You can't be expected to know much, being a foreigner. After we're married, you'll get to know everyone. The hostess with the mostest, right?"

She smiled at his joke without understanding it.

"Anyway, I talked to Rockwell's agent today. He says he might be able to stage the wedding at Rockwell's house!" He grinned at her, waiting for a response. "Well? What do you think about that?"

"At his house?" Mireille said finally. "Not in a church?"

Mohl made a face. "Nobody gets married in church anymore. But Peter Rockwell's lawn! Think of it! Every reporter in town will be there. We'll decorate the whole place with gardenias. I'll leave that all up to you, but you get the picture: flowers everywhere, a string orchestra in tails, striped tents for the food and bars . . . It'll be sensational."

"Is . . . is this man a good friend of yours?" Mireille asked, still bewildered.

"Yeah, pretty good," he waffled. "I've run into him." Victor declined to mention that the only places he'd ever run into Peter Rockwell were public restaurants, where Rockwell and his entourage had roundly ignored him. "He's up for an Oscar, and he can use all the publicity he can get. I told his agent I'd plug his last movie like it was my own."

"I see," Mireille said.

"That's it? I go to all this trouble, and all you can say is, 'I see'?"

"I'm very happy, Victor. I'll try to make it a nice wedding."

"Just don't get fat," he said. "Once they see you, they won't be able to avoid taking my picture with you." He grabbed her possessively and planted a big wet kiss on her lips. "Wait and see, baby. You won't be sorry you married me. I'm going to invite every famous name in Hollywood."

His attitude depressed Mireille. "Does your family live here?" she asked pleasantly, trying to change the subject.

"No. They're still in New York."

"Will they be staying here, then?"

"What for?"

"For the wedding, Victor. I'm looking forward to meeting them."

"Jesus, they're not coming, for Christ's sake," he said. "They wouldn't know what to say to these people. None of them even went to high school. They'd embarrass me." He turned away toward the window as he spoke. When he turned around again, he was beaming. "Oh, baby, this is going to be big. Just wait and see."

By the following week, Victor's hopes had been dashed. "Rockwell won't go for it," he said glumly. "He probably doesn't think I'm big enough. I'll show him. One day he'll be begging to be in one of my films. I'll show him."

Mireille rose to make dinner.

"The wedding's going to be at John Reynolds's house," he said as an afterthought. "I don't suppose you know who he is, either."

"Another famous actor?" Mireille guessed.

"A has-been. Reynolds hasn't made a movie in five years, but the public still remembers him. He's got the same agent Peter Rockwell has. The slime. I bet he never even mentioned the idea to Rockwell. He just led me on to get some publicity for that booze-hound Reynolds."

"Victor, we don't have to be married in anyone's house—"

"Just take care of your end of things, okay?" he snapped. "November first. John Reynolds's house. Make sure that gets on the invitations."

"Yes, Victor."

"Do you have a dress?"

"I will." She smiled. "It was going to be a surprise."

Mohl made a face. "Don't tell me you're going to wear your mother's wedding gown."

"No. My parents' home was burned, and—"

"So what are you going to wear, already?"

"My dressmaker in Paris is making a gown for me."

"Jesus! How much is that going to cost? Do you think I'm made of money?"

"It will cost you nothing, Victor. The dress is a gift from my friend Barbara. Barbara Ponti. You remember, from *Lone—*"

"Yeah, yeah. Well, it better not be a piece of shit. My wife's not going to look like a ragpicker."

"No, Victor."

She swallowed. *How can I marry this fool?* she thought angrily, then immediately felt ashamed of herself.

Victor wasn't a fool, she told herself, not really. He was a man of reasonable intelligence, with a good heart and a willingness to work. In a town like Champs de Blé, he would have made a fine baker or mason. But this wasn't Champs de Blé. This was Los Angeles, California, America, where success was measured in dollars and proclaimed in newspapers. It wasn't his fault.

"I'll have the invitations made up right away," she said.

Stephanie was going to have a home. That was what mattered. Nothing else.

Victor was on edge for the next six weeks. During that time, Mireille hardly saw him.

He had installed her in a small apartment near his house. He objected to the price, but felt that their living together without being married would not be wise for someone in his position.

The break was a relief for Mireille. Between her visits to the florist, the caterer, the musicians, and John Reynolds's publicist, who complicated matters considerably by not allowing Mireille to visit the grounds on which the wedding was to be held, she wrote a steady stream of letters to Stephanie extolling the virtues of Los Angeles.

Actually, she saw little of the city, traveling to her appointments by taxi, too busy to venture beyond the wide streets clogged with fast-moving automobiles. Los Angeles was, it seemed, a city of cars, anonymous and hurried. Some of the buildings were painted in pastel colors like the quaint houses she remembered from childhood vacations in the South of France, but they were surrounded here with garish signs and buried in litter.

Still, her daughter was going to live here, and Mireille was determined to bolster Stephanie's enthusiasm as much as she could. She made a special trip to Hollywood just to describe it in her letters. She wrote about the beautiful theater that resembled an ancient Egyptian palace, and the Chinese one with the handprints of film legends embedded in the cement walkway.

Film legends, she thought. Mireille had never heard of most of the actors and actresses who were so revered by these people who spent so much time in cars. The only actor she'd heard about in her youth was Charlie Chaplin, whom the French adored as their own "Charlot." She remembered seeing pictures of Chaplin in magazines her mother had brought home. After her parents' death, though, the only magazines in the house were the pornographic ones old Valois used to stash behind the cushions in the sofa.

She shook the thought away. Stephanie's upbringing would be different from her own. It was a different age, a different country. Her daughter could not be raised as she had, in a quiet country house with only a piano and books for entertainment. She would be an American.

As Mireille walked along the handprints in the sidewalk, she stood aside for a group of young people bustling forward together, talking animatedly about an audition. They all clutched envelopes—filled, Mireille guessed from her experience at Cinecittà, with glossy photographs of themselves—and their hopeful young faces were filled with dreams.

What happens when the dreams don't come true? Mireille asked herself. Did they harden into despair? Or did the dreamers, like Victor Mohl, go on dreaming until their dreams poisoned them?

"Oh, Victor," she said aloud.

Slowly, she walked back to the bus stop. Who was she to judge him? And for what? His ambition? His dreams? At least he had them, she thought bitterly. Mireille's own dreams had vanished long ago, in a field of flowers. They had died before the first frost had touched the blossoms.

Chapter Thirty-Four

The ceremony took place on John Reynolds's lawn, presided over by a minister who boomed his remarks over a sea of empty white chairs.

From his place beneath an archway of white gardenias, Victor Mohl twitched and fumed, openly surveying the scattered guests with undisguised rage. Beside him, dressed in a shimmering gown of silk and antique lace, Mireille tried to calm her mind. There was no more time for guilt anymore, or fear, or for childish dissatisfaction. She had chosen to marry Victor, and she had to accept her choice.

He's a good man, she told herself, a mantra she felt compelled to repeat almost daily. *We'll make a life together. We'll be a family.* As the minister's voice droned on, her thoughts ossified into a numbing litany:

It's not real . . . Nothing that's happening is real . . .

And for a moment she was back in Paris, sitting in the back of a limousine with a stranger who had paid to use her body.

Then the minister stopped speaking and Victor was pulling her toward him in a perfunctory embrace.

Mireille backed away, wanting to bolt, wanting to think.

It's not real . . .

But it was. She was married, not to Stefan, but to Victor Mohl. She belonged to Victor now. That was real.

A door clanged shut in her mind as the string quartet began to play.

"Three thousand bucks' worth of food," Victor declared, looking around at the sparse crowd. Even John Reynolds, ostensibly the host of the affair, only made a brief appearance in search of photographers. When he saw none, he quickly withdrew back into his house.

"Most of the bastards didn't even bother to say they weren't coming."

"Many people are here, darling," Mireille said, trying to comfort him.

"Nobody that counts. The only ones who showed up are moochers looking for a free meal. Do you see any press here? Do you?"

She looked around. "No . . . Maybe if you talked with some of your friends—"

"What friends? I've never laid eyes on most of these slobs." He brushed the air with his hand. "Leave me alone, will you? Go circulate or something."

Mireille walked over to the banquet table, feeling awkward. She had been given no say about the guest list. Not that she could have contributed names, anyway. Her world was an ocean away. The only one she would have wanted to attend, Stephanie, had been excluded from the beginning.

She had hoped that Victor's friends would become her own, but it seemed Victor had no friends, only potential contacts.

"Mrs. Mohl?" A fresh-faced young man extended his hand to her. "Best wishes. I'm Jim Allerton."

"How do you do?" Mireille said.

The young man laughed. "I can see you're not from around here. Usually, the first question is 'What do you do?'"

"I don't think I'll ever get used to the way things are done here," she said.

"The accent's French." He grinned. "Are you from France, or somewhere more exotic?"

"Paris."

"That's exotic enough for a boy from Virginia." He squinted, straining for a thought, then looked up eagerly. *"Vos fleurs sont comme le halo d'un ange,"* he said.

Mireille gasped. *L'Ange!* Did this boy know her? Through his father, perhaps, or during a visit to Paris? Oh, she must have been crazy to think she could hide her past from Victor. *L'Ange!*

"Did I say something wrong?" Allerton's face crumpled. "I'm terribly sorry. I only meant that your flowers were lovely. Like an angel's halo, I was getting at."

"My flowers . . ." She touched the arrangement of blossoms in her hair absently, searching desperately for a place to run.

"Please, Mrs. Mohl, I meant no disrespect by my gruesome French. If I've been swearing like a polecat trapper, it was completely inadvertent, I promise you. And I apologize from the bottom of my heart, even though I'm too dumb to know what I said."

Mireille looked at him. The young man seemed genuinely puzzled by her reaction.

"No," she said finally. "There is no need for you to apologize. It was I who . . . misunderstood. My English is still so poor."

"Your English is gorgeous." He blushed. "It sounds like velvet. Liquid velvet." The words caught in his throat.

Mireille half expected his voice to squeak.

He cleared his throat. "Please don't think I meant that in any sort of . . . inappropriate . . ."

She smiled at him indulgently. "Thank you. You have the words of a poet."

"Shhh." He looked around in an elaborate charade of furtiveness. "Don't use words like that around here. I'm a screenwriter. Being known as a poet could ruin me."

She laughed. "Have you written many movies?"

"A couple. Both bombs, I'm afraid."

"Bombs?" She wrinkled her brow.

"Failures. But then, I'm only twenty-three years old. Around here, you're not considered a failure until you're at least twenty-four. Can I get you a drink?"

The two of them milled around the outskirts of the crowd while Victor pulled himself together and forced himself to greet the guests he did not know. Allerton was young, but it had been so long since Mireille had anyone to talk to that she was soon caught up in conversation with him.

With Victor, she could only listen. He was not a man who gave time to idle chatter, and his attitude about Mireille seemed to be the less he knew about her, the better. The Allerton boy was different. Perhaps because he was a boy, Mireille thought, then remembered that he was about her age. Still, there was something quintessentially childlike about him, an unspoiled naiveté that made her feel comfortably maternal.

She told him about her family and their experiences during the war, about her mother, even about Stefan as a child, and how he had secretly learned to read.

During it all, Jim Allerton listened raptly. "What a great character," Allerton said. "What happened to him?"

The question about Stefan came at Mireille with sudden ferocity.

"He was killed during the war," she said quietly. "He worked for the Resistance. He was trying to blow up a bridge the Germans used."

"And they caught him?"

She shrugged. "I suppose so. He never came back." She turned her face away. Mireille had never mentioned that she and Stefan had been lovers, but it was clear from Allerton's expression that no elaboration was necessary.

"I'm sorry," he said. "I didn't mean to upset you. Certainly not on your wedding day."

"My wedding . . ." She looked around at the scattered strangers, at the would-be actor who had served as the minister, at the home of the "friend" she had never met, and suddenly burst out laughing. "Yes, it is my wedding day!" She had forgotten, and the thought made her laugh even more.

"I'm glad to see you're enjoying yourself so much," Victor Mohl said with a scowl. Mireille looked up and saw him standing next to her, glaring at the young man.

"Oh, Victor," she said. "May I present Mr. Allerton? My husband, Victor Mohl."

"Congratulations," Allerton said, extending his hand.

Mohl ignored it.

"Mr. Allerton is a writer," Mireille said, hoping to cover up her husband's rudeness.

Victor stuck his hands in his pockets. "Never heard of you," he said.

Allerton laughed. "I think that's my cue to get myself a drink."

Mohl stared after him as he left.

"He was only trying to be friendly," Mireille said.

"Yeah. Real friendly. Look, that bum is a nothing. I don't even know how he got here."

"He was courteous and kind," Mireille said.

"He only wants to get into your pants." Mohl yanked her elbow. "If you're going to come on to somebody, at least have the brains to make it somebody important." His grimace switched suddenly to a broad, patently phony smile. "That's a publicist at Metro," he whispered as he led her over to an overdressed woman who'd had too much to drink. "Try to be nice to somebody who's worth something for a change."

Mireille felt a fury rising inside of her, but she squelched it. *I'm his wife,* she thought, feeling as if a weight had settled in her chest. *Oh my God, I'm his wife.*

After an hour, most of the guests had already left, even though the bride and groom were still present. The caterers stood near the table of nearly uneaten food, and the orchestra continued to play.

"Get rid of them," Victor snarled, and walked away toward his car. When Mireille caught up with him, he was tearing the tissue-paper flowers off the automobile. "Get in," he said flatly.

"Victor, I know how hurt you must be. It's really not so bad, though. The caterers will bring the food to your house—our house. We'll have another party, for your friends."

"I said get in."

They drove to the small Brentwood house in silence. Victor unlocked the front door and sat down heavily on a chair. "Get me a drink," he said.

She looked around. This was her home now, yet she knew where nothing was. "Where do you keep it?" she asked.

"In the bar," he said exasperatedly, waving toward a piece of wooden furniture in the corner of the room. "The ice cubes are in the kitchen. Think you can figure out where that is?"

She had seen him order scotch in restaurants, so she poured some into a glass with ice and handed it to him.

He drank it in one swig. "Bastards."

Mireille sat down on a chair and looked at the gold band on her finger. There had been no laughter between them, no celebration, not even a dance to commemorate their wedding.

All for lack of an audience, she thought sadly.

"Well?" Victor said, sighing as he swirled the ice cubes in his empty glass. "How do you like being married to a nobody?"

"Oh, Victor, it's not like that."

"What do you know? You don't know this town. If you don't belong, you're nothing."

She put her arms around him. "Victor, please stop . . ."

He pushed her away. As he did, his hand got tangled in her wedding veil. Her headdress pulled away, scattering flowers on the floor. Victor looked down at the tulle in his hands, then up at Mireille, his wife, her carefully done hair now falling loose. A flower hung on one side of her face. He approached her slowly.

Mireille saw the wild look in his eyes and backed up. "Victor," she said softly. "Victor, no. Not this way."

He grabbed the high lace collar of her gown and ripped it open down to her waist. "You wish I was someone else, don't you? Like that waspy punk you were dangling your tits in front of."

"No, Victor . . ." She tried to pull the torn lace up to cover herself.

"You'll do what I tell you, understand?" He grabbed her arm and yanked her toward him.

Mireille tried to push him away. He slapped her face with the back of his hand, and her head sprang backward as she lost her footing. In an instant Victor was on top of her.

This was just the way it had been with Valois back in the kitchen in Champs de Blé. Mireille wanted to scream. She could almost feel the shards of glass cutting into her back, almost feel herself reaching for the piece she would use to cut his throat, almost hear the gurgle of the old man's blood as it bubbled up out of the gash in his neck . . .

"No!" she screamed. "You're my husband! My *husband*!"

Victor stopped. He rolled off her slowly, then curled into a ball at her feet.

"How can you think to do this to me?" she asked, her voice unsteady.

He hid his face. "I'm sorry," he muttered into his sleeve.

Mireille plucked, sobbing, at the torn pieces of her wedding gown.

He looked up at her. His knees were pressed together, pulled up almost to his chest. His face was a mask of misery and humiliation. "Oh God, I'm so sorry." He reached out to caress her face.

"Don't touch me," she said, pulling away from him.

He closed his eyes in anguish. "Mireille . . ."

She stood up, clutching the rags of her dress around her. Victor lunged toward her with a cry and wrapped his arms around her legs. "Please forgive me," he moaned. "I'm begging you. I'll never do that again. I'll never touch you unless you want me to. Don't hate me." A deep sob seemed to rip out of him. "Goddamn it, you're all I have."

Mireille looked down at him, small, wretched, sobbing into her skirt like a child. How could she call this man—this creature— her husband?

But no one had forced her to marry, she knew. She had understood that from the beginning. And now it was done. For better or worse.

"Please stand up," she said.

He scrambled to his feet, hopeful and smiling through his tears. His lips were dark, formless. "I'll make it up to you, you'll see. I'll get another movie, a good movie, and a studio will sign me on. God knows, I've been to see them all a dozen times since I've been back. But my luck's going to turn, I've got a good feeling about that."

"Victor—"

"Things are going to be different around here, baby. That's a promise. Once I get a break, everybody'll know my name. Headwaiters will show you to the best tables when they hear you're Mrs. Victor Mohl. You'll be the first to be invited to those hotsy-totsy charity balls—"

"Stop it!" she shouted. She wiped her forehead, trying to rid herself of the headache that was starting. "Don't you see, I don't care about those things! I want my daughter."

"Sure, baby, sure," Victor said. He held up both hands in surrender. "Didn't I already say we'd bring her over? Christmas. Sooner, if I get a movie. You can count on it." He was talking in a frenzy now. "We'll move out of this house, too, get a bigger place, with a chandelier in the foyer. You'd like that, wouldn't you? A Rolls in the garage, a maid just to look after you . . ."

Mireille gathered up the remnants of her dress and walked out of the room.

Chapter Thirty-Five

The big studios did not hire Victor. Each day he went out filled with confidence that this contact, this agent, this producer, this department head, this actor, would be the comet whose tail he would ride to glory. And each evening he returned to the Brentwood house with tales of betrayal.

"How do you like that Dallas Cole," he said, throwing his hat onto the sofa. "Thanks to the break I gave her, she's getting offers right and left. All she's got to do is drop a word with her agent at William Morris . . ." He looked over at Mireille. "Aah, forget it. You don't understand anything about this business."

He picked up the scotch Mireille had set before him and drained the glass. "So what'd you do all day, fix your makeup?"

Mireille turned away from the window. Outside, in the starless night, the wind was bending the trees on the empty residential street.

"I would like to get a job, Victor," she said.

"Oh, great. That'll make me look just great, won't it? My wife, lining up for extra work at MGM. No, thanks."

"I could do something else."

"What? Model clothes in restaurants where the other wives are having lunch? Or were you thinking about waiting on their tables?"

She sighed. "I only wanted to help."

"Well, I don't need your help, all right? I need a studio. Oliver Jordan, that's whose help I need."

She looked away. "Perhaps after *Lone Gun* is released—"

"*Lone Gun* isn't going to be released. Not in this country, anyway. The distributors don't want any more Westerns. That's what they think I am, a Western director. Jerkoffs."

"But couldn't—?" She bolted up from her chair and rushed over to the window. "Victor, there's a tow truck outside. Two men are doing something to your car."

She ran to the front door and opened it. "What are you doing?" she shouted to the men who were hitching the second-hand Mercedes to the truck. "Stop, or I will call the police!"

Victor closed the door. "Don't do that," he said.

"But your car . . ."

"I can't pay for it anymore." He retreated without looking at her.

Mireille held her head. She'd had no idea their finances were so bad. Victor had never mentioned anything to her about money, except that he would take care of their bills. In the small room he used as an office, he kept all of the bankbooks and financial statements inside a desk that Mireille had been instructed never to open.

It didn't make sense. From everything Barbara had told her, film directors were well paid. Victor had finished *Lone Gun* in September. It was now December. He had been out of work for scarcely three months. They lived modestly. Neither of them had bought anything except necessities since the wedding.

That must have been expensive, she knew. Parties like that were costly, but . . . *everything*?

She followed him into the kitchen, where Victor was rummaging through her handbag. He looked up, red-faced. He was clutching a twenty-dollar bill.

"Is this all you've got?" he asked, scowling.

She nodded.

He stuck it in his pocket. "I'll see you later."

"Please don't go now."

"I've got things to do."

"What about the car?"

"I'll grab a cab at the corner." He moved past her and slammed the door.

With a sigh, she sat down at the kitchen table. At first, Victor only went out a few nights a week. Drinks with important contacts, he insisted; dinner with his agent. Lately he was gone every night, returning in the small hours looking disheveled and despairing.

It might have been another woman, Mireille supposed. They'd had sex only a few times since his attack on their wedding day, and each of those times had been quick and perfunctory. It was as if the love-struck man who had wooed her had vanished before her eyes, replaced by an angry, nerve-wracked neurotic. Still, she did not believe that Victor was seeing anyone else. His frustration and rage went beyond the longing for a mistress.

In the past couple of weeks, Victor had not risen until noon. Then, with trembling hands, he left the house in a rush, barely speaking to Mireille, sometimes looking surprised to see her. He had, it seemed, forgotten her existence.

It was the money. It had to be. How had it gone so quickly?

Christmas was less than a month away. There would be no presents for Stephanie when she came.

Mireille's face softened. *When* she came. Victor would have nothing to do with that. He had promised that Stephanie would live with them, and though he dodged any discussion Mireille brought up about her daughter's move to America, he would not forbid it. Mireille herself would buy the plane ticket, just as she sent Stephanie her living expenses each month, from the money she had earned working on *Lone Gun*.

It wasn't much. Her elevation to second lead in the movie brought her only as much money as an extra with one line to speak. Still, that money was her own, budgeted to last until the school's holiday break. Mireille had never asked her husband to support Stephanie. She wanted nothing to sour his reception of the child.

She went to a baseboard in the kitchen and carefully lifted out a segment. *Like a frightened old woman,* she thought, *hiding her money from thieves.*

The envelope was there, a neat brown rectangle filled with Swiss franc notes. Mireille reached for it, then stopped. She knew exactly how much money it contained. Enough for Stephanie's airfare home.

She would fly to California on her birthday. At last, Stephanie would be coming home.

Mireille replaced the floorboard and went to bed.

Victor was still gone when she woke up. By noon, she was worried. By midafternoon, she had begun to think the unthinkable. Victor had been filled with despair when he left. He had no money. His prospects for work were not good. His car had been taken away. His wife had caught him taking money from her purse.

I've got things to do, he had said.

What things? Had he felt so hopeless, so trapped, that he had wanted to end his life? The thought made Mireille shudder.

When the front door banged open, she jumped up with a gasp as Victor bounded in, happy as a schoolboy.

"Get your coat, baby, we're going to Vegas!"

Mireille ran to him, her legs feeling weak. "Are you all right?"

He laughed raucously. "I couldn't be better," he said, picking Mireille up by the waist and swinging her in a circle.

"What—what is it? Did you get a job?"

"Better. Come on, we can hop a plane in an hour."

"To Las Vegas? Now?"

"Right now."

"But I haven't packed."

"Forget about that. I'll buy you anything you need."

"Victor, this is crazy. We don't even have a car."

"Tomorrow I'm buying you a Rolls." He kissed her. "Don't you see, baby? It's happened. My ship came in." He stood back from her and smiled. "I told you it would, didn't I? Let's go."

That night they checked into the Presidential Suite at the Dunes.

"Well? How do you like it?" he asked triumphantly.

"Victor, look at this room!"

"Get used to it. We're going to have nothing but the best from now on." He looked like a proud bantam rooster, strutting through the elegant hotel room.

"Tell me about the movie you'll be making," Mireille said excitedly. "Did you get a studio contract, or will we be going back to Italy? I'd like that, seeing my old friends. We could bring Stephanie with us, and show her Rome—"

"We'll talk about it later," he said brusquely. Then he smiled again. "What say we go downstairs to the casino? Try our luck at the tables, okay?"

"Now? We haven't eaten, and I'm not dressed for a casino."

"Never mind that. We'll just go for a few minutes, then I'll buy you the biggest steak in the hotel." He took her by the hand and rushed her out the door.

In the casino, Mireille marveled at the grand scale of the ostentatious finery that was on display everywhere. She had been to the casino in Monte Carlo, but even the glittering Hôtel de Paris offered nothing like the orgiastic grandeur of the great Las Vegas gambling dens. Behind the tables stood the croupiers in crisp starched shirts under black tuxedoes, while multilingual waitresses in the briefest of costumes offered drinks to the players.

"You know how to play roulette?" he asked. She nodded.

They sat down at a twenty-five-dollar table, and he bought in for five thousand.

"Victor!" she whispered. "So much money!"

"This is just the beginning, sweetheart," he said as he placed stacks of chips on the board. "Here, have some fun." He slid a pile of chips over toward Mireille. "Go on, put them on the board."

Hesitantly she placed a single chip on red.

"What are you, cheap?" He grabbed six chips out of her hand and placed them hurriedly on the board as the croupier set the ball in motion on the wheel.

The ball slowed, then came to rest on one of the two green spaces at the top of the wheel. The other players gave a groan.

"Double zero!" Mohl shouted exultantly, jabbing a fist into the air. "Over here, baby," he said as the croupier pushed two stacks of chips toward him. Mohl took two chips off the top and tossed them to the croupier. "That's for luck."

"Thank you, sir," the young man said.

"That was fifty dollars," Mireille said, but her husband did not hear her. He was already spreading chips around the board.

"Eight black," the croupier said. This time another player whooped in excitement. All of Victor's chips were swept away.

"Nineteen red." Another loser.

"Thirty-six black." The stack of chips grew shorter.

Within ten minutes, they were gone.

"What have you got?" Mohl asked Mireille. She counted through her chips. "Two hundred," she said.

He took them from her. "Double zero. Let's see that green!"

The ball rolled in agonizing slowness. "Five red," the croupier said.

Victor reached into his pocket and took out another thousand dollars. "Chips," he demanded.

"Victor—"

He shook her hand off.

"Miss?" the croupier asked.

She shook her head and slid off the chair. Victor didn't seem to notice that she was no longer beside him.

Silently, she watched as he lost the thousand and exchanged another thousand for chips. When that, too, was gone, she left.

Victor came back to the room just after three in the morning. He was disheveled and wild-eyed. Mireille sat on the bed, waiting.

"Is it all gone?" she asked quietly.

He nodded.

"Where did you get it?"

"Poker game," he said. He lay down on the bed with his shoes still on. "I won eleven thousand dollars."

"Is that where you went every day?"

"Get off my back, will you?"

"Answer me, Victor."

He turned away from her, then, with his clothes still on, fell into a weary, indifferent sleep.

They flew back to Los Angeles the next day. Victor had the taxi drop Mireille off at the house. He did not tell her where he was going. Hungry, still in the clothes she left in, Mireille walked woodenly into the small den Victor used for an office. What she had seen in the past twenty-four hours had negated, in her mind, the promise she had made her husband not to look through his papers. For once, she was going to know exactly what their financial situation was.

The figures in his books and files stunned her.

Victor's salary for directing *Lone Gun* was enough for the two of them and Stephanie to live in comfort for years. Yet it was all gone. Throughout the records of his bankbooks were listings of cash withdrawals totaling nearly eighty thousand dollars for the past three months alone. And there were debts incurred long before that.

In his desk drawers she found a racing form from Santa Anita, a ticket stub from the dog track, and chits from various lotteries. There were also eviction notices from a housing agent.

So the house is rented, she thought. Another thing she never knew.

She felt herself trembling with anger and fear. How could she have married a man she knew so little about? How could she have allowed things to go so far?

In his phone book were dozens of names—first names only, all male. She called a few. One was a candy store, the other a grocery. She did not know the word for "bookie," but she knew what they were. And after seeing her husband's bankbook, she knew what her husband was, too.

A great well of pity threatened to burst inside her. This man, with all his vain dreams, had gambled away every cent he owned, and much more. How long would it be before they were forced to leave their rental house? What would she be bringing Stephanie to?

When Victor came home, his watch was gone. "Get me a drink," he said.

Mireille did not move. "I've seen your books," she said simply.

"What are you talking about?"

"Your bankbooks. And other things, too. I know what you've been doing with your money."

He was silent for a moment, then stared up at her defiantly. "That's right," he said. "*My* money. And what I do with it is none of your business."

"Victor, you need help—"

"I pay the rent, don't I?" he shouted. "You sure don't. I've never seen a dime of your money help us out. No, that all goes to your little brat in her fancy Swiss school."

"Someone has to pay for it," she said. "You don't."

"Hey, smart-ass, I don't keep a stash hidden in the floor."

Mireille froze. Knowing he had said too much, Victor stood up.

"How do you know about that?" she demanded.

"Don't you cook anymore?"

"How do you know?" she repeated.

He didn't answer.

She walked into the kitchen to the baseboard. With a knife she popped off the loose piece, then snatched the brown envelope behind it.

It was empty. It fluttered out of her hands.

Mohl stood in the doorway, his hands in his pockets. He did not meet her eyes. For a long moment they remained frozen in that tableau, Mireille on her knees with the torn brown envelope beside her, looking with disbelief up at her husband.

"I needed a stake for the poker game," he said finally. "I was going to put it back when I won." His hands formed into two fists. "And I *did* win, damn it. I won eleven thousand dollars. I was on a streak, baby, I couldn't lose! I thought that in Vegas—"

"Is it all gone?" she asked dully.

He hung his head.

"Oh, Stephanie," she whispered.

Her daughter would not be coming home. And would not be able to remain in school. Where would she go now? The child was nine years old and entirely alone.

While her husband made himself a drink, Mireille remained where she was on the kitchen floor, staring numbly at nothing.

Ma chère Stephanie . . .

Stephanie handed the letter to Nora. "Can you read this?"

Nora clucked. "You're almost nine. You should be able to read it yourself."

"But it's curly writing."

"Cursive," Nora said. "I was reading it when I was five."

"Okay, I'll ask Sister Marie-Thérèse to read it to me."

Nora snatched it. "I'll read it. I always do," she mumbled as if in an afterthought.

Stephanie giggled. They went through almost the same ritual with each letter from her mother. The Sisters always offered to read them, but Stephanie steadfastly refused, preferring to share their prized contents only with her friend. Together they dissected each sentence, daydreaming about the idyllic life in southern California, imagining themselves on the arms of movie stars at grand galas.

"The only thing is," Nora had said soon after Stephanie's announcement that she would be leaving La Voisine to live with her family in America, "you're really going to be doing the things we talk about. I'll still be here."

"But you can visit," Stephanie said. "We can spend all summer together."

"Bullshit." Nora lit a cigarette. "You'll forget me. People always forget when they don't see someone."

"Oh, no, Nora," Stephanie said solemnly. "You're my best friend. I'll never forget, not ever."

"Bullshit," Nora repeated.

Still, Nora always read the letters.

"There's no plane ticket in here," Stephanie said, peering into the empty envelope. "Maybe it fell out."

"It couldn't have fallen out. It's a great big thing."

"Did you ever ride on an airplane, Nora?"

"Sure. Lots of times. By myself."

"Is it scary?"

"Of course not. Don't be such a baby." She squinted through her glasses at the writing.

Stephanie looked through the window at the falling snow outside. "Maybe she sent it to Sister Marie-Thérèse. I'll go ask her after you read me the letter."

"You're not going to America," Nora said.

Stephanie whirled around to face her.

"Your mother can't send for you until later. She's mailed you a birthday present instead."

"Liar!" Stephanie's soft features were twisted in rage. "You're a liar!"

"Holy Jesus, Steff, I wouldn't lie about that."

"Liar!" Stephanie screamed. She grabbed the letter and struggled over the words herself.

It is so hard for me to write this, my darling . . .

Stephanie looked up silently, her eyes welling with angry tears.

"It's not so bad," Nora offered. "I spend every Christmas here."

"But she promised me! She promised!"

Nora shrugged. "Grown-ups do that," she said.

Tight-lipped, Stephanie turned to the small altar of the wishing place she had made and swept it to the floor. The tiny stone horse spun off and whirled at her feet. With a sob, she picked it up and bolted out of the room, down the long corridor and onto the snowy lawn. She ran through the deep drifts, the cold reddening her bare legs, her tears streaming hotly down her cheeks.

"Steff," Nora called, running after her.

Stephanie threw the stone horse as far as she could, then collapsed in the snow, crying out in anguish and betrayal.

Wordlessly, Nora lifted her up by her shoulders.

"She promised me . . ."

"Yeah," Nora said.

"But she didn't mean it."

Nora's breath came out in a mirthless white cloud. "They never mean it," she said. "Let's get inside."

Chapter Thirty-Six

Oliver Jordan smiled as he walked to the other side of his polished mahogany desk. He was holding a blue-bound screenplay in one hand, and placed the other on the shoulder of the young man who had just come in.

"James Allerton," he said affably, reading from the cover of the screenplay. "What do I call you—James? Jim?"

"For what you're paying me, you can call me anything you like," the young man said with a smile of his own.

Jordan chuckled. His assistant, a diminutive man with trim, thinning hair of a decidedly unnatural color, rolled his eyes.

Allerton saw him and cleared his throat. "Jim would be fine."

"Jim it is. Please don't mind Adam. He's just as nasty to me. Jim Allerton, my assistant, Adam Wells."

Wells screwed his face into a caricature of a bitchy smile, then turned to the coffeepot and the two Limoges porcelain cups in front of it.

"Would you care for something stronger?" Jordan asked.

"Is he of legal age?" Wells chimed in.

"Just get the coffee, Adam."

"Yes, massa."

Jordan ignored him as he motioned Allerton to an overstuffed leather chair and sat down behind his desk. He leafed through the screenplay in front of him. "This is good, Jim. Very good. Sam

Hope's already agreed to direct, and he's in love with it. He says he's not going to change a word."

"I appreciate that, Mr. Jordan."

"Oliver." He closed the folder. On its cover was the screenplay's title, *Field of Glory*. "We were talking about a cast. Sam's pretty sure he can get Peter Rockwell for the part of the Resistance fighter. We don't know about the girl yet. I think she ought to be French. The characters are French, but it'll be *too* French if the leading man and the leading lady are both really French, and not French enough if neither of them are. We thought about Bardot, of course, but she's tied up for the next two years. Any ideas?"

Allerton smiled uncomfortably. "Actually, that character's based on a real woman. It's her story, in fact. The most beautiful woman I've ever met. To tell the truth, I never saw anyone except her in my mind while I was writing *Field of Glory*."

Jordan leaned forward, immediately interested. "Is she an actress?"

"I don't know. I don't even remember her name. She's married to Victor Mohl."

"Who?"

"Oh God," Adam Wells said dryly. "The Mole."

Allerton laughed. "That pretty well describes him, I guess. A mole with a short mole complex."

Wells frowned at him over the silver coffee service he brought over.

"Is he in the business?" Jordan asked.

"Loosely speaking," Wells said, pouring. "He directs B's for Republic. Spaghetti Westerns, mostly, although he's been on the beach for a few months. Or should I say at the track." He rubbed his fingers together. "Money goes through his fingers like water. That's why no studio'll have him."

"Is he talented?"

Wells made a face. "That's another reason, a secondary one. This is Hollywood, after all."

"Adam knows everything," Jordan confided, although Adam was well within earshot. "That's why I tolerate him."

"You mean why you need me," Wells said primly.

Jordan grunted. The peculiar relationship between one of Hollywood's great cocksmen and his effeminate assistant was a source of constant speculation in film circles. Oliver Jordan was among the titans of the industry, yet the most casual observer could see that he permitted Wells liberties that other studio executives would not have tolerated with visiting heads of state.

Jordan was well aware of the gossip, but he was above rumor. He couldn't have cared less what anyone thought about himself or Adam Wells. The truth was just as he always stated it: Wells knew everything. And he told Jordan everything. And he was never wrong. And Jordan did need him.

"I'll check things out and see if this woman—Madame Mohl—ever made a movie," Wells offered.

"The most beautiful woman you ever met, you say?" Jordan inquired, too casually.

"Oh God," Wells muttered.

Allerton smiled. "She was hypnotic, mysterious, sad, elegant . . . I don't know. I only met her once, on her wedding day eighteen months ago. It sounds insane, but I've never been able to forget her, or a word she said. I began writing this screenplay on the same day I met her. It was as if I had to write her story . . . had to." He laughed softly. "I suppose it's a declaration of love, in its way."

Jordan smiled. "For someone you only met once," he mused.

"And whose name you can't remember," Wells added.

Allerton blushed. "I told you it was insane."

"Not insanity," Jordan said with fabricated sagacity. "Art. The name wasn't important. It was the essence. Am I right?"

"Just which art are we talking about?" Wells asked.

Allerton ignored him. "Yes, that's it. Her essence. There's something about her that makes you fall in love with her."

"I'm sure," Wells said. "That's why she ended up with Victor Mohl."

"I believe we're discussing the character in the screenplay, Adam," Jordan said.

"You got an invitation to that wedding, you know," Wells said.

"I did? I don't even know the man."

Allerton shrugged. "I don't think many of the guests did know him. It was a strange affair. Sad. There was seating for three hundred. Almost no one showed up."

"He's reaching beyond himself," Wells said, comfortable now in the thick of gossip. "Why, Mohl's the biggest name-dropper in Hollywood. And believe me, that's quite a distinction."

Jordan brushed the conversation aside impatiently. "At any rate, we'll find someone for the part. There's a young French actress named Leslie Caron—"

"Mireille," Allerton said, his boyish face suddenly lighting up as if by an epiphany. "Mohl's wife. I just remembered. Her name is Mireille."

"Ah," Wells mused. "Mireille Mohl. Has a kind of ring to it, don't you think?"

"Mireille," Jordan said, almost in a whisper.

Wells turned slowly toward his boss, one plucked eyebrow raised.

Jordan stood up quickly. "I'm looking forward to making this picture," he said, terminating the interview. "By the way, my wife, Anne, and I are giving a party in a couple of weeks. You'll get an invitation. Hope you can make it."

Allerton nodded as they shook hands. After he left, Adam Wells turned to Jordan and said, "And Mrs. Mohl?"

"Mireille," Jordan said, feeling himself harden beneath his trousers.

Except for one week in Sardinia, he had not experienced a spontaneous erection for five and a half years. Five and a half years of almost constant depravity, without a glimmer of pure, abandoned pleasure. For an instant, he could almost hear the warm Tyrrhenian waves slapping the rock shore; could almost smell the salt of the sea and the green grass and the fragrance of white-blonde hair entwined like spun starlight in his fingers. The perfect woman, she of the emerald eyes with their tragic depths, of the lips that had invited him to languish forever in her perfection.

Her name had been Mireille.

"Excuse me," Wells asked. "Is this artistic contemplation or a stroke?"

Jordan blinked.

"You know her?"

"No. That is . . ." He shook his head. "It's a common enough name, I suppose."

Wells snorted.

The day following the Mohls' return from Las Vegas, Mireille took a job selling cosmetics in a department store.

She made a deal with Victor: since she had no money to her name, she would remain in the Brentwood house to cook and clean for him until she could save enough to leave. And when they divorced, she would make no claims on him.

In exchange, Victor was never to touch her again. Mireille got a lock and a bolt, and put them on the door to the guest bedroom. There she lived as if she were in an apartment, eating sparingly and alone, meeting Victor only when their proximity to one another in the house demanded it.

After her first payday, she had saved forty-four dollars—much more than she could have earned as a salesclerk in Europe. It was decided, then: she would remain in America, and bring Stephanie over as planned. Her daughter would not have the home or the stepfather Mireille had promised her, but at least they would be together . . .

Forty-four dollars. It would be months before she saw Stephanie again. The Sisters at La Voisine would not send the child out in the snow, but they would have to be repaid for their charity. And there would be no Christmas for them. All that was over now.

Three days after the second eviction notice came in the mail, Victor returned, flushed and heady, just as Mireille was leaving for work.

"We're set now, baby!" he shouted. "Three thousand smackers! Look at it." He pulled her inside. "Come on, honey. This has gone on long enough. I'm a winner now, and this is just the beginning. Wait and see, I'm going to buy you—"

She took the money, counted out the month's rent and the money owed to the landlord, and threw the rest on the floor. "I'll mail this," she said.

So they had a place to stay for another month.

When Mireille got home from work, Victor was waiting with a bottle of chilled champagne. "Honey," he said excitedly. "Sit down. I've got something to show you."

She groaned. "Please, I'm very tired—"

"Take a look at this!" With a look of childlike triumph, he handed her a stiff white card. It was bordered in gold, and printed in the center were the words:

Mr. and Mrs. Oliver Jordan request the pleasure of your company . . .

That was as far as she read. The card fell out of her hand. Feeling faint, she sat down heavily on the sofa.

"Knocked you for a loop, didn't it?" Mohl said, mistaking her shock for elation. "Oliver Jordan! Do you believe it? I told you things were turning around for me." He picked up the card and shook it at her. "Do you know what this means? An invitation to one of Oliver Jordan's parties carries the kind of clout an Academy Award does. I've got it made now, baby." He crumpled the card in his fist and punched into the air in a sign of victory. "Didn't I tell you I'd make it? Didn't I?"

He grabbed Mireille in a bear hug and tried to kiss her, but she pulled away.

"Hey, don't be like that," he said. "Okay, we went through a rough time, maybe. Let's put that behind us. This is my big chance, honey. That's how things are done around here. I get close to a big shot like Jordan, and the doors swing wide open. Hey, with your classy looks, how can I lose? What do you say we bury the hatchet, okay?" He grabbed for her again.

"Go away," she said with annoyance, standing up.

"Bitch," Mohl said. She walked away. "You're going to that party," he called out to her back. She didn't turn around. "Please." He ran after her and caught her by both arms. "Please, Mireille."

"I can't. I . . . I don't want to go."

"I've got to have you there. I want everything to be perfect."

"I won't help your chances with Oliver Jordan," she said levelly.

"Sure you will. You're beautiful. You always knock everybody out. And a guy's got to have a wife. You don't bring your wife, people think something's wrong."

"Something *is* wrong, Victor."

"Maybe, maybe not. Appearances are what matter."

"Victor, you don't understand." She was on the verge of saying she knew Oliver Jordan, then decided against it. The marriage was over. There was no reason to complicate things. "I'll rent you some jewelry," he said. "Good stuff. And a limo. We'll look like we belong there. Please, Mireille. It's the biggest thing that's ever happened to me."

She shook her head sadly. How had this little man become so warped that he believed, as he did from the bottom of his heart, that attending a party was the most important thing that had ever happened to him?

"Victor—"

"I don't care what your reasons are. Please go with me. I'm begging you. Afterward, you can do anything you want. Just do this one thing for me, Mireille."

She knew she had no choice. Victor was like a dog with a bone. He would never stop hounding her until she gave in. "All right," she said at last.

He beamed. "You won't be sorry, baby. This is it. I can feel it. This is the big score. It's all going to come together now, honey, just wait and see . . ."

The Jordans' Holmby Hills mansion was set on a high hill with a long driveway illuminated by gaslights. At the door, a butler greeted the guests and showed them into a huge marble-floored ballroom.

"How do you like this?" Mohl whispered to Mireille as if he were showing off his own treasures.

Towering over her husband, she flushed with embarrassment. The diamonds Victor had rented were too gaudy. For a gown, she had removed the skirt of her wedding dress, taken off the tulle, dyed what was left, and sewn on another strapless top. The overall effect was attractive, but anyone who knew clothes would recognize it for the handmade make-do thing it was. To cover it, Mireille sewed a taffeta cape with a hood, taking pains with every stitch.

She was reminded of the time when she and Madame Racine had stayed up all night remodeling that old velvet bustle dress for a job interview. She hadn't fooled even the personnel manager. Among these glittering nouveaux riches with eyes honed to the price of everything, she and her unsophisticated husband would be laughingstocks.

And there was Oliver Jordan. The shame of seeing him again was too great for words.

Well, she reasoned, she had faced worse things. The reporters outside her Paris apartment had been worse. The police taking her away in the presence of her daughter had been worse. Saying good-bye to Stephanie had been worse.

Waiting for Stefan in the early morning, knowing that he was dead, had been much worse.

She would face Jordan. Whatever cruel gossip circulated about Victor Mohl's choice of marriage partners would soon quell after the divorce. As for herself, Mireille would soon be done paying for the mistake she had made by marrying Victor. She had a job; not a wonderful job, but it was honest work. Soon, within a few months, she would be able to leave Mohl and send for Stephanie. They would start with nothing in a foreign country, but they would be together. That was what mattered. Now, she knew, it was the only thing that mattered.

She lifted up her chin and walked into the ballroom.

"Oh my God," Mohl exclaimed. "There's Peter Rockwell. Rocky, baby!" he shouted, leaving Mireille standing alone.

A few people stared at her. It was not, she knew, the same sort of stare she used to elicit, when people watched her because she was l'Ange, notorious and dazzling. Now they were watching her because they found her amusing. She worked her way toward a corner as unobtrusively as possible.

No one stopped to talk with her. Sometimes, through the crowd, she could see Victor approaching one celebrity or another.

Usually the person he was trying to engage in conversation struggled visibly to get away from him, but he never seemed daunted. There were apparently many people to impress here.

Maybe he was right. In this shallow place, perhaps an invitation to the "right" party was the most important thing in the world. Maybe he would find a way out of the hell his obsessive gambling had created.

Suddenly, Mireille was aware of a hand touching her.

She looked up, startled, and saw him. Oliver Jordan's eyes were looking straight into her own.

A flood of emotions raced through her. Anger, fear, shame, and even a sudden, unwelcome strain of pure sexual excitement. When their eyes met, she felt as if she had seen him only yesterday. Nothing had changed. Their animal response to one another was unmistakable.

"You must be Mrs. Mohl," Jordan said pleasantly, belying the mocking knowledge in his eyes. "I'm delighted to meet you. Oliver Jordan."

He was introducing himself! *He doesn't remember,* she thought with astonishment. Yet his eyes had looked so sure . . .

"Hello," she said, extending her hand politely.

"I understand you're French. Have you met François Truffaut? A marvelous young filmmaker. Come, I'll introduce you."

As he led her across the room, Mireille felt as if she were burning with fever. She went through the motions of meeting several people, although she barely saw their faces or heard their names.

How could he have forgotten?

Then a lonely, ineffable sadness drained the febrile energy out of her. *Why should he have remembered?* she asked herself. To Oliver Jordan, she had been no more than an expensive call girl.

She struggled to make small talk with the new people until Victor came over at a trot, barely able to contain his excitement at meeting the head of Continental Studios.

"Mr. Jordan, my husband, Victor Mohl," Mireille said miserably. "Excuse me." She walked away.

Jordan found an excuse to escape Mohl almost immediately. The others in the crowd dispersed as if the small man carried a plague. Within a few minutes, Mohl had sought Mireille out and grabbed her firmly by her arm.

"What's the idea?" he hissed. "Running out like that. The man's a legend in his own time, and you act like he's a nothing. It didn't look good."

"I'm sorry," Mireille said, squeezing her eyes closed. "I . . . I don't feel well. Please, Victor, could we leave?"

"Are you crazy?" Mohl's eyes bulged. "Leave? I've waited ten years for an invitation to Oliver Jordan's house. Now you expect me to leave just because nobody's paying enough attention to you?"

"It's not that, Victor."

"I don't give a shit what it is," he said. "You're staying, and you're going to make a good impression, understand? I didn't bring you here so you could hide behind a potted plant. Get out there."

He grabbed her arm and shoved her toward the middle of the room. She collided with a dancing couple and apologized while the couple scrutinized her disdainfully.

Gathering what little stores of dignity she had left, Mireille turned and walked toward the door.

"Get back here!" Mohl snarled. Several of the couples on the floor stopped dancing to stare at him.

Mireille never looked back as she swept away.

"Rather a boor," Adam Wells said, watching Mohl.

"Ummm." Oliver Jordan was not looking at the rude little man standing alone on the dance floor. He was watching Mireille. "Where's John Ford?"

Wells tore his eyes away from what he knew would be a juicy piece of tomorrow's gossip. "Ford? He's in Wyoming. He's started the location shooting on the Greg Peck Western."

"How much longer will he be there?"

"At least three more weeks," Wells said.

Jordan rubbed his immaculately shaved chin. "Have him replaced."

"Replaced?" He looked at Jordan as if he were insane. "When? Who with?"

"Immediately," Jordan said with his usual pleasant calm. "With Victor Mohl."

Wells took a deep breath. He was paid well for keeping Oliver Jordan's secrets. This, he knew, would be another one of them. His gaze strayed to the bank of French doors.

Outside, Mireille was standing, her cloak billowing behind her, looking like some illusory spirit. Jordan seemed to be transfixed by the sight of her.

Wells had met many of Jordan's women, but he had never seen his employer exhibit so much interest in any of them.

"The dress is a horror," Wells said. "But she's got a certain quality, I agree." He looked down at Jordan's crotch. A noticeable bulge was growing there. "Oliver, really," he sighed.

Jordan never answered. He watched Mireille until a taxi came and took her away. And then he continued to stare at the place where she had been, as if it had been touched by magic.

Chapter Thirty-Seven

That weekend Victor Mohl was assigned to take over the location shooting of the John Ford Western.

Although he would receive only second-unit credit and would not be able to participate in the editing of the film, he was thrilled to finally have an "in" with Continental Studios.

"No thanks to you," he said to Mireille while he was packing for his three-week stay in Wyoming. "See? I told you I was going to make it, even if you never had any faith in me." He shut his suitcase with a bang and marched toward the door. A cab was waiting outside.

"I'm very happy for you, Victor," Mireille said wearily.

"Sure you're happy, now that I've got a contract. The perfect little wife, aren't you?"

Mireille sighed. "Your taxi's waiting."

"Yeah, I'll bet you can't wait to get rid of me. Well, the feeling's mutual." He stormed past her, bumping her deliberately with the suitcase. "See that you're out of here before I get back."

A jolt swept through Mireille. "Out? But our agreement—"

"You should have thought of that before you walked out on me in front of half of Hollywood." He slammed the door behind him.

In the ensuing silence, she leaned against the door, surveying the room. *So even this will be taken away,* she thought.

Slowly, she wrapped a cloth around her head and began to clean the house. When she received her next paycheck, she would have enough money to move into a room in the city. With the added expense of rent to pay, it would take even longer to send for Stephanie.

Outside, some of the neighbors had put up Christmas decorations. She remembered another Christmas, in Paris, and the lit windows of the beautiful shops in the distance as she ran from the bony arms of the drunken clochard to have her baby in the snow.

That was always how things seemed to be. A while here, a while there, always one step ahead of the clochard in the park. In all these years, nothing had changed.

She felt the sting of tears. When the doorbell rang, she wiped her eyes quickly and walked over to answer it. It would be another of Victor's creditors, no doubt. They were the only people who visited them anymore.

Mireille opened the door and froze. Oliver Jordan was standing in front of her.

"May I come in?" he asked, his blue eyes crinkling in a smile.

She stood still for a moment, unable to move. Then, wordlessly, she shuffled back from the door. "Victor's already left," she mumbled.

"I know," he said. He took the kerchief off her head slowly and watched the long white hair swing free. "It's been a long time, Mireille." Jordan closed the door behind him. "L'Ange," he whispered.

She trembled. "You did recognize me, then."

"More easily than I would now."

Her face flushed with embarrassment. Her swollen eyes, her old clothes . . . She had come down a long way from the twenty-year-old who had gone to Sardinia with him.

He touched her face. "I've missed you so." For a moment his touch electrified her. It was Oliver, larger than life, Oliver who had made love to her on a rock by the sea . . .

"Please don't," she said, moving away from him.

"I've never stopped thinking about you."

"I'm married," she said.

He sighed, the mood broken. "Yes, I know. I've just put the weasel on my payroll."

She cocked her head. "Why, Oliver? Why did you do that?"

"So I could see you."

"For another eight days?" Her eyes flashed. "I'm afraid you've wasted your time, Mr. Jordan. I'm not for sale anymore."

He laughed. "Good. I didn't come to buy you." He leaned against the wall, smiling. "Whatever possessed you to marry him, anyway?"

"Nothing I'd care to discuss with you."

"Was it love, Mireille?" The corners of Jordan's mouth twisted cruelly. "Did your heart hammer in your perfect breast at first sight of that odious creature? Or was it the fellow's legendary charm?"

"That's none of your concern."

"Look at how you live!"

"And how do *you* live?" she snapped. "Still playing your little-boy games, I suppose. Surrounding yourself with whores you pretend are real people until you grow tired of them—"

"Ah, that's the spirit I hoped to see! Suburban life hasn't broken the Angel after all."

"There is no more Angel!"

"Marvelous. Even that dreary housewife disguise can't change you."

"What do you want, Oliver?"

"I've come to do business."

"I told you. I'm not in business anymore."

"My business, not yours. I make movies."

"And?"

"I saw you in *Lone Gun* yesterday. My assistant came across an English-language print. I didn't know you'd become an actress."

She laughed suddenly. "You saw that?"

"You were good, actually. The movie was abysmal, but you were quite enchanting."

She shrugged off the compliment with a subtle Gallic gesture.

"The point is, I'd like you to test for a role in a film I'm producing."

She eyed him levelly. "Is that the approach you use with your starlets?"

"I'm serious."

"Then you're crazy."

"That's a matter of opinion. Nevertheless, the screenplay was written about you, and I'd like to see how you test in it."

"Written . . . about me?" *About l'Ange?* The catch in her voice was audible.

"That's what the screenwriter says. A kid named Allerton. James Allerton. He met you at your wedding."

"James . . . Yes, I remember. How could he write a movie about me? How did he find out—?"

"Stop panicking. He doesn't know a thing. What he's come up with is a hearts-and-flowers wartime romance. It's a beautiful screenplay, titled *Field of Glory.* The heroine is a sort of latter-day Cinderella whose gypsy lover turns out to be a dashing Resistance fighter."

Mireille's hand went to her mouth.

"Is any of this ringing a bell? Allerton says he got it from you."

"I . . . Yes, perhaps," she said, composing herself. "But there are many actresses—"

"I don't need another actress," Jordan said. "I need someone to put magic onto the screen. The kind of magic you've always possessed." He leaned forward in his chair. "Mireille, you have a quality I've never seen in another woman. Allerton thinks it's a spell of some kind, something that makes men fall in love with you. He certainly did, and he only talked with you for twenty minutes. And

I know I did," he added. "I think that's the reason I left you the way I did."

"Because you couldn't bring yourself to love a whore?"

He smiled bitterly. "You were never the whore, Mireille. I was. I needed my wife's money."

"And now?"

He smiled ruefully. "Nothing's changed."

They were both silent. Mireille looked at him, at the handsome face just beginning to show the first signs of age, at the tamed wildness of his mouth, and understood. A lot of time had passed, much more than five chronological years.

"Anyway," he said, "it's a quality that can be exploited, if it transfers to the screen. I think it does, after seeing that Western of Mohl's." He grinned. "Let's find out, Mireille."

She smiled slowly. "My God, Oliver, you're serious."

"Then you'll test?"

She hesitated.

"Please, darling. For old times' sake."

"Old times," she repeated. "Not good times."

"But you'll do it," he said, willing her to agree.

She sighed. Then she shrugged, as if it were a matter of no importance. "Why not?" she answered. "I certainly don't have any other plans."

"Good. I'll make all the arrangements." He stood up. "Don't let anyone touch your face. If those makeup people get at you, they're going to make you into a copy of Lauren Bacall. Do your face yourself, and keep it light. The camera will pick up on everything."

She nodded silently and rose to let him out. "I suppose I should thank you, Oliver," she said at the door.

He reached for her hand, and she let him take it. "How could I have let you go?" he whispered.

They stood in silence for another moment before she stepped away from him. "It wasn't convenient for you," she said finally.

He winced. "Ouch."

"It's the truth."

"I suppose so," he said. "I did love you, though. The best I could."

She smiled sadly. "I know."

Outside, Jordan took a deep breath. He felt dizzy and disembodied, as if he were made of helium.

The question he had asked was still crashing around in his mind. *How could I have let her go?*

Confused and apprehensive, he wanted to both laugh and cry. By the time he reached his car, he decided that it was a marvelous sensation, the emotional equivalent of the moment just before orgasm. He hadn't felt this way since he was a child reaching his tentative, frightened hands toward a pair of budding breasts.

Angel. Only you could make me young again.

He drove to his office and called Adam Wells at home. "Get me a woman. Someone tall, with long blonde hair."

"What?" Wells answered with annoyance. "Now?"

"Platinum. Monroe's color. Long hair, not too much curl. Green eyes, if possible."

"Mr. Jordan, it's Saturday, and I happen to be on my way out."

"And a blonde bush."

"A blonde—"

"Bush," Jordan finished. "Within thirty minutes." He hung up and put his palm around the biggest boner he'd experienced in years, then laughed out loud.

Oliver Jordan was back in form.

Mireille's screen test for *Field of Glory* took place on December 15, 1955.

The director, Sam Hope, was a lean man with a long, serious nose and the eyes of a bird of prey, and Mireille knew instinctively that he was a man she could trust. Even though he hardly spoke to her, Mireille could feel him studying her the way a sculptor studies a piece of marble.

Peter Rockwell, who had been cast in the role of the Resistance fighter, arrived late. Swaggering and arrogant, his face gray from a late-night party, he made no attempt to conceal his resentment at being called in for an unknown actress's screen test. He would not have come at all if Oliver Jordan had not demanded his presence and assured the actor that he himself would be on set to watch him read through his lines with Mireille.

The scene was a two-shot in a wheat field between the young French heroine and her guerrilla fiancé. He was to bid her good-bye before making a dash across the field toward a bridge in the distance. During his run, Nazi soldiers would rise like monoliths out of the earth and shoot him down as the girl watched, calling his name in anguish.

"We'll only use the first part of the scene for the test," the director said. "Places, please."

Reluctantly, Rockwell moved next to Mireille on the bare set. "I've got a tennis date in half an hour," he growled. "Try not to fuck up."

The boy with the clapboard announcing the first take stood between her and the camera.

"Camera . . . Action!"

The boy skittered away, and Mireille was left facing the actor, who looked more like a hungover college student than a Resistance fighter.

"I don't want to go, Simone. I'm afraid. We're all afraid." Rockwell spoke in a monotone, his face registering pure boredom. But it was not the actor Mireille was seeing. Somehow, in a process even she could not understand, the bare soundstage vanished. In its place was a waving field of wheat, golden and fragrant as the lavender hills where she had lived with Stefan. And it was Stefan who was leaving, going away from her forever, knowing he would die, but too kind to warn her. Stefan, whose baby she carried in her womb; Stefan, who had held her and loved her, who would never come again.

The memorized words flowed out of her as if they were her own. They were the words she would have spoken if she had been able to see the future as clearly as the past. In this script, the name of the man she loved was different, but it was Stefan. It was always Stefan, only Stefan . . .

"Come back!" she called as Peter Rockwell lumbered away from her. "Come back!"

"Cut!" the director called.

Mireille never heard him. Stefan was leaving, walking into the darkness with his rifle, and in the morning the candle on the table would flicker and go out. "No!" she screamed, and she heard the fire from the soldiers' guns exploding outside her window. She clutched her hair as she imagined him falling, shot by the Nazis along with the other wounded, and she screamed again, her soul naked with grief. "Kill me too!" she raged at the invisible soldiers. "For God's sake, kill me too!"

As she sobbed, she began to realize where she was. The studio was dead silent. Peter Rockwell was staring at her with a look of disgust. The boy with the clapboard watched her with frank wonder. Sam Hope's face was expressionless.

In front of Mireille, the camera's red light shone, unblinking, as it continued to roll. After a moment, it went off.

"Sorry," the cameraman said.

The director never moved his eyes from Mireille. "Did you get all of it?" Hope asked.

"It's there," the cameraman answered.

Then, from out of nowhere, someone began to applaud. Others joined in. The sound echoed through the big studio.

Mireille had never heard applause for herself before. Was that what always happened at a screen test? Blushing, she looked over to the director.

Sam Hope said nothing. He lit a cigarette, still studying her with his knowing eyes. Then slowly, through a cloud of smoke, he turned to Oliver Jordan and nodded.

Chapter Thirty-Eight

Mireille's screen test was such a spectacular success that to show a print of it at one's home momentarily became the new measure of a person's inclusion in the Hollywood "in" circle. Not since Vivien Leigh's test for *Gone with the Wind*, Hedda Hopper wrote after an invitation to the first private screening of the test at Oliver Jordan's home, had an actress conveyed such magnetism on the screen.

Jordan had arranged for it all, of course. As soon as he heard the burst of spontaneous applause, he knew that Mireille's star quality worked as effectively in public as it had in bed. *Field of Glory* had everything it took for a major hit: a brilliant screenplay, an Oscar-winning director, America's most popular matinee idol, and a face that could seduce a million people at once.

Three days after the test, Adam Wells showed up at the Mohl house in Brentwood carrying a black Lanvin dress with matching hat and shoes.

"Mr. Jordan wants you to wear these," he said haughtily. "You're meeting him at the Polo Lounge at one o'clock."

Mireille bristled. "Who are you?"

"I'm Mr. Jordan's assistant," he said, pushing past her into the house. "Chop-chop. We've got to get you moved out of here, and there isn't much time." He clapped his hands impatiently.

"I'm afraid you've made a mistake," she said, bewildered. "I have to be at work soon."

"Work? He didn't tell me you worked. What do you do?"

"I'm a clerk at I. Magnin."

"A . . ." He burst out laughing. "Well, those days are over, honey. Where's your phone?"

"What do you plan to do?"

"Just get your personal things together, doll. I'll take care of it." He picked up the telephone and dialed the number of the store. "Please inform the personnel department that Mrs. Mohl . . ." He covered the mouthpiece. "Is that the name you're using, darling?"

"*Non*, just a moment!" Mireille said, rushing toward him.

"Mrs. Mohl will no longer be working for you." After he hung up, Wells cast around nosily, finally picking up an airmail envelope addressed to Mireille de Jouarre. "Pretty name," he said, waving the envelope. "You should have kept it."

"Give me that," Mireille said, snatching it out of his hand. "Is this some sort of joke?"

"Only in the broadest sense. Look, whatever plans Mr. Jordan has for you, you can bet your bazonkas they don't include clerking at Magnin's. I'll pack for you." He darted up the stairs.

"Pack . . ." Under her breath, she let out a little shriek of frustration. "Mr. . . ."

"Call me Adam," he said over his shoulder. At the top of the stairs, he paused. "Oh, I almost forgot." He took a long velvet box from a pocket of his sweater and tossed it to her. "Catch."

"What's this?"

"Mr. Jordan told me to give it to you." He disappeared into the bedroom.

Mireille looked at the box in her hand. It was green velvet, trimmed in silver. Slowly, she opened it. Inside was a three-strand diamond bracelet.

"Need help with the clasp?" Wells called out. He appeared at the top of the stairs with two of her blouses on hangers.

"What are you doing with my clothes?"

"Just my job, babes. This is all we can keep." He hoisted the blouses. "And your underthings, for the time being. I know what Oliver likes. Everything else has got to go."

"Please stop what you're doing at once," she said angrily.

Wells placed his hand on his hip. "Look, Fifi, my orders are to check you out of this dump. Now, are you going to get your expensive little butt moving, or am I going to have to punch you out?"

She sighed with exasperation. Things could be straightened out later, she supposed. There was no point in arguing with this maniac. "I'll come," she said. "Where does Mr. Jordan propose to take me?"

Wells smiled. He sauntered down the stairs and put his arm around her. "On the roller coaster ride of your life, baby doll."

Jordan was waiting for her at the bar of the Polo Lounge. He smiled with approval as she walked in, dressed in the clothes Adam had brought. "This is the Mireille I've been waiting for," he said. He gestured around the room. "So have they all, whether they know it or not."

"Oliver . . ." she began, trying to contain her anger. "That man you sent . . ."

"Shall we?" He gestured toward the maître d', who was gliding toward a table in the center of the room. It was a conspicuous table, and Mireille felt the eyes of everyone in the place on the two of them.

"Champagne," Jordan ordered. The maître d' nodded and snapped his fingers at the sommelier. When he had gone, Jordan took an envelope from his jacket.

"These are copies of your divorce papers."

"Victor divorced me?"

"In Mexico. It's all quite legal."

She looked through the Spanish carbon copies. "How is it you had these?"

"Well, I am his employer," he said. "And—"

"And you arranged it."

"Well, yes." He took in her air of irritation. "Damn it, I did you a favor and you know it. Mohl would get in your way. You can't have that albatross around your neck, not where you're going."

"And just where am I going, Oliver?" she said hotly. "Not home, certainly, since I no longer have a home."

"Patience, patience," he said, smiling. "I'll explain everything in time. By the way, where is the bracelet I sent over? It would have complemented the dress nicely."

She placed the velvet box in front of him. "Please take this back," she said. "I can't accept it."

He laughed. "How Victorian. Wishing to keep your reputation intact, no doubt."

"I don't want the bracelet," Mireille said.

"Nonsense. We're not in Paris anymore. Diamonds are a measure of status in Hollywood, nothing more." He took the bracelet out of the box, held it up for a moment to appreciate its shimmering beauty, then clasped it on her wrist.

A low murmur circulated around the room.

"Don't look up," Jordan said. "They're watching."

"Is this part of the show?" she seethed.

"Of course. Mireille—*my* Mireille—must have diamonds."

"*Your* Mireille?"

"Mine. The one I'm going to create. A woman made of stars and dreams, a creature out of a fairy tale. A princess, perhaps, from a castle in a faraway land . . ." He smiled. "Leave that to me. Ah. Here's something else for you."

He produced another sheaf of papers as the champagne arrived. "Your contract."

She looked up, her breath suspended.

"It's for five films. *Field of Glory* will only be the beginning."

"Oliver . . ."

"I lost you once. I won't make the same mistake again." His eyes swept her face. "Sign it, darling. Sign it here, where everyone can see you." He handed her a gold pen.

She accepted it reluctantly.

Jordan stared at her, annoyed. "Really, Mireille," he murmured. "Do you honestly believe you have anything to lose?"

As she signed the document, he raised his glass.

"Ah," he said, satisfied. "To Mireille."

"Which one? Yours or mine?"

"Mine, of course." He smiled. "You'll like her. She's going to give you everything you've ever wanted."

After lunch he drove her to Beverly Hills along the same route she and Mohl had taken to go to the party at Jordan's home.

"Are you taking me to your house?" she asked.

He shook his head. "Better than that." He pulled into a driveway that was obscured from the road by a flowering hedge. Beyond it was a white brick bungalow, small but lovely, with lattice windows and a gabled roof.

"Who lives here?" she asked as he helped her out of the car.

He opened the door. "You do," he said, handing her the key. "Welcome home, Mireille."

She could scarcely believe her eyes as she walked through the rooms. They were filled with furniture and appointed beautifully. In a corner of the living room was a Christmas tree, completely decorated with silver ornaments.

"Oliver! I don't understand . . ."

"It's yours," he said. "I bought it for you right after your screen test."

She looked around in wonder. "But I couldn't . . ."

"Consider it a loan," he said. "My Mireille can't live on the street, can she?" He squeezed her hand. "Come. There's one more thing I have to show you."

He led her past the master bedroom, done in peach peau-de-soie and mirrors, to a closed door at the end of the hall. "Where is your daughter?" he asked.

She looked down. "She's at a boarding school in Switzerland."

"Maybe she'd like to come home for the holidays." He swung open the door. The room inside was a girl's bedroom, all pink and ribboned, with stuffed animals on the bed and ruffled curtains.

"Oliver . . ." she whispered. "I don't know what to say, how to thank you."

He stroked her long hair absently. "Just don't forget who you are."

"Who . . ." She forced her eyes away from the beautiful room. "I don't understand."

He smiled in his sensual, ironic way. "In a few days, we're going to tell the press all about you. It will be tailored to an American audience, naturally, so it'll have nothing to do with the truth. America has never been very fond of that. But I don't want you to believe your own press."

She laughed. "That I'm a fairy princess?"

"That you're anything except l'Ange," he said.

She inhaled sharply. "I've told you. There is no more l'Ange."

"Yes, there is." He spoke very softly, close to her ear. "I saw her in your test. No matter how you try to bury her, she's there, behind your eyes. And the audience will see her, too. And they'll want her, the way I want her."

He kissed her mouth. The taste of him, the heat of his lips, sent a wave of passion through Mireille's body that made her feel ashamed. He had abandoned her, used her body like he'd wanted, and then left her to find her own way home. And yet his touch still made her wet between her legs. As memories of their lovemaking came roaring back like the sound of the sea where they'd first had one another, her body responded with throbbing urgency.

Her thin will broke. She opened her lips and took his probing tongue, feeling the sleek hardness of him against her, the pressure of his sex beneath his clothes.

Slowly, with practiced fingers, he unzipped the black dress until it fell to the floor like liquid. He smoothed his hands over the silk of her lingerie, made hot by her flushed skin, and lowered the straps of her brassiere until her full breasts spilled out. He played them with his tongue, tasting her sweetness, sucking them into his mouth while her legs trembled with need.

"Have me, Angel," he groaned. "Have me now." He stepped out of his trousers, his erection stiff and purple, and eased Mireille toward the wall. "Here," he said thickly. "I want to do you here."

He grasped one of her legs and pulled it behind his back as he pressed her against the wall. He felt the slick wetness between her legs and shuddered.

"Take it deep," he whispered as he entered her, smoothly, urgently.

She gasped.

"You've wanted it, too, haven't you?"

"Yes . . . Yes, I've wanted . . ." Then there were no more words.

Their bodies moved in a rhythm that beat faster and faster, his meat thrusting deep, the sounds of their breathing harsh and rasping as they writhed together.

Mireille wrapped one leg around his back to join the other, and they rocked, moaning, until the wild music inside her shrilled and screamed.

They sat in a heap on the floor afterward. Jordan ran a finger down Mireille's spine, making a runnel of her sweat.

Silently, she turned away and gathered her clothes together.

"Don't," Jordan said, holding her wrist. He took her face in his hands and kissed her. Even now her mouth opened slackly to take his tongue. "You're mine," he said. "My Angel."

"Your whore," she corrected, feeling small.

Jordan smiled like a big, hungry cat. "Don't forget it," he said.

Chapter Thirty-Nine

Adam Wells crossed his arms and looked at his watch.

It was nearly seven o'clock on Christmas Eve. The Continental Studios complex was deserted except for one security guard, Wells himself, and the two rutting fools in Jordan's office. From behind the closed door issued squeals of delight and an occasional baritone grunt.

"Disgusting," Wells muttered.

After a few minutes, a blonde starlet emerged, rumpled and giggling. It was Dallas Cole. Wells recognized her from the abysmal spaghetti Western he'd been obliged to watch several times while Jordan took his measure of Mireille.

"Oh," she said breathlessly. "What are you doing here?"

"I was just standing by in case Oliver fell in."

She turned up her nose and minced toward the door.

"Merry Christmas, Angel."

Dallas stopped in her tracks. "What did you call me?"

"Angel. That's what Oliver calls you, isn't it?"

Her red lips formed a practiced pout. "How did you know? Were you listening?"

"He calls all of you Angel. And I only listened when you screamed, 'Ball me, Daddy, I need a big one.'"

"Pervert," she said, slamming the office door behind her.

"Well, I could hardly help overhearing," Wells muttered. He walked over to Jordan's door and knocked. "Okay, the coast is clear."

Oliver Jordan was standing by the bar in his office, drinking a martini. His grin was wide and satisfied. "You're a good man, Adam," he said.

"Just call me Bob Cratchit," Wells said. "Do you suppose I can take Christmas Day off, or will m'lord be requiring a blonde in a Santa Claus suit?"

Jordan laughed. "I really ought to fire you."

"Hah! I'd like to see the job description you send to the employment agency for my replacement." Wells walked back out to his cubicle and put on his coat. "I used to do respectable work."

"And I used to pay you a respectable salary." Jordan sauntered over, holding out an envelope. Inside was a check. "Bonus."

Wells peeked at it. "Well, every man's got his price," he said. He put the envelope in his pocket and patted it. "And you've met mine. Thanks, Oliver."

Jordan set down his glass. "Did you get everything I asked for?"

"Right here." Wells picked up a stack of wrapped packages. "Party dresses, dolls, a game of Cootie . . . Here, you can carry this." He slapped an enormous stuffed panda into Jordan's arms. "Now, it's none of my business, but it seems to me that whoever you're seeing might be a tad young for you."

"You're right. It's none of your business. Where's the necklace?"

"In your pocket. I wrote out a card for Anne, too."

"Anne?"

Wells rolled his eyes. "Your wife."

"Oh." With a scowl, Jordan pocketed the card. "Anne and I don't usually exchange cards," he said.

Wells uttered a sound of dismay. "Don't tell me the necklace is for one of the blondes."

"I don't plan to tell you anything," Jordan said.

The door to Mireille's new home seemed to open all by itself. Raising his chin to see above the pile of parcels in his arms, Jordan saw nothing but the far wall of the vestibule.

"Hello?" he ventured tentatively, bending forward.

"Hello," a lilting voice with the trace of a French accent answered.

He saw the top of a child's head: long black tresses tied with a blue velvet ribbon. Slowly, the little girl lifted her face to reveal a pair of smoky-gray eyes fringed with thick black lashes. "You've come," she whispered almost reverently.

Then, without another word, she hurled herself at his legs, hanging on tenaciously as the packages tumbled out of his arms. Jordan gave a yelp as he lost his footing. He twisted and turned like a dervish before landing seat-first on the floor, his eyes on a level with the girl's.

"*Mon Dieu! Qu'est-ce qui s'est passé?*" Mireille shouted, running toward them.

"It's quite all right," Jordan said, bemused by the child's ardor. She was still holding onto his legs. "I believe I've just made the acquaintance of your daughter."

Stephanie looked adoringly at him. "I knew you would come, Saint George."

"Saint George? Stephanie, this is Mr. Jordan," Mireille said, helping him to his feet. "Oliver, I'm so sorry."

Jordan laughed. "Don't be. I've been called a lot of things, but never a saint." He picked up the giant stuffed bear and gave it to Stephanie. "This is for you, sweetheart."

Stephanie's face lit up with indescribable joy as she struggled to get her arms around the huge panda.

"Please come inside," Mireille said. "I'll make you a drink. I'm afraid you've missed dinner."

"No need. I can't stay long."

"But you have to," Stephanie cried. "You have to stay forever. It was part of the . . ."

"Part of what?" Mireille asked as she led Jordan toward a sofa. She forgot the question almost as soon as she asked it, but when she saw Stephanie's flushed face, she frowned and knelt beside her. "Part of what?" she repeated.

"The wish," Stephanie said, so quietly that Mireille had to lean over to hear her. "The first year I was at school, I saw his face on Nora's magazine wall. I thought he was Saint George, the Red Cross Knight, and I wished for him."

Mireille stared at her in bewilderment.

"And he came to us," Stephanie finished.

"Maybe you'd better open some of these presents," Jordan said, interrupting their tête-à-tête. "Saint George has waited a long time to give them to you."

"Oh, yes," Stephanie answered breathlessly. She tore open the wrapping paper, shrieking gleefully as Jordan teased and flattered her. Afterward, when Mireille put her to bed, Stephanie insisted that Jordan tuck her in.

"She's already in love with you," Mireille said after Stephanie was asleep.

Jordan smiled. "And I'm in love with her mother." He gave her the velvet box. "Merry Christmas, darling." Sixty-five diamonds twinkled out of the slim golden filigree necklace. "They match the bracelet."

She looked at him for a moment, then shook her head.

"No, Oliver." She snapped the box closed and handed it back to him, then stood up and walked to the fireplace where the bracelet lay, still in its box. "Take this back, too."

"Why?" Jordan asked, hurt.

"Because we have no future."

"How can you say that? We're going to be making five films together."

She shook her head again.

"Oh, that sort of future," Jordan said with dismay. Shades of all the grasping coeds who had tried to strong-arm him into marriage filled Jordan's mind. "Don't be silly, Mireille."

"You have a wife."

"I have an arrangement!" Jordan shouted. Suddenly, he laughed. "Am I to understand you've never slept with a married man before?"

"You know I'm not proud of my past."

"Then live in the present, for God's sake," he said angrily. "Or is this some kind of tart's ploy to get me to leave Anne and marry you?"

"I don't want you to leave your wife. And I don't want to marry you. Things shouldn't go on between us. It's not right. It's too . . . too strong . . ."

He swept her up in his arms. "It's bad sex, you mean? Bad, dirty, what-would-Mama-think sex?" He laughed, a low, gravelly sound. "That's what makes the Angel so good."

He kissed her, languidly, teasing. "Don't be ashamed of your past, not with me. Because it's what you are. A soiled, corrupt thing, Mireille. Just like me." He thrust his tongue deep into her mouth. "And this is what you want."

He led her into the master bedroom and flopped down on the bed. All four walls were paneled with thin strips of mirror. "Now undress for me," Jordan said, propping himself up on a pillow. He tossed the diamond necklace to her. "And wear that."

Mireille put on the necklace. Then slowly she took off her clothes.

"Suck me off," he said.

Obediently, she knelt between his legs, feeling like a whore, Jordan's whore. But God help her, despite her shame, she still moaned when she took his cock in her mouth.

Anne Rutledge Jordan was reading a magazine when her husband walked in. A snifter of brandy was on the onyx end table beside her. She tossed down its contents and turned to him, glassy-eyed.

"You're home early, Oliver," she said. "Should I be flattered, or is Christmas Eve just a slow day on the casting couch?"

"You're drunk."

"Shhh. The servants will hear." She aimed her empty glass toward the end table and missed. "They hear so much."

He sighed. "Is there something you'd like to say to me, Anne, or are you just goading me out of habit?"

She set her hand over the arm of the sofa and rested her head on it. "Just happy to see you," she said. "I miss you sometimes."

Jordan felt a twinge of annoyance. In twenty-four years, he had hardly given his wife a thought, and he liked it that way. Anne had been easy to live with, her casual cynicism lending tacit approval to his wandering ways. She had fulfilled her part of their marital bargain, as he had his. It was, as he had told Mireille, an arrangement. A trade. His freedom for her fortune; her pride for his name.

The arrangement was clean, well balanced, and fair, as long as neither thought about it too much. But Anne was breaking the rules now. Her face showed every one of her fifty-three years, and there was a wronged-wife look in her gimlet eyes that set Jordan's teeth on edge.

"I miss you, too, Annie girl," he said, putting on his most expansive smile. "It's been busy."

"I saw the screen test for that French actress."

Jordan felt the hair prickle on the back of his neck.

"There was a lunch at Pamela Rockwell's—Peter's ex-wife. Most of the women there were divorced. Movie divorcées."

"How charming," Jordan said. "What did she serve, bitter herbs? Or sour grapes?"

Anne smiled. "Salmon, I think. In curry. She has a Thai cook." She doodled on the carpet with her toe. "Everyone howled at the girl's theatrics in the test. What's her name? Mirabelle?"

Jordan didn't answer.

"That was for my benefit. The laughter. A show of support from a roomful of aging, overdressed ex-wives." She put her hand over her eyes. "It was a mistake for me to go."

"Now, Anne," Jordan said in his most conciliatory voice, "this is completely unnecessary. I am not involved in any way with that woman."

She laughed, her eyes still covered. "How you can lie!" She pushed herself off the sofa and fixed another drink. "You were always such a good dissembler, Oliver. I suppose that's one of the things I used to like about you. I never had to face the truth, as long as you could come up with a good enough lie. And you always could."

She drained her glass. "They say that even the women you cheat on her with look like her. 'Oliver's Obsession' is how the ladies refer to your little romance. Isn't that quaint? My Oliver, who was never obsessed with anything besides himself. Certainly not with me."

Jordan sniffed disdainfully. "Forgive me, darling, but you've never given the impression of requiring a faithful husband. Only a presentable one."

"Oh, yes, I did give you permission to philander, didn't I?" She smiled. "That's been the whole basis of our marriage, in fact. Ever wonder about that? Ever wonder why I consented to your count- less betrayals, the constant humiliation?"

"Well, what you said was—"

"Because you wouldn't have married me otherwise!" She sat down and folded her hands in her lap. "Even for my money," she added.

Jordan shifted uneasily on his feet. "You should be above this sort of thing," he said.

"Ah, yes. I almost forgot. Rich girls don't make noise. Even when they're dying."

"Please. You're becoming melodramatic." He poured himself a glass of gin. "Go to bed, Anne. You'll feel better in the morning."

She looked up at him. "Like an idiot, I thought that if I waited long enough, you would come to love me." Suddenly, tears coursed down her haggard cheeks. "But you can't. Of course you can't. And I've waited so damned long."

Jordan knelt beside her. "Anne . . . Annie girl . . ."

"Oh, don't bother being solicitous. I'm sure it's too much of an effort this time of night. Besides, it wouldn't change anything." She dried her face with a tissue. "At least I know you're as unfaithful to her as you are to me."

She started to cry again, then pounded on her knee with a fist and brought herself under control. "Why is that, Oliver? Why do you have to fuck over everyone who cares for you?"

"That's really rather base."

She barked out a short laugh and stood up. "Well, we can't have that, can we?" She headed unsteadily toward the stairs.

"Wait. Anne." Jordan remembered the card Wells had bought. He took it out of his pocket and gave it to her.

"Merry Christmas," he said.

Anne opened it and read it. "Signed by Adam Wells in your absence. How thoughtful."

She dropped the card onto the carpet. On her way upstairs, she made a point of stepping on it.

Chapter Forty

"She was divine even then," the Comte de Vevray recounted wistfully.

Louella Parsons swiveled her head toward the entryway in the Jordans' immense salon, looking to see if Mireille had entered yet. The photographer for the *Los Angeles Times* took a photograph of the diminutive Count, who looked like Marcel Proust with his effete airs and continental clothes. Jack Moffitt of the *Hollywood Reporter* sipped his bourbon and smiled. The Frenchman was a weirdo, but he made good copy.

"At fifteen, Mireille was the best horsewoman in Champagne. Lovely, charming, witty . . . Ah." Vevray's eyes twinkled behind his quaint glasses as he pretended to remember.

"After her coming-out party, three young suitors committed suicide." He shook his head sadly. "She was too beautiful, you see. But Mireille never wanted to marry. She wished only to care for her beloved grandmother at the ancient family villa in the Pyrenees."

Jim Allerton nearly choked on his drink across the room. "Isn't he laying it on a little thick?"

"They're buying it," Jordan said. "The public needs Mireille." He smiled. "So I've manufactured her."

"How much of her?" Allerton asked. "I mean, is she some hat-check girl from the Bronx? Is none of it real?"

Jordan set his ice-blue gaze on the writer. "Why, I do believe you *want* her to be real."

Allerton made a dismissive gesture he did not feel. "I guess I'd like for there to be some actual magic in the world," he said.

Jordan laughed. "And you've come to Hollywood to look for it?"

At that moment Mireille entered the room on the arm of Peter Rockwell, and the reporters scrambled toward her, flashbulbs popping. Jordan went forward to introduce his protégée to the press.

From across the room, the Comte de Vevray winked at Allerton and popped a chocolate into his mouth before sauntering over beside him.

"The legend begins," he said, sliding off his pince-nez.

Allerton looked over to Mireille, dazzling in a pale-pink Charles James dress studded with pearls. She was a unicorn, he thought, a creature from an enchanted realm come to drink from Oliver Jordan's golden waters. For a mad instant, he wanted to scream at her, tell her to go home to whatever secret place she'd come from, pull her away from the sorcerer and his sycophants before they painted her with their cheap glitter and attached ungainly artificial wings to her perfect body.

But the moment passed. This was Hollywood, after all. It was no place to look for real magic.

"To the legend," he said, raising his glass in a quiet toast with the Frenchman.

HOLLYWOOD PRINCESS

LOS ANGELES (AP) — Mireille, the stunning Hollywood new-comer everyone's talking about is, it seems, a lady with a past. And what a past!

Her full name is Baroness Mireille Orlande de Jouarre. Yes, a baroness, complete with a chateau on the Rhone, family jewels, etc., according to close family friend Anatole Jean-Claude de Balfours, 53rd Comte de Vevray. The Count, currently visiting Los Angeles as

a houseguest of Continental Studio head Oliver Jordan and his wife,
socialite Anne Rutledge Jordan, described his childhood with the
magnificent Mireille during an informal tea in the Jordans' palatial
home in Holmby Hills . . .

"That dreadful little man," Anne Jordan said, smoothing out the newspaper with white-gloved hands. There was a picture of Mireille beside the article. "He hasn't awakened before two in the afternoon since he got here."

"The Count's a good friend, Anne. An old friend."

"And bosom buddies, apparently, with your French starlet."

"That's just show business," Jordan said, rising. "Now, if you'll excuse me, dear . . ."

"What does she have?" Anne asked quietly.

"I beg your pardon?"

She looked up, smiling. "Who is she, really?"

"I haven't the faintest idea. A real baroness, for all I know."

"Come now, Oliver. You don't need to keep secrets from me. You must know all about her. After the great lengths you've gone to with her publicity . . ." She heard the edge in her voice but couldn't stop. "Even Louis B. Mayer wouldn't hold a press party in his own home for an unknown actress in a movie that hasn't even begun filming."

"That was perfectly appropriate, under the circumstances. I couldn't very well drag the Count to a press conference in some hotel, Anne. It had to be done informally, in a casual setting."

"In my home," she said, her voice raw. "In my home, in front of me."

Jordan gripped the table edge to control his anger. "You seem to forget, darling, that *Field of Glory* will cost more to produce than any film in the past five years. If the public isn't in love with Mireille before it's released, we're going to end up with a very expensive bomb on our hands." He tried a smile.

She tried to return one. "*Your* hands, Oliver," she said tightly. "My money is guaranteed. That's something you seem to have forgotten."

"You mean the terms of our marriage? No, I never forget those." His knuckles were white. "See that you don't, either. *Darling.*"

After he left, Anne looked at her gloves. They were black with newsprint. While she had been speaking with her husband, she had unconsciously tried to rub Mireille's picture off the page. But it was still there.

She folded the paper, removed her gloves, and made herself a drink.

Mireille felt a small shiver of fear as she looked at the picture of herself in the *Los Angeles Times*.

The last time her image had appeared on a printed page was when she had been arrested for assaulting a newspaper reporter. True, Oliver had guaranteed that her past would never resurface again, but a lifetime of hiding had conditioned her to balk at the sight of her uncovered face.

"Maman, that's you," Stephanie said, pointing to the photograph. "What did you do?"

"Well . . ." She thought about it. "Nothing," she said finally.

It was true, she realized. She had done nothing, said nothing, accomplished nothing to become a celebrity. All of her fame was based on pure fiction, thought up by Oliver Jordan.

My Mireille, he was fond of saying. *His* Mireille, the baroness from the Pyrenees. It was *his* Mireille the reporters were after, not the one who had scandalized Paris. That Mireille had disappeared with the name l'Ange, long ago in a faraway place.

"Absolutely nothing." She hugged her daughter.

"What a funny place this is," Stephanie said. "Is Saint George's picture in the paper?"

"His name is Oliver Jordan, Stephanie. And he is a movie producer, not a knight."

"Are you going to marry him?"

"I am not. He is already married."

The little girl's face fell. "He can't be. It's not part of the wish. You have to marry him."

"Why, darling?" Mireille knelt down. "Why is that important?"

"So that . . . so that . . ." *So that I can stay with you,* she wanted to say. But instead she smiled and shook her head. "Can't tell," she said. "It would break the wish."

The doorbell rang. Without waiting for someone to answer, Adam Wells stepped inside. "Anybody home?" he called. He was wearing a long woolly sweater and a muffler wrapped around his neck. "Sorry to barge in, but it's freezing out there."

"You must not be very strong," Stephanie said.

"Stephanie, please," Mireille chided, glaring at Adam.

"At school, we call this warm," Stephanie said.

"Then you won't have any trouble readjusting," Wells snapped. He handed an envelope to Mireille.

"That's the return portion of her ticket."

Mireille blinked. "What?"

"*Field of Glory* starts shooting next week, dollface."

"That has nothing to do with—"

"Oh, yes, it does. Mr. Jordan's got a busy schedule for you, and lots of publicity. If you're going to play movie star, you can't have a kid hanging around your neck. Especially not . . ." He turned to look at Stephanie. "Well, you know."

"No, I don't know," Mireille said hotly.

"Look. All I know is that you've got to be single, sexy, and ready to work by next week. No kids, okay?"

"I won't do it," she said, amazed by the man's effrontery.

"Ah-ah-ah. That's what contracts are for, sunshine. Besides which, you owe Continental Studios a bundle for clothes, rental limos, a diamond bracelet—"

"That was returned!"

"Not to mention this house."

"What?"

"Pay it off and you can get out of the contract. Problem solved. Go back to Magnin's."

"I'm calling Oliver Jordan."

"You do that, hon."

"Get out of my house."

"Nice to see you again, too," he said, and whistled his way out the door.

Immediately, Mireille called Jordan. "There must be some mistake," she said, trying to keep calm. "My daughter—"

"She's better off in Switzerland," Jordan said.

"Better off? How can you say that? Everything I've done for the past year has been to get her back!"

"Mireille," he said in a soothing voice. "Think for a moment. What kind of life can you give her, with the hours you'll be working? Do you really want Stephanie to stay alone with a nanny all day and all night? At school, she'll have friends, a regular routine, all the things children need. It's better, darling."

"But that man . . . Adam Wells . . ."

"Whatever he said, it was probably pure theater."

"Then it isn't true? That I owe you for the house?"

"Not me."

She hesitated. There was something about his answer that alarmed her. "The studio, then?" she ventured.

Jordan waffled. "It's only true on paper. For bookkeeping purposes."

"I never signed anything."

"You signed a contract," he said. "It was in there." For a moment his words seemed to ring in her ears. "Mireille—"

"You bastard."

"Mireille, listen to me—"

She hung up.

Stephanie was standing against the wall. "It was my fault, Maman," she said quietly. "I threw the stone horse away." Her eyes welled with tears. "The wish was no good."

Chapter Forty-One

Continental Studios produced no other film during the making of *Field of Glory*, and the schedule proceeded at a furious pace. Oliver Jordan worked Mireille relentlessly, from six in the morning until ten at night, making sure that every moment she didn't spend in front of the camera was devoted to the studio publicity machine. On the set, she was permitted to see no one except Jordan himself, who bullied her like a belligerent father, and an "assistant" he hired for her, a burly, taciturn giant named Leo who served as Mireille's bodyguard, chauffeur, and chaperone.

Jordan did not attempt to bridge the rift between himself and his embryonic star. Mireille was angry, both with him and with herself, and Jordan wanted to keep her that way. Her anger lit her eyes like green fire, and the camera captured it. Once, while watching the dailies, Jordan had found himself in a state near orgasm simply by looking at an extended close-up of her face. He was embarrassed when the lights came on, until he saw the faces of the other men in the room. Even Sam Hope sat mesmerized.

"Remember 'it'?" the director asked languidly. "That indefinable quality some people have that makes the rest of us turn to Jell-O?"

Jordan nodded and looked to the blank screen. "She's got it."

"You bet your balls."

By March, *Field of Glory* was half-shot and under budget.

By April, Mireille was being touted as the new Garbo, and Oliver Jordan as the genius behind the biggest movie of the year.

By May, everyone of note on the West Coast was looking at Continental as the harbinger of a new era in filmmaking.

One man, one movie, eliminating the deadwood of the big-studio apparatus. It was the only way the film industry would ever be able to recoup the loss of its audience to television. Darryl Zanuck had known that on some instinctual level when he'd left the country to produce independents in Europe, but even he had not been able to turn things around with the behemoth American studios. Only a maverick like Jordan, who had always been an independent, could have found a way to make money at a time when MGM and 20th Century Fox and Paramount were turning their executives white-haired with worry.

"And it was an accident," Jordan declared at a dinner party. "I'd never intended to become a pioneer of American filmmaking, or whatever they're calling me."

"No," Anne said dryly, hefting a Lalique glass filled to the brim with bourbon. "Oliver only intended to sleep with the leading lady."

A deathly silence fell over the room. Jordan scowled into his soup. The other diners, fortunately, were not involved in the movie business. Mostly they were Anne's socialite crowd, gone momentarily bohemian in deference to their hostess's new passion, which was postmodernism.

The dining room, once furnished in authentic Louis XV antiques, was now starkly bare except for a black lacquer floor, a massive slab of white marble that served as a table, some uncomfortable chairs composed of spindly pieces of chrome, and four walls covered with abstract expressionist paintings.

The guest of honor, a Romanian artist possessing both the table manners and aroma of a goat, was the only one to appreciate his patroness's humor. "Aaarg!" he roared, slapping Anne's skeletal back. "Is good! Is America, is Hollywood! Everybody make love, eh?"

He shook Anne's chair until her very bones seemed to rattle. "To freedom!" he said, and took a deep, emotion-filled breath. "Is wonderful."

He raised his glass of vodka with one hand. With the other—and Jordan couldn't be sure of it, stationed as he was at the far end of the marble slab—the hairy Romanian appeared to grab Anne's thigh.

She gave a little shriek and jerked upward in her chair. The guests to the immediate left and right of Anne and her artist pointedly averted their faces.

Jordan grinned. "Well, well." So his wife hadn't been the long-suffering victim he'd imagined. In that moment, he was able to cast away the last frail shred of guilt about his extramarital indulgences.

Beet-faced, Anne tinkled a little silver bell to summon the maid.

Jordan raised his glass. "To freedom," he repeated, smiling.

After Anne's unspoken confession at the dinner table, Oliver felt like a new man. Not that he'd ever considered being faithful to his wife; but now, knowing that Anne was spending her days frolicking in bed with a Romanian and a wineskin, he went about his sexual hobby with renewed vigor.

At Continental Studios, the half hour between four thirty and five p.m. was set aside as sacred. Jordan took no calls, scheduled no appointments, and did no work during the sanctified thirty minutes of every working day. That time was reserved for leggy blondes with long hair and green eyes. An endless parade of them went through Jordan's mahogany doors: starlets, shopgirls, housewives, hookers. The incestuous bisexual twin prostitutes of days gone by were brought back, albeit with wigs and peroxided pubic hair. Ditto the actress who had once specialized in playing Jordan's gray-haired grandmother. Now she called herself Angel and spoke with a French accent so convincing that Jordan signed her to play a small part in a forthcoming movie.

And there were happy accidents, too. Once, when the adolescent shampoo girl at his hairstylist's leaned over him at the sink, he felt a vague stirring in his loins as she creamed conditioner onto his head.

The sensation came as a shock to him, since she was not a beauty. She was plump as a pumpkin, and had crooked teeth. Her fingernails were short. She appeared to have no eyebrows. And during the course of an inane monologue, she confided that dressing hair was her destiny.

"My mother's a beautician. My aunt's a beautician," she said proudly. "I guess it must be in my blood."

Nevertheless, she was blonde and green-eyed, and the vague, hot scent of clean sweat in her armpits combined with the jiggle of her soft, oversized breasts temporarily caused Jordan to lose all control of himself.

She has pink nipples, he thought wildly. *I know it. Pink and big as saucers, with a little jujube on the end that puckers when her panties get wet.*

Unthinking, he opened his mouth while she lathered his head. He sucked in the tip of the breast, pencil-tip bra and all.

Immediately, he opened his mouth with a great sense of mortification, waiting for the inevitable scream. The shampoo girl just smiled. And he smiled back.

The next day at 4:50, he'd had his fill of the big pink nipples— he'd been right—and the bouncy round hips and the wet pussy that rode him like a jackhammer.

"Angel," he breathed.

"Am I crushing your balls or something?" she inquired politely, never missing a beat.

Adam Wells stared at the young hairdresser-in-training as she left the office. "What in hell were you doing with her?" he whispered harshly to his boss.

"What do you think?" Jordan said testily.

"She can't be sixteen years old. Are you crazy?"

"Oh, I don't think she's—"

"And a dog. Thighs like steel girders. She's even worse than the Amazon you crashed into on Santa Monica Boulevard."

"The—oh, yes." He smiled, remembering. He and the big blonde on the freeway had exchanged insurance cards, then retired to his dented Jaguar, where they remained, four-way flashers blinking, for twenty minutes of ecstasy before a state trooper pulled up to assist.

"Really, Oliver, you haven't just lost your mind. Your taste has gone down the toilet, too."

Jordan laughed. "Get me a driver. I want to go to the location shooting."

"Oliver, this is a mental thing, I tell you. It's sick. They all look alike." He stole another glance at the door. "Well, more or less. Actually, they're getting uglier and uglier."

"Make me a martini for the road."

"If Mireille's the one you want, why don't you just go after her?"

"Shut up, Adam," he said. "I've already had her." He thought for a moment. "I suppose I don't want her to have me," he added.

Wells walked over to the bar. "And they call me queer," he muttered. He opened a bottle of gin. "Anyway, everybody knows what goes on here."

"So?"

"So they're all doing it, too. The whole studio's like Pavlov's laboratory. The clock strikes four thirty, and everybody gets a hard-on."

"The driver, Adam."

"All right. I heard you." He picked up the telephone, stirring the martini at the same time. "Sick," he said.

Mireille was resting in her trailer when Jordan arrived at the location shooting in the foothills of the San Gabriel Mountains. Her chauffeur was standing guard at the door.

"Any problems, Leo?" Jordan asked the silent giant.

"No, sir."

Jordan nodded and went into the trailer without knocking.

Mireille was going over her lines at a small Formica-topped table. She looked up with a start.

"Surprised to see me?"

Mireille went back to her script. "Not at all. No one else is allowed to come in here. You arranged that yourself."

"For your own good. You shouldn't be disturbed while you're working."

"Is that why I have a twelve-hour bodyguard?"

"Really, Mireille, Leo is for your convenience."

"And I'm for yours."

Jordan smiled. "You're beautiful when you're angry."

She flushed. "I'm quite busy, Oliver."

"You'll have plenty of time for the movie. Come sit over here." He sat down on the small sofa in the trailer and patted the spot beside him.

Setting down the script with barely concealed annoyance, she obeyed.

"Have you missed me, Angel?"

"I miss my daughter."

He laughed. "Ah, yes. The good mommy. That's all sweet Mireille ever wanted to be, wasn't it? With a clerking job at Magnin's and a child in rags. Poor but happy."

"What do you want?"

He stretched his arms along the top of the seat. "I've come to invite you to a party."

"No, thank you. I've heard about your parties."

"Oh?"

"Even Leo can't protect me from everything. I know about the women."

"And you're jealous?"

"No. I never loved you."

"Yes, you did. And you still do." He rucked up her skirt and slid a finger into her slit. "You're already wet for me." He forced her hand around his erection. "And I'm hard for you."

She looked away.

"I'm going to need to fuck you," he said as he unzipped his trousers.

She struggled to stand up. "I'm expected outside."

"Not with me here." He spun her around, holding her wrists behind her back.

"You're hurting me."

Slowly, he pulled her to the floor. "I've got to have you, Angel. It's been too long."

"I don't want you."

"Liar." He spread her legs and tongued the swollen button of flesh above her opening.

"No," she moaned. "Not like this."

"Just like this," he said, and sucked her until she cried out, bucking her hips.

"Now take the cock," he whispered as he thrust inside her, listening to her groan as he galloped her, spreading her legs even wider. "Look at you," he breathed into her ear. "Fucking like a wild thing."

"No . . . no . . ." she whimpered. "I don't want to . . . to be like this . . ."

"But this is exactly what I want," he said, shooting his load into her.

When it was over, he kissed her face. It was wet with tears. "Please, Mireille," he said with more than a touch of impatience. "Stop pretending some sort of injured innocence. We both know what you are." He got dressed and combed his hair. "Now dry your face and get ready for the cameras."

Still lying on the floor, Mireille felt tears crawling from the corners of her eyes into her hair. There was no use in protesting. In the end, Jordan would always have her, any way he wanted. And she would always be Angel, waiting for him with her legs open.

When Jordan left, Sam Hope nodded to Jordan, a wry recognition of his accomplishment. Peter Rockwell slid his gaze in the direction of Mireille's trailer and formed an "o" between his index finger and his thumb. A blonde bit player with big breasts smiled.

"I've always wanted to meet you, Mr. Jordan," she said.

"Really?" He touched her hair. "I'm free at four thirty tomorrow."

Chapter Forty-Two

Like his workaday frolics, Jordan's parties also took on a different aspect.

The Jordans still held their famous soirees, but insiders knew that the real parties didn't begin until Anne—by now constantly accompanied by one starving artist or another—retired for the evening. Then, one by one, the guests who had left at ten because of "heavy shooting schedules in the morning" slipped back into the guesthouse, where a score of women, including at least three striking, long-limbed blondes, sat waiting.

The themes of the "cottage parties," as these late-night celebrations in the guesthouse were called, were always different. It was where Adam Wells's master touch showed. Thanks to Continental's props and costumes, the cottage was transformed into an Arabian harem, complete with belly dancers and couscous, or a replica of the court of Louis XIV, with dazzling prostitutes posed decorously in satin gowns and powdered wigs.

Shortly after their inception, the cottage parties dictated a new level of sophistication on the social scene. It was no longer enough to be invited to Jordan's home. Now, the true measure of a celebrity's worth was to attend the midnight bashes at the cottage, where members of the press were never invited and movie stars were often seen cavorting in a fantasy of nudity and various stages of drunken oblivion.

"Good heavens, isn't that Peter Rockwell?" the Comte de Vevray asked, perching his pince-nez on the end of his nose. It was a comical gesture, since all he was wearing at the time was a necklace of daffodils to go with the evening's Garden of Eden motif. Peter Rockwell was not even wearing that much, having degenerated during an orgy of sloe gin fizzes. The movie star sat hip-deep in a vat of water lilies while one starlet straddled his face and another gyrated on his lap.

"He does the gender proud, wouldn't you say?" said Jordan.

"Mmm." The Count lay back on his cushions beside Jordan. Two women knelt astride them, undulating with exquisite languor. "Mercy, Oliver, why didn't you invite me earlier?"

"Couldn't reach you," Jordan mumbled, crossing his arms behind his head. "That's fine, dear," he told the blonde who was sliding up and down on him with quick, bouncy strokes.

The Count frowned momentarily, then brightened. "Oh, yes. I was touring. I got married, in fact."

"Really?"

"Her name was Raynu. A Sikh. I met her in Kashmir. Lovely."

"*Was?*"

"Her parents objected. A whole squadron of turbaned swords-men came to fetch her in Morocco. Seems she was betrothed to someone else. I suppose they burned her at the stake or some-thing," he said thoughtfully. "Pity, really. She was only fourteen."

"You're a swine," Jordan said, moving his hips and grunting.

Vevray laughed. "And you're a pillar of rectitude, I suppose. I say, I believe you've outdone even Madame Renée in her heyday with this. You know she's in jail again, poor dear."

Jordan made a sympathetic sound.

"It's too bad those days are gone," the Count sighed.

"I remember there used to be a girl—the most stunning red-head in the entire world, Oliver—who sat on a velvet swing in a room filled with rose petals." He closed his eyes in appreciation. "Buttocks like pure alabaster. Oh, yes."

He tweaked the nipples of the woman ministering to him. "Say, here's an idea," he said engagingly. "Oliver, do you think we could come together?"

"Angel . . . Oh, Angel," Jordan sighed, pumping rhythmically.

"Won't you, as an old friend? There's so little that's new."

Oliver shivered and sucked air through his teeth.

"Damn," the Count said.

"Sorry." With great reluctance Jordan sat up and tapped each girl on the shoulder. "Thank you very much," he said, waving them away.

"I beg your pardon!" Vevray sputtered indignantly. As he frantically called back his fleeing partner, Jordan rose, stretched, and slipped on a satin robe embroidered with gold thread that had been used in an epic about the life of Moses.

"Mr. Jordan," a bass voice rumbled from the foyer. It was Mireille's chauffeur, red-faced, shifting from one foot to the other as Jordan strode, barefoot, toward him.

"What the devil do you want?" he asked irritably.

"Someone brought this to my house, sir." He produced a fine deckle-edged envelope with the words "Oliver Jordan—Urgent" typed on it. "I thought I'd better get it to you."

"Who brought it?"

"Don't know, sir. My bell was ringing like crazy, so I jumped out of bed and ran to the door. But nobody was there. Just that, lying on the mat."

"Oh, Christ. It's probably some crazed actor." He tore it open and read.

I'll come to the cottage at one o'clock. Can you meet me alone?
M.

Jordan stared at it stupidly for a moment, feeling his pulse race.

"Anything I can do, Mr. Jordan?" the chauffeur asked. The man was a beefy ex-marine, who, Jordan knew, wouldn't mind lending a little muscle if that was called for.

"No, Leo, thank you," Jordan said, tapping the note against his palm. "It's from a friend. What time is it?"

"About a quarter to one, sir."

A naked woman darted across the doorway behind Jordan.

Leo cast his eyes toward the floor.

"Er . . . good work," Jordan said. "That will be all."

"Yes, sir," the big man said.

Alone, Jordan read the message again. He could scarcely believe it. Grinning, he walked back into the party and told some of the hired prostitutes that as soon as the guests were gone, they could collect their pay and go home.

There was a mad scramble as a half dozen of Hollywood's elite were given the bum's rush by the professional ladies.

Peter Rockwell had to be rolled to the front door, where his chauffeur was called to carry him back to his car. Then the girls were paid in cash. Smiling, each with a kiss for Oliver, they also left.

The Comte de Vevray sat on his pillow, twirling his garland with a look of disgust on his face. "I'm afraid your charms as a host leave something to be desired, Oliver," he said.

Jordan dumped the Count's clothing on his lap. "Something's come up."

"Yes, and gone down again." He sighed at the mass exodus. "You should have told me you were looking for a speed record."

Jordan laughed. "I'm sorry, Anatole. I promise to find you someone wonderful tomorrow."

"*Merde.* By tomorrow I will be dead of the blue balls. Call back the women."

"I can't." He leaned forward. "Mireille's coming."

The Count raised an eyebrow. "Ah? Then perhaps I should stay. The two of us . . ."

"Forget it," Jordan snapped. "Not with her."

Vevray turned down the corners of his mouth exaggeratedly, hunched a shoulder, and raised a palm. "What is this? She's not really a baroness, you know."

"I want her alone."

The Count gave a delicate snort. "Decidedly unsporting, I'd say."

Jordan got up and fixed himself a drink. His hand trembled slightly. He felt giddy. Proud Mireille, who always pretended to spurn his advances, was coming to him, sniffing like a bitch in heat.

And he would make her visit worthwhile, he thought as he turned off the already dim lights in the cottage, replacing them with the glow from a few candles.

Oh, yes.

The front door closed with a soft click. Jordan snapped his head in the direction of the figure dressed in a gossamer-hooded burnoose.

Slowly, he walked toward her, his arms outstretched. She melted into them. As she raised her face to kiss him, the iridescent hood fell away.

Jordan let out a small quavering sound. "Anne," he said.

His wife's eyes flickered with pain for an instant. "You love her, don't you?" she said.

"Oh, Jesus God."

She untied a silk cord around her waist, and the robe she wore fell open to reveal a desiccated, aging body.

"Make love to me, Oliver," she said, her voice cracking with humiliation. "Make love to me the way you make love to her."

"Anne, stop it—"

"You never touch me anymore. I want to know how it feels to be loved, even if I have to pretend to be someone else."

"Well, what about your damn Hungarian, or whoever the artist of the week is?"

"Don't make fun of me, Oliver. I need you. Just this once, and I'll never ask again, I promise. Love me. Love me like I'm your mistress." Her eyes were shining with tears.

Jordan put his hand over his mouth in disbelief.

Anne's small breasts quivered beneath the exquisitely sheer fabric of her costume. In the candlelight he took in the sight of his wife's xylophone ribs, the flaccid belly, the white thighs beginning to dimple, the corded neck. He touched her hair and smiled, swallowing. He was never going to be able to perform.

He reached out to hold her, nevertheless. Women were easily satisfied. A pat, a hug, a few words of endearment might be enough to get her off his back. If there was anything he couldn't stand, it was a beggar.

"Sweet Annie," he crooned.

Gently, she pulled away from him. "Close your eyes," she said.

She kissed his neck and worked her way down his body. The flamboyant Pharaonic robe he was wearing slid off his shoulders. His wife had learned something from the goatish Hungarian, he decided. This might not turn out to be a total loss, after all.

By the time she slid her lips over his member, it was nearly erect. "Yes," he whispered. "Oh, my, Anne, lovely."

"Call me Mireille," she said. Involuntarily, he shied away, but Anne pulled him back, her hands digging into his buttocks. She flicked her tongue over him with soft, teasing strokes. "Say my name. Say my name."

Jordan groaned.

"Say it, Oliver."

A tide flooded over him. "Mireille," he sighed, and his organ swelled to fill the unseen mouth. Lips, her lips, sucked him in a frenzy, swallowing deeper, pulling him into her as his legs brushed against her breasts. He groaned low in his throat. "Yes, Mireille, my darling. My whore. My angel."

"Your angel," Anne repeated, opening her mouth around the throbbing, erect phallus. She tasted a drop of semen as it oozed from the head. Then, as he whimpered for her to take him again, she wrapped her mouth around the massive penis and bit down hard enough to make up for all twenty-four sour years of their marriage.

"I'm getting a divorce," she said through Jordan's screams. "And you owe me five million dollars, you son of a bitch."

Chapter Forty-Three

Still aching and swathed in bandages that made him appear to possess the genitals of a horse under his trousers, Jordan was released from the hospital in time to attend to the final details of *Field of Glory*. By the time the film premiered in September of 1955, the wound had healed but the legend lived on.

Word about Jordan's spectacular injury (brain surgery, Hollywood-style, was how one comedian described it) traveled like wildfire. Many of the female stars at the opening had once done duty on Jordan's famous casting couch, and there was more than one triumphant snicker as he walked into the Pantages Theatre with Mireille on his arm.

Most of those present had come to see the film. It would be abysmal, of course, the insiders whispered. Movies hyped as hard as *Field of Glory* were always stinkers. The French girl was an unknown, and Jordan's mistress, to boot.

Jordan had lost all perspective; back in the days before Anne's *bacio della morte*, the little head had done the thinking for the big head. All of his eggs, as it were, were in one multimillion-dollar basket.

Even under budget, *Field of Glory* was one of the most costly films ever made, and it was no secret that Anne Rutledge Jordan, who had financed much of it, was demanding more than the pound of flesh she had almost succeeded in extracting. She wanted her money now, as well as half the worth of Continental

Studios. As for the Jordan mansion, the house in Sardinia, and the apartments in New York and Paris, Anne's lawyers had skirted the community-property laws long before. When the divorce became final, Jordan would be homeless and indebted to his ex-wife for several million dollars, and his business in a state of forced liquidation. Unless *Field of Glory* turned out to be the biggest box-office smash of the decade, everyone knew the golden boy from Oregon would be run out of town, as one Hollywood pundit liked to say, "with nothing but the shirt on his back and the teeth marks on his prick."

The gala was in the finest Hollywood tradition, with the beams from klieg lights windmilling through the night sky as one limousine after another stopped to discharge its illustrious passengers. The biggest names in Hollywood showed up, each with a smile for Jordan and a kiss for Mireille in front of the cameras. Hordes of adoring teenage fans screamed and swooned when Peter Rockwell appeared. Adam Wells had ensured that Mireille would receive a similar welcome by hiring a claque of good-looking men to shout her name as she walked into the theater.

"Bet you had fun rounding those boys up," Rockwell said snidely as he passed Wells in the theater.

"Sure did, Peter," Wells answered in a shrill voice that carried through the lobby. "Thanks for lending me your address book." He gave him a big malicious grin.

Jordan and Mireille took their seats. The lights came down. Mireille folded her ice-cold hands in her lap as the credits began to roll.

The first shot in the picture was a close-up of Mireille's face. She was sleeping, and she looked like an innocent child. Then, when she awoke, her eyes opened slowly to fill the screen with their dazzling emerald sensuality.

At one look, the audience stopped shifting in their seats. Greetings to corporate acquaintances were forgotten. Every eye was on the screen; every heart was pounding in the dead silence of the vast theater. Jordan looked at Sam Hope and grinned. In one shot, without any dialogue or action, the director had captivated the audience simply by showing them Mireille's extraordinary beauty.

"We've got them," Jordan whispered. He closed his eyes. The gamble had been a big one, and he knew it had paid off.

Unconsciously, he covered his crotch with his hand. The doctors had assured him that he had suffered no permanent damage and that he would be back in action in a matter of weeks, but he had not disclosed this information to Anne's lawyers. As far as they were concerned, he would be a cripple for life. In exchange for not being charged with criminal assault, Anne had privately agreed to waive her right to half of Jordan's property. Despite the racy speculation of the film industry, Continental Studios would remain in his sole possession, and as long as it continued to produce hit movies, Oliver Jordan would be a rich—and single—man.

All in all, he thought, one bite had been a small enough price to pay.

When the film was over, the thunderous applause was nearly drowned out by cheers from the usually jaded Hollywood audience. Women wept openly. Peter Rockwell rose from his seat and bowed.

"The idiot thinks it's for him," Jordan said. He squeezed Mireille's hand. "Go ahead. Stand up."

"Me?"

"Do it." He smiled. "It'll feel like nothing you've ever known."

Slowly, flushed with embarrassment, she stood up, and the decibel level of the applause tripled.

She smiled hesitantly. *For me,* she thought.

Then she looked around at the sea of faces turned toward her. Stephanie's was not there. She had not been permitted to attend the opening, because Mireille the movie star, that good-hearted princess from the Pyrenees, had never given birth to an illegitimate child.

Mireille had not seen her daughter in nine and a half months. *No, not for me. They're applauding Oliver Jordan's creature.*

When she sat down, Jordan squeezed her hand. "This is just the beginning," he said. His words made her shiver. She turned away from him.

"My, my, we're playing the princess to the hilt tonight, aren't we?"

"I'm very tired, Oliver."

Sam Hope stood up and offered Mireille his hand. "Good job," he said.

"Thank you, Sam. Thanks for everything."

He nodded curtly. "Coming to my place for the celebration?"

"Of course," Jordan said. "We'll be there shortly."

"Please go without me," Mireille said after Hope left. "I don't feel like going to a party."

"Fine." He stood up and led her through a throng of celebrities, all of whom swore that they had believed in Mireille's talent and Jordan's genius from the very beginning—meaning, presumably, all of three months ago.

"Where are we?" Mireille asked as the Rolls pulled into a gas station in the seamiest area of the city she'd seen since she arrived.

"East LA," Jordan said. "Picturesque, don't you think?"

Mireille took in the litter-covered streets, the crumbling buildings smeared with graffiti, the knots of teenage boys in tattered clothes, smoking cigarettes in darkened storefronts, staring at Jordan's beautiful automobile.

"What are we doing here?"

"You'll see."

The chauffeur got out as the station's night attendant trotted up to the pumps. "Fill 'er up, sir?"

Mireille laid her head on the seat back. Behind her, the attendant fiddled with the gas-tank cover. Suddenly, her window rolled down, letting in the odor of gasoline mixed with the ripe scent of neighborhood garbage.

"Oliver," she protested.

Jordan's smooth voice overrode hers. "Excuse me, boy."

"Sir?" In a crouch, the attendant lifted his head so that his face was exactly parallel with Mireille's.

It was Victor Mohl.

Her mouth opened, but she was unable to speak. Mohl straightened, his face a blank.

"Victor, what a pleasure," Jordan said with utterly false sincerity. "Is this place yours?"

Mohl's gaze drifted toward the dingy tiled attendant's shelter. His skin looked yellow under the harsh light. "Sure is," he said, slapping on a grin. "Well, pretty soon, anyway." His hand rubbed over the oval patch on his coveralls on which "Joe's Esso" was embroidered. "We're changing hands now, you understand."

Jordan nodded.

"Hey, you've got to have something to put your profits into, right?"

"Of course."

"Mae West got rich on real estate."

"She certainly did," Jordan concurred.

In the ensuing silence, Mohl made a little mime of surprise at seeing the gas nozzle in his hand and proceeded to fill the tank. "So how you been, Mireille?" he asked, trying to sound offhanded. "Been reading about you in the papers."

"I'm . . . fine," she answered in a small voice. "Victor, how . . . ? Your career . . . ?"

"Hey, I'm doing great, believe me. After the Gregory Peck Western, I was getting offers from everywhere. I'm just closing a deal with MGM." He peered into the window. "That is, unless Mr. Jordan here wants me back. Maybe he'd like me to direct your next movie. After all, I was your first director, right?" He laughed heartily. Jordan joined him, and Mohl laughed harder, trying to turn his plea into a joke.

Finally, the pump clicked off. He replaced the nozzle. "Yeah, there were some good times, weren't there?"

No one answered. Mexican music and the roar of a bad muffler filled the silence as a dilapidated '49 Chevy pulled up behind them honking.

"I got to go, I guess," Mohl said. He smiled and pointed a finger at Jordan. "We'll have lunch sometime, okay, Mr. J?"

Jordan only stared at him.

Mohl spoke to the chauffeur. "That'll be eight dollars," he said.

The chauffeur took out a ten. "He can keep the change," Jordan called out.

Mohl took the money, looked at it for a moment, then stuffed the bill into his pocket as the Rolls pulled out.

"How could you do that to him?" Mireille asked quietly, her anger threatening to explode.

"I?" Jordan was a picture of outraged innocence. "I didn't force the man to gamble away every cent he owned."

"He worked for you."

"For three weeks. Three weeks longer than he would have worked otherwise. And he was very well paid."

She stared at the floor. "Why did you bring me to see him?"

"So that you'd remember," Jordan said. "I warned you once about believing your own press. The applause of the crowd is very tempting, Mireille." He ran his hands slowly up her legs, beneath her dress. She tried to squirm away from him, but he pressed her against the door. "Very tempting. Just don't listen too long."

Carefully, deliberately, he pulled off her panties and spread her legs. "Because the frog princess can become a frog again." He unzipped his trousers and entered her while the car raced over the wide streets of the city. Between her open thighs, he shuddered and came while she tried to bury her face in the seat.

"Thank God," he said at last. He pulled himself off her. "It still works. For a while, I was afraid Anne had killed it." He reached into the bar for a bottle of scotch and a glass of ice. "Twelve weeks. Can you imagine how long that is to go without sex?"

He sipped his drink, then raised his eyebrows in question. "Would you like one?" he offered.

"I hate you," Mireille said.

"Fix your hair, darling."

By the time they arrived at Sam Hope's sprawling ranch house in Malibu, the party was in full swing.

"I told you, I don't want to go to a party," Mireille said.

"Nonsense. You'll love it." Jordan got out and waited while the chauffeur opened the door for Mireille, his eyes carefully averted. Finally, Mireille stepped out.

"Good," Jordan said, patting her fanny. "You really do have to make an appearance. After all, you're a star."

Chapter Forty-Four

At the age of twenty-seven (although the press releases insisted that she was twenty-five), Mireille won an Academy Award for *Field of Glory*. So did Sam Hope for his direction, James Allerton for his screenplay, and Oliver Jordan for producing the best picture of the year.

Scripts came flooding in, including one from MGM called *Gigi*, based on Colette's novella about a young girl reared to be a courtesan.

"It's too close to the truth," Jordan said when Mireille asked him if he would loan her to MGM for one film. "Ingrid Bergman's been crucified just for taking a lover, for God's sake. If the Bible-thumpers in the Hays Office ever get a whiff of how you used to amuse yourself, you'd be run out of town on a rail."

He laughed, but the remark froze Mireille to the bone. "You promised me that would never happen," she said.

"And it won't. The press likes you, and I'm going to see to it that they keep on liking you. But we've got to be careful about your roles. If you play Gigi, the tabloids are going to want to draw comparisons with your own life, and your life can't stand that sort of scrutiny."

"Ingrid Bergman played Saint Joan and a nun," Mireille said.

"And then she ran off with an Italian in pointed shoes. That's not going to happen with you."

He also refused to loan Mireille to Otto Preminger for *Anatomy of a Murder*. When star Lana Turner walked out because of Preminger's intimidating style of directing, the part was left open. Despite Mireille's accent, Preminger wanted her in the film.

"Your face is like the sun," Preminger pronounced during a cocktail party. He spoke without the slightest trace of flattery, as if he were merely expressing a fact. "One is compelled to look at it, even though one knows one may go blind." He looked at her body frankly, his breathing coming rapidly. "I can take you to another level," he said. "Would you like that?"

"She would not," Oliver Jordan said at Preminger's back.

The director turned slowly. "I see," he said, his great wise gaze swiveling from Jordan to Mireille and back again. "She is special, yes? For you?"

"Yes," Jordan said.

Preminger nodded. He understood everything.

Even so, the director continued to urge her to accept the part until he saw Jean Seberg, an entrant in a talent search.

"She's nearly as beautiful as Mireille," Jordan conceded when Preminger showed him Seberg's photograph.

"Mmm. And she has a moral quality about her. Upright."

Jordan laughed. "You think you're going to insult me into giving Mireille to you."

Preminger shrugged. "If I can take her from you, I will."

"Not for your films," Jordan said. "Too controversial."

Preminger shrugged. "They are art. The French girl ought to have the chance to participate in them."

Jordan laughed. "She's mine, Otto," he said.

Preminger's offers reinforced Jordan's belief that Mireille was more than a blonde bombshell. Monroe, dazzling in *Gentlemen Prefer Blondes*, would have no competition from Mireille in sex comedies. Oliver Jordan's protégée was more than a celebrity with a good body; she was a star with substance.

Once Preminger gave up, Jordan finally agreed on *Lady Marguerite*, a modern-day remake of *Camille*, as Mireille's second film. It won her a New York Film Critics Circle Award.

The movie was nominated for best picture by the Academy, but lost out to *The Bridge on the River Kwai*'s Oscar sweep. Her third movie, *Day Without End*, in which she played a deaf-mute, sealed Mireille's reputation as a serious artist.

By her fourth film, *Forever*, Mireille was voted the most popular woman in America, leading Mamie Eisenhower in a Gallup poll by a slim margin.

"She is so luminous an actress that one very nearly forgets her beauty," one columnist wrote. But the fans didn't forget. "Mireille" became a look unto itself, consisting of pastel chiffon dresses accented by diamonds. All over the country, women let their hair grow to their waists and dyed it platinum blonde. A phrase from Mireille's Academy Awards acceptance speech, "you have seen me with your heart," became a hit song chanted by blonde teenagers everywhere. A Parisian perfumer created a fragrance for her. Called simply "M" and packaged in a green bottle that was ostensibly the exact shade of Mireille's eyes, it created a sensation in department stores from coast to coast.

Through it all, Jordan worked Mireille mercilessly. In five years, the only time she was not working were the two weeks each year when she was allowed to visit Stephanie at school, and the two weeks each Christmas when Stephanie was permitted to come home to see her mother.

During these times, Jordan vanished into his cottage parties (which had recommenced with renewed vigor following his divorce from Anne) and a spate of new women whom he impaled with his relentlessly tumescent appendage with tireless dedication.

Yet he missed Mireille during these times, missed her with a frenzy. It annoyed him to admit this weakness to himself. After all, he reasoned, he had not been faithful to Mireille for even one day since their sojourn to Sardinia years ago.

He no longer even demanded that the nameless women he called "Angel" be blonde, or tall, or resemble Mireille in any way. He no longer insisted on the optimum age range between nineteen and twenty-nine. The sanctions against thin hair, small eyes, visible gums, and poor posture were abandoned, as were Jordan's qualms about nail-biters, heavy perspirers, and flat-chested women. He had them all.

Still, he missed Mireille with an aching need when she was not available to him, and suffered nightmares that she might leave him.

Part of his paranoia was due, no doubt, to the fact that Mireille was the lifeblood of Continental Studios. By now, Oliver Jordan was not only the trailblazing independent producer of Hollywood; he was the one whose entire output depended on one star. If Mireille betrayed him, as he had betrayed her from the first day of their relationship, he would be ruined.

There was another dynamic at work, too. Sexually, he could not get along without her. There was only one Mireille, and Jordan knew it every bit as much as the screaming fans in the theaters did.

She was the prize to be discarded, the masterpiece to be defaced. Without her, the women Jordan bedded became a reflection of him, and all of them reflected him badly. To treat with disdain a flat-chested nail-biter with visible gums and a carriage like a question mark meant nothing if he could not also treat the most beautiful woman in the world in the same manner.

When Mireille was in Switzerland visiting her daughter, Jordan's bedroom performances flagged noticeably. More than one sallow-skinned, myopic creature had dared to suggest that he might be impotent. He! Oliver Jordan, cocksman extraordinaire! He had hastened to remind these modestly endowed ladies that his lack of response had nothing to do with *his* capabilities, thank you.

Nevertheless, he promised himself fervently during those absences that when she returned, he would treasure Mireille as never before. He wrote her passionate letters, sent gifts of diamonds by personal messenger, called her every evening after the last woman, her face already forgotten, left his bed.

When Mireille finally did return, he was thrilled. He was overjoyed, a man mad with romance. Until he made love to her. Then she was his again, and he was hungry for new flesh. All was right with the world once more.

As for Mireille . . . Well, Mireille was French, he told himself. She was, above all things, practical. One did not work as a Parisian prostitute for as long as Mireille had without learning the value of money. He made sure she got plenty of that, and a great deal more, besides. Mireille had fame, honor, public adulation and respect for her work, a splendid education for her daughter, and the best roles in Hollywood. Unlike the other studios, Jordan never made his star swallow an insipid script in order to save a mediocre movie. Continental made the best pictures in the world, and everyone knew it.

The most expensive original screenplay ever bought was a property of Jim Allerton's, whose success in *Field of Glory* had skyrocketed his career. Since then, Allerton had written two other films—one for MGM, the other for Paramount—and both had been among the top grossers of their years. Now he had a new screenplay that his agent promised was better than anything Allerton had yet written.

"The finished screenplay?" Jordan waved the script in the air. "Why wasn't I given a treatment to read months ago?"

"Jim doesn't work with treatments," the agent said. "This is it. Except for minor changes, it stays the way it is. That's the condition of sale."

The twerp, Jordan thought. Five years ago, nobody knew the kid's name. "I'll read it and get back to you if I have time," Jordan said.

The screenplay was magnificent. Titled *Josephine*, it was a huge historical about Napoleon. Allerton had given the part of Joséphine de Beauharnais an almost mystical quality, foreshadowed in Napoleon's dreams since his childhood. It was a great vehicle for Mireille, and Jordan was pretty sure he could get a commitment out of Devin Miles, a British stage actor whom the critics were already calling a cross between Richard Burton and Sir Laurence Olivier.

Jordan snagged Allerton in the steam room of the Beverly Hills Athletic Club. "Why are you offering this around?" he asked sharply.

Allerton smiled boyishly. "It's how I make my living, Mr. Jordan," he said.

"You know what I mean. Only one actress can play this part."

"I know," Allerton said. "That's why I'm hoping you'll buy it."

He did, at a cost of a quarter million dollars.

It was Mireille's last film under her contract.

And her best. From the beginning, there was magic in her performance. Relentlessly, Jordan drove her, alternately tyrannizing and worshipping her. By the end of filming, she was exhausted.

"You're going to take another Oscar for *Josephine*," he said by way of consolation as they sat near Mireille's candlelit pool. "I'd love to make a sequel, but Allerton wants to go back home to ole Virginny to write novels." He poured himself a glass of champagne from a bottle he'd brought out. "I imagine he'll be back as soon as he finds out what book publishers pay. Meanwhile, though, I've been looking at another screenplay. It's called *Mozambique*. Kind of a cross between *Pillow Talk* and *The Third Man*. Not very original, but it's a sure moneymaker—"

"No, Oliver." She spoke softly, and her smile was faint and serene in the candlelight.

"No?" Jordan asked, amazed. "You haven't even taken a look at the part."

"I don't care what sort of part it is. My contract with you is finished."

He looked at her, his face aghast. "You're not serious."

"Oh, yes. Quite serious."

"But everything has worked out beautifully. I've made you famous, Mireille."

"I never cared about that."

"And me? You never cared about me, either, I suppose."

"I've told you how I feel about you."

He drained his glass and refilled it. "Temperament no longer becomes you, darling," he said maliciously. "It makes you look old." Jordan poured more champagne into Mireille's glass, even though she hadn't touched it. "Has another studio made you an offer?"

"That's none of your business."

"It damn well is my business! Don't try to—"

"I made a deal with you," Mireille said, her voice rising. "Five pictures. That was six years of my life. Six years of being your 'baroness' and your whore, and you took advantage of every minute. Well, that's over now."

"Mireille . . . Angel . . ."

"I won't discuss this any longer."

Jordan's eyes glazed with rage. "You slut," he whispered.

"Is that supposed to insult me? You've called me a slut for years. You've treated me like one since the moment we met."

"I've given you everything!"

She smiled. "And I've given you everything. That sounds fair to me."

He ran his fingers through his hair. "We shouldn't talk about this now. It's late. You're tired. We'll say things we don't mean."

"Such as how the way you make love sickens me? No, I would mean that. Or that you're a despicable man without any sense of decency?"

"Or that I love you!" he shouted.

Mireille laughed. "Yes, I suppose in your way you do," she said. A silence passed between them. "No regrets," she said finally. "Six years was a long time to live your lie, but no regrets, not really." She stood up. "Good-bye, Oliver."

"I simply will not believe this," Jordan said, dusting off his trousers as he rose. "You're a star, for God's sake, the biggest star in the fucking world! You can't just—"

The telephone rang.

"Ignore it," Jordan demanded. "You can't—"

Mireille walked inside to answer it. She passed him without a glance.

"Shit," he muttered.

Through the glass doors, he saw her pick up the phone, shout something into it in hysterical French, then slowly lower the receiver into its cradle.

Jordan stood in the doorway. Mireille was pale and trembling. "What's wrong?"

"It's Stephanie. She's in the hospital. The police are there . . ." She looked up at him with panic in her eyes. "I've got to get to Geneva right away."

"I'll arrange it," Jordan said. He retrieved her mink coat from the closet and wrapped it around her. "Don't worry about a thing."

"Oliver . . ."

"I'll call from the car. By the time we get to the airport, my plane will be ready for takeoff."

"Oh God," she said. "Oh my God. Stephanie . . ."

"Everything's going to be fine, darling." He bundled her into the back of the Rolls. "Just promise me you'll think about a new contract."

BOOK III

New York

1960–1962

Chapter Forty-Five

Stephanie screamed.

She felt a needle puncture her arm; something warm and viscous poured out of it and filled her up. She sobbed, her breath catching raggedly, her hands clenching into fists.

"It's all right. Relax now," a disembodied voice said from somewhere above her. The voice was distorted, like a record played at too slow a speed.

"It's . . . all . . . right . . . Stephanie . . ."

"Nora?" she called.

"Ste . . . pha . . . nie . . ."

She whirled slowly down, down, while the voice droned senselessly above her. She was lost. Something terrible had happened, but in the confusion of her fall through empty space, she had forgotten what it was.

"Stephanie . . ."

"Nora?" The darkness of the tunnel into which she was falling cleared away, and she found herself, surprisingly, standing in the hallway of the school dormitory, turning the knob on a door. "Nora, is that you?"

Her mind reeled back. It was the previous summer, when Nora was still protected from her demons, and the world seemed like a place that was almost safe to live in.

"Who'd you expect, Quasimodo?"

That was how the conversation had begun.

Yes: *Who'd you expect, Quasimodo?*

Nora stepped back from her wall, where the photographs of Robert Walker had been replaced by those of James Dean and Elvis. Now the King himself was slowly being papered over by a gigantic collage of Mireille.

Nora tacked a full-page close-up with the legend "Hollywood Princess" beneath it on the center of the wall and blew a smoke ring toward it. "Well? What do you think?"

Stephanie sighed. "It's okay, I guess."

"'It's okay, I guess,'" Nora mimicked. "Jeez, how blasé can you get? If my mother were the biggest star in the world, I'd shit a brick."

"Yeah . . . well, shit one for me," Stephanie said. She took one of the Gauloises out of the blue pack on the windowsill and lit it.

At fifteen, she was as graceful as a dancer, with long limbs and agile fingers. While Nora, well past puberty, had retained all of her childhood awkwardness, Stephanie had already blossomed into a beauty. She sat on the deep windowsill, looking out at the budding trees.

"Okay," Nora said. "What's with you?"

"Nothing."

"You get your period?"

Stephanie rolled her eyes. "No." She took a drag on the cigarette and blew out the smoke in a long blue stream. "I won't be going home this summer," she said. "Again."

"Oh." Nora wiped her glue-covered hands on the white lawn curtains—now a mucoid-gray mass—and sat down beside her. "I'm sorry, Steff."

Stephanie shrugged. "I wasn't counting on it, anyway. She's always too busy for me."

"You went home at Christmas."

"Big deal." Stephanie tucked her knees beneath her chin.

"And the Christmas before that."

"So?"

"So you know how many times I've been home since I got here? Once. For one day. My brother Neil came home and smashed the Mercedes. Drunk. The next day Daddy's secretary came to take us both to the airport." Nora shook her head. "One day in eight years."

"At least you didn't have to spend last summer here."

"Yeah. I got shipped off to camp." She twirled her index finger above her head.

Stephanie laughed. "Listen to us," she said.

"Sister Theresa's Lonely Hearts Club," Nora said, convulsed with mirth. Suddenly, she straightened up. "Hey, I've got an idea."

"What?"

"Since you won't be going to California this summer, why don't you come to camp with me? My dad's secretary will take care of everything. Just give me your passport number."

Stephanie blinked. "My passport? Where is this place?"

"Maine. It's in the States, but far enough away from everything so that your parents don't have to visit you."

"Said in the true spirit of Sister Theresa's Lonely Hearts Club."

"So? Will you go?"

"Is it fun?"

"It's fabulous."

"Last year you said you'd never go back."

"It'll be different this year."

"How's that?"

Nora smiled, cryptic and hopeful. "Because we'll be there together."

During the weenie roast on the first night, a fourteen-year-old camper stabbed one of the counselors in the eye with a stick. Following the arrival of the ambulance, the summer residents of

Camp Hope were lined up at the infirmary, where everyone except Stephanie was given some sort of medication.

"What'd they make you take?" Stephanie asked.

"Antidepressants, tranqs . . ." Nora shrugged. "They keep you pretty stoned here."

At ten o'clock, they were locked into their cabins.

"They've bolted the door," Stephanie said, trying the latch.

Nora examined her nails. "They always do that."

"What?"

"I guess I didn't tell you this was a psychiatric retreat."

Stephanie stared at her for a full five seconds before plopping leadenly onto a cot. "No. No, you didn't tell me that, Nora."

"I guess I didn't think you'd come if you knew."

"Oh, where would you get an idea like that?"

"It's really quite exclusive," Nora said. "Only three beds to a cabin."

"Now, that's what I call a selling point."

"Oh, try to look on the bright side, Steff," the older girl pleaded. "We've got this place all to ourselves."

"Only because Jackie the Ripper was supposed to be our roommate!" Stephanie covered her face with a pillow.

"Well . . . she's not coming back. They don't let you come back if you try to kill people."

"Lucky, lucky us."

"What I mean is . . . Well, shit." Nora flopped down on her bunk. "I know I shouldn't have brought you to crazy kids' camp. I'm sorry, Steff. I just . . . I guess I just didn't want to be alone here." She laid her head down and stared at the log wall.

Stephanie removed the pillow. One of the lenses of Nora's glasses covered the bridge of her nose; the other her right temple. Nora didn't seem to notice, any more than she noticed the rip in her shorts above her gangly, bruised legs or the fact that her hair hadn't been washed for days. The sight of her filled Stephanie with a surging, protective love.

"I'm glad you're not alone here," she said. "It'd be hell without a friend."

"You're telling me." Nora sat up and smiled crookedly. "Thanks," she said. "I mean that." She produced a pack of Winstons she'd bought at the airport and offered one to Stephanie. "Go ahead. The next bed check isn't until one a.m. And the counselors don't care if you smoke, anyway."

"With campers like our ex-roommate, I guess they've got other things on their minds."

"Something like that."

The two girls smoked in silence, listening to the chirp of crickets outside the sealed window. "Why are you here?" Stephanie asked finally.

"I told you. It's easier on everybody not to have me at home."

"I mean why *here*? At crazy kids' camp?"

Nora pulled the skillet out of her mess kit to use as an ashtray. "I tried to kill myself."

"That was when you were eight years old."

"Yeah, well, that was the first time. And the bloodiest. Jeez, there was a lot of blood. Did I ever tell you—?"

"How many times were there altogether?"

Nora rubbed her hand over her face, squashing her features. "Five," she said. She looked tired.

"Five? I've known you for eight years. When—?"

"There were three more times before I got sent to La Voisine. I guess my father didn't want to find me dead in the bathroom at home."

"That's four," Stephanie said.

"Yeah. Well, there was one other time."

"Since I've known you?"

Nora shrugged. "It was when you went to LA. I thought you were going to stay there."

"Nora," Stephanie whispered. "Oh God . . ."

"Don't feel bad about it. That's why I never told you."

Stephanie was too horrified to answer.

"Whatever you do, don't try it with pills. They make you puke, and then you choke on your own vomit. At least—"

"Why?" Stephanie asked. "Nora, why?"

"Christ, I don't know." Nora rolled her shoulders, as if trying to shrug off an unpleasant layer of skin. "You don't really think about *why* so much. Not while it's happening. You just want to get out, you know what I mean? Just get the hell out."

She stubbed out her cigarette in the skillet, then slid it over to Stephanie. "Stash that under your bed when you're through," she said. "I've got to get some sleep." She took off her glasses, folding the earpieces carefully, and placed them on the floor. Then she pulled the blanket over her.

"Aren't you going to change into your pajamas?" Stephanie asked.

"Forgot to pack them."

Stephanie watched her for a few minutes.

You just want to get out, you know what I mean? Stephanie didn't know. She never wanted to know the horrible things Nora accepted as truth.

She looked at the crescent moon out the scratched window. She longed to open it, at least long enough to clear the smoke out of the room, but it was sealed shut. She felt like screaming.

No wonder Nora's nuts, she thought. *She's spent her whole life locked up in prisons disguised as places for kids.*

Stephanie thumped on the window with her fist. "Camp Hope," she muttered.

Chapter Forty-Six

Stephanie was still unresponsive. A nun from La Voisine was ordered to remain by the girl's bed until she regained consciousness. After five hours, the nun slept.

And Stephanie remained in the past, engulfed in memory.

There had been five counselors at Camp Hope, all of them post–medical school students specializing in pediatric psychiatry. Their main function was the dispensing of medication to the fifteen psychologically challenged children and adolescents whose parents had paid thousands of dollars each to keep them in a state as near to comatose as possible.

Medication was the watchword at the camp. Drugs were dispensed after breakfast, before Group Therapy, during Nature Trails and Exploration, throughout Outdoor Skills, during lunch, at Individual Therapy, before Crafts, during Campfire, and before Lights-Out. By the end of the first week, there was absolutely no possibility that the stabbing incident of the first night would repeat itself. The campground resembled a nursing home.

Hour after hour, Stephanie watched Nora sleep.

Activities were not enforced at Camp Hope, and naps were always viable options instead of making knots or climbing trails.

Stephanie stared out the sealed window. There were no activities going on outside. The counselors were conducting their daily conference on the status of their patients.

You just want to get out, you know what I mean? Nora's words repeated in a numbing drone through the silence of the room.

Stephanie took one of Nora's cigarettes and smoked it while tapping absently on the windowpane with her nails. *If I'm not crazy now, I'm going to be by the end of summer,* she thought. Camp Hope was quickly turning into the worst experience of her life, and she'd only been there two weeks.

Almost three months to go. Three months in the outdoor version of *The Snake Pit.*

Outside, some tall trees rustled in a breeze she could not feel. Just beyond the glass pane—just out of reach, it seemed—were air and water and freedom.

She didn't belong here, she knew. Nora was her friend, but enough was enough. She threw the cigarette on the floor and stomped it out. "Sorry, Nora," she said aloud. She picked up her suitcase, wrapped her blanket around it, shut her eyes tight, and rammed the window until the glass exploded.

Nora didn't stir.

Stephanie draped the blanket over the broken glass. Watching the cinder-block building where the counselors were holding their meeting, she climbed onto the sill carefully, then took a final look at the room where Nora lay on her cot, oblivious.

If there were a fire, she'd burn to a crisp, Stephanie thought. Suddenly, her eyes filled with tears.

You just want to get out, you know what I mean? Just get the hell out.

Nora had gone through this year after year, spending the summer drugged into unconsciousness. Strangers with pills had taken her life away one day at a time. How many years had she lost on that cot? How much of her time on earth had Camp Hope stolen from her?

Stephanie climbed down from the window and walked over to her friend. "Nora. Wake up," she said.

"What . . . what do you want?"

"Just wake up." She shook her. "Do you hear me? Make yourself get up."

"Blow off, Steff." She tried to turn away in her bunk, but Stephanie pulled off the blanket.

"What the hell are you doing?"

"Nothing. I'm not doing anything, and neither are you. That's the point. You're all like a bunch of zombies here." Nora tented her hands as if she were praying, then splayed them over her face while she yawned.

"What are you talking about?"

"We're getting out of here."

"What?"

"The counselors are all in the medical building, comparing notes. They'll be there for at least another hour. I've been watching them."

"But the door's still locked," Nora said.

"I broke the window."

Nora looked over to the open square, its sill draped in a blanket. "Are you crazy?"

"I guess so. Are you coming or not?" Stephanie asked. "Either way, I'm leaving."

Nora adjusted her glasses. "Where are we going to go?"

"Does it matter?"

The tall girl sat up. "You mean just blow this pop stand? Eat berries and kill sparrows, sleep on the ground with mice running over our bellies?"

"Would that be worse than staying in this hellhole?"

Nora put on her glasses and her shoes, then grabbed her mess kit. "Lead the way, Kemo-Sabe."

By midafternoon the next day, they were starving. Neither of them could identify edible berries, and killing sparrows was more easily said than done.

"Think they've sent out a search party for us yet?" Nora asked, sitting on a rock.

"Who'd come?" Stephanie panted. "Most of the counselors haven't set foot outside of a classroom since they were in first grade."

"The kids, maybe."

"Are you kidding? They're too blitzed to blow their noses."

Nora cracked her neck. "I've missed two Group sessions."

"Thank God. All anybody talks about is how they hate their parents."

Nora laughed. "That's because nobody in your group has big problems."

"My biggest problem was being there," Stephanie said. "And that's been solved."

"Yeah." Nora rummaged through her mess kit. "I wish I'd brought some Valium with me."

"What for?"

"It makes me feel better."

"So does a ham sandwich."

Nora packed up her kit again. "None of those in here, either," she said.

"Maybe we'd better go on."

Nora stood up, took a few steps, then stopped. "Stephanie . . ."

"What's the matter?"

"I'm going to die out here."

"No, you're not—"

"Yes I am." Nora was sweating. "You don't know, you don't understand . . ." Her voice echoed through the steep wooded hills. She covered her face with her hands. "I'm sorry. It's just that I've missed all my medication. If I'd stayed for Group yesterday . . . oh, Jesus Christ . . ."

Stephanie put her arm around her. Nora hugged Stephanie back, her birdlike arms evincing a ferocious strength. "Sit down," Stephanie said. "We'll stay here together."

"No one's held me like this since I was a little kid," Nora said, shivering. "D-Don't g-get me wrong. I'm not q-q-queer or anything."

"Shhh," Stephanie said, rubbing Nora's arms to warm them up.

"And I'm not a drug addict, either. Not like . . . like some people."

"I know."

"I guess you think this is really stupid, right?"

"No," Stephanie said. "It's what friends are for."

Slowly, she felt the tension leave Nora's body, and the girl relaxed, laying her head on Stephanie's shoulder. They stayed just so for a long time.

"My mother used to hold me," Nora said finally. "I'd climb up on her lap, and it always felt cool and smooth, because she wore satin all the time. Satin dressing gowns. I guess she was pretty much an invalid even then, only I didn't know it." She closed her eyes and breathed deeply. "And she always smelled like perfume. The scent wasn't flowers or anything. It smelled like gold. At least that's how I remember it."

"You've never mentioned your mother before."

Nora rolled off Stephanie onto the grass and lay looking up at the clouds. "She isn't my mother anymore."

"You mean she died?"

Nora thought about it. "I guess so, in a way. God knows, she tried often enough. The overdoses got to be so routine my dad actually bought a stomach pump for her. After a while, my mother's suicide attempts were just conversational items at breakfast. By the time she went into the loony bin, she didn't even know our names. It was pretty much of a relief to see her go."

"But . . . why'd she do it?"

Nora sighed. "Why, why, why . . . Shit, who knows? Because she was crazy. Everyone in my family's suicidal, except my father. It's in our genes or something. We're like lemmings, swimming toward the deep water from the day we're born."

She twirled a twig. "My grandfather hanged himself in the garage. He had cancer. That was like a disgrace back then, so I guess he sort of had a reason. And my brother—my oldest brother—he killed himself, too. Gun to the head. Blam. I didn't know him very well, since I was only four years old when he ate the barrel. Nobody talked about it much. His friends in prep school held a big memorial service for him, and we all went. I guess that's when my mother started really falling apart."

"What about your other brother?"

"He's too much of a jerk to do anything." Absently, Nora turned her pockets inside out, then looked through her mess kit again. "Once I found a Seconal—an actual *red*—inside my empty canteen." She held the canteen upside down. "Crap. No such luck."

She tossed the cap away. "My brother lives with a fifty-year-old woman in Venice. Can you believe it? They probably do it and everything. El Disgusto. Neil's been . . ." Suddenly, her face went pale. She swallowed audibly, groaned, then spun away on her knees and threw up.

"Nora, what's wrong?"

Nora pushed Stephanie away. "Fuck, I wish I had something for my nerves," she said.

"Maybe we should go back."

"Do you know the way?"

Stephanie looked up at the sun. It was reddening, but she really had no idea in which direction the camp was.

"Sure," she said blithely. "We'll walk back the way we came."

They headed down the trail they had made through the tall grass. It ended in deep woods.

"I think we went through here," Stephanie said uncertainly.

"It looks pretty dark."

Stephanie felt a momentary wave of fear, swallowed it, and forced herself to look confident. "We'll be okay," she said.

Nora smiled back, although her lips were an unwholesome dark color, and she rubbed both her arms. "You're cool, you know that?"

Yeah, I'm great, Stephanie thought. *We're starving to death, it's getting dark, my friend's sick, and I'm leading us both into the woods. Real cool.*

Nora lit a cigarette, then retched immediately. "Want this?" she asked, holding the cigarette behind her bent back like a torch.

"No, thanks. Whatever you've got, I wish you'd keep it to yourself."

"I'm not sick," Nora insisted, heaving again. "It's withdrawal. I've been through it before."

"Jesus, how much stuff do you take?"

"About twenty pills a day."

"Are you kidding me?"

"They keep me alive. The last time I OD'd, the hospital tried to dry me out. Strapped me into the bed."

"What'd you do?"

"Nothing. My heart stopped." She straightened up with a loopy grin. "That showed them."

"Oh, shit," Stephanie said.

"That won't happen for a while, though. Days and days."

"Wonderful. What happens between now and then?"

Nora put her arm around Stephanie's shoulders. "Nothing. I live clean and die brave."

Stephanie looked over at her. Nora's face held a ghastly radiance.

"That's bullshit," Stephanie said. She forced them to walk faster.

By nightfall, the girls had no idea where they were.

Exhausted, Stephanie sat down on the leaf-covered ground. Nora leaned against a tree, her eyes fixed and glassy, her body trembling out of control.

"I think we're going to have to sleep here," Stephanie said. "We can get a fresh start in the morning."

"Mice running over our stomachs . . ."

"Nothing's going to run over our stomachs," Stephanie said.

Nora slid down the tree as if she were boneless. "I've never had a friend before," she said.

"Me neither. We're Sister Theresa's Lonely Hearts Club, remember?"

"Hold my hand."

Stephanie groped in the darkness and found Nora's bony fingers.

"Don't let go, okay?"

"I won't."

Nora shivered. "If I die, will you tell my father?"

"You aren't going to die, Nora."

"No, I know. It's just that I wonder . . ."

"Wonder what?"

"If he'd be sorry."

Stephanie put her arm around her. "Let's get some sleep," she said.

When Stephanie awoke at dawn, Nora's eyes were large and staring. Sweat poured off her waxy face.

"Nora?"

"I'm okay," she answered in a whisper.

Stephanie stood up, brushing leaves off herself, and extended
her hand to Nora. "Let's go."

Nora looked up at her, blinking away tears. "I've wet my pants."

"Doesn't matter." Stephanie slung the older girl's arm over her
shoulder.

"Christ, I'm nothing but a junkie," Nora said, stumbling.

"It isn't your fault."

Nora's tears fell on Stephanie's shoulder. "When we get back,
I'm not going to take any more medicine."

"I think you need it."

Nora shook her head. "It's never been what I needed. But it's
the only thing anyone was willing to give me. Until you."

"Me?"

"To make the pain go away. A friend is better. I'm not going to
take any more pills."

"Let's just think about getting back, okay?"

"Okay," Nora said. "At least we never have to go back to crazy
kids' camp."

"Yeah? What are we going to do to get out of it, stab a
counselor?"

"Don't have to. Automatic expulsion. That's the punishment
for running away."

Stephanie stopped in her tracks. "Are you kidding?"

"Nope."

"Jeez." Stephanie shook her head. "I wish you would have told
me that before. What's that?"

"Where?" Nora adjusted her glasses. "What are you—?"

"Quiet!" Gently, she set Nora down. Through the silence, she
heard the faraway call of voices.

"Somebody's come!" She jumped up and down, waving her hands over her head, even though she knew no one could see her through the thicket of trees. "Here we are! Over here!" She screamed herself hoarse until three figures in orange striped jackets appeared.

"Nora, they've found us!" she shrieked.

"Great." Nora sat on the ground.

"What's the matter? Aren't you glad? We could have stayed in these mountains forever."

"Yeah, I'm glad." She looked up at the dark trees around her. "It's just that . . ."

"What?"

The older girl took a deep breath. "Well, I was sure I was going to die."

"And?"

"And I wasn't afraid." She smiled. "It's like that afterward. After the pills, the razors. When you start to see the tunnel."

"The tunnel?"

"That's what I see, a tunnel. And it's leading somewhere."

"Heaven?" Stephanie asked in a whisper.

"I don't know. Freedom, I think."

Stephanie's eyes met hers. She took Nora's hand.

"Call out!" a man's voice boomed. The three figures moved closer. They were policemen. They would take Stephanie and Nora back to the life they knew.

Nora sniffled. "Yeah," she said. "It felt like freedom."

"Over here!" Stephanie called.

Nora was silent. When Stephanie looked back at her, she only smiled through her blue lips and pushed her glasses up the bridge of her nose.

Chapter Forty-Seven

"Nora!" Stephanie's scream pierced the din in the hospital emergency room.

The nurse attending to her checked the drip in her arm. "Shall I increase the drip on the diazepam, doctor? We're at five milligrams."

"Another five ought to do it," the doctor said. "Are her parents here?"

The nurse shook her head. "Her mother's flying in from America. She won't arrive until tomorrow."

The doctor lifted Stephanie's eyelids. "That's just as well. She'll be fine by then. Just keep her quiet, and transfer her to a regular room for the night."

"The police want to talk with her."

"No. Nothing like that, not until she's released. Tell them to speak with the school authorities."

The nurse nodded.

"She's the movie star's daughter, isn't she?" the doctor asked.

"I believe so, yes."

"Was it some sort of suicide pact?"

"I don't know, Doctor."

"You can up the diazepam to fifteen if she needs it," the doctor said.

Stephanie slept. Nora appeared again, deep in the thoughts that swirled and faded inside her shock-numbed mind.

Nora, smoking cigarettes inside her room papered with magazine pictures of movie stars. They had changed over the years. Natalie Wood's platter of mashed potatoes had been covered over by a full-page *Life* close-up of Mireille's face.

It had become an irritation to Stephanie that her best friend had chosen to immerse herself in her mother's images. She sensed a certain betrayal in that, as if Nora's adoration of the blonde movie goddess lessened her friendship with Stephanie.

"Don't take it personally," Nora said with the all-encompassing disdain of a high school senior.

"How can I not take it personally? She's my mother."

"Yeah," Nora said abstractly. "That doesn't mean anything, though." She fell back on her bed and sprawled out in what Stephanie had come to recognize as Nora's "thinking" position.

Stephanie sighed. "All right. What's that supposed to mean?"

The tall girl's cheeks colored. They were actually *pink*, Stephanie thought. Ever since midterms, Nora had been looking better. She had put on some weight. Her hair looked shiny. Most of her nervous mannerisms were gone. At last, at the age of eighteen, Nora seemed to have grown into herself.

"It means that this," she said, pointing to the photograph on the wall with her white-stockinged toe, "is not your mother. It's Mireille. She's nobody's mama. She's not even real, not exactly. She's just this perfect thing. Your mother's a whole other person. Get it?"

"No." Stephanie sat down on the bed next to Nora. "I don't know what you're talking about most of the time."

Nora sighed. "To be great is to be misunderstood," she said wearily.

"Oh, brother."

"Ralph Waldo Emerson said that." She flicked Stephanie's leg with her finger. "Can't you see I'm kidding?"

"About what?"

"About everything," Nora said. "You take life too seriously."

"Me? Since when did you become the Pollyanna of the Alps?"

Nora laughed. "I've changed."

"So I've noticed. What is it—the doctor giving you new happy pills?"

Nora gave her a sidelong smile, then reached over lazily to the small table beside her bed and pulled it open.

It was filled with prescription containers. "Untouched. Each and every one of them," she said.

Stephanie blinked. There must have been a hundred vials in the drawer. "You stopped taking your medication?"

Nora nodded. "Five months ago. I told you I was going to do it."

"But why didn't you say anything? It must have been rough."

"It wasn't too bad, after the first week. They kept me pretty doped after we got back from camp, but by Christmas vacation everybody sort of lost interest in counting my pills." She grinned. "So I stopped taking them a little at a time. I stayed in my room till I got over the shakes."

"God, I'm sorry. I never knew."

Nora shrugged. "I didn't want you to. It would have depressed you."

Stephanie thought back to last Christmas. Her mother had been shooting a film then. The preceding summer, when the administrators at Camp Hope called to tell her that her daughter had been thrown out, Mireille had promised to spend more time with Stephanie at Christmas.

That had come to nothing, of course: with her shooting schedule, she was gone most of the time. In the end, Stephanie had spent the rest of the holidays in the childishly decorated pink room in the Beverly Hills house, reading books and watching television until Mireille came home, dead tired and ready for bed. Stephanie had been glad to fly back to La Voisine.

She smiled now. "Come to think of it, you do look a little better."

"Gained fifteen pounds," Nora said triumphantly. "Not in the boobs, though." She smacked Stephanie. "Not like you." They both laughed.

"Wait a second," Stephanie said finally. "If you're not taking all those pills anymore, why do you keep refilling the prescriptions?"

"It would just cause a stink if I didn't. You know, the infirmary, my psychiatrist—God, I've got to make up things these days to keep him interested—and Daddy's secretary. She'd have a cat if she didn't think I was drugged to the gills."

"But, Nora, wouldn't they all be glad?"

"Not in this life. The last headshrinker I saw before I came here told Daddy that medication was the only way to control my incipient psychosis."

"What?"

"They think that if I ever approach actual consciousness, I'll off myself."

"But you haven't. You've gotten better."

"Damned right. But the only way Daddy's going to believe me is if he sees me for himself."

"Well, there's graduation . . ."

"Bingo," Nora said. "And something else, too." She leaped off her bed and rummaged through a stack of papers on her desk. She found one and threw it over to Stephanie. "Take a look at that."

"It's from Barnard College."

"I've been accepted," Nora said breathlessly.

Stephanie squealed with joy. "Barnard! Nora, I can't believe it!"

"New York City, here I come." Nora beamed. "I think I've finally got my act together."

"That you have. From Sister Theresa's Lonely Hearts Club to class valedictorian."

"Much to the regret of the good Sisters," Nora added. "If they had their way, I'd skip college and go straight to jail."

"Or hell," Stephanie said.

They both laughed. "We're going to have a blast in New York, Steff. You can come stay with me on holidays. And during the summers, we'll take off to Coney Island. We could even go to California, the way we used to talk about. The two of us, on our own. How's that sound?"

"Sounds great," Stephanie said, already feeling the first twinges of loss. The school had been home for so many years that it was hard to imagine anywhere else. It was especially difficult to picture life at La Voisine without Nora. "I'm glad for you." She took Nora's hand. "For both of us."

A look of relief passed across Nora's face. "Yeah, well, it'll be okay, I guess." She sniffed indifferently, then laughed. "God, what a gas. I'm finally going home." Her smile faded slowly, and she tugged at her hair. "Do I look all right?"

"You look terrific," Stephanie said.

"I mean . . . Well, can I pass for a typical sane eighteen-year-old girl on the brink of womanhood? I don't want the old man to be ashamed of me or anything."

"Your dad's going to be really proud of you," she said.

"I wrote him today. I told him about Barnard in the letter. When he comes up for my graduation, I'll fly back with him. Jeez, I wish I had a picture of myself to send him. Last year's class picture made me look like the Bride of Frankenstein."

"Don't worry about it. It'll make the surprise better."

"Class valedictorian . . . He'll come for that, don't you think?"

"For sure," Stephanie said. "Take it easy, will you?"

Nora lit a cigarette. "It's a pain to grow up," she said between two blue plumes of smoke.

On the hospital bed, Stephanie thrashed until the IV ripped out of her arm. The nurse assigned to her picked up the disturbance on the monitor and rushed into the girl's room, then increased the dosage of intravenous diazepam to fifteen units.

That's some dream she's having, the nurse thought, looking at the beautiful young girl on the bed. Movie star's daughter. She shook her head. She had a fifteen-year-old daughter of her own.

You can't protect any of them, she thought, shivering as she left the room.

Inside, deep inside the thick darkness of Stephanie's memory, Nora stood in the doorway of her dormitory room. The pink cheeks were now ashen. Her hands hung at her sides. In one of them was a thick envelope.

"Airmail special delivery," she said, tossing the packet on the floor.

Stephanie picked it up circumspectly. It seemed to be filled with brochures written in English and French. On top of them was a letter that began: "Welcome to the University of Geneva."

"What's this?" Stephanie asked.

Nora smiled crookedly. "It's my official acceptance to Switzerland's best college. Note the enclosed application form."

"I don't understand . . ."

"Don't you? I never applied to Geneva," Nora said. "Dear old Daddy obviously developed a bad case of the heebie-jeebies after finding out that his ugly, crazy daughter was planning to come out of hiding after nine years of nuns' school and crazy kids' camp."

"Nora—"

"So he gets on the horn quick to his banking buddies in Geneva, and together they make sure I stay safely tucked away in the Alps, where no one will ever lay eyes on me." As she spoke, two

spots of color appeared high on her cheeks. Her eyes grew shiny
with tears. "He never even said congratulations."

"There must have been some mistake—"

Nora pushed her arm away. "Oh, quit the crap," she said. "My
dad hasn't given me a thought since he dumped me here. And
nothing I do is going to make him remember me. As far as he's
concerned, I'm just like my mother." She stubbed out the cigarette
she'd been smoking. "She's dead, by the way."

Stephanie gasped. "Your mother?"

There was a silence. Then suddenly Nora bent forward, sobbing. She let Stephanie put her arms around her. "She died over
a month ago," she said. "In the booby hatch. Nobody told me
until now. My father's secretary put it in a postscript in her letter.
Lawrence Stillwell's letter, signed with a rubber stamp."

"Oh, Nora, I'm sorry."

"That's what they do to the lemmings in my family," Nora said
quietly. "They pretend we're not here. And then one day we're not,
and nobody notices."

Stephanie held Nora then, just as she had in the forest the
summer before, and rocked her, rocked her like the mother who
had smelled like gold.

Nora extricated herself from Stephanie's embrace. "I'm okay,"
she said, and gathered up her things. "Go on to dinner."

"I don't want dinner," Stephanie said.

"Suit yourself." Nora shrugged wearily and went out.

Stephanie followed her to her room, but Nora closed the door
in her face.

"Nora?" Stephanie called tentatively.

"Go away."

With a sigh, Stephanie walked listlessly back to her own room
to wait for Nora to cry herself out.

She went back after lights-out. "Nora?" she whispered.

There was no answer, only a bar of light from the room that spilled out from beneath the door. She knocked. The silence frightened her. Slowly, she turned the knob and pressed open the door. Nora lay on the floor, surrounded by open bottles. Their contents, colored like bits of confetti, lay all around her.

"Oh God," Stephanie whispered, running to her. "Nora! Oh God, Nora . . ."

Nora squinted, laboriously opened one red eye, and grinned. "Nosy little shit," she said thickly.

"Jesus!" Stephanie sat upright, angry with relief. "I thought you were dead."

"You always did have a dramatic turn of mind." She raised herself up on her elbows and swung her legs around. "Sleepy, that's all."

"What did you take?"

"The regular stuff I've been taking all my life." She shook her head. "Guess I wasn't used to it. Kicked the habit."

"Let's go to the infirmary, just the same," Stephanie said.

"Get lost."

"No. We ought to go."

"'We ought to go,'" Nora mimicked. "Get off my back, will you?"

"I was only—"

"Please shut up."

Stephanie sat silently on the floor as Nora stood shakily upright. She blinked. "I hate the goddamned light."

"Want to take a walk?" Stephanie offered.

Nora sighed. "Where? To the infirmary?"

"Anywhere."

"We're not allowed to go anywhere," Nora said. "That's part of the problem."

Stephanie looked out the window. Nora was right. The restrictive rules at La Voisine didn't permit much movement after lights-out.

"Then again . . ." Nora said.

"What?"

"How about the roof?" she suggested. "I could at least get some air up there."

Stephanie felt her belly tightening. Not only would they both be in trouble if they got caught, but the roof struck her as a dangerous place for someone on the verge of unconsciousness. "Uh, I don't know," she said. "Maybe we could break into the kitchen—"

Nora grunted in a harsh, bitter laugh. "I don't feel like eating. And quit saying *we*. *We* could go to the kitchen. *We* should see a doctor. Damn it, there's no *we*. I'm the one who's fucked-up. Me. Not you. Not *us*." Woozily, she looked down at Stephanie. "You've got a really stupid face sometimes."

Stephanie stood up. "So you want to go?"

"To the goddamn kitchen?"

Stephanie shrugged. "Wherever."

"Okay. The roof." Nora grinned maliciously. "Is that too scary for you?"

"I guess not," Stephanie said.

Nora staggered into the hallway. "It's dark as the inside of an asshole out here."

"Keep your voice down," Stephanie whispered.

"Sure." Nora shambled through the double doors leading to the stairway. "Wouldn't want to piss off the nuns."

It was cold on the roof. The night was starry, and the moon was almost full. "We should have brought jackets," Stephanie said, rubbing the gooseflesh on her bare arms.

"It's May. Almost time for summer vacation," Nora said. "You'll be going home soon."

"You can come with me. My mother won't even notice you." Stephanie blushed. "I mean us."

"You were right the first time."

"No, Nora, I didn't mean—"

"That's okay," Nora said. "I've gotten used to being invisible." She sat down on the foot-wide ledge surrounding the roof. "I guess that's how my mother felt at the end. Like nobody even knew she was there." She looked up at the stars. "I wonder if she even knew it herself."

"I think you'd better get off of there, Nora."

"You know who I really feel sorry for?"

"Who?" Stephanie asked, moving closer to her.

"My father. He's surrounded. It must be like living in the plague ward of a hospital. People dropping right and left. No wonder the poor bastard doesn't want to see me." She stood up, balancing shakily.

"Nora, get down." Stephanie's voice shook. She reached out her hand. "Listen to me. We'll fly to New York together, you and me. And your dad will see how terrific you look . . ."

Nora shook her head. "I'm through forcing myself on him."

"It wouldn't be like that. It'd really just be us. Like you said, we'd have a blast in Manhattan."

Nora took a deep breath and closed her eyes. "I love the cold," she said. "Come up here with me, Stephanie."

Stephanie hesitated.

"Come on. It's almost like flying." She spread her arms.

Stephanie clambered up the knee-high brick ledge, sucking in her breath as she caught a glimpse of the miniature trees in the courtyard below. "Yeah, it's great," she said. "Let's go back down, okay?"

"It feels free up here," Nora said, swinging her arms from side to side. "Steff, remember those two days when we were lost in the woods?"

"How could I forget it?" Stephanie swallowed. "Listen, do you think we could talk about this back in your room?"

"No, you couldn't remember. Not the way I do. Everything was so magnified, so bright. The air was so clean it almost hurt my chest. The sky was so light one minute, and then as dark as outer space the next."

"That was the drugs. You were withdrawing."

"I was dying," Nora said. "And it felt free. Like this. Weightless. Painless. As if I didn't have a body anymore."

"Nora, I want to get down from here."

"No." Suddenly, she clasped Stephanie around her shoulders, pinning her arms at her sides. Stephanie bobbed, off balance for a moment.

"Don't worry. I've got you," Nora said. Her face looked serene and radiant. "Then again, we could jump," she said quietly.

Stephanie was too horrified to move.

"It wouldn't be so bad. A second of pain, that's all there would be. Then nothing. No more disappointments. No more waiting. No more wishing. Just free, free as the wind. That would be something, wouldn't it, Steff? Steff?" She was smiling, the same dreamy, contented smile Stephanie had seen just before they'd been spotted by the police in the Maine woods.

"No," Stephanie said, trying hard to keep her quavering voice under control. "We've got to go back. We'll talk. We'll buy a bottle of brandy from the janitor. We'll have a meeting of Sister Theresa's Lonely Hearts Club. We'll—"

"Come with me, Steff."

Stephanie's shoulders were trembling violently. Her face twisted into a mask of fear and revulsion. "Please don't," she whispered. "I don't want to die. Please—"

Then, with a force that sent Stephanie flying almost halfway across the rooftop, Nora pushed her back over the parapet onto the roof.

Even before Stephanie hit the pebbled cement surface, she saw Nora tumbling backward, over the far side of the wall.

For a moment, Stephanie's scream was the only sound in the still night. Then, more softly, distant, there was the dull, almost wet thud of Nora's body as it struck the concrete walkway below.

The lights came on one by one, twinkling beneath Stephanie like a miniature village under a Christmas tree. Nuns in habit ran out, only their large white wimples visible, turning this way and that. A small crowd gathered around Nora, lying in an impossible position on the stone courtyard. They looked down at the body, then up, slowly, at her.

And still the scream went on, filling the sky like a ragged banner.

Chapter Forty-Eight

She awoke with a start, her throat painfully dry. "Nora," she rasped. "Nora is dead."

The nun, who had sat at Stephanie's bedside for nearly forty-eight hours, spoke quietly but clearly. "Your mother will be coming, but you'll have to answer some questions first."

Stephanie struggled to see through the fog of drugs she'd been given. The nun—Sister Bernadette, she remembered—was looking back at her with eyes as hard and cold as ice.

The Sister had taken over the position as dormitory housemother when Sister Marie-Thérèse retired at the end of last term. It was Sister Bernadette who had received the call when Stephanie and Nora were expelled from Camp Hope.

The Sister had first met Nora in the school infirmary after the girl had been flown back from Maine nearly comatose with medication after her painful withdrawal. At the beginning of the school year, she met with Stephanie personally to warn her that any further antics such as the occurrence at summer camp would result in immediate dismissal from the school.

Sister Bernadette sat straight and still on a wooden chair, her hands folded inside the sleeves of her habit over her bosom. Beneath the enormous white wimple that seemed to fill the room, she reminded Stephanie of some ancient tribal priestess.

"Dead," Stephanie whispered.

Her eyes stung as they filled with hot tears. She wanted to run away somewhere, hide in a place where no one could find her, even though she knew there was no such place. Nora continued to tumble to the concrete inside her mind, releasing her as she fell. Even in the farthest reaches of her subconscious, smothered by intravenous tranquilizers, she had been unable to escape that image.

"The police want to speak with you," Sister Bernadette said. Stephanie drew her legs up to her chest and whimpered. The nun blinked in annoyance. "However, I feel that may not be necessary. Not if you talk candidly with me."

Stephanie peeked out above the sheets. She nodded. "Yes, Sister," she croaked. She reached for a glass of water, but there was none on the small bedside table. "I'm so thirsty," she said.

When Sister Bernadette did not respond, Stephanie's hand retracted back under the bedcovers.

Finally, the nun spoke again. "Were you taking drugs with her?"

"Drugs?"

"There's no point in lying about this. The police will find out, whatever you say."

"No . . . We didn't take drugs."

"Pills were found all over the floor of Nora's room," the nun said, her steel eyes narrowing.

"Those weren't—"

"There were duplicates of every prescription. Some had been refilled ten times or more."

"That was her medication," Stephanie said. "She was supposed to take it. But she didn't. Not for months. She wanted to stop."

"The vials were open, Stephanie."

"She got a letter from her father. She was upset. She wouldn't let me in her room." Stephanie sniffed and looked around for a tissue, aware that she sounded as if she were covering up for some wrongdoing, one lie at a time.

"I said the vials were open."

Stephanie noticed the wall behind Sister Bernadette. It was stark white. A wooden crucifix hanging from it appeared to rest on the nun's shoulder.

"Stephanie, look at me."

"Yes, Sister." She forced her eyes to meet those of Sister Bernadette. "Nora opened the bottles. She took . . . I don't know. She said it was the normal dosage."

"But she hadn't taken it for months, you said?"

Stephanie nodded. "Not since she got back from camp."

"Ah, yes. Camp Hope. That was the first time you made Nora stop taking her medication."

"I didn't make her—"

"But it was your idea to leave the camp, wasn't it? That's what you told me at the beginning of term."

"Yes." Stephanie bunched the sheet in her fist. "It was my idea."

"And even though you saw with your own eyes that Nora nearly died last summer because of a lack of medication, you once again encouraged her to stop."

"It wasn't like that," Stephanie said.

"Tell me, did you enjoy seeing Nora suffer?"

"No! I didn't want her to suffer! I wanted her to get well!"

Sister Bernadette paused dramatically. "So did her family," she said. "But she won't, will she? Not anymore. Her so-called *friend*—"

"I *was* her friend, damn you!" she shouted. "I loved Nora more than anyone in the world!"

"Don't you dare use that language around me," Sister Bernadette commanded, her eyes glinting.

Stephanie felt her heart thudding. "I'm sorry, Sister."

The nun took a deep breath. "How was she when you visited her in her room?"

"She was okay," Stephanie said.

"*Okay?* She killed herself. That doesn't seem okay to me."

"She was groggy. I thought if we got some air . . ."

"On the roof."

Stephanie hesitated. "Yes," she said finally.

"After hours."

"Yes." Stephanie looked at her warily.

"You were aware, I assume, that students are not permitted on the roof under any circumstances."

Stephanie hung her head.

"Also, that students are not permitted to leave their rooms after lights-out."

"I know," Stephanie whispered.

"And yet you took a girl who was obviously in need of medical attention to a prohibited area."

"I didn't *take* her—" Stephanie began to shake. Her eyes lost focus. A dull, insistent ringing grew in her ears. She felt nauseated.

Dimly, she saw Sister Bernadette, sitting so still that she might have been carved from rock, each fold in her habit solid and permanent, her hands invisible, with the dying Christ rising inexorably out of her right shoulder.

Then, mercifully, Stephanie fainted.

"Stephanie."

Nora was falling, falling, the strangely contented smile still on her face; and behind her was Sister Bernadette, shrieking an accusation.

Tell me, did you enjoy seeing Nora suffer? she shrilled.

"I thought she should get some air . . ."

Nora fell, the cold wind whistling around her face, blowing her hair around it like a halo.

Yes. Some air. She's only getting some air . . .

The nun's face broke into a wide black-toothed grin. *You did it, Stephanie. You made sure she got some air.* Then she grasped the crucifix on her shoulder and held it in front of Stephanie's face. The small gold Christ on it writhed in pain. His eyes opened as the nun dropped it and Jesus tumbled around and around. He pulled his hands away from the cross and held them, bleeding, out to her. *Come with me, Steff,* he pleaded in Nora's voice. He was smiling. Then there was laughter, Sister Bernadette's high, screeching cackle, her breath cold as an ice storm.

"No," Stephanie screamed.

"Stephanie." Hands were touching her, wiping her face. "Stephanie, please. It's Maman."

Familiar green eyes. A beautiful, perfect face. A face from a magazine. Stephanie touched the white-blonde hair. "Mireille," she said.

"Dieu merci," the blonde woman whispered. She smiled at Stephanie.

What was a movie star doing here? She belonged on Nora's wall, next to Grace Kelly on her wedding day. "Are you real?" Stephanie asked.

"She'll be disoriented until the sedative wears off," the doctor explained. "But she's fine otherwise."

The woman smelled like gold. "We're going home, Stephanie," she said, and wrapped her arms around her.

Stephanie sat like a rag doll in the woman's arms. Two fat tears rolled down her cheeks.

Home?

Where was that?

Chapter Forty-Nine

"Oliver, you must understand—"

"I do, darling. But this delay has cost me more than a half-million dollars already."

"I can't leave Stephanie alone."

"She doesn't have to be alone," Jordan explained patiently. "You have many options. However, refusing to finish the movie is not one of them. Not with only a month of filming to go."

Mireille rubbed her forehead.

"Be reasonable," he said. "Your daughter needs time. It doesn't matter whether it's with you or without you."

"Oliver . . ."

"I did help you when you needed it," he reminded her.

"Yes, yes," she said wearily. It was true. Oliver had given her use of his plane to get to the hospital in Geneva. And afterward, he had gone along with her refusal to return to work until Stephanie showed some sign of recovery. That had been more than two weeks ago.

Stephanie still had not spoken since they left Switzerland. She would not eat voluntarily, or brush her teeth, or comb her hair, or leave the bed in the frilly pink room. She had been seen every day by Dr. Mark Cole, a prominent Beverly Hills psychiatrist who had agreed to visit Stephanie at home.

"These things take time," Dr. Cole had told Mireille earlier that day. "From what I've been able to learn from the doctor who treated her at the hospital in Switzerland and the nuns at the school, her reaction to her friend's death was very severe. A clinical setting may be a better environment for Stephanie right now."

"She's not leaving home," Mireille had said. "I'm not going to abandon her again."

"Mrs. Jouarre, this is hardly a question of abandonment—"

"Stephanie is staying here."

The doctor had accepted her decision, but Stephanie had made no progress since then.

"Mireille." Oliver's voice was a command, cutting through her thoughts about the meeting with Stephanie's doctor. "One month. That's all I'm asking." He might as well have added, *And if you don't do what I say, you can expect a breach-of-contract suit.* Smiling, he added, "Then you'll have the whole summer free."

Mireille turned away.

"Look, do you really think you're helping Stephanie by keeping her locked up in your house? Christ, even the shrink thinks she'd be better off among professionals who understand her condition."

"*I* understand her!"

"Do you?" Jordan snapped. "Exactly how much time have you spent with your daughter in the past year, Mireille?"

"That was your doing, not mine!" she shrieked, covering her face with her hands.

Jordan put his arm around her. "Shhh," he said placatingly. "I'm just asking you to think clearly. For Stephanie's sake. Give her a month, darling. That's all it'll be. One month."

One month. It would seem like forever.

"Please. Do it for her."

Mireille hadn't thought about it in those terms before. He was making a terrible kind of sense. And to be fair to all the people whose livelihoods depended upon it—the crew, the other performers—she *had* agreed to do the film.

"All right," she answered at last.

"Thank you. Your call is for six tomorrow morning."

After he left, she walked down the hall to Stephanie's room. The girl was lying in bed, her eyes unfocused. She had lost weight. The prominent cheekbones, once obscured by a healthy layer of baby fat, now stood out beneath her pale skin. Her lips were chapped, white-caked.

Mireille forced herself to smile. "It's going to be a beautiful day," she said, opening the window.

Stephanie pulled the covers higher. She never moved her head.

Mireille sat down beside her on the bed. "Darling, is there anything you need?"

There was no answer.

She stroked the girl's long dark hair. "Oliver Jordan stopped by. Do you remember him? You used to be quite mad for him."

She waited for some flicker of recognition, but there was none. Stephanie only stared. Mireille went on, quickly, looking down at her hands. "Well, I'm making a picture with him now. We'll be finished next month. I have to go to work tomorrow. Will you be all right here?"

The girl did not blink.

"The housekeeper will be with you all day. Her name is Mrs. Rodriguez. And of course, if you'd ever like to call me . . ." The sentence died on her lips. Stephanie would never call. She might never even speak again.

Mireille stood up. "I'll be back in a few minutes," she said, hearing the catch in her voice. She would not let her daughter see her cry. Not out of pity.

She walked out of the bedroom and leaned against the cool wall of the hallway. Would Stephanie ever be herself again? The doctor at the Swiss hospital had assured Mireille that her daughter had been physically unharmed by the incident. But who could calculate the emotional damage to a fifteen-year-old girl who had watched her best friend kill herself?

She peeked into the room. Stephanie's eyes were closed, as usual.

The movie would be finished by late summer. Perhaps Stephanie would be well by her birthday in December. They would celebrate together, just the two of them, the way they had when Stephanie was a small child.

So many birthdays missed, Mireille thought. Stephanie had spent her last eight birthdays at La Voisine. Mireille had always sent lavish gifts to her and saw her soon afterward for the holidays, but for eight years the girl had spent her special day alone . . . or with Nora.

She would not be alone anymore. This film would be Mireille's last. The two of them would leave California and go back to France, perhaps, or to a place where no one knew her either as l'Ange or as Mireille, and they would start over. But first Stephanie had to get well.

How long would it take her to get over Nora's death? Mireille had been only a year older than her daughter when she'd lost Stefan. How long had it taken her to forget?

Never, she answered herself. *I've never forgotten.*

But she had never willed herself to die, as it seemed Stephanie was doing.

One month. She prayed that it would pass quickly.

There was a stack of mail on the breakfast table. Mireille hadn't bothered to look at it for days. Idly, she sorted through the envelopes. She tossed the invitations to one side. Her secretary would send her regrets. Her bookkeeper would pay the bills. She never even saw the huge bags of fan mail that arrived every day. The studio took care of that.

After she was finished, there was only one piece worth looking at, a thin blue airmail envelope from Paris. The return address was in the area of the Rue Pigalle. Above it was scrawled the name "Ponti."

Mireille tore it open. She had written to Barbara several times since her wedding to Victor Mohl, but Barbara had not responded. Her last two letters had been returned, stamped "Address Unknown."

My darling Mireille, the letter began. *Has it really been so long? I suppose I've gotten caught up in my adventures again . . .*

It went on to sketch out a madcap whirl of decadent parties, world travels, and liaisons with mysterious men, then ended with a casual request for money:

By the way, little cabbage, I'm afraid I've got the teeniest case of the shorts. Could you see your way clear to advance me a little pocket change—say five thousand francs—for a week or two? I hate to be a bother, but Hermès has a pair of stunning red gloves that I really can't do without. You do understand, don't you?

Mireille laughed out loud. Beautiful, shallow Barbara, the grasshopper who fiddled the summer away. No doubt she had spent the month's rent money on a new outfit and was now in hock up to her ears.

What was it like never to change? Mireille wondered. Never to regret or worry, never to find yourself in a place you didn't intend to go . . .

She wired Barbara the money, along with a telegram. Their lives were far apart now, but Barbara was still Mireille's only friend in the world. One day they would see each other again, even if they were both old crones at the time. They would laugh all day, as they had in Rome, and Barbara would find an easy solution to everything, as she always did.

Mireille sat with Stephanie the rest of the evening. She had
Mrs. Rodriguez bring in a tray with soup and bread, and set it on
the bed. Automatically, Mireille picked up the spoon.

"An old friend of mine sent a letter," she said chattily, bringing
the spoon to the girl's lips. "Barbara. I don't imagine you remember her. We all lived together when you were small—"

Stephanie swallowed the soup, vacant-eyed.

The following month was maddening. The director, Sam Hope,
was conducting the final principal shooting for *Josephine* at a
furious pace, probably to make up for time lost during Mireille's
absence. Mireille worked until late into the evening, arriving home
exhausted, to hear that miracles had happened with her daughter.

Twelve days into shooting, Stephanie fed herself. On the sixteenth day, she got out of bed for the first time. By day twenty, she
had watched *Leave It to Beaver* on television.

Mireille listened to Dr. Cole's reports with a combination of
exultation and envy. She knew she had been right to keep Stephanie
at home, yet she had seen none of Stephanie's first steps toward
recovery. They had occurred while she was at the studio, where
she had been for every major event in Stephanie's life for the past
eight years.

After her last day on the set, Mireille came home to find
Stephanie dressed in a pair of jeans and a sweatshirt. She was sitting in the rocker in her room, reading. Her hair was brushed. Her
bed was made.

"Stephanie," Mireille whispered.

Stephanie's head snapped up.

For a moment Mireille stood in the doorway, blinking incredulously. Then she ran over to the girl and put her arms around her.
"You heard me."

The girl pushed her away. Her eyes were frightened.

"No, no, I'm not going to hurt you," Mireille said.

Don't run, she thought. *Oh, please don't run away from me.*

Stephanie remained just as she was for some time, her fingers splayed, her eyes wide and unblinking. The book sat open on her lap, where it had fallen. A breeze from the open window ruffled the pages.

Mireille backed away silently. *She doesn't know who I am yet.* The thought hurt like a physical pain. Her daughter was healing at last, healing on her own. She neither needed nor wanted the person who called herself her mother to help.

For the first time in years, Mireille thought of Madame Renée. She, too, had abandoned her daughter to save her from shame. At least she'd had the wisdom to leave completely.

Mireille shook off the thought. "I'll go," she said quietly, moving slowly toward the door. "You see? I'm going now."

Stephanie watched her warily. Then, when Mireille reached the threshold, the girl relaxed. She picked up the book and found the page she had been reading. With a careless, automatic gesture, she pushed her long dark hair behind her ear.

When did she become so grown-up-looking? Mireille wondered. She wished she could remain where she was, watching the beautiful young woman who was her daughter.

But it was best not to stay. Stephanie did not want her now. The movie was finished; there would be time for them to be together. At last, there would be enough time.

If it wasn't already too late.

The doorbell rang, sounding violently loud. Mireille held her breath, watching to see if it frightened Stephanie. The girl went on reading, indifferent as ever to any activity in the house.

"I'll check in on you again at bedtime," Mireille said.

Stephanie did not respond.

Mrs. Rodriguez was arguing with whoever had rung the doorbell.

"No, I'm sorry," she said in her accented contralto voice. "The *señora* is not expecting visitors."

"But I tried to explain . . ." The voice that spoke now was a raspy croak. *"Merde! Salope!"*

"Who is it?" Mireille said, moving quickly toward the door.

"Mireille," the woman at the threshold said. She was skeletally thin, an aging caricature of a young girl, with long straw-like hair dyed red, thick kohl rimming her frantic eyes, and a smear of bright lipstick that accentuated her bad teeth. She was wearing a thin dress of cheap fabric, covered by what had once been the top half of a suit. In her hands was a tattered hatbox.

"I beg your pardon?" Mireille asked.

The woman smiled nervously. "Don't you remember me?" she asked. "I'm Barbara."

Chapter Fifty

"Barbara," Mireille whispered incredulously. "I mean . . . Come in. Please."

The redhead pushed snootily past Mrs. Rodriguez. *She looks like a streetwalker,* Mireille thought, then felt ashamed of herself. "I'm . . . I'm so glad you came." She nodded to the housekeeper in dismissal.

"Sorry I didn't give you any warning, but you know me." Barbara laughed, and it turned into a hoarse, phlegmy cough. "Got any scotch, honey?"

Mireille snapped to. "Yes, of course." She rushed over to the bar to pour a glass. When she turned around, Barbara was sitting on one of the sofas, rummaging in her small shoulder bag for a cigarette. She tried to light it with the big table lighter, but her hands were shaking so badly that the flame never connected with the cigarette.

Finally, Mireille steadied Barbara's hands with her own. "All right," she said gently. "Tell me what's wrong."

Barbara inhaled deeply and squinted. "Nothing. I got tired of Rome, that's all. Went back to Paris . . ." Her words trailed away. She seemed to be staring across the room without seeing. She blew out the smoke in a noisy stream. "I know I don't look like much. I've been sick a little. You know all the viruses you pick up in the winter."

Mireille nodded, not believing her. "What have you been doing?"

"Oh, this and that. Some extra work, a little modeling . . ." The cigarette fell out of her hand onto the carpet as she doubled over, clutching her abdomen.

"Barbara!"

"I need to use the toilet."

"I'll take you. Are you all right?"

Barbara nodded. Thin mucus seeped out of her nostrils. "It must have been the food on the airplane." She got shakily to her feet and picked up the old hatbox she had brought.

"You can leave that," Mireille said. She reached for the box, but Barbara yanked it out of her grasp.

"The bathroom. Hurry, all right?" Barbara walked slowly but frantically, droplets of sweat standing on her forehead and cheeks. Mireille put her arm around her shoulders for support as they walked.

"I think I should call a doctor," she said.

"No!" Barbara's eyes flashed at her like those of a frightened, starving animal.

"But food poisoning—"

"I told you, I've been sick for a while," she muttered crossly. "Christ, you need a golf cart to get to the freaking john in this house."

"It's not much farther—" Suddenly, Mireille stopped.

Stephanie stood in the hallway, directly in front of them. She was staring at Barbara, two deep creases between her eyes.

Barbara looked up woozily.

"Excuse us, Stephanie, please," Mireille said, but the girl did not move. Instead, she lifted her hand to Barbara's sweat-slick cheek.

"Nora," she whispered. It was the first word she had uttered in a month.

Mireille swallowed. "No, darling, this isn't—"

"You've come to die again, haven't you?"

Barbara's eyes squeezed shut. Mireille could feel her trembling.

"I'll come with you this time," Stephanie said.

"Stephanie, please," Mireille pleaded, terrified of the words her daughter had finally chosen to speak. Stephanie did not even seem to be aware of her mother's existence.

"I love you, Nora."

Barbara tore herself away from Mireille's grip and pushed past the girl into the bathroom, slamming the door behind her.

Mireille watched after her anxiously for a long moment, then turned toward Stephanie. The girl was paying no attention to her whatsoever. When Mireille touched her arm, Stephanie flinched.

"Darling . . ."

"She's going to go to the roof," Stephanie said. "I let her go there. I did it wrong. I didn't mean to kill her—"

"You didn't kill anybody!" Mireille threw her arms around the girl. Stephanie fought her off with the strength of a grown man.

"I did! I killed her, and Jesus, too!"

"Stephanie, please listen to me—"

With a roar of rage, the girl hurled her mother against the wall. Mireille gasped with the shock of the blow, then fell to all fours.

Mrs. Rodriguez rushed into the hall, but Mireille waved at her to stay back. "Stephanie," she whispered, getting to her feet. "Stephanie . . ."

But Stephanie had already forgotten the incident. She was standing where she had been, her face blank, her eyes glazed, once again staring at the closed door where the woman she believed was Nora had gone.

Mireille closed her eyes, trying to blot out the truth that stood not five feet in front of her: her daughter had disappeared somewhere inside her own madness. The only thing that was real to Stephanie now was the horror of Nora's death.

Quietly she walked to the library and called Dr. Cole.

As she hung up the telephone, she heard the bathroom door open. She rushed out into the hall to see Barbara slouched against the door frame, her head lolling, her gaze calm and unfocused, her too-red lips curled into a sardonic smile against a dead-white face.

Mireille stopped in front of her, frowning with alarm. "Barbara?" she whispered.

"I'm fine now," Barbara said, slurring her words. "Everything's . . . fine . . ." She made a small gesture with her hand. The hatbox slid off her wrist. It popped open when it fell to the floor. Some clothes, wrinkled and not too clean, spilled out, along with a cosmetic bag and a small black rectangular case.

Beside it was a hypodermic syringe.

"Everything's . . . fine . . . now," Barbara said, and slumped to the floor, unconscious.

Stephanie screamed. She threw herself on Barbara's motionless body. "Don't die again! Don't die without me! Nora! Nora, wait for me!"

She would not allow Mireille to come near. When the ambulance arrived, shortly after Dr. Cole, Stephanie was still screaming.

"What's her name?" one of the paramedics asked.

"Barbara . . . No, it's Létitia. Her real name is Létitia Pauchon."

The paramedic wrote it down. "Is she going to be all right?" Mireille asked as they placed Barbara on a stretcher.

"She's an addict," the young man said. "From the looks of things, she's had the habit for some time." He showed Mireille her friend's arms. They were pitted roadways of track marks. Seeing Mireille's stricken face, he added, "I think she's going to be all right, though. You didn't let any grass grow under her."

Dr. Cole was with Stephanie. He had injected her with a sedative so that the paramedics could pry her away from Barbara.

"She mistook my friend for Nora," Mireille said numbly. "She thinks Nora is going to kill herself again. When Barbara collapsed . . ."

Dr. Cole touched her arm. "Let me take Stephanie to Whitefield Sanitarium," he said gently. "It's a good facility. We can arrange for your friend to go there, too, after the crisis has passed." He paused. "They're both going to be all right in time."

Mireille nodded woodenly.

The doctor cleared his throat. "I'm going to recommend that Stephanie remain under fairly heavy medication for a time. I think it would be best if you didn't see her for a week or two."

"But I'm her mother," Mireille protested.

"Sometimes strangers can be of more help to a patient than family," he said.

Tears welled in Mireille's eyes.

"Try to distract yourself with work," Dr. Cole said encouragingly. "That would be the best thing for you now."

The ambulance carrying Barbara rolled away, its taillights growing small down the long driveway. Following behind was Stephanie in Dr. Cole's car.

The house seemed terribly quiet, so when the telephone rang, the noise was terrifying. Her heart thumping, Mireille forced herself to sit down and breathe until Mrs. Rodriguez, who had stayed unobtrusively out of the way during all the commotion, entered the room.

"Señora, the phone," the housekeeper said. "It is Mr. Jordan calling. He wishes for you to attend the party."

"Party?" Mireille asked incredulously.

"He say the party for finish the movie. You will come? He want to know."

Mireille sat, stunned, for a moment. A cast party. Oliver Jordan was calling to summon her to a cast party.

She closed her eyes. And then she laughed. She laughed so hard that Mrs. Rodriguez came to sit beside her and wrapped her arms around Mireille like a mother comforting a child.

Then Mireille cried, sobbing into the woman's shoulder.

Mrs. Rodriguez stroked her hair. "You would like some tea, maybe?" she asked quietly, her soft voice filled with concern.

Mireille pulled away from her. "No, thank you," she whispered. "I'm going to bed." She wrung her hands together to stop them from shaking. "I'm tired," she said.

Chapter Fifty-One

After two weeks at Whitefield, Stephanie was more of a stranger to her mother than ever. During Mireille's first visit, her daughter stared blankly at her. She was wearing a bathrobe and slippers. She wet herself when Mireille touched her.

"Give her time," Dr. Cole said as he walked Mireille to the elevator. "She's safe here. At the moment, that's what we're interested in most. Once she learns that, we'll see some progress." He smiled, but Mireille knew it was no more than a professional bromide.

"Meanwhile, our other patient is doing quite well," he went on, more cheerfully. "Barbara—she insists we call her Barbara—is recovering nicely. She isn't ready for release, of course, but the worst of her withdrawal symptoms seem to have passed. Why don't you pay her a visit?"

Mireille nodded. Barbara had been admitted to Whitefield a day after her collapse. Her stomach had been pumped at the hospital. Then, during the full throes of heroin withdrawal, she was brought to the sanitarium by ambulance. Mireille had come to visit her then, but Barbara, shaking and wild-eyed, had not recognized her.

"How's the new movie coming?" the doctor asked genially.

"My part in it's finished now."

"Oh. Is that good?" He was a perceptive man. It was supposed to be good.

Finishing *Josephine* was something Mireille had looked forward to for months. It was to be the end of her Hollywood career, the long-delayed beginning of her life with Stephanie. Now, alone during the holidays, with the two people she loved most locked away in this fearful, antiseptic place, this milestone seemed no more than another part of an endless nightmare.

"I don't know," she answered truthfully.

The elevator door opened. "You know, you're welcome to come see me if you need someone to talk to."

Mireille forced herself to smile. She wished she could afford the luxury of telling the truth, but that door had been closed for too long. She dared not open it now.

"Thank you, Doctor," she said, pressing the button to separate herself from him.

Barbara was sitting up in bed, drinking a soda. She made a face when she saw Mireille.

"Caught guzzling warm ginger ale. Now this is humiliating."

"How are you, Barbara?"

"Oh, great. Just great. Can't you tell by the way I look?"

Her eyes were hollowed and dark, her skin pasty. The improbably red hair stood out wildly on her head like a fright wig. On her arms were the needle scars, traveling along her veins in rough ridges. There was so little of the old Barbara left that Mireille found it difficult to meet her eyes. "You look fine," she said.

Barbara snorted. "You never could lie worth a damn. Get me a cigarette."

"I don't have any."

"Well, get some."

Mireille lowered her head. There was a long silence.

Finally, Barbara spoke. "I'm sorry," she said hoarsely. "I didn't mean to make you take care of me." She sniffed. The corners of her mouth turned down. "So what are you doing here, anyway? I thought movie stars had better things to do than hang around drunk tanks."

Mireille smiled. "Maybe not." She took a small gaily wrapped package out of her purse and gave it to Barbara. "I brought you something."

"I hate sentimentality," Barbara said as she pulled off the ribbon.

Inside the box was a silver compact engraved with the words "For B with love, M."

"Aren't you afraid I'll hock it for a quick fix?" she asked quietly, touching the compact. "That's what I did with the dildo necklace the girls at Madame Renée's got me. The diamond earrings, too. Remember them? My old-age pension." She rubbed the silver absently with her thumb. "They kept me high for two solid months."

"Do what you want with it," Mireille said.

Barbara held it tightly for a moment. "Thank you," she said. She opened it and looked at her reflection in the mirror. She seemed mesmerized by the sight. Then her hands began to shake, and Mireille saw that she was crying. She went over to the bed to sit with her.

"How did this happen to me?" Barbara whispered. "It was good times . . . real good times . . ." She dropped the compact and clung to Mireille.

"At first it was just the parties, the drinking. There was a lot of drinking. I missed a few calls." She laughed bitterly. "When you're a star, you can be late or miss a day, but they don't put up with that from bit players. We're too easy to replace."

She coughed, and the coughing wracked her body. "After a while, I packed it in—I was kicked out of my apartment—and went back to Paris. I tried to get back with Madame Renée, but she said I was too old." She toyed with the bedcovers. "I was thirty-two."

"It's all right," Mireille said. "Don't say any more. You don't have to talk."

"Yes, I do. I want to. Maybe it'll get me to think, for a change. I never did much thinking about my life. I just figured things would go on forever, somehow." She waved her hands, as if she were trying to erase whole blocks of her life. "Anyway, I had it out with Renée. Pulled out a handful of her hair." She laughed sharply. "That felt pretty good. Then I went to work for Phillippe Martine. Do you know him?"

Mireille shook her head.

"Maybe he was after your time. High-class pimp. What a contradiction that is. Anyway, he's got good girls, beauties, except he didn't put me into the good work. He sent me to parties. *Ménages à trois*," she said with distaste.

"Two guys and me. That was my specialty. Two, or more. Five men, sometimes. Once, a whole roomful, one after the other. After the first four or five, another girl offered me a Demerol to get me through the rest. After that I used them all the time."

She seemed to calm, but it was an eerie, lackluster quiet. "They were good. The pills, I mean. I almost forgot what was happening to me. And then one night Phillippe gave me a shot of morphine. It was even better." She looked out the window. "I remember thinking, *This is the answer.* You wonder what you're going to do with your life, you give in so much, hoping for a change in things, a chance at something, and then . . . it doesn't matter. With the morphine, it just didn't matter. There were no more problems. I was getting old—so what? I have to fuck eighteen dirty boys who slap me around?" She shrugged.

Mireille put her hand over her mouth.

"Do you understand? Do you?"

Mireille nodded mechanically, remembering the first night she became l'Ange in a limousine with a nameless, faceless man. "Nothing that happens is real," she said.

"Nothing." Barbara picked up the compact and toyed with it. "Do you think Ankha knew that?"

"Yes," Mireille said. "We all do."

Barbara blew her nose. "Anyway, after a while Phillippe stopped getting me the stuff. He said I was an addict. He batted me around pretty badly, too. Broke one of my teeth once." She opened her mouth in a grimace to show a jagged broken molar, untreated and blackening.

"He said I was ugly. He said he couldn't use me anymore. He said nobody would want to stretch out next to me, even in the dark. He said . . . Well, a lot of things. I guess you can say anything you want to a used-up whore."

She blew her nose again. "So I worked the streets. I found a connection. Heroin. It was even better than morphine. Every cent I had went to get more. I spent thirty days in the slammer once. I thought I'd die, until they put me in a hospital. I could at least get sleeping pills there."

She looked down at her hands. "I did one of the orderlies there for some extra pills," she said quietly. Her eyes were wide and swimming in tears. "Every day at five p.m."

"Oh, Barbara," Mireille whispered.

"This is what the bottom of the barrel looks like, sugar."

Mireille tried to comfort her, but Barbara shook her off. "Don't waste your time feeling sorry for me. I only wrote to you so I could get high again."

"Then why did you come? Five thousand francs buys a lot of heroin."

The silence filled the room. "That's what I thought at first," she said. "Damn, I was one happy scaghead when that money order came. I picked up a little stash—if I could have gotten more, I would have. And then I saw where it was all going. I wasn't going to stop till I was dead." She took a deep breath. "So quick, before I could change my mind, I bought a plane ticket with what was left of the money. A new life in a new country—that was what I told myself. I didn't even get high on the plane. That was a mistake, I guess. I was already sick by the time I got to your house."

"And then you saw Stephanie."

"Who?"

"My daughter. The girl in the hall."

"I don't remember."

"You don't . . ."

"Sorry, honey. Things were so bad by the time I got to your place, I didn't know what was going on. There were voices. Crazy voices . . ."

She saw Mireille stiffen.

"I'm sorry I couldn't meet her," Barbara said. "Guess I embarrassed you pretty badly."

Mireille shook her head.

"How old is she now?"

"Fifteen." Her voice was quavering.

"Is anything wrong?"

Mireille shook her head again and swallowed.

Barbara touched her hand gently. "Look, I may be the lowest form of life around these parts, but I'm not really stupid."

Mireille bit her lip. "She's here," she said.

"Here? In the joint?"

Mireille nodded slowly. "The doctor keeps promising me that she'll get better, but she hasn't. She never gets any better." She spoke numbly, without expression.

"Hey. Hey," Barbara said, bringing her old friend back from whatever terrifying place Mireille had gone. This time it was Barbara who reached out in an embrace.

Mireille accepted it, taking consolation in the pallid and bony, yet familiar, arms. "God, it's been so long," she said.

"For me, too."

Twenty minutes passed before Mireille spoke again. "Is there a way out, Barbara?" she asked. "For any of us?"

"I don't know." Barbara sighed. "Maybe we should try to find it, though."

The two remained holding each other silently for a long time. Then Barbara pulled herself away. "I'll start the ball rolling by talking to her."

"That won't be easy," Mireille said. "Except for the outburst on the night you came to my house, she hasn't spoken a word for nearly six weeks."

Barbara shrugged. "No harm in trying, is there?"

"No," Mireille said, making an effort to sound hopeful. "No harm."

"It'll give me something to do. This place isn't exactly bristling with activity. How much longer am I in for, anyway?"

"The doctor said six months."

"Six months! Oh, Christ, Mireille! I can't let you pay for these quacks to keep me like a rutabaga for six more months!"

Mireille opened the silver compact idly, then snapped it closed again. "If you can get Stephanie to talk, it'll be worth every cent."

Barbara smiled. "Really?"

"More than you know."

Barbara snatched the compact out of her hands. She tossed it high in the air and caught it with a wicked laugh. "Honey, in six months I can do anything," she said. "It's a deal."

Chapter Fifty-Two

Barbara was never meant to be an invalid. Within weeks, she had organized the patients in Whitefield's alcohol-and-drug recovery program into a volleyball league. She turned her group therapy sessions into forums for planning the next day's extracurricular events. She took a fallen pop singer under her wing and taught him bawdy French sailor tunes in exchange for instruction in current American slang. She talked a wealthy and depressed socialite who had been wearing the same bathrobe for a year into giving Barbara half her wardrobe. After three days of looking at her own clothes on Barbara's body, the socialite began dressing again.

There were evening dances, weekend picnics, and talks by the patients about their areas of expertise in the outside world, all under Barbara's aegis. Her own lecture on the life of a Parisian call girl packed the recreation room. She persuaded the sanitarium authorities to donate a quarter acre of ground for a flower garden, which the patients tended. She directed a show in which the patients satirized the medical personnel at Whitefield.

But she could not get Stephanie to talk to her.

Day after day she approached the pale, silent girl in the east wing, where potentially suicidal patients were kept in doorless rooms equipped with television monitors.

Stephanie almost never left her room. When Barbara came in to visit, the girl never turned her face toward her or acknowledged her presence in any way.

"She's that way with everyone," confided a nurse's aide. "It's like she's got her own little world to live in."

"It's probably a hell of a lot better than this one," Barbara said.

And she kept trying. For a month she paid the girl daily visits. She brought her candy that remained untouched in a pile on her dresser. She told her jokes in English and French. Stephanie's blank stare never changed.

Barbara offered to brush her hair, but at the touch of the hair-brush, Stephanie began to scream.

Something. Barbara wracked her brain. There had to be something she could do to reach her.

Then she had an idea. Mireille had told her that Stephanie had confused her with someone else, a friend who had killed herself. What was her name? Nora. Yes, that was it. Nora. Stephanie had talked to Nora once. Maybe she would talk to her again.

Early in October, Barbara dressed herself in a pair of flowing white Courrèges palazzo pants and a diaphanous white silk top—both gifts from the now-released socialite—and floated down the long hallway toward Stephanie's room.

Careful to stand in the open doorway out of range of the monitor, she slowly raised her arms to her sides, so that the wide silken sleeves of her blouse hung down like an angel's wings.

"Stephanie, it's Nora," she said in the voice she used to reserve for casting directors.

Stephanie's head snapped toward her, her gray eyes large and frightened.

Oh, shit, Barbara thought. *She's going to go over the edge.* Panic fluttered inside her stomach. Should she back out now, tell the girl it was all a joke? Should she call a nurse? *Damn it, I should have asked her doctor first!*

She glanced over at the window. Bars. Well, at least Stephanie couldn't jump. There were no sharp objects in the room. Even the drinking glasses were made of paper. There was no way the girl could kill herself in this room. You couldn't take a piss without somebody watching.

Suddenly, Barbara's heart welled with pity for the girl. "It's like a cage in here," she said.

Stephanie blinked. For the first time, she seemed to hear what Barbara was saying.

"Come on, kid. Let's get out of this place for a while."

She held out her hand. Stephanie refused it, but when Barbara walked out of the room, she followed her. Stephanie hesitated at the outer door, squinting into the sunlight.

"It's all right," Barbara said. Slowly, Stephanie walked onto the brick patio. It was the first time she'd been outside since her arrival. "Pretty brisk." Barbara rubbed her arms. "I always thought California was supposed to be warm."

"It was cold on the roof, too," Stephanie said. Her voice was rusty from disuse. "Remember?"

"Er . . . right," Barbara said. She wished she had a cigarette.

"It's not dark anymore."

"It's daylight, honey. This is what it looks like. Not that I'm much of an expert, but I've seen more of the sun since I got to this dump than I ever did before. It kind of grows on you."

Stephanie was watching her with fascination. "You don't look the same," she said.

"The same as what?"

"As you did when you . . . left." She looked frightened again. "How long has it been?"

Barbara sniffed. "Too damned long, Steff," she said. "You understand me? You've been hurting too long, cooped up in this hole. It's time to get out."

Stephanie stared at her for a moment, blinking, her face expressionless. "Yes," she said at last. "Sometimes you just want to get out."

"Don't I know it," Barbara said.

Slowly, Stephanie moved her hand toward Barbara and touched her arm. It was the first time she'd made conscious physical contact with another human being since the incident on the roof. "I'm afraid of dying," she whispered.

"I can think of more fun things to do, myself," Barbara said. Stephanie's mouth opened in bewilderment. "Look, dying's easy," Barbara went on. "It's living that's a bitch."

Stephanie frowned, looking as if she were contemplating "Nora's" message. Then, after a moment, she nodded and asked hoarsely, "Do you still want me to come with you?"

"Come with me?" Barbara looked at her for a moment before understanding what the girl was saying. "No, baby," she answered in a whisper. "I want you to live."

"But you said—"

"I said living was tough. But it can be wonderful, too. Ever eat so much ice cream you thought you'd burst?"

Stephanie shook her head.

"Well, that's reason enough to go on, if you ask me. As soon as we get out of here, I'll take you for the biggest ice-cream sundae you've ever laid eyes on. We'll eat like pigs and get chocolate all over our faces. People will look at us and shake their fingers in shame."

"Is that good?"

"You bet. How about dancing? I'll bet you're a dancing fool when you cut loose."

Stephanie smiled shyly. "I've never danced. There were some dances at school with boys from Saint Augustin in Geneva, but . . ." She shrugged.

Barbara slapped her forehead. "What? You've never done the boogaloo?"

"The what?" Stephanie giggled at the strange word.

"Ever hear the Drifters?" Barbara vocalized the first deep notes of "This Magic Moment," punctuating it with finger snaps. "No? Honey, you can't even think of leaving this planet until you've boogied with the Drifters! And what about boys? You said you didn't dance with them. Could it be . . . you've never kissed one, either?"

"Oh, no!" Stephanie blushed. "Never."

"Well, shit," Barbara said. "No wonder you're in the nuthouse. We'll have to take care of that, too." She gazed at the girl steadily. "Time. That's what you need, Stephanie. You've got to give yourself some time."

"But you died."

Barbara looked away, then back at Stephanie. "I don't suppose you've got a smoke on you," she said.

The girl shook her head.

"Okay. Look, I've got to tell you something." She led Stephanie to a chair, then knelt down close beside her. "Take a good look at me, kid," she said. "I'm not Nora, okay? But I do know how you feel."

Stephanie's face, for so long an expressionless mask, now ran through a gamut of strong emotions—fear, hatred, joy, relief—as if she didn't know how to respond to the stranger who had crashed down her defenses in such a vulgar and friendly way.

"My name is Barbara. I was a heroin addict. I wanted to die, too, for a long, long time."

Stephanie looked away.

"But you don't really want to die, do you?" When Stephanie didn't answer, Barbara kept talking. "No." She shook her head. "No, you don't. I've seen lots of losers. I know what they look like. You're not one of them."

"She asked me to go with her," Stephanie said.

"And you didn't."

The girl blinked back her tears. She shook her head.

"That's because it wasn't your way out. It was Nora's, not yours. There are other ways to find what you're looking for besides taking the pipe."

"The what?"

Barbara clasped both hands around her own neck and feigned an agonizing and comical death.

Stephanie gasped. It was something Nora would have done. But this wasn't Nora. It was . . . Barbara? Yes, someone named Barbara. Someone who could look at death and laugh, just like Nora.

"Other ways out," Stephanie said.

"Yeah. That's right."

"Like what?"

Barbara took a deep breath. "Like what we're doing now, maybe. Trying not to be alone in the shit heap."

Stephanie stared at her, blinking. Then, tentatively, she took Barbara's hand in her own.

Once Stephanie began to talk, her recovery was rapid and spectacular. Dr. Cole was astonished; Mireille was ecstatic. Barbara had become the center of the girl's life.

For the next six weeks they spent almost all their free time together. Stephanie became involved with Barbara's myriad projects at the sanitarium. When she wasn't gardening or playing volleyball, she could always be found in Barbara's room, listening to the older woman's outrageous stories about her past, although Barbara was careful not to mention Mireille's connection with it.

By December, the two of them were permitted outside the sanitarium, and they spent Stephanie's birthday and Christmas with Mireille. By mid-January of 1962, they were both released.

Mireille celebrated by treating them all to a day at Elizabeth Arden, getting facials and manicures and makeup. Stephanie had her long hair shaped into a more mature look, and Barbara's red mane was at last restored to its former beauty.

"Knockouts," Barbara said, admiring their reflection in the mirror. Stephanie only stared, looking bewildered. "Well? What do you think, kid?"

"I . . . I don't know. I look so . . ."

"So what?"

"So *pretty*."

Both Barbara and Stephanie melted in laughter. "Of course you're pretty. You're gorgeous. Didn't they have mirrors in that convent you went to?"

"Some. But I didn't look like this."

"You've grown up, honey," Barbara said. "This is your face now. And the boys will be fighting duels over it, believe me."

Then Mireille came to stand beside them, and the joy in Stephanie's face visibly faded. Next to the most beautiful woman in the world, Stephanie looked childish and Barbara looked haggard.

"You're lovely," Mireille said, putting her arm around her daughter. Stephanie shrugged out of her grasp.

"What's the matter, Stephanie?"

"I'd like to go now," the girl said shortly, then left the room.

Mireille looked at Barbara. "Have I said something wrong?"

"No. You can't help being perfect." She smiled and elbowed Mireille's ribs. "Let's go."

Chapter Fifty-Three

Perfect. If Stephanie only knew just how imperfect her mother was!

But then, hiding herself from Stephanie was what Mireille had built her life around. It was no wonder that Stephanie would open up for Barbara rather than Mireille.

Barbara was open herself. She was vulnerable, fallible, *real.* For eight years, Mireille had been no more real to Stephanie than she was to the screaming fans who'd lined up outside the movie theaters chanting her name.

Fortunately, though, those years had finally come to an end. There would be no more films, no more Hollywood, no more Oliver Jordan. Her daughter was home at last, and well.

And her best friend had come back into her life. Into both their lives.

Please let it last, she prayed silently. *This time, let it last.*

"Hey, sleepyhead, get up." Barbara tossed a wet beach ball toward the chaise longue. Mireille caught it, smiling.

"God, I don't know how you Americans can stand these gigantic bathing suits," Barbara said, snapping the stretchy fabric of the tank suit she'd borrowed from Mireille. "You stay wet for hours."

"Oh? What are they wearing in Paris?"

"Bikinis. A little stripe here, a little triangle there, and nothing in between. Much more comfortable."

"Sounds scandalous," Mireille said.

"Don't be square," Barbara said in English. "This is nineteen sixty-two! Modern times, baby. I'm going to get one for Stephanie as soon as I get back."

"Oh?" Mireille had never thought about Barbara's leaving. "I . . . I was hoping you would stay."

"No, Barbara's going back to Paris," Stephanie said, running up beside them to grab a towel. She gave Barbara a big grin. "And we're going with her."

"We are, are we?" Mireille asked archly. "What about school?"

"School? God, Maman, I've already missed nearly a whole year! It's going to be completely humiliating as it is, being a sopho-more next fall instead of a junior."

Mireille looked at her skeptically. "What does going to Paris have to do with starting high school?"

"Everything! Don't you see? It will lessen my suffering. Tell her, Barbara."

"How could I come up with a better argument than that?" Barbara said. "We don't want the girl to suffer, do we?"

"Oh, Maman, I've always wanted to see Paris, and Barbara's my very best friend in the world. Of course, we haven't got any money, but since you have so much . . ."

"Well, now at least I know why I've been invited," Mireille said.

"Don't be stupid, Mireille." Barbara lit a cigarette. "Okay, you happen to be the one with the bucks at the moment. It wasn't always that way, if you can bring yourself to remember back a few years."

Mireille did remember. The borrowed clothes, the borrowed apartment, the nanny for Stephanie, the movie job in Rome . . . They had all come from Barbara. "You even supplied my wedding dress," she said.

"Damn right. So don't get snooty about a trip to Paris. We need it. All of us do. What do you say?"

"Yeah," Stephanie chimed in. "What do you say?" They both smiled, a familiar, ever-shifting, growing grin.

"You've taught her the lollapalooza," Mireille said.

"I plan to teach your daughter all sorts of depraved things. The only way to control me is by coming along."

Mireille sighed. "I'll never be able to control you," she said. "Either of you."

"Well, Maman?" Stephanie asked hopefully.

A moment passed. "Okay," Mireille said. "It's about time we saw Paris again."

Stephanie and Barbara cheered. And when Mrs. Rodriguez came out to the patio carrying a silver tray piled with mail, Stephanie grabbed the rotund woman around the waist and danced with her around the table.

"I'll take that." Barbara scooped the envelopes off the tray and riffled through them. "Let's see. Southern California Edison. Dieter Brothers Fuel. Tom's Pool Cleaning Service. Gee, your mail's just like other people's."

"What did you expect?" Mireille laughed.

"Well, fan letters or something. Don't people write to movie stars?"

"That goes to my manager. I never see the fan mail."

"Are you kidding? That's the first thing I would read. Oh, here's something. The return address is in Beverly Hills." She tore the envelope open.

"Barbara!"

"Hey, it's an invitation to a party!" She gasped. "At Peter Rockwell's house! Ooh, I've seen all his movies."

"He was one of Nora's favorites, too," Stephanie said, taking the card. "Oh, look, it's a birthday party for Oliver Jordan."

Mireille felt herself freeze.

"Uncle Oliver. He used to come to the house at Christmas," Stephanie said. "I thought he was the handsomest man in world."

"So did I," Barbara quipped. "I think I still do. Oh, Mireille, do you suppose you could take us?"

Mireille's eyes flashed. "What?"

"Well, all the magazines say that you and Oliver are inseparable. He wouldn't mind if you—"

"The magazines are wrong."

Barbara frowned, puzzled. "Well, you don't have to get testy about it."

"I think I understand," Stephanie said, her eyes narrowed. "Mother isn't supposed to have a child. That's part of being a movie star. They don't have kids. At least not kids as old as me."

"No, that's not it. That's not it at all. It's just—"

"Don't bother trying to spare my feelings. I've known for a long time that I wasn't part of your life. Nobody knows I exist, and you want to keep things that way."

"Stephanie, that's not true!"

"Aren't you supposed to be the Baroness Something-or-Other?"

Mireille was stunned by the anger in her daughter's voice.

"I guess it would be hard to explain why a baroness would marry an ordinary Frenchman. My father wasn't good enough for you, either, was he?" Stephanie ran into the house.

For a long moment, Barbara and Mireille stared at each other. Finally, Barbara broke the silence. "I know what you're thinking," she said flatly. "You want to tell her the truth."

"Yes. Though I wouldn't know where to start."

"Then don't do it. You stayed away from Stephanie to protect her. Try to remember that, Mireille."

"I know. I know. But it's gotten to be so hard . . . All the lies . . ."

Barbara touched her hair. "Everything you had to lie about is over now," she said. "Everyone's forgotten about l'Ange. We can go back to Paris. And if movie stars aren't supposed to have children—"

"I couldn't care less about being a movie star! I'm never going to make another film again, anyway."

Barbara raised an eyebrow. "What happened between you and Oliver Jordan?"

"Nothing. Nothing's happened."

"I mean way back when. What put him on your permanent shit list?"

Mireille blushed.

"Okay, you don't have to talk about it. You're not the only babe who ever went back to a guy who treated her like dirt." She looked around at the expensive house. "Seems like he's tried to make things up to you, at least."

Mireille didn't answer.

"So what do you want that he won't give you?"

"A normal life," Mireille said. "I just want to lead a normal life, for once. And I'm going to."

"Then there's no problem. Let's go to the party."

Mireille knew she had been foolish to react so strongly to Oliver's name. Her contract with him was over; he had no hold on her anymore. She did not have to hide from him. "All right," she said. "We'll go if you want to."

Barbara leaped up. "Great. I need to go through your closets." She paused in the doorway. "And you need to tell Stephanie about the party. Let her know you're proud of her and want to show her off."

Mireille nodded. She was right. Stephanie had been in hiding long enough.

The party was an afternoon luau, with pretty girls dressed in sarongs serving drinks and finger food. Peter Rockwell's own lady of the moment, a twenty-year-old blonde, with a face that was interchangeable with all of Peter's former girlfriends', presided over the event in a gold lamé slit skirt that matched her gold bathing suit.

"Is she a hooker?" Barbara asked.

"That's how they dress out here," Mireille whispered. "She's an actress, I think."

"Darling Mireille!" the girlfriend gushed, strolling toward them in her imitation of a human panther. She thrust her lips in the general direction of Mireille's cheek. "You still look so wonderful. You must tell me your secret."

"Maybe she'll give you the name of her dressmaker," Barbara said caustically.

Mireille couldn't stifle a laugh. The girlfriend looked icily at Barbara. "I guess French people have a funny sense of humor," she said.

"Ah, non, chérie." Barbara looked thoughtful. "I don't know any Frenchwoman funny enough to wear the costume you have on."

Mireille stomped on her foot.

"The bar's over there," the girlfriend said, and turned away.

"Why did you have to say that?" Mireille hissed.

"She rubbed me the wrong way, the bitch," Barbara muttered.

Stephanie giggled. "I thought it was hilarious," she said. "Oh, look, there's Uncle Oliver."

The hostess was scampering toward Jordan, arms outstretched. Mireille swallowed.

"I wonder if he'll remember me?" Stephanie waved hesitantly. "Maybe we ought to say hello."

"I don't think so," Mireille said. Rockwell's blonde appeared to be holding him in a death grip. "He looks busy just now."

But Jordan had noticed them. "He's coming this way," Stephanie said cheerily. "Uncle Oliver!" She intercepted him. Jordan kissed her briefly on the cheek, then sent her off to the bar and continued toward Mireille, his face dark with anger.

"What is the meaning of this?" he rumbled fiercely. "That girl—"

"That girl is my daughter," Mireille said coolly. "Surely it's no longer necessary to keep her existence secret," she said, "since I'll be making no other films."

"That's inane, Mireille. We'll have to discuss this . . ." He cast a glance at Barbara, then squinted into her face. "I believe I know you from somewhere," he said.

"Oliver, I'd like you to meet an old friend of mine, Barbara Ponti. We worked together in *Lone Gun*."

"Oh, yes," he said abstractly, still staring, trying to place her. "Ponti . . . You're from Italy, then?"

"Paris," Barbara volunteered. "We met once, at a party at the Comte the Vevray's in London." She extended her hand.

Jordan did not take it. He looked up slowly at Mireille. "How dare you," he said. He grabbed her by the arm. "It wasn't bad enough to bring your teenage daughter here, I suppose. You had to bring an aging trollop, too? She's probably already sold her story to some rag."

Mireille gasped at the phenomenal rudeness of the remark. "You . . . you owe us both an apology," she managed finally.

"*I?* I owe *you*? If this . . . this *person* opens her mouth about you, you're finished, do you understand? Do you understand anything?"

"How dare you say such a thing!"

"Well, apparently someone has to explain the obvious to you."

"Let's go," Barbara said quietly.

"I've staked everything on you. Absolutely everything. And this is how you repay me!"

"I've repaid you a thousand times over," Mireille said. "In a thousand degrading ways. You're worse than anything I ever was—"

"For God's sake, keep your voice down. People are staring."

"Let them! I wish everyone could know the kind of monster you are!"

"Get out of here before you make a fool of yourself." He released her arm with a shove. "And take your friend with you."

"Not until I've told you exactly what I think of you."

"Mireille, please," Barbara pleaded. Her hands were trembling. Stephanie came over.

"Here's your drink, Uncle Oliver . . . Barbara, what's the matter?" she asked. "Are you sick? Mother, what's wrong?"

Jordan took the drink from her, murmured his thanks, then turned on his heel and walked away. He was the picture of serenity as he greeted Peter Rockwell.

Mireille could barely drive home.

"What happened?" Stephanie asked, confused. "Why did we have to leave so soon?"

Mireille tried to speak but couldn't. Finally, she patted Stephanie's hand in a gesture asking for a few moments' grace.

"You can tell me, really. I'm not a child—"

"Your mother had a falling-out with Mr. Jordan," Barbara said from the backseat. "He wants her to make another movie, and she doesn't want to. She'd rather go to Paris with us." She smiled.

"Oh," Stephanie said with understanding. "Well, you could have told me that." Mireille looked in the mirror at Barbara. The woman was a marvel. Nothing upset her, utterly nothing. Just thinking about Oliver's overt cruelty made Mireille want to scream with rage, but Barbara just sat calmly, smoking and looking out the car window.

"I'll never speak to him again," Mireille said.

Barbara shrugged.

At home, Mireille suggested they call for pizza, but Barbara begged off. "I think I'll just go to bed," she said. She kissed Mireille and Stephanie good night.

The next morning, she was gone.

Chapter Fifty-Four

Adam Wells knew everything.

That was a premise that Oliver never questioned. Wells knew about Peter Rockwell's luau, of course; half of Hollywood knew about the reclusive Mireille's brief appearance, even before the *Hollywood Star* published a photograph of her driving through the gates of the Rockwell estate with two unidentified "friends." And he knew about the spat between Mireille and Jordan—an observation that could have been made by anyone who had seen the two of them together.

But Wells was the highest-paid producer's assistant in the business because he was supposed to know more about everyone's private affairs than anyone else. In this he had failed.

"Why wasn't I told she'd be bringing someone?" Jordan bellowed into the phone.

"Oliver, be reasonable. I checked the invitation list. Mireille didn't respond. She never goes to parties. You know that. No one expected her to show up."

"Well, she showed up, all right. And she brought her nearly grown daughter and a streetwalker with her!"

"A what?"

"Shut up," Jordan commanded. "From now on, I want to know everything Mireille does. Everything! Do you understand?"

"But . . . Oliver, really. Isn't this going a bit far?"

"Do it!" Jordan slammed down the receiver.

Two days after Barbara's disappearance, Jordan knew about it. He sent five dozen calla lilies for Mireille and a yellow chiffon dress for Stephanie, along with a note apologizing for his lamentable behavior at the party.

One hour after Mireille hired a private detective to search for Barbara, Jordan knew about it. He sent the screenplay of *Mozambique* to Mireille's home, along with a note begging her to reconsider her decision to retire.

Thirty minutes after the detective informed Mireille that he had found no leads whatever, Jordan knew about it.

"Adam," he said smoothly into the intercom.

When Wells came into the office, Jordan was sitting with his feet on his desk. He was smiling. "I want you to find me a woman," he said.

"My, what a novel request."

"A particular woman." He wrote down a name on the back of a still from *Lone Gun*. "She looks considerably older than the photograph."

"Barbara Ponti? How am I going to find her? A detective couldn't."

"The detective's livelihood wasn't at stake."

"That sounds like blackmail."

"Call it what you like. By the way, she's a hooker."

"Oh, well, that makes things so much easier. I'll just look her up in the yellow pages."

Jordan didn't catch the humor. "Call me when you've found her."

"Care to discuss the screenplay?" The voice needed no introduction.

"I told you what my plans are, Oliver," Mireille said coldly.

"Ah, yes. I'd forgotten. Garbo vants to be alone. Nevertheless, I'd like to see you in my office."

"That's out of the question."

"I've found Barbara Ponti," he said softly.

There was dead silence on the line.

"Her real name is Létitia Pauchon."

Mireille swallowed. "Where is she?"

"Shall we say four thirty? I'll see that she's here." He hung up.

The redhead stepped out of the bathroom onto the plush carpeting, tottering on her high heels.

She must have been pretty once, Jordan thought.

The woman held onto the doorway unsteadily. Her eyes were glazed and sleepy. There was sweat on her upper lip. The flesh on her arms stood out in goose bumps, and had a bluish cast.

"Damn it," Jordan muttered. If Wells gave her too much, this junkie was going to die right in his office. "Here, drink this," he said, offering her a glass of water.

She waved it away. *"Ça va,"* she said dreamily.

"I said drink it."

She obeyed. *"Tu as l'envie, chéri?"* she asked, forming a curlicue on his face with her stubby fingernails. Jordan recoiled from her touch. "You have a nice face," the woman said in thickly accented French. "A nice face. Not a kind face." She shrugged and smiled. *"Je m'appelle Barbara."*

Jordan looked at his watch, then buzzed Wells.

"Mireille just came in," Adam said.

"Have her wait for ten minutes, then send her in." He turned to Barbara and cupped his hands over her breasts. She responded with professional enthusiasm, running her hands down his body, caressing the swelling in his pants.

"Get on the floor," he said.

The teddy she was wearing had thoughtfully been designed with a snap crotch. Jordan yanked it open to expose her white buttocks. They were still round and smooth, unlike her face. From this angle, he thought, she wasn't half-bad.

He knelt over her, licking the porcelain skin of her ass, flicking his tongue over her. She moaned and raised her buttocks high to expose a wet vagina surrounded by labia shaved smooth as a child's.

"That's my girl," he said, taking his cock out of his trousers. The thought of Mireille finding him this way excited him more than the flesh of any woman could. Guiding it with his hand, he rubbed the throbbing organ over Barbara's glistening wetness. She tightened her buttocks around it and released it rhythmically, squeezing it with her body.

Jordan felt himself flushing with excitement. One thing he had forgotten during his infatuation with Mireille was how proficient an experienced hooker could be. They were trained to fuck. In becoming a star, Mireille had forgotten how to service a man with no thought for herself. It had been good, glorious at times, but there was something special about a mindless, uncommitted rut.

"Fuck it," he said, grabbing hold of Barbara's buttocks. She continued to sway and push, exposing the parted lips of her pink pussy, the round aureole of her anus, shining with his juice. Then, with one violent thrust, he shoved the whole of his huge prick inside her.

She gasped and tightened her muscles so that every movement was like a long, hard suck. Her dangling breasts jiggled. She thrashed her head so that the long red hair spread across her shoulders. Jordan gathered it up and yanked it hard as he galloped her, slamming deep inside her flesh again and again.

"Fuck it," he whispered. "Fuck it . . . fuck it . . . fuck it . . ." He exploded in an ecstasy of light and helpless release. He cried out, jerking the girl onto him in a frenzy.

As he unloaded into her body, the door opened and Mireille walked in.

She said nothing, but her face was a kaleidoscope of changing expressions: First, disgust, then recognition as she saw Barbara's face. She put her hand to her mouth. Her eyes flashed with anger. Then an ineffable sadness overtook her as Jordan pushed Barbara aside on the floor.

Barbara, she knew, recognized her, too. She moaned softly when she saw Mireille's face. Then she turned away, pulling down the crotch of her teddy. She tried to stand up, but she was too drugged to keep her balance and fell to the floor again.

"Hello, Mireille," Jordan said affably. "Perfect timing. We're all through."

Slowly, Mireille walked over to Barbara and knelt down beside her.

"Mireille . . ." Barbara's face was contorted grotesquely. She raised one hand off the floor in an attempt to rise. Mireille caught her, but her eyes were fixed on Jordan.

"How could you do this?" she demanded.

"I didn't force her to come."

"I'm sorry," Barbara said in a small voice. "I didn't know."

"Of course she knew," Jordan countered. "She didn't expect to see you, of course, but your friend here would hump a donkey for a shot of heroin."

"And you gave her one, I suppose," Mireille said through clenched teeth.

"So would any newspaper in the country." He stood up. With a few adjustments, he was once again impeccable. "I trust I've made my point."

He walked to the door. "See that the ladies have whatever they want," he said to Adam on his way out.

Alone in the office, Mireille pulled Barbara to her feet. "We're going home," she said. She took her into the washroom and got her dressed. When she came out, supporting Barbara, Adam Wells was waiting for them.

"I can call a car for you," he offered, avoiding Mireille's eyes.

"Get out of my way."

"I'm so ashamed," Barbara said. "You can't forgive me for this. Don't even try."

"That wasn't you," Mireille said, pulling the sheets over Barbara. "It was the drugs—whatever Oliver gave you."

"I didn't have to shoot up!" Barbara cried. "I didn't have to . . ." She covered her eyes with clenched fists, trying to blot out the memory of the act she had performed in front of her best friend. "I should have been stronger," she finished weakly. "You would have been."

Mireille closed her eyes. "No," she said. "Not with him." She remembered all the times she, too, had been humiliated in Oliver Jordan's perversion of the act of love. "He makes you forget everything good about yourself."

Barbara buried her face in the pillow. Mireille kissed the back of her head. "Sleep now. We'll talk tomorrow."

It was the last time she saw Barbara alive.

The police called three days later, asking Mireille to identify a woman in the morgue. A redhead who had died of a heroin over-dose in a seedy downtown hotel.

"You probably don't know her," the morgue attendant said tim-idly, staring at the movie star as he pulled open the metal drawer containing the woman's remains. The corpse's face was bloated. Flecks of dried vomit still clung to her hair.

Mireille touched her friend's gray face. "I know her," she said quietly.

"Sorry we had to trouble you, ma'am," the police officer with her said. "She didn't have any other identification. Just your phone number in her pocketbook. That right?" He directed his last remark to the young attendant.

"There was one other thing," the attendant said, retrieving a plastic bag from his files. "This." He took out a silver compact and handed it to Mireille.

She opened it. *For B with love, M.* Mireille looked at it for a moment, then ran her fingers over the tarnished silver. An anguished sob spilled out of her. The two men, experienced witnesses to grief, stepped back silently to give her the illusion of privacy.

After a moment, the morgue attendant cleared his throat. "Can you give us the name of someone who'll claim the body?" he asked. "A relative, or—"

"There isn't anyone else," Mireille said. Through her swimming eyes, Barbara's face became Ankha's, then Sonja's and Denise's and Nicole's . . . "Our kind always die alone."

"I beg your pardon? I didn't quite—"

Mireille took a deep breath. "I'll claim the body."

After filling out a form, she took a last look at the compact. *For B with love, M.*

She closed it with a soft click, then dropped it into the wastebasket on her way out.

"Ma'am, we can have the undertaker see to it that she's buried with that," the attendant called after her.

Mireille didn't turn back.

After she had gone, the young man retrieved it. "I'm not proud," he said to the police officer, a little embarrassed. "I just don't know why she didn't want it. It looked like they were friends or something."

The policeman shrugged. "What would she want with it? The lady's got everything."

Chapter Fifty-Five

Mireille and Stephanie passed the two months after Barbara's funeral in a silent fog. The question of Stephanie's returning to school was never mentioned. Their plans to go to Paris were discarded without a word. Both of them seemed to sense the nearly overwhelming grief in the other, and struggled to live through each day like the passing moments of a ticking clock: uneventful, empty, blessedly predictable.

Mireille did not read her mail; her manager paid her bills and answered her correspondence. She did not take phone calls. Mrs. Rodriguez protected her from the unwelcome voices that intruded into her static nonexistence. She saw no one except Stephanie. She went nowhere; she did nothing. She had stepped out of time, and taken her daughter with her.

In early April, Barbara's gravestone arrived. It was a white marble cube on which a brass insert inscribed with Barbara Ponti's name had been placed. Mireille did not remember ordering it. Only at the insistence of Mrs. Rodriguez, who regarded the artifacts of the dead with reverent awe, did she consent to have it placed on Barbara's grave in a small ceremony.

Stephanie and Mireille were the only ones in attendance at first. Then slowly, as if they had grown out of the graves themselves, the photographers began to appear. They moved around the gravesite like jackals at a kill, invading the women's grief with their clicking cameras, talking among themselves with the ease of workingmen on a routine job.

Stephanie looked around, first in bewilderment, then in panic. "Maman," she whispered, seeking shelter in her mother's arms.

The photographers knelt in position. "Good one," one of them shouted encouragingly. "Could you do that one more time?"

"Over this way, Mireille."

Stephanie's eyes were frantic. "What are they doing here?" she asked shrilly.

Instinctively, Mireille covered the girl's face with her shawl and led her back toward the car. They left the cemetery like thieves—quickly, warily, dodging the shouted questions and the naked, staring eyes of the cameras.

RECLUSIVE STAR GRIEVES FOR MYSTERY FRIEND said the *Los Angeles Times*, along with its picture of her on page two.

HEARTACHE IS HER ONLY COMPANION NOW was the cloying headline in the *National Enquirer*.

MIREILLE ODDS-ON OSCAR FAVORITE trumpeted *Variety*, true to its single focus.

A *New York Post* photographer, armed with a telephoto lens on the branches of a tree, had taken a picture of Mireille and Stephanie at the gravesite, and had identified the second mourner as Stephanie Giroux, a "family friend."

"Why can't they leave me alone?" Stephanie complained, placing the *Post* on the pile of newspapers stacked on top of the kitchen counter. "I'm not the movie star."

"Stephanie, I'm so sorry," Mireille said. "I don't know how those reporters found out about the stone." *Or why they would care,* she thought.

"Don't you?" Stephanie looked up suddenly, and her eyes were angry.

"No," Mireille answered, bewildered. "What are you getting at?"

Stephanie didn't answer. She was thin and drawn-looking. She had handled the ordeal of her friend's death better this time; still, Mireille noticed, it had obviously taken an act of will for her daughter to get through the aftermath of the headstone ceremony.

"Please tell me, Stephanie. I don't understand."

The girl stared at her savagely. "You've been nominated for an Academy Award, haven't you?"

"Yes . . ."

"Well, the awards ceremony is tonight. Even I knew that. Don't pretend you didn't."

"What are you saying?" The implication finally dawned on her. "Do you think *I* called those photographers?"

Stephanie made a dismissive gesture. "I just think it's funny that one of those papers printed my name—my *full* name— without mentioning that I'm your daughter." Her cheeks reddened. "It was good publicity for you, wasn't it? Sweet, considerate, *young* Mireille at the grave of her mystery friend. That's better than a billboard on Sunset Boulevard."

"Stephanie, you can't think—"

"I *can* think, Mother. You might have shut me away for most of my life, but I'm not stupid. The whole point of the Oscars is publicity."

"I don't care about that. Or the award. You know that."

"Oh, that's right. You're not just any actress, are you? The great Mireille wouldn't stoop to publicity gimmicks. The baroness from the Pyrenees is far too well bred for that. When she wants people to notice her, all she has to do is invite the press to watch her emote over death." With a swat, she swept the pile of newspapers to the floor. "I'm glad Barbara was finally useful to you," she said as she stalked out of the room.

Stunned and shaken, Mireille looked at the litter of newspapers. *That's better than a billboard on Sunset Boulevard* . . .

Stephanie was right about one thing. The publicity had been engineered, and carefully: Stephanie's relationship to Mireille had been studiously avoided while Mireille's exposure was maximized. All in time for the biggest television event of the year.

Because Oliver Jordan always got what he wanted.

Mechanically, Mireille stood up and reached for the telephone.

"Mr. Jordan's office," the secretary's voice said.

"This is Mireille. Tell Mr. Jordan I'm on my way to see him." She hung up, her hand still trembling.

"Darling, you're still upset over your friend," he said sweetly. "Death is hard."

"Not for you, Oliver. You thrive on it."

He looked hurt, his eyes full of false sincerity. "That isn't fair, Mireille. It was a lovely stone. And frankly, you really left me no other choice."

"Go to hell."

"Be reasonable. *Josephine* is one of the most expensive motion pictures ever made. Publicity is essential to its success."

"I don't give a damn about your movie."

"You've made that clear enough. By refusing a publicity tour, you've badly damaged its chances."

"You've already made back your money a hundred times over. You didn't have to bring my daughter into it."

He waved her objection away. "The *Post* reporter found her name by himself. Got into the records at the funeral home or something. When he called me for a quote, I tried to minimize the damage by saying she was a family friend." He straightened his tie. "And I didn't give him a quote, either."

"How very kind," she said acidly.

"What's her name again?" he asked. "Your daughter."

She only stared at him.

"Look, Mireille, whether you care about it or not, *Josephine* just may be one of the great films of all time. It deserves an Oscar. *You* deserve it."

"I don't want it!" Mireille spat. "And if you interfere with my personal life ever again, I'll have you arrested."

"All right, all right," Jordan said calmly. "I apologize about the photographers. But I promise you'll change your mind about me after you win the award."

"It would take more than that to make me change my mind about you."

He stood up and walked around his desk to her. "Be ready by six," he said, his expression unchanged.

"For what?"

"Darling, this pretense is becoming a bore. You must attend the Awards. I'll send Adam to your house with the stylist. Now go home and get some rest."

Mireille took a deep breath. "Perhaps I haven't made myself clear in the past," she said. "I will not attend the Academy Awards. I will not make any more films. I will not see you, personally or otherwise, again. Do you understand, Oliver?"

He touched her hair. "Of course you'll attend," he said softly.

She slapped his hand away.

Jordan's laughter followed her as she passed Adam Wells's office.

"Can I see you for a second, hon?" Wells called as she walked by.

She sighed. "What do you want?"

"Just one question, sweetie. Do you want the black limo tonight or—"

She rounded on him. "As I have informed Mr. Jordan," she began, "I do not intend . . ."

The words died on her lips.

"Yes? Is something wrong?"

Slowly, she walked into the office. Propped in front of Wells's desk was a framed watercolor of a blonde nude. Scrawled across the bottom of it were the words *Fortune's Child.*

Her mouth went dry. "Where . . . where did you get this?" she asked.

"Oh, that. We're waiting for the maintenance men to come hang it in Oliver's office. You know, you can't even hammer a nail anymore without the unions—"

"Anne sent it to me," Jordan said from the doorway behind her. "It rather resembles you, don't you think? Probably a fan."

She knelt down to examine it. It was Stefan's painting; she could not be mistaken about that.

Then she saw something in the lower right corner, and gasped. "It's signed."

You didn't sign the painting, she had said.

It's not good enough, Stefan had answered.

Oliver arched his eyebrows and peered down at the painting. "Giroux. Never heard of—Oh. That was the name in the *Post,* wasn't it? Stephanie's name?" He thought for a moment, smiling. "A relative?"

She stood up. "Your ex-wife sent this to you?"

He nodded. "Of course, Anne's much more au courant about the New York art scene than I am. She regards sleeping with starving painters as a civic duty."

You're fortune's child. The world is going to belong to you.

Mireille backed up against the wall, trying to catch her breath.

"Is she all right?" Wells asked quietly.

Jordan said something to her, but Mireille was unable to concentrate on the words. All she could see was the small, bare cabin near Champs de Blé where she had waited all night by the light of a candle for Stefan to come back to her. Once again she could smell the dried lavender she had hung in the rafters of that room; once again she saw, through the cracked windows, the field of flowers where he had captured her soul in a painting.

A painting that had not been signed when Stefan went out to die.

He's alive. Those words rang in her ears like pealing bells.

"Good God, Mireille," Jordan said, alarmed. "What is it? Tell me!"

She ran from the room. Ran, back to a past she had thought was lost forever.

Jordan followed her as far as the stairs, then gave up. "Didn't even wait to use the elevator," he said.

"What was that all about?" Wells ventured.

"Damned if I know." He glanced at the painting. "Giroux," he said slowly. "That's the painter's name, Giroux . . ."

Wells made a face. "What are you on about now?"

"I need to find him."

"Oh, no, you don't." Wells backed away. "I've already staged one manhunt for you, and I'm not doing it again. That's final, Oliver." He folded his arms over his chest.

"It won't be necessary," Jordan said. "I'll take care of this myself."

Chapter Fifty-Six

The Hollywood Beat
Noni Walker, syndicated columnist

Garboesque star Mireille, seldom seen outside of Oliver Jordan's closely guarded circle, surprised everyone last week by disappearing just before last Tuesday's Academy Awards ceremony.

Although the police deny receiving a missing persons report, sources close to the powerful and enigmatic producer say that Jordan has been "terribly distraught" over Mireille's unannounced departure.

Our own sources claim to have spotted the incognito actress entering the prestigious Pierre Hotel in New York.

Oops, have we let the "chat" out of the bag?

Mireille sighed as she read the article. Now that her address in New York had been published in all the papers, Mireille and Stephanie would have to move to another hotel right away.

She was tired. She felt guilty dragging her daughter around with her. And Mireille's fame had proven to be a monumental hindrance in her search for Stefan.

He was one man in a city of eight million. The odds were actually worse than that. Who knew when the painting had been bought, or where? Stefan could be anywhere in the world. All

Mireille knew was that he had lived through the skirmish in the fields outside Champs de Blé.

That was enough. Hopeless and foolish as her search might be, she had to try to find him. She set down the newspaper on the luncheonette counter next to her half-finished coffee, assumed her thin disguise—an ordinary trench coat, a head scarf, and rather unfashionable dark glasses—and walked back out onto the street.

It had probably been a mistake to bring her daughter to Manhattan. The weather had been rainy and cold since their arrival, and stomping through the wet streets had put Stephanie in bed with a cold. She was at the Pierre now, alone, while her mother combed the city in what was beginning to look like a futile search.

Five more galleries to visit. The last five. She'd spent a full week looking, with no results. None of the gallery owners she'd checked with knew of an artist named Stefan Giroux, and none had sold any of his paintings.

Mireille tried to buoy up her hopes, telling herself that the joy of seeing Stefan again would be all the better for the disappointments along the way, but it was becoming more difficult to fight off the nagging feeling that she and Stephanie would be returning to Los Angeles with only each other for company.

Her feet were burning from the endless hours of walking on the city sidewalks. Now it began to rain, as it had intermittently for days, piercing needles of water that sent people scurrying toward cover and slowed traffic to a crawl. Mireille walked on doggedly, checking small shops and restaurants she passed between the remaining galleries on her list, on the off chance that someone might remember an artist who walked with a limp sometime during the past sixteen years.

It was useless, of course. Her search had been nearly hopeless right from the beginning, but after the last five galleries had been crossed off the list, Mireille knew for certain that her efforts were pointless.

Well, what did you expect? she railed at herself. Truthfully, she knew next to nothing about the man she was looking for. How long had it been since he had been in New York? Five years? Ten? More? Had he ever even lived in the city at all? There was no Stefan Giroux in the phone book, and no listing for him in any of the artists' associations she had scoured.

Hopeless. Hopeless and stupid.

Still, the knowledge that he might still be alive was almost more than she could bear. Even walking in circles was better than doing nothing, knowing that Stefan could be around the next corner, in the next building . . .

If he's alive, why hasn't he come to you? She faltered momentarily, just as she had when Stephanie had first said it.

Why hasn't he come?

The blouse Mireille had been stuffing into her suitcase dangled in her hands. "Why hasn't he come?" she had repeated.

Stephanie sat on the edge of the bed and spoke quietly, sensibly. "You're famous, Maman. He would have heard of you. If he hasn't tried to reach you, it probably means he's married or . . . I don't know." She had shrugged in an attempt at indifference, yet Mireille knew that Stephanie's excitement at learning that Stefan might still be alive had been almost as great as her own. When Mireille had rushed in the door with the news about the painting in Oliver Jordan's office, Stephanie had nearly cried, her anger with her mother forgotten.

"My father? My real father?" she had asked, stunned.

"The painting was signed," Mireille had said, feeling her throat go dry. "It wasn't signed when I left."

"Was it his signature? Are you sure—?"

"Yes, yes! Oh, I know it isn't very much to go on, but I've got to find out."

"Mother . . . Maman . . ." Stephanie bit her lip. "Please, could I come with you?"

"Of course you'll come," Mireille had said. "We'll find him together."

She had run to her bedroom to pack, hurriedly, mindlessly. And then Stephanie had asked the question that they both realized was the key to everything:

Why hasn't he come?

Stephanie was right. Stefan would have heard of her. Nearly everyone in America had heard of her. If he hadn't made contact with her in all these years, it must have been a conscious choice.

Mireille stuffed the blouse into the suitcase. "I don't care," she said. "He should have a chance to see you. He doesn't know about you. And I . . ."

I have to see Stefan again. Nothing else matters.

Now, walking on the puddled sidewalks in Midtown Manhattan, she pulled her raincoat close around her and wondered what she would do if she did find Stefan. What if she scoured the city, every city, in every country of the world, and finally found the only man she had ever loved? Would he even know her? Would he *want* to know her?

Seventeen years had passed. A lot could happen in seventeen years. Stefan was probably married, as Stephanie had suggested. Mireille herself had been. He had probably made a new life for himself. Mireille might now be no more than a ghost from the past, someone to greet with embarrassed cordiality, a quick hello, a promise to catch up on old times, a hurried good-bye on his way to see his kids in their school play.

"For Christ's sake," someone groused as he bumped into her from behind. "If you're just going to stand there, get off the sidewalk, huh?"

Mireille mumbled an apology.

Yes, it had probably been hopeless right from the start . . .

There was, of course, one person who might be able to help find Stefan—if Mireille really wanted to find him badly enough.

She had hoped that it wouldn't come to this.

Let him go, a voice inside her pleaded, and she was sorely tempted to listen. He didn't want her. She would be an unwelcome intruder into his life. And this last means of locating him would be so hard.

Her hands shaking, she opened her handbag and took out a piece of paper on which an address on Sutton Place had been scribbled. Anne Rutledge Jordan's address.

As the first clap of thunder pealed, Mireille steeled herself and began walking.

The butler answered. "Yes?" he asked condescendingly, eyeing the bedraggled-looking woman in the soaked raincoat.

"Is Mrs. Jordan in, please? My name is—"

"I know perfectly well who you are," Anne said, appearing at the far end of the foyer. A highball glass was in her hand. She swirled the ice cubes distractedly. "Let her in, please."

The butler backed away deferentially, then took Mireille's coat. Through the process, Anne stood silently, sipping her drink occasionally. The three of them remained in the entranceway for what seemed like a long time, the butler looking to the lady of the house for his cue. Finally, she waved him away with an irritated flutter, and he left discreetly. Anne herself did not move.

"Oliver told me to expect you," she said.

"Oliver?" How had Oliver known she would visit his ex-wife? According to the column in the newspaper, he hadn't even known she was in New York.

"He called after you left his office."

Then she understood. He had made the connection between Mireille and the painting immediately. The blather in the press was just more publicity for *Josephine*. Oliver had probably leaked the story himself. "I see," Mireille said.

"He does have an uncanny knack for knowing what one is going to do." Anne's alcoholic gaze was cold. She moved out of the foyer, her shoes clicking smartly. "Come along." She went into the salon and sat down on an exceedingly uncomfortable-looking chrome chair. "What do you want?" she asked flatly.

"I . . . I'd like to know about a painting."

"Oh, yes. He did mention that. The nude. Did you pose for it?"

"Yes. That is . . ." Her thoughts were suddenly jumbled.

"I thought it resembled you," Anne said. "At a younger age, of course."

"How did you acquire it?"

Anne sat back. "Let me see. It was some time ago. I'd had it hanging in one of the guest rooms in the house I shared with Oliver." Her knuckles whitened as she gripped the arms of her chair. "When I found out about you and my husband, I put it into storage."

Mireille looked away, ashamed. "I'm sorry," she said.

"That apology comes a bit late, wouldn't you say?"

"Mrs. Jordan—"

"Please don't explain. It probably wasn't your fault. There were others." Her mouth twisted bitterly. "Many others."

Slowly, she looked over the rim of the glass at Mireille, meeting her eyes for the first time. "Oliver was obsessed with you. He loved you, I think."

"I don't think it was love."

"It was as close as Oliver could get," Anne said dryly. "He has limits."

"Mrs. Jordan, the painting . . ."

"Ah, yes. I bought it—when? Ten years ago? In nineteen fifty-one or fifty-two. The artist was French. Quite handsome. Lame, though. A pity. He walked with a noticeable limp."

Mireille sucked in her breath.

"Is he the one, my dear?"

Mireille nodded. "His name is Stefan. Stefan Giroux."

"Yes, I remember now. He was selling his canvases on the street in the Village. The nude wasn't among them. It was hanging in his bedroom." She smiled again, a predatory smile. "There's a kind of justice in that, isn't there? You took my man. I took yours."

"Mrs. Jordan, I don't care what Stefan's done, or with whom," she said patiently. "I just want to find him. Please help me." Her voice was hoarse. "Please."

"Why should I?" Anne's eyes flashed maliciously. "This isn't Hollywood. Your looks don't count with me."

Mireille closed her eyes, trying to pull her thoughts together.

"Oh, the poor dear. Suffering so, just because there's one man in the world she can't get. Have you ever thought that he might not want you?" She paused. "Could there be someone, some perverse creature so demented that even the heaving bosom of Hollywood's sexiest starlet can't stir him?"

Mireille stood up. "I'm sorry to have taken your time," she said.

"He was very tender," Anne went on, unperturbed. "Rather slight, but well muscled. Soft lips." She looked up. "Oh, will you be going now?"

Mireille walked to the closet where her coat had been hung and retrieved it herself.

Anne stood up languidly and sighed. "This is where I'm supposed to tell you he's dead."

Mireille whirled around.

Anne was poised for attack, her eyes glinting. A second went by, then two. Then she exhaled slowly, appearing to deflate like a balloon. "That's a lie," she said, with a small dismissive gesture. "He's alive. At least as far as I know." She pressed her lips together. "I'd wanted to get even with you for so long that I rather relished the idea of taking away your hope. Oliver was counting on that, no doubt."

"Ol . . . Oliver?"

The older woman sighed. "It was his idea to tell you that your Frenchman was dead. And that he was my lover. Neither is true." She walked over to an ebony bar and poured herself another drink. "I did visit his home—a room, really, somewhere in the East Village, not that I'd ever remember the address now—but nothing happened. Except that I bought the painting."

Mireille frowned. "Why would Oliver ask you to do such a thing?"

Anne gave a ladylike snort. "You really don't understand the man at all, do you?" She drained off half the glass in one pass. "Oliver needs you, dear. He needs the actress. And I suspect he needs the woman as well."

"My contract with him is over," Mireille said. "In fact, I plan to leave the country soon."

Anne leaned against the wall between two violently colored abstract paintings and sipped her drink. "May I surmise that it was you who ended the romance?"

"I did."

"It was what you wanted."

"I . . . Yes."

"Well, there you have it." She stepped shakily from the wall and bent to take a cigarette from an ivory box. When it was lit, she reassumed her position between the two paintings. "Haven't you learned by now that what you want isn't of the slightest importance to him? All Oliver cares about is what *he* wants."

She blew a stream of smoke toward the ceiling. "He does believe he's in love with you, you know. I found out when I sent him the painting. I hadn't expected him to like it. To tell the truth, I passed it along to him out of a sort of petty vengeance. I wanted to remind him that you were the reason he lost me . . . and my money, which was a considerably greater loss to him," she said. "I wanted him to regret throwing me away for you."

A long ash fell from her cigarette onto the white carpet, but she didn't seem to notice. "He didn't get my message, though. He adored the painting. He even called to thank me for it. Imagine, after all this time. I think that hurt more than everything else— knowing he still loves you more than he ever pretended to love me."

Mireille shook her head. "Mrs. Jordan, please believe me. There's nothing between Oliver and me."

"Yes, there is," Anne insisted. "You may not feel it anymore, but he does." She took a quick drink to calm herself. "And I'll tell you another thing. He'll never let you go. You're his property, Miss Movie Star, and Oliver will do anything he must to keep you. I wouldn't be surprised if he's found your Frenchman already."

"And done what?"

"Paid him off. Threatened him. Appealed to the man's nobler instincts, or baser ones. Oliver's very persuasive. He almost talked me into helping him against you." She barked out a short laugh. "I would have, too, if I hadn't remembered that I loathe him even more than I do you." She narrowed her eyes. "He won't need me, though. He'll find another way to get you back." She stubbed her cigarette out in a silver ashtray. "Oliver always gets what he wants."

There was a moment of silence between the two women. At last Mireille spoke. "Do you know where Stefan is?"

Anne shook her head. "I haven't seen him since I bought the painting. Frankly, I doubt if he's still in New York. I'm fairly well acquainted with the art circles in the city."

Mireille stood, swallowing her disappointment, then nodded curtly.

"Who is he to you, if I may ask?"

"He's the father of my child," Mireille said.

"Ah. Well, don't hope for too much," Anne said. "That's always a mistake with Oliver." She opened the door for Mireille. Outside, the rain was crashing white onto the street. "I'll call a cab for you," she offered.

"I'd rather walk."

"Then please take an umbrella." She thrust her hand into the stand by the door and yanked at several handles, spilling her ice cubes and cursing under her breath.

Mireille pulled out a plain black one. "This will be fine," she said.

Anne weaved where she stood, her eyes glassy. It occurred to Mireille that the woman probably began every day with a hangover.

"You've been very kind to see me," Mireille said. "I appreciate it."

Anne shrugged, the movement loose, sloppy. "Sorry I couldn't be of more help. I would love to watch Oliver fail, just once." A lock of hair fell over one booze-bright eye as she opened the door.

He's ruined her, too, Mireille thought. Even a woman as intelligent and rich as Anne Rutledge had no chance against Oliver Jordan. What chance, Mireille wondered, did she herself have?

She turned and walked into the storm.

By the time she reached Midtown, the rain was falling so hard that Mireille didn't even notice the two teenage girls who passed her until they turned around, shrieking and pointing excitedly.

Both were bleached platinum blondes, with their long hair styled in a parody of Mireille's. Their eyes were made up heavily to resemble the smoky softness of her own, except in the light of day, the girls looked garish and ridiculous.

"It's Mireille!" one of them shouted.

"No . . . you must be mistaken," Mireille said, turning her face.

"Yeah, it is!"

Mireille looked for an exit in the tight knot of people suddenly crowding the sidewalk, hurrying to escape the worsening downpour.

"Mireille!" The two girls circled around her like sharks. Their hair was stuck to their faces in long wet strings, yet neither seemed to mind the rain in the least. All they were aware of was that a movie star was standing in their midst.

"Please," Mireille said. "Go away."

"Listen to that," one of them said. "What a bitch."

"Hey, we only want to talk to you, okay? Can I have your autograph?"

Mireille squirmed through the tangle of pedestrians and dashed across the street as the light turned green. The two girls came running behind her. She looked back over her shoulder, feeling a moment of panic. The faces of the girls were caricatures of her own, demonic and cruel.

They caught up to her at the corner, slapping their hands all over her. One of them snatched Mireille's handbag from her shoulder. "I got it!" she screamed. With a parting slap at Mireille's face, they ran away.

"My bag," Mireille said, looking around helplessly, but no one seemed to be paying the slightest attention to the bewildered woman whose purse had just been stolen.

She ran after the girls for a block and a half, past a row of stately old buildings, onto a side street, through an alley, and onto another street. The rain was sheeting now. The crowds of people had disappeared from the sidewalk, seeking refuge in the doorways of shops and office buildings.

Gasping for breath, Mireille followed the teenagers into one of the parklets that crop up unexpectedly in the city. "Please come back," she called. But her voice seemed to get lost in the wall of rain as the two girls vanished out the other side of the tiny park.

Exhausted, she sat down on one of the stone benches. It was wet, but Mireille was already too soaked to care. With her pocketbook had gone all her cash, her driver's license, her checkbook, and the return plane tickets for herself and Stephanie. It was the perfect ending to her fool's journey.

Well, she thought, at least now Oliver wouldn't have to place any more newspaper stories about his missing movie star. Like an errant schoolgirl, she would have to call him and ask him to wire enough money for her to go home.

A gust of wind came up, spraying water in her face. At the same time, something cold wrapped around her ankle. With a start, she saw it was a page from a magazine. She peeled it off, only to see her own face staring back at her.

THE OSCARS it read beneath the *Life* logo.

In her despair, the sight of the soignée blonde in the photograph struck her as terribly funny. Here she was on the cover of *Life* magazine, and the only person on earth she knew well enough to ask for a one-day loan was a man she hated.

With the rain streaking down her scarf into the collar of her coat, she threw back her head and laughed. *Fortune's child*, she thought. *Oh my, yes.* What a charmed life she led.

The rain swallowed her laughter, just as it blocked out the noise of traffic. Slowly, she sat up, listening. There was no sound except for the splash of water on the pebbled pavement. Beside her, rain bounced off the delicate pointed leaves of a Japanese maple tree, surrounding it with white mist.

Almost unconsciously, she began to notice how beautiful the parklet was. It was circular, surrounded by a wrought iron fence with two exits. Art nouveau–style lamps like those found near the Métro entrances in Paris stood unobtrusively between rounded hedges. The bench she was sitting on was shaped in an arc, part of a circle of stone around a central fountain that formed the centerpiece of the little park. The concrete of the fountain was broken, and the hedges had grown rangy with neglect, but the inherent perfection of the design saved it from shabbiness. It was a place out of time, serene and unreal, a misty fairyland where the bright spots of green from the maple shone through the silver sheets of water. Atop the graceful spokes of the iron fence stood whimsical animals that seemed to come alive in the pelting rain: bears and giraffes and monkeys . . .

She leaped up, her heart suddenly pounding, and ran to the gate. She recognized these animals, because they had once been carved for her in stone by a fourteen-year-old boy.

It can't be, she thought, feeling her knees start to buckle as she stood up to touch a miniature ironwork elephant so smooth and majestic that it seemed to have been made out of ebony. She had tried once to describe the animals to another artist to reproduce, but he had never been able to capture their essence.

She ran to the next animal figure, and the next. They were the same, identical in every detail to the beasts Stefan had made out of stone back in a time when everything, even happiness, was supposed to last forever.

The last of the twelve creatures was a unicorn. It was running, its lush mane streaming, its fragile lines taut with tension, as if this desperate run were the last of its life before being killed for its magical horn.

He had remembered. He had lived and, for a time, at least, he had remembered her. Mireille grasped the bars of the fence and rested her face between them, feeling comfort in the cold metal.

She had no idea how long she remained there. The rain was subsiding, sending steam rising up from the pavement as the sounds of city traffic again swelled around the tiny oasis. She became aware of bursts of conversation carrying from the sidewalk nearby, and the clack-clack of walking feet.

Time had caught up with her, she thought sadly. It had stopped for a while in this place, and she'd had a moment alone with her memories. God had given her that much. But now the rain had ceased, the streets were once again filled with people, and life went on. Her time here was over, and Stefan was forever lost to her.

When Mireille turned away from the fence with its wonderful ironwork animals, she saw a man wearing a fedora standing at the far entranceway. He looked as rain-soaked as she was. She gave him a brief nod, then walked slowly toward the other gate.

"Wait," she heard the man say. "Please."

His voice was so soft that she wasn't certain if he'd spoken or not. Of course he had, she realized. Her private moment here had passed. She was Mireille the movie star again, and someone had recognized her. She turned toward him reluctantly.

She could not see the man's face beneath the shadow of the fedora, but he seemed harmless enough. At least he didn't have a camera. Then he began to walk toward her haltingly, with the gait of a man who did not have full use of his legs.

No. Don't even think it, she told herself. *It's just this place, the animals, the memories . . .* She swallowed as he moved closer, past the fountain. *When you see his face, you'll feel like a perfect fool.* And yet her heart hammered in her chest as she watched him, his walk as familiar as the ironwork animals on the fence.

Don't want this so much! she commanded herself. *Don't imagine . . .*

"Dandelion?"

A small cry escaped from her lips. He stopped where he stood. Slowly, almost humbly, he removed his hat, and she saw that his dark eyes were filled with tears. *His eyes,* Mireille thought. Eyes that had seen her as none other had, beautiful eyes shining out of time, out of the distant, broken past.

"Stefan," she whispered, running to him, and suddenly his arms were around her, holding her, enveloping her in their warmth and sureness and love. "I didn't think I'd ever find you again," she sobbed, her hands touching his face.

"I was afraid."

"Why?" she asked. Then, before he could answer, she brought her fingers to his lips. "No. Don't explain. Don't say anything."

Shivering and wet, she brought her face close to his and kissed him. She tasted his mouth, and behind her closed eyes the sky grew clear and blue again, and the air was scented with lavender, and she found herself awakening to love once more in a field of flowers.

Chapter Fifty-Seven

A flashbulb popped nearby. Mireille looked over in alarm. The young photographer smiled at them.

"Hope you don't mind," he said. "It was a really good shot." Suddenly, his face blanked. "Holy cow, you're Mireille."

"Don't use that, please," she said. The young man turned and ran, clutching his camera in front of him like a stolen treasure.

"Just an amateur photographer," Stefan said.

Mireille sighed. "There's no such thing."

"Is there someone who shouldn't see you with me?"

"No, nothing like that. I guess we don't know very much about each other, do we? It's been a long time."

"Too long," he said. "Look, I know you must be busy, but I live nearby. In case you'd like to dry off," he added.

His awkwardness touched her. "I would like that," she said.

Stefan's apartment in the East Sixties was sparse in furnishings but filled with exquisite artwork. In the living room, beautiful impressionist sculptures stood atop small black display tables. A figment of a Greek frieze hung over a doorway. Near the curved staircase was a Byzantine icon heavy with gold embellishment. An immense postmodern painting by Jean Negulesco covered one wall. The others sported a wild variety of paintings of every style imaginable yet somehow remaining compatible with everything else in the room.

"This place is so much like you," Mireille said, marveling at how the space fairly burst with ideas, indiscriminate in its embrace of beauty. "Stefan, the iron animals in the parklet . . . Were they yours?"

He nodded. "A commission, some time ago. I didn't think you'd ever see the animals."

"I wouldn't have, if . . . if . . ." She paused, thinking. "I was looking for you, Stefan. I'd been walking all over New York for a week."

"I know."

"You *know*? But I didn't find you. You found me."

Stefan set a log and some kindling in the fireplace and lit it.

"Was it just a coincidence, then?"

He jabbed the new fire with a poker. "No." He set down the tool. "I spoke with Stephanie." Mireille heard the air rush through her lips.

"About a week ago I saw your picture in the paper. You were at a cemetery with a young woman. There were only the two of you there, apparently. I couldn't make out her face very well, but the story said her name was Stephanie Giroux." Two red blotches appeared on Stefan's cheeks. "At first I didn't know what to think. I'd been reading about you for years, like one of those demented fans people are always making jokes about. There had never been anything about a child. But the name . . . *my* name . . ."

Mireille began to tremble violently.

"Oh God, I'm sorry," Stefan said. "You're freezing. This can wait."

"Stefan—"

"I'll get you some dry clothes." He pushed away without looking at her.

Mireille followed him into the bedroom. He was holding a pair of neatly folded pajamas. "You can put these on if you like," he said, avoiding her eyes. "I'll dry your other things by the fire."

She took the pajamas. "How did you find her?"

He spoke almost in a whisper. "This morning I read about you in the paper again. The article said you were staying at the Pierre Hotel. I hadn't wanted to pry. I know you've made your own life. A good life, a wonderful life. I wouldn't have interfered . . ." He looked out the window. "I went to the Pierre. I don't know what I'd hoped for. To see you in the lobby, perhaps. Or maybe I was just waiting to come to my senses." He shook his head. "Then I saw Stephanie's name in the guest register. I thought you'd just checked in under her name, so I called the room. And I spoke with her."

Mireille took his hand. "She's yours, Stefan."

He blinked away the tears in his eyes. "I know. She came downstairs. I knew as soon as I saw her face."

They found one another's arms again, and this time it was Stefan who wept. "All these years," he said. His lips were hot against her mouth for a moment. Then he let her go.

"What is it?" Mireille asked, certain that he was about to tell her that he knew all about her past and was disgusted by it.

"You're exhausted," he said.

"Is that all?"

"What do you mean?"

"I mean . . ." She couldn't meet his gaze. "Is there something wrong with me?"

Stefan blinked. "You? Something wrong with *you*?" He shook his head. "There's nothing about you that isn't perfect, Mireille."

She released the breath she didn't know she'd been holding. Then, slowly, she unbuttoned her wet blouse and let it drop to the floor. Her breasts were slick, the nipples puckered with cold. Stefan's hands reached toward her and touched them, the tips of his fingers soft as kisses.

A low moan escaped Mireille's lips. She wanted to take him into her body, to feel the rhythm of his desire inside her.

"Will you make love to me, Stefan?" she asked. "Will you, please?"

He hesitated for a moment. Then, inexplicably, he wrenched himself away from her.

"What is it?"

He turned away, leaning against the bureau.

"Stefan—"

"It's nothing to do with you."

"Then I don't understand. Stefan, please . . ." Then she understood. "Is it your leg?" she asked.

He didn't answer.

"You know I've never cared about that, Stefan. Don't you remember? Even when we were children—"

"My leg is *gone!*" Savagely he swatted at his trousers. A dead sound came from the hollow limb inside.

"Oh, Stefan, that doesn't matter," she said, relieved that the problem was so minor.

"It matters to me!" He turned around. "I'm sorry. This wasn't the way I wanted things to turn out. Seeing you . . . For a moment, I forgot. I'm sorry."

"But—"

He limped out of the room.

Mireille sat on the bed for a long moment, dazed by his rejection. She had waited so long for him, spent so many years remembering the smallest detail about him, reliving a thousand times each precious moment they had spent together, and now . . .

Resolutely she stood up and gathered her clothes around her as she strode into the living room. Stefan was poking at the fire. He did not look at her.

"Don't you dare do this to me," she said. When he didn't answer, she grabbed his arms and shook them violently. "Look at me, damn you!"

"Mireille—"

"I've spent my whole life loving you. Do you understand? Every minute of my life! When I was pregnant with Stephanie, the only thing that kept me alive was knowing that your child was in my belly. Because she was all I had left of you. The first time she smiled at me, all I saw was you. You, Stefan. Always, only you."

Tears were streaming down her face. "Do you think I care whether you have a leg or not? Do you think anything matters to me more than seeing you again?"

Slowly, his gaze moved toward hers. "I've missed you so much."

She closed her eyes. He came to her then, in front of the fire, and solemnly, almost ritually, they undressed each other. "I love you, Mireille," he said.

"And I love you."

The play of the fire reflected on Stefan's skin reminded her of a night in Sardinia. Another man had held her then, as Stefan held her now, but she knew that this was what she had longed for: this place, this night, this man.

She melted into his arms, feeling freer than she had ever felt in her life. There was none of the shame that had plagued all her encounters with Oliver Jordan. Stefan didn't look upon her as l'Ange. For him, she had never been an object for anyone who could meet her price to use and discard. When she gave Stefan her body, he accepted it as a gift, a treasure.

Does he know? she wondered, suddenly feeling her belly clench with fear. Tears sprang from her eyes before she could stop them.

"What's wrong?" Stefan asked gently, moving her hair away from her face and touching her eyes with his soft lips.

"I . . . I want you to think kindly of me," she said, knowing that he could never understand.

"What are you talking about?" He laughed. "Of course I do. More than kindly. I worship you, Mireille."

She bit her lip. *Maybe he doesn't know,* she thought wildly, hopefully. Maybe he'd never heard of l'Ange.

Was that possible? Could it be that he thought of her as clean? As a good woman, worthy of a good man's love?

"You're such a mystery," he said.

Mireille kissed his cheek, and he smiled at her, brushing her damp hair off her forehead. "You're everything I've ever wanted," he said. "I've dreamed of making love to you again. You don't know how long."

"I think I do," she answered. "Because I have, too."

He pulled a blanket from the sofa and flung it over them. It was to cover his leg, Mireille knew. She leaned over and threw the blanket aside.

"No!" He tried to move away.

She stopped him. Then she knelt beside the artificial leg and kissed it. "There's nothing you have to hide from me," she said. *If only you could feel the same way about me.*

Stefan lay back on the floor.

"How exactly did it happen?"

"Oh, the war. The damn war," he said wearily. "It happened the day I left you. We were stupid. We should have known the Nazis would be prepared. There were land mines surrounding the bridge. The others with me were killed, either by the mines or the German soldiers who swept the field afterward."

Absently, he stroked her face. "I suppose I was lucky. When the mine took my leg, I lost consciousness. The Nazis must have thought I was dead. When I finally came to, I managed to crawl as far as a farmhouse. I guess the people there got me to a hospital, but I don't remember any of that. I was in Saint Mathilde's for eight months." His gaze focused again on Mireille. "Thank God you escaped. I sent a man—"

"He found me."

"I prayed that he would. You were the first thing I thought of when I came to."

She felt as if a metal band were wrapped around her heart. While she was giving birth to Stephanie in the snow, Stefan had been struggling for life in a hospital not more than twenty miles away.

Suddenly, Stefan laughed. "Afterward I was decorated by the government. Can you imagine? Me, a war hero."

"Yes," Mireille said, her eyes glistening with pride. "I can imagine it."

"I could have gone to school in Paris, I suppose. I'd wanted to be a painter." He shrugged.

"You mean you're not? You're not an artist?"

"No." He grinned. "I don't know if I might have been or not. Probably not. At any rate, I'm an architect."

"Then the park . . . You didn't just make the iron animals?"

He laughed. "No, the whole place is my work," he said. "For what it's worth."

"It's beautiful. I loved it as soon as I saw it."

He looked down. "It was for you. It's where I go to think. It's where I went after seeing Stephanie." He touched her nose. "And look what I found."

"Are there others like it?"

He shook his head. "No. Unfortunately, that was the only creative endeavor of its kind. Mostly I design gas stations and tract houses." He spread his hands. "Alas, fourteen years in New York has made me an American capitalist."

"But why, Stefan? Why didn't you paint? Why didn't you go to Paris?"

His expression sobered. "I didn't want to stay in France anymore. I couldn't." He looked up at her face. "I found your gravestone in Champs de Blé."

"What?"

"The body of a girl was found in a field near the road to Paris about a month after my accident. It was too badly decomposed to identify, but she had blonde hair, and Dr. Lacroix said she'd died after being molested and tortured." He raised his eyebrows. "I was certain it was you."

"Oh my God," Mireille said. "I believed you were dead, and you—"

"I wanted to forget everything that had to do with my past. Because it was all you, Mireille. All you." They held each other then, tightly, as if afraid that the treasure they had found might disappear again. "That was why I came to America. This country is new. It's a good place to forget. Sometimes."

A powerful thought crowded out everything else in Mireille's mind. *He hasn't been in Paris since just after the war,* she thought. "Then . . . you've never been back?"

He shook his head. "No."

"And you didn't know about me?"

"Not then. Not for years."

He's never heard of l'Ange.

"Mireille, are you all right?"

"Yes, of course. So . . . is that when you decided to become an architect?" she asked with false brightness.

"Oh, that just sort of happened," he said. "At first I painted. Not very successfully. The portrait of you was one of the few I sold. Funny, I thought that getting rid of that painting would help me to forget you. It didn't.

"So I worked at this and that. Odd jobs. One of them was as an office boy at an architectural firm. They liked me there. After a time, they sent me to school part-time for seven years. A university, no less.

"I told them that my academic records had been burned during the war. No one knew that I hadn't had one day of formal schooling. So when I graduated—*voilà*! The French gypsy turned into a white-collar American man."

"When did you design the park?"

"It was my first job. A freak accident. The land was donated by a rich woman in memory of her husband, and she wanted something special. The firm I work for came up with a dozen plans, all very traditional, and she rejected all of them. Then one day she passed by my desk—I didn't even have an office then—and she saw something I'd been doodling. The animals. She wanted them in her park. I made the molds myself. It was like making them for you again."

He stood up and added a log to the fire. Mireille watched him as he moved, the ungainly limb juxtaposed against the smooth flesh of his body.

We can go back, she thought. *It can be just the way it was, as if the years in Paris had never happened . . .*

The prospect made her heart pound. He would never have to know about l'Ange, just as Stephanie had never known. Mireille would never be a whore in the eyes of the only people who mattered in her life.

"It was while I was making the animals that I saw you in a movie," he said. "It was called *Field of Glory.*"

"But . . . why didn't you come for me then? You might have called, or—"

"Look at who you are," he said, brushing off his hands as he turned around. "Even then, the newspapers and magazines were full of you. Mireille, the most beautiful woman in the world. They'd made you out to be a princess or something, if I remember."

"That was just publicity," she said. "It's all so stupid."

"You'd been married to a movie director. A famous producer was in love with you. You won an Academy Award." He smiled sadly. "How could a nobody from your childhood compete with that?"

"Oh, Stefan, if you only knew how little those things mean," she said.

He knelt beside her. "They may seem little now," he said gently, "but in the morning you'll see things differently."

"What—what are you saying?"

He touched her cheek with the backs of his long, slender fingers. "You don't know how many times I've prayed for this night. One night, I would bargain, just give me one moment in exchange for the rest of my life." He kissed her forehead. "And I got it. For that, I'm forever grateful."

"We have the rest of our lives, Stefan." Her brow furrowed. "Together. This is just the beginning."

He cradled her in his arms. "Maybe." He drew the blanket around them.

He'll see, Mireille thought. This is the way he was about his leg. In time, he'll know. "I love you, Stefan."

"Yes, Dandelion," he said, "I believe you do. For now."

"Forever," Mireille said, and pulled him close.

They made love, sweetly, languidly, with none of the frenzied urgency of the sex she had shared with Jordan. Instead, it was dreamlike, respectful. *Loving.* He kissed her arms, her ears, her elbows. They took their time, as if they had a lifetime ahead of them to love one another. When they came, together, it was a revelation.

Then Mireille curled up in his arms and slept.

For now, Stefan thought.

One moment in exchange for the rest of his life.

Yes, it was enough.

Chapter Fifty-Eight

Mireille brought their daughter to Stefan's apartment that same night—the first night of his life, Stefan liked to think. From that night on, the three of them had been a family. To have seen Mireille again had in itself been a miracle. To find his daughter as well was more than Stefan could possibly have hoped for.

The girl showed no reticence at all toward him from the beginning. They talked and laughed together like old friends over his makeshift spaghetti dinner. While she told a story about her school in Switzerland, Stefan noticed the girl's hands, clever hands with calluses between the first and second fingers.

"I'll bet you draw," he said.

When Stephanie admitted that she did, he brought out a sheet of drawing paper and taught her the "mouse game," in which each player drew a mouse that was somehow connected to all the other mice drawn. Mireille managed four mice before running out of ideas, but Stephanie seemed to have an inexhaustible supply of funny drawings, from mice fighting over a piece of cheese to a mouse hurtling forward in a catapult. In the end, her imaginative doodles outshone even Stefan's.

"These are great!" he shouted. "Look at the expressions on their faces!"

Quickly, Stephanie drew one last mouse, this one with a caricature of Stefan's face on it.

"You're good, Stephanie. Really good." He passed the sheet to Mireille.

She examined the cartoons with something like wonder. "Stephanie, I had no idea . . ."

"Maman's never seen my drawings," Stephanie said.

Stefan looked up in amazement.

"I've been away at school for a long time."

"Ah, yes," Stefan said, trying not to embarrass Mireille further. "Have you ever used pastels?"

The girl brightened. "A little."

"I'll clean up the dishes," Mireille said, managing a smile.

"Don't be silly," he said. "They'll keep until morning. And besides, that's my job."

But Mireille held up a hand, signaling that she wanted no more discussion of it.

Later, while Stephanie was absorbed in copying a small Boulanger drawing in chalk, he joined Mireille in the kitchen. "Please," he said, "I didn't invite a movie star to my apartment to wash dishes."

She made a deprecating sound, and he put his arms around her waist. "Tell me what's on your mind," he coaxed.

"The drawings."

"It was only a game."

"They were good."

"So? Aren't you pleased?"

"With her, yes." She went back to the dishes.

"And with yourself?"

"Oh, I'm just wonderful. I haven't spent enough time with my daughter to know she could draw." She put a dish into the cabinet with a clatter.

Stefan took the towel from her and held both her hands in his. "You can't change the past," he said.

She turned her face away. "I know."

"But it doesn't have to destroy your future." He kissed her gently.

A month later, Stefan was still in a state of uncertainty. For sixteen years he had felt as if he were standing still in the midst of the passage of time. He had never married, never dreamed, never aspired to anything since Mireille vanished from his life.

Now she had come back, and their child had come with her. For the past month, the three of them had lived together like ordinary people, with Stefan going to work while Mireille and Stephanie took in the sights of New York. When he returned, Mireille would invariably have begun preparations for dinner and tidied up the place. It was insane in its way, he knew, having one of the most famous women in the world iron his shirts, yet Mireille had not complained. She seemed, in fact, to enjoy being anonymous.

"I don't like living like a princess," she'd said tersely when Stefan objected to her labors. She made her point by taking the photograph of the two of them in the park, which had appeared in a newspaper the day after they met, and using it to wrap fish heads.

"Well, I don't like having you wait on me. Do you think I want you to spend your life doing housework?"

"My *life*, Stefan?" she asked coyly, and he bit his tongue.

That had been boorish and presumptuous of him, he thought. Of course she would never spend her life with him, no matter how much he desired it. She was Mireille, *the* Mireille.

She never talked about Hollywood . . . or anything else about her past, for that matter. When the subject came up, she always found some excuse either to change the subject or leave the room.

"You're too mysterious," he told her one night in bed.

She laughed. "Me? I'm the least mysterious person on earth. The happy peasant, that's me."

"Hardly."

"You're not going to start asking questions again, are you?"

"I want you to tell me about yourself. We've been apart for seventeen years, and all I know about you is what I've read in gossip magazines."

"Well, none of that is true."

"Then what is?"

She put her arms around him. "That I'm going to trick you into marrying me."

Stefan blinked. "Marrying? You would do that?"

"Is this a proposal?"

"I'm serious, Mireille. Would you . . . ? If circumstances were right, would you . . . ?"

"I would marry you tomorrow," she said. "Tonight, if you ever got around to asking me."

Then she kissed him with such passion that the past disappeared, as it always did with her.

It was difficult for Stefan not to run down the crowded Manhattan streets as he made his way home from work the next day. He wanted to jump up and click his heels in the air.

I would marry you tomorrow . . .

The words seemed hard to believe. They may not have been true, he told himself prudently. You didn't decide to marry a person in thirty days. Of course, he had decided just that, but then, he had spent the better part of two decades thinking about Mireille. He had not lived the life she had. He had never possessed what she did. Still, she had said the words, and Stefan had acted on them.

He fingered the small velvet box in his pocket. He would ask her tonight. He would tell her that it wouldn't have to be soon, that she wouldn't even have to answer until she was certain, that he would move back with her to California, if that was what she wanted . . .

He stopped and laughed at himself. Stefan had never thought of himself as a fool before. But what else did you call a man who would change his entire life for a woman?

A man who's had a second chance, he answered himself.

And then he did run, like a deer, back to his apartment—*their* apartment—and into Stephanie's open arms.

"Maman had to go back to the hotel," she said.

"Why? You've checked out, haven't you?"

"Sure, the first night we came here. She got a phone call today."

"Here?" That was odd. "On my phone?"

She nodded. "I don't know who it was, but she didn't look happy about it."

"Oh. Business, maybe. She must have given someone this number." He took off his hat and wiped the sweat off his forehead.

"Why were you running?"

"I wanted to see you."

"And Maman," Stephanie said.

"And Maman." He grinned. "But especially you. How about a walk in the park, just the two of us?"

"Ice cream on the way home?"

"Why not?"

"Perfect. Let's go."

Mireille recognized the voice on the telephone at once.

"Playing housewife again, darling?"

She felt her heart sinking into the pit of her stomach. "How did you get this number?"

"I can do a great many things," Oliver Jordan said. "Perhaps you've underestimated me."

"Leave me alone, or I'll call the police."

"Now, now, there's no need for histrionics. I've flown across the country to see you. Won't you give me a few minutes? I'm just down the street, at the Plaza."

"There's nothing to discuss, Oliver. My contract with you is over."

"Surely we mean more to one another than a piece of paper. Or did you only feel that way when you needed to get to Switzerland?"

Mireille clenched her jaw. "A lot has happened since then."

"If you're referring to Barbara—"

"I'm not going to talk to you about her. Or anything else."

He sighed. "Very well. I'll just have to try later. Say, this evening? Mr. Giroux's apartment is on Sixty-Sixth Street, I believe."

"You're not coming here!"

"Why not? I'm sure your young man and I will have a great many things to discuss."

The telephone shook in her hand.

"Mireille? Are you there?" he asked smoothly.

"I'll meet you at the hotel," she said.

"Splendid! I'll be waiting in the Palm Court at two. We'll have a late lunch."

He hung up before she could answer.

Mireille walked with dread past the rows of starched white tablecloths. Jordan was seated in a corner, sipping something pink. "You're late," he said, waving to the waiter. "I've already ordered for us."

"I'm not hungry."

"Alas. The cuisine here is excellent."

"What do you want, Oliver?" she asked flatly.

"I want you to come to your senses." The sommelier brought over a bottle of champagne on ice. "No one leaves Hollywood after winning an Academy Award."

"I did."

"Don't be a ninny, Mireille. You've only been working in films for a few years. In that time you've won two Oscars, two New York Film Critics Circle Awards, a Golden Globe, and the Palme d'Or. You're in every magazine in print. You earn more than any other actress on earth. Are you sure you want to leave all that to go back to stepping and fetching for another Victor Mohl?"

"Save your insults, Oliver."

"Forgive me. My mistake." Jordan paused to think. "That's right, your housewifely days were fairly recent, after all, weren't they? Back when I found you, you were still the great whore of Paris."

"That's always been how you've operated," she said. "Find a person's weakness, and then you own her. Only it isn't going to work this time."

He smiled, innocent as a schoolboy. "Why not?"

"Because I won't let you own me anymore."

"I see. You'd prefer to be owned by someone else, apparently. What does he do, this vanishing lover of yours, park cars? Or does he merely sire your offspring?"

She ignored the remark, refusing to give him any more fuel. "I'm sure you already know," she said wearily. "Not that my life is any of your business."

"Oh? I beg to differ. You *are* my business. A great deal of it, at any rate. It's much more difficult to make money in movies than it used to be, particularly for a one-man operation like mine."

"I don't give a damn about you. Or your operation."

The waiter came with two salads. Oliver ate quietly, unruffled. He sipped his champagne. "Well, then," he said finally, "perhaps you might bring yourself to care about someone else. Your daughter, possibly."

"Don't even mention her."

"Good heavens. There are so many things I dare not mention. Unfortunately, others already have." He reached into his pocket and took out a handful of yellowed newspaper clippings. "We're simply full of nasty little secrets," he said as he tossed them at her.

The brittle scraps of newsprint floated around her like confetti. One of them landed on top of her salad. It carried a photograph of l'Ange, one of the originals that ran in the newspaper *L'Etoile*. Beneath it, in French, read the caption "Parisian Call Girl at Play."

A waiter came to pick up the pieces that had fallen to the floor while a dark oil spot grew over the picture on her plate.

"May I get you another, madame?" he asked.

Mireille shook her head. She did not look at him. She did not look at Oliver Jordan. She could see only into the misery of her own heart.

Jordan waved the waiter away. "You might as well face me," he said. "Surely you must have known it would come up sooner or later." He reached toward her. "You have a loose hair."

"Don't touch me!" She slapped his hand away.

Jordan's calm features hardened. "I suggest you stop deluding yourself, Mireille," he said with growing intensity. "You are my property. I created you, and I intend to keep you. If you dare to walk away from me, the Hays Office will crucify you after the newspapers get wind of this. And not only will the press have a field day with your sordid past, not only will you never work again except as a streetwalker, but Stephanie's name will be smeared through the mud, right along with yours."

Mireille fought to keep her anger in check.

Jordan spread his arms as if he were reading a banner head-line: "'former prostitute hides illegitimate daughter in posh board-ing school.' And those will be the conservative papers." He folded his arms. "Yes, they'll love that, won't they? You'll be lucky not to have her taken away from you."

Mireille balled her hands into fists.

"And you might as well forget about your long-lost love," Jordan went on. "I trust you haven't yet filled him in on all the lip-smacking details of your eventful life since your daughter's conception."

She didn't answer.

"I thought not. At least you're not a fool." He sipped his champagne. "Look, it's not as if I'm tying you up forever. You did get a late start, after all. I'd say you've got two years before you start to show your age, maybe three." He smirked. "Well, I won't be greedy. Two years, all right? I'll even put it in writing."

"You're blackmailing me."

"Mmm," Oliver said, digging into his Caesar salad. "Delicious. Sure you wouldn't care for some?"

Mireille felt numb. "I'll tell him," she said. "I'll tell him everything."

"Do that, Mireille. I'd love to see the expression on his face when he finds out that his famous paramour has a nodding acquaintance with every set of cock and balls in Europe." He guffawed, nearly choking on his lettuce. "Be realistic," he said finally, having brought his mirth under control. "If Mr. Giroux isn't merely after your money—which you must admit is a distinct possibility—how could he accept you if he knew what you were really like? How could this upstanding fellow want you? The girl he remembers is a teenage virgin. At least the girl in the painting looks like a virgin."

She looked him straight in the eyes. "And what am I now, Oliver?"

He paused for a long moment, studying her. "You're a survivor," he said at last. "Just like me." He touched her hand. This time, out of inertia, or despair, or simply numb indifference, she did not move it away. "There aren't going to be any rides into the sunset with our true loves for either of us."

He patted her hand. "Be strong, Mireille." He raised his glass to her. "To success. You can learn to like it. I have."

She slid her chair back from the table. "I hope you burn in hell."

Oliver Jordan stood as she left, then nodded to some people he knew at the next table.

Chapter Fifty-Nine

Almost as soon as she met her father, Stephanie used him to fill the void left first by Nora's death and then by Barbara's, although in Stefan, she found more than a friend. She was more like him, she knew, than she had ever been like her mother. Maman was strong, practical, realistic. She didn't indulge in useless fantasies, while Stefan . . . Stefan was made of dreams.

They showed in his speech, his looks, even in the artwork that filled his apartment, but mostly in his drawings. He didn't have any paintings—he said he didn't paint anymore—but in the evenings they usually doodled together, and Stephanie always looked on with wonder as he hastily turned three or four lines into a swan or a tree or a woman.

"You're the best artist I've ever seen," she said.

He made a face. "Then we'd better expose you to some real art before long." He raised his eyebrows. "Ever been to the Metropolitan Museum?"

That had begun their excursions alone together. At lunchtime, Stephanie would meet Stefan at his office, where he introduced her as his daughter, and then the two of them would take off exploring the galleries and exhibits in the city. Mireille was always invited to come along, but she sensed that Stephanie's time alone with her father was precious to her, and usually managed some sort of excuse.

Stephanie's noon meetings with Stefan were the highlight of her day. At first they only discussed art—she was an apt pupil, talented and eager to learn—but as they got to know one another better, Stephanie began to open up to him, spilling out all the thoughts she'd been unable to share with anyone since Nora's death.

Stefan listened carefully to her, marveling at the intelligence and sensitivity of this daughter who, a month before, he had not known existed.

"I like being with you," she said as they passed the children's carousel in Central Park. She blushed as she spoke, and did not look at Stefan.

He put his arm around her. "I like you, too," he said. "I only wish I'd been around when you were little."

"You wouldn't have seen me anyway. I've been in Switzerland since I was seven years old, remember?"

Stefan couldn't offer her any comfort, because he had difficulty understanding the situation himself. Why Mireille had placed her daughter in a school so far away was a mystery to him. He had asked her about it and, as usual, she had avoided answering. He hoped that with time, with trust, she would open up to him as Stephanie had, but he knew that it was pointless to demand an accounting of Mireille's past until she was ready to give one.

"Well, you and your mother have been together since you left school. That ought to make up for some things," he said as he led her to a bench near the carousel.

Stephanie sat between her father and a woman moving a stroller back and forth. "I've only seen her when she wasn't working." She rummaged in her bag and took out a small sketchpad and a pencil. "She doesn't see me while she works. Uncle Oliver—that is, Mr. Jordan—says it would distract her." She looked up at him. "Do you know Mr. Jordan?"

"I've heard of him," Stefan said. "He's Maman's boss."

"I used to think he was my father." She blushed. "I mean, we didn't have any pictures of you—"

"That's all right," he said. "I'm glad you had someone."

"Well, not exactly. I've never spent much time with him, either. It was just his picture. I pasted a photograph of his face onto a drawing I made of my family, and kept it on an altar. I thought that would make Maman come back to me. It didn't work, though." She dropped the pencil.

Stefan picked it up. "Maybe it did work. You're both together now."

"Until she makes another movie."

"I thought she wasn't going to make any more. It's what she said."

Stephanie sighed. "Right. That's what she said. If you believe her."

"Don't you?"

"Please." Stephanie made a disgusted sound. "If I hadn't gone crazy, I'd still be in Switzerland, watching my mother on a movie screen."

Stefan gave the pencil back to her. "You have two parents now," he said. "I can't be your mother, but whatever happens, you've got me."

She regarded him solemnly. "Do you mean that?"

"Yes, Stephanie. Always." He craned his neck to see what she'd drawn. "Hey, that's pretty good."

"It's Maman."

"I know. You've caught a likeness. A little broader around the chin, maybe . . ." He held out his hand. "May I?"

She handed him the pencil and pad, and he drew two lines that made the drawing come to life.

Stephanie nodded her approval. "I wish I knew how you do that."

"I think of the spaces, not the lines," he said. "This is a face against the sky, not a line on a piece of paper." He held up his hand. "Draw this. Not lines, but a hand. Or, rather, the planes that make up a hand." He gave her things back to her. "Have you taken lessons?"

She shook her head. "Just classes at school."

"Well, I'll see that you get them. A few lessons would have saved me years of effort, even though I didn't have your gift."

Her eyes shone. "Do you think it's a gift? Really?"

He laughed and ruffled her hair. "Yes, I do. Now are we going to have ice cream or not?"

When they got back, sticky-fingered and silly, Mireille was waiting for them.

"Maman, you should have seen . . ." Stephanie's words died away as she took in the expression on her mother's face. Four suitcases were standing by the door. "What's wrong?"

"I want to talk with your father alone," Mireille said. "Would you mind going to your room for a few minutes?"

Stephanie was about to protest when Stefan gave her a silent nod. She retreated, frowning in bewilderment.

It took Mireille a moment to find her voice. Stefan waited patiently, his eyes searching her face. "I've . . . been called away," she said with great effort. "Stephanie and I have to go back to Los Angeles. "There's a film . . ."

"A film?"

"Yes. A new script. I really can't turn it down, you see . . ."

Stefan could see the tears in her eyes. "You don't have to lie, Mireille."

Yes, I do! she wanted to scream. *I've had to lie all my life!*

"Just tell me the truth."

Tell the truth! The truth was why she had to leave him. Oliver Jordan had told the truth: *Come back to me, or I'll destroy all three of you.*

"I wish I could tell you," she said in a dead voice. "But I can't. I . . . I can't."

He was silent for a long time. Finally, he spoke. "Is there another man?"

She looked at him. Oliver Jordan was not a man. He was a monster. "Something like that," she said.

Stefan bowed his head.

"I'm so sorry," she said.

He turned away.

"Stefan—"

"What about my daughter? *Our* daughter?"

Mireille hesitated. "It might be better if she went back to school—"

"Let her stay with me."

"We should be going," she said, and called Stephanie.

"Mireille, please," he said urgently. "Don't keep her from me." He grew silent as Stephanie entered the room.

"Maman?" Stephanie looked from Mireille to Stefan. "What's going on? Tell me!"

With an effort, Stefan kept his voice steady. "Your mother has to go back to Los Angeles," he said.

Stephanie's face was incredulous. "What about—?"

"We'll discuss this later," Mireille said. "Please help me with these bags."

Stefan took her arm. "Mireille, I'm begging you."

She picked up the largest of the bags herself. "Come with me, Stephanie."

"We're leaving?" Stephanie asked. "Just like that?"

Silently, Stefan took the bag from Mireille and went into the hall.

"What did you do to him?" Stephanie asked her mother accusingly.

"I don't want to talk about it now."

"Well, *I* want to!" Her eyes were furious. "What is it, another movie? Has it been too long since you've been the center of attention?"

"Stephanie—"

"Or is it that you just can't stand that my father likes me?"

"What?"

Stephanie's face was twisted with anger. "Maybe you'd have kept him around longer if he'd ignore me the way you always have. But he's proud of me. Stefan's proud to be my father, even though you never bothered to tell him I was born." She spat the words out of her mouth. "To him, I'm not the little bastard who has to be hidden out of the way."

Mireille blanched. "Don't say that!"

"What, 'bastard'? That's what I am, Maman. I'm a bastard. And you're a bitch."

Mireille slapped her.

When Stefan came back in, the two women were standing facing one another. There was a dark red mark on Stephanie's cheek. "I'm not going with you," she said defiantly.

Mireille stood staring at her, blinking, for a moment. She opened her mouth to speak, only no words came. Finally, she moved two of the suitcases with her foot.

"These are Stephanie's," she said, her voice unsteady, her eyes unable to meet Stefan's. "She can stay with you until school starts. But she has to be back at La Voisine in the fall. Agreed?"

Stefan and Stephanie exchanged a look.

"It's the best place for her," Mireille shrilled. "You know that, Stefan."

"Mireille—"

"I am her legal parent, not you. I can make her come with me now if I want to."

"Don't listen to her," Stephanie began, but her father silenced her with a gesture.

"Agreed," he said quietly.

Mireille glanced at the two of them, then picked up her other bag and closed the door behind her without another word.

Stefan stared after her for a moment before turning to Stephanie. "At least we'll have some time together," he said. His hands were trembling.

Slowly, Stephanie went to her father and put her arms around him. "I love you," she whispered.

"I love you, too." He could not control the catch in his voice.

"Why does she do it? She'll say she loves you, and then . . ." She buried her face in Stefan's shirt. "Why is it always so easy for her to leave?"

Stefan stroked her long hair. *One moment,* he thought. That's what he had asked for, and he hadn't expected more. He hadn't had the right to want more. But Stephanie had.

For a blinding instant, he almost hated Mireille. He wanted to hate her. Anger would burn him clean, rid him of her forever. But then, he realized, he could never be rid of the pain she caused, no more than he could forget the joy she brought. He could never hate someone he had spent his whole life loving.

He held Stephanie close to him. "We'll find a way through this," he said.

Chapter Sixty

Eighteen months later, Oliver Jordan and Mireille sat across a long wooden table from one another. "This is the last one," she said, leafing absently through the script he'd given her.

"We'll talk."

"It's in writing, Oliver. Two more films. That was the agreement. *Mozambique* and . . ." She tossed the bound screenplay onto the table. "And whatever this is. The last one. The last time I'll ever work with you."

"Fine, fine. Whatever you say." He held up his hands in surrender. "It's a pity, though. The public still adores you." He tapped on the script. "What do you think?"

She turned her head away in disgust. "Does it matter what I think? Has it ever mattered?"

"Please. You're not going to start that song and dance again, are you? Read it, darling. It's fabulous. Jim Allerton wrote the screenplay." Jordan chuckled. "He says he wrote it for the money. He's still hoping to turn into a literary lion, I suppose."

He took the script from her and began flipping through it. "Marvelous," he said. "We're calling it *Filigree*. It's a spy thriller set in Berlin."

"I really don't care what it's about," Mireille said wearily. "Let's just get it over with."

Even though shooting on the film was not scheduled for some weeks, Jordan saw to it that Mireille's time was filled. *Mozambique,* the film she made after *Josephine,* was being released around the country. Jordan arranged for a thirty-city promotional tour for Mireille before beginning work on the Allerton screenplay.

Mozambique was not good. The film was a desperate clone of the new genre of glamour/espionage movies that substituted exotic locales for quality. It had made money, though. Since Oliver Jordan no longer had the luxury of using his wife's money to bankroll his films, *Mozambique* marked the wave of the future for Continental Studios. No longer could Jordan gamble with an unknown foreign actress as he had with Mireille in *Field of Glory,* nor could he pour eight million dollars into a lavish costume piece like *Josephine.* From now on, he knew, it would be incidental whether the films produced by his studio were artistic masterpieces or banal imitations of other movies. The important thing was not to lose money.

With Mireille as his star, he knew he wouldn't—not until her appeal with the public wore off.

Despite receiving a beating by the critics, *Mozambique* played to full houses all around the country. In the cities Mireille visited on her promotional tour, talking on local radio and television shows, signing autographs for fans, making personal appearances, the movie was booked for twice its normal run. Her magic hadn't faded, not by an iota. People wanted to see her, feel the magic of her, no matter what she was in, as long as there were enough close-ups of her face.

Jordan joined Mireille at the end of the *Mozambique* tour in New York, where she dutifully accompanied him to nightclubs and press-infested private parties, as per her contract. When they were alone, they stayed in separate rooms. Mireille refused even to eat breakfast with Jordan. Nevertheless, the gossip columnists engaged in their usual orgy of speculation.

Wedding bells for Mireille? the tabloids asked under photographs of the movie star with her handsome escort as they made their dazzling way through the city's hot spots.

Producer Oliver Jordan, en route to Berlin to finalize locations for his new film, Filigree, *has squeezed in a one-week stopover in New York to wine and dine—and possibly propose to—the leading lady in both his films and his life, Mireille. Rumor has it that the dashing Hollywood mogul has already purchased an engagement ring fit for the reigning Queen of the Silver Screen.*

"What is this nonsense?" Mireille asked, reading the newspaper in a limousine on the way to her hotel.

He grinned. "Marriage to me, nonsense?"

She folded the paper with disdain and placed it on the seat between them.

"It wouldn't be a bad idea, Mireille. In fact, I think it's time." He placed his hand on hers. She retracted it.

"I'm finally coming to the end of my last contract with you," she said. "What a coincidence that you would want to marry me now."

"Don't be harsh, darling. We've had our differences, but you've always known that I love you."

"Yes. You've shown me in so many ways," she said coldly.

"Mireille, please." He took a small box out of his pocket and opened it. Inside was an enormous diamond solitaire ring. "I'm serious. Marry me. You won't regret it, I promise."

With barely a glance at the ring, she snapped the box closed and left it in Jordan's hand. "I've regretted every moment I've known you," she said. She leaned forward and tapped on the glass partition. "Driver, stop the car."

The limo pulled over to the curb and Mireille got out.

"Mireille . . ."

"Get out of my life." She slammed the door and walked toward the windblown flags of the Plaza Hotel.

She went to her room and took a steaming shower, trying to wash the dirt of Oliver Jordan off her. The doorbell rang, and she stepped out.

"What is it?" she called through the door with annoyance.

"Room service."

"I didn't order anything," she said.

"Mireille, please let me in."

She sighed. Pulling on a hotel bathrobe, she wound a towel around her head and went to the door. Jordan strode in, as elegant and in command as ever. "I would have liked to finish our conversation in the car," he said. "Your departure was rather abrupt." There was a strong taint of alcohol on his breath.

"All right," she conceded. "I'm sorry I was rude. Now—"

"It's not your rudeness that offends me, Mireille. It's your stupidity. It's becoming rather tiresome to have to constantly bully you into acting in your own best interests."

"Really," she said flatly. "Like marrying you."

"Yes, damn it, among other things. You objected when I arranged for your divorce from that embarrassing fool of a husband, whom you detested. You complained because I wanted you to concentrate on your work—work that won you two Academy Awards. You went berserk when I suggested that you disassociate yourself from drug addicts and prostitutes, heaven forbid."

"Barbara was my friend," she said, feeling her jaw clench.

"You see? You're ready to attack me all over again, despite the fact that I saved your career, and probably your life, which was also the case when you were about to run off with that gold-digger artist chum of yours—"

"Go away, Oliver."

"Why? Have you got some stablehand here to satisfy you? Some sweating mill worker, perhaps, to give you the life you so long for?"

"I said get out."

"Oh, stop it. You've never known what's good for you. You've never shown a lick of appreciation for what I've done for you."

"What you've done!" She could hardly believe it. He actually expected her to be grateful that he'd stolen her life from her.

"Yes, you addle-headed idiot! In case you haven't noticed, I'm the one who made you the biggest star in the world. Because of me, you're richer than you ever dreamed possible. But that's so inegalitarian, isn't it? Our sweet Mireille wouldn't deign to marry a man who offered her anything so mundane as money. And then we all know how she loathes the attendant fame of her calling."

"You're wrong, Oliver," she said. "The only thing I loathe is you."

"Bravo. Hilarious. Get me a bourbon on ice."

"There isn't any."

"Then be a dear and order some. This has all been so upsetting, and I've got to go to Berlin this afternoon." He fluttered a hand over his forehead. "There are a million details to take care of before *Filigree* can go to camera. The last thing I need is more trouble from you."

"Oliver, please go," she said wearily. "I'm tired."

"And I'm brokenhearted." He flopped down on an overstuffed chair. "I do want to marry you. At least I did in the car."

"I'm sure the urge will pass," she said, unraveling the towel from around her head. He grabbed the towel as she walked past and yanked her toward him. Mireille lost her balance and fell into his lap. Instantly, he reached his hand into her bathrobe.

"Oh, the memory of it! I always loved this breast particularly." He wiggled his tongue and bent down over her.

She shoved the wet towel in his face and wriggled free, but he caught hold of her waist and pulled her back.

"Oliver, you're drunk."

"Let me make love to you, darling. I've missed you so." He nuzzled her neck.

"Stop it," she said, trying to push him away. "I don't like this."

"Tell me," Jordan whispered in her ear. "What does your artist do? Fuck you on a dirty floor? Does he keep his boots on?"

She twisted in an attempt to get out of his grasp, but he shifted his grip to pin her arms at her sides.

"I mean it, Oliver. Let me go."

"Unhand me, suh!" he crooned in a high falsetto. "You have no raht to mah body!"

"You're hurting me."

"That's what you like, isn't it? The fabulous Mireille, just waiting for a man with calluses to slap her silly." He spun her around and pressed his lips on her mouth. Mireille struggled to get away from him, but her protests only seemed to excite him.

She began to scream. He slapped his hand over her mouth. "Shut up, you magnificent bitch," he said.

She tore at his shoulder with her teeth. While he roared in anguish, she wheeled away from him. He caught her by her hair. "If you insist on acting like a slut, I'm going to treat you like one." With a violent jerk, he sent her to the floor, at his feet. He still held her long hair, now smeared with blood from the wound on his shoulder.

He was standing over her now, and Mireille was seized by panic. This was clearly not loveplay, even for Oliver Jordan. With his predatory instincts, this was sport.

And she was his prey.

"Oliver, please . . . please . . ."

"Oh, yes. Beg, Mireille. I want to hear you beg." He pushed her head to the floor, until she felt the bristles from the carpet digging into her face.

Her arms were twisted behind her at a painful angle, and it felt like her neck was breaking. She tried to speak but found she could not. Then she felt him roughly pulling up the skirt of her bathrobe. With all her strength, she bucked him off, crashing her elbow into his face. Mireille got to her knees, but he came after her again. This time she picked up a lamp and threw it at him. It missed, shattering against the wall.

Now she was standing in a corner, her breathing heavy and labored. "Get . . . out . . . of here," she panted.

Jordan smiled. Slowly, he took off his belt. "You always knew how to keep me interested," he said. "As soon as I got bored, you had something new to give me."

"No!" she shrieked, but he rushed at her, looping the end of the belt around her neck.

"Here's something new for you," he said. "See if you like it."

He pulled the belt taut, choking her. As she struggled to breathe, her eyes bulging with terror, Jordan ripped the linens off the bed with one hand while he held onto the belt, like a leash, with the other. With his teeth he tore a strip of cloth from a sheet, then slammed Mireille against the closet door while he bound her hands behind her back.

In the past, he had allowed himself some rough play with hookers, but that had been nothing like this. The women he had paid to accept a little physical punishment hadn't fought back with any sincerity. Their hearts hadn't pounded with fear the way Mireille's did now. Jordan could even smell her sweat. It drove him to a frenzy.

He shoved her onto the bed. Tying the belt to one of the corner posts, he took two other strips of cloth and tied her ankles, then attached them to the legs of the two nightstands on either side of the bed. When he was finished, he stood back to admire his work.

Mireille was lying spread-eagled and naked, her face swollen, barely conscious. He made a low sound and touched the swelling in his pants. It was the hardest erection he had ever experienced.

"Angel of night," he whispered. He took off his clothes. His penis was surging.

Two tears squeezed out of the corners of Mireille's eyes as he mounted her. He tore into her with wild need, holding onto her hair, riding her.

"You like this, don't you?" he taunted. "Yes. Your kind likes this. It's the only thing you understand." He jammed himself even more deeply into her flesh. When she tried to scream again, he covered her mouth.

He's going to kill me, Mireille thought.

Just as this new panic was beginning to well inside her, there was a timid rap on the door.

Please help me, she pleaded silently. *Whoever you are, please . . .*

"Are you all right?" Adam Wells asked.

She tried to shout for help.

"He can't hear you," Jordan said.

Wells spoke again. "For God's sake, Mireille, what are you doing in there? The racket's unbelievable." He knocked again.

Jordan thrust again, oblivious now to the intrusion. His passion mounted in a sick crescendo.

"Mireille," Wells whispered harshly behind the door. "Just say you're all right, okay?"

Twisting around painfully, she lurched her head out from under Jordan's grip and screamed. With the leather belt around her neck, the only sound that came out was a forced, harsh rasp ending in a choking spasm, but it was loud enough to be heard.

Jordan remained unaffected. Dull-eyed, he yanked the belt tighter. For a few seconds, Mireille struggled against the airless blackness that was enveloping her. She felt her tongue lolling out of her mouth, felt her bulging eyes roll back into her head. Then she fell back.

The sight fueled Jordan's uncontrolled passion. He climaxed with a moan deep in his throat just as the heavy hotel room door began to shake in heavy thumps.

He rolled off her, breathing spasmodically. For a moment he lay beside her, blinking up at the ceiling. Then he turned to her and flicked open the belt buckle. He was zipping his trousers when the door crashed open.

Adam Wells stood in the doorway, holding his shoulder and grimacing. "What the hell are you doing here?" he began. Then he saw Mireille lying on the bed.

"Jesus Christ," he whispered, carefully closing the door behind him. He ran to her and pulled the belt from around her neck. He slapped her face gently. When she did not respond, he put his lips to hers and blew a puff of air into her mouth, then another, until a rush of breath escaped from her and she began to gasp.

"Mireille?" he asked, his voice on the edge of hysteria. "Mireille, can you hear me?"

After a few moments, her breathing began to sound normal again, but the color had completely drained from her cheeks, leaving her ashen except for the bruises that were already darkening.

"She's all right," Jordan said.

Wells only stared at him.

Finally, Mireille's eyes opened, groggy and unfocused. Wells untied her hands. Slowly, she brought them to her neck, touching the rough red welts left by the belt.

"Take her somewhere," Jordan said, buttoning his shirt.

"Where? Back to LA?"

"Of course not." He scowled in annoyance. "Somewhere in the country. Don't you have a summer house?"

"Yes, but—" Wells looked at his watch. He had planned to go to Germany with Jordan.

"See that she gets there. Anonymously."

Wells sighed. "All right. I'll bring over your passport and ticket. The plane to Berlin leaves at three."

"You're going with me. I don't intend to handle the German bureaucracy alone."

"Then what's *she* going to do?" Wells shrieked. "Wheel herself over to Idlewild on a gurney?"

"Adam," Jordan said calmly, "there are ways. Find someone to accompany her. Arrange for a series of small planes, or something. Better yet, find someone nearby who'll take her in until she's well enough to travel." He thought about it. "Yes, that's it. Someone discreet."

"Who's going to be discreet about this?"

"Well . . ." Jordan brightened. "Doesn't Jim Allerton live around here?"

"He's in Virginia."

"That's close enough." He smiled mechanically. "I'm sure you can do it, Adam."

"Oh God." Wells turned to Mireille. Her left eye was swelling noticeably. "She's going to have you arrested," he said.

"No, she won't." Jordan slipped on his jacket and walked toward the door. "Meet me at the airport in two hours."

"Where are you going?" Wells asked, wild-eyed.

"Downstairs for a drink."

"Oh, for God's sake, Oliver!"

"Please, Adam, don't make more of this than there is."

"Look at her! Look at what you've done!"

"The tour's over," Jordan said expansively. "No one has to know."

He checked himself briefly in the mirror, ran a hand through his wavy golden hair, then let himself out of the room.

BOOK IV

Berlin

1962–1963

Chapter Sixty-One

The first face Mireille recognized was Jim Allerton's.

"Adam Wells called me," he said as he walked beside her wheelchair. The nurse who had accompanied Mireille from New York pushed the chair toward a comfortable old house surrounded by large pine trees. "We're at my place," Allerton said. "You'll be able to rest here."

Mireille didn't answer. She had not spoken since the beating. To avoid publicity, Adam Wells had arranged for a Mireille look-alike wearing a scarf and sunglasses to leave the hotel with him in a chauffeured limousine while the real Mireille, barely conscious, was carried through the hotel's back door late at night into a waiting taxi with the hired nurse inside.

She had not spoken a word then, nor throughout the trip to Teterboro Airport in New Jersey, nor during the flight to Richmond. She had greeted the nurse with only a blank stare. When she saw Jim Allerton's bewildered, stricken face, she was silent.

She said nothing, ate nothing, showed nothing.

During the days that followed, she had to be fed intravenously. She never seemed to look at the apparatus over her bed, or at the face of the nurse who ministered to her every day and night, or at Allerton, who watched sadly as the once radiant features of Mireille's face grew hollow and sunken.

After four days, Adam Wells called from Berlin.

"Mireille doesn't seem to be getting better," Allerton said. "She won't eat. She's lost twenty pounds and aged ten years. I'm going to call a doctor."

"Don't do that," Wells shouted. Then, more calmly: "I'm telling you, she's fine. There's nothing wrong with her that a little rest won't cure."

"Then why won't she talk?" Allerton pressed.

Wells took a deep breath. "I've told you, Jim. She picked up some stud who thought it would be fun to turn her into a punching bag. She's probably too ashamed to discuss it."

"Is she too ashamed to take nourishment from anything except a needle?"

"She's French, Jim. She's emotional. What she needs most is a friend."

"What she needs is a hospital," Allerton said.

"We can't risk that. The publicity—"

"Fuck the publicity! Don't you hear me? She may die!"

There was a pause on the phone. "Hang on a minute," Wells said before covering the receiver. Allerton heard muted voices. Then Wells came back on the line. "No hospital," he said.

Allerton slammed the phone down.

He went into the room where Mireille was staying and sat on the bed beside her. The bruises around her neck were beginning to turn yellow at the edges. One eye was still black and swollen, and her high cheekbones were pale and shiny, giving her a skeletal appearance.

"How could they have let this happen?" he asked, knowing that she could not, would not, answer.

Wells, in a frantic telephone call from New York, had told Allerton the bizarre story of Mireille's encounter with an unknown man who had left her for dead in her hotel room. No one had seen him come or go, Wells had said.

"Then how do you know he was a date?" Allerton had asked.

"She'd mentioned that she was meeting someone," Wells had extemporized, adding, "she doesn't always choose her friends with the best of care."

Allerton hadn't been aware that Mireille had any friends at all. "I see."

"Which is why I'm calling you. Jim, you've got to help Oliver out here. We're on our way to Berlin, and we can't leave Mireille in this condition."

"It sounds like she needs a doctor."

"She's seen one. He says she's got to rest. She can't go home, naturally. It's too far, and the publicity would be awful. I was about to check her into a sanitarium upstate when I thought of you out there in Virginia."

Allerton had been shocked. "You want *me* to look after Mireille?"

"She'll have nurses, of course—I'll make all those arrangements, and you'll be reimbursed for any expenses, but . . . yes."

Allerton had taken a moment to answer. "Does she want to stay with me?"

"Sure," Wells said. "She asked for you herself."

"Well, I'll do my best," Allerton said hesitantly.

"Jimmy, you're a lifesaver, believe me. Oh, one thing. Not a word about this, all right? I wouldn't even talk to Mireille about it if I were you. She's embarrassed enough as it is."

"I understand."

Still, he had not been prepared for the sight of the woman who had been wheeled off the plane. She lay on a bed near him now, almost visibly willing herself to die.

And he understood now that she had never asked for him. Mireille had not been well enough to ask for anything. Adam Wells and his master had only wanted to get her out of the way until she was presentable again.

They never gave a damn about you, he thought.

He remembered the press party at which Mireille had been introduced. Oliver Jordan had sprinkled her with stardust, and she had glittered for everyone. What no one had noticed, though, was that Mireille the woman was far more interesting than the glamour queen that Continental Studios had created.

"I'll see that you're not hurt here," he whispered, close to her ear. He took her hand in his. Almost imperceptibly, he thought he felt her respond with a faint movement of her fingers.

"Allerton may have a point," Wells said. "If she dies—"

"She won't." Oliver Jordan folded the *International Herald Tribune.* There was a picture of Mireille inside, along with a story about Jordan's visit to Berlin. "She wasn't hurt that badly."

"But he said—"

"I know what he said. Forget it, all right?"

Wells set down his coffee cup. "Look, Oliver, I'm worrying about this for your sake. You may think she loves you enough to get over this and come back to work as if nothing happened, but personally, I have my doubts."

"She'll come back to work," Jordan said stolidly. "Besides, what can I do about anything now?"

Wells shook his head. "For starters, you might try to make amends."

"I will. When she's able to appreciate them."

"Oh, for—well, can I at least call her daughter?" he asked in exasperation. "Maybe that would help her snap out of it."

"Her daughter? Where is she?"

"Back at school in Switzerland, I imagine."

"Stephanie," Jordan mused. "How old is she now? Fourteen, fifteen?"

"Seventeen, I think, or nearly so. Do you think that might be worth a shot?"

"What?" Jordan asked distractedly. "Oh. No, don't call her daughter. I will. In fact, I'll go speak to her personally." He stood up. "Make me a plane reservation for Geneva. Today, if possible."

"What are you going to tell her?"

"No idea," Jordan said with a smile. "But I'll see to it that Mireille goes back to work."

"How?"

"Stop fretting. She's going to get better. She's a survivor."

The boarding school parlor was elegant and old-fashioned. Jordan waited with a cup of tea while a nun called Stephanie from her room.

"She will come soon," the nun said, struggling with her English. "I know Stephanie will be pleased to have a visitor." She didn't mention that Stephanie had rarely spoken to anyone since she'd returned to La Voisine. She did well in her classes, but she had no social life whatever. Even the letters she received regularly from her mother remained unopened in a pile in her room.

Sister Bernadette, the new housemother, was tight-lipped about Stephanie's radically changed demeanor, but most of the faculty and staff at the school attributed the girl's silence to the tragic death of her best friend nearly two years before. Stephanie had not been forced to participate in school events or to speak up in class. Yet everyone had watched her, waiting patiently for her to regain some of the cheer and vitality she had once shown. She never did.

"She is a somewhat reticent adolescent," the nun explained. "A good student, however. And a good girl."

"I'm sure she is," Jordan said in a fatherly tone.

"Ah, here she comes." The nun clasped her hands together when Stephanie came into the room. "Isn't this a pleasant surprise, Stephanie?" she said encouragingly.

"Hello, Mr. Jordan," Stephanie said, inclining her head slightly.

"It used to be Uncle Oliver," he said for the benefit of the nun.

The Sister smiled. "Pour some tea for your guest," she whispered, then discreetly left.

While Stephanie poured, Jordan studied her. He had not expected her to blossom as she had. The girl was tall, at least five eight, and every inch as beautiful as her mother, although she didn't particularly resemble Mireille. Stephanie's coloring was startling, her dark hair hanging in long loose waves around the white skin of her face. Her eyes were large and slightly elongated, giving her an almost sultry look, but the pale-gray irises inside were as innocent as a fawn's.

Good God, Jordan thought. *In five years, this girl could own Hollywood.*

"Lemon?" Even her voice was beautiful.

"No, thank you, Stephanie."

She sat down in a hard chair, her hands folded in front of her. "All right," she said. "What does she want?"

"Your mother didn't send me."

She raised her eyebrows.

Jesus, I'm getting a hard-on, Jordan thought. The girl was perfect. Her face was both innocent and knowing, fresh and exotic. And shining through it was a sort of . . . distance. Yes, that was it, a distance, an aloof quality even more pronounced than Mireille's. She was an ice princess, carved of perfect marble.

What would she be like when she melted in passion? he wondered. Unreal. Perfect. He could hear his own breath quickening.

"Mr. Jordan?"

He blinked. "Stephanie," he said. "I'm simply stunned by how beautiful you are."

She blushed, and suddenly Jordan could see the child still living behind those sophisticated eyes. "I'd like . . ." He smiled. He saw its effect. *Oh, goodness me, yes, yes, yes!* "May I take you to dinner?"

Stephanie swallowed. "I don't know. The Sisters . . ."

"I'll speak with them." He gave her a reassuring look as he went to fetch the sweet-faced nun.

Not too fast, Ollie boy. Take your time with this one. Take your time and savor every moment.

"More champagne?" Jordan held the bottle above Stephanie's glass. She nodded demurely.

Soon the last remnants of childish roundness would leave those cheeks, he thought. She would be ready for the camera then. "To you, *ma belle*." He touched her glass with his own.

The tip of Stephanie's nose reddened. Jordan wanted to lick it. *Take it easy. She's young, this succulent, unplucked peach.* He loosened his tie. "Let me come to the point," Jordan said.

Stephanie cocked her head, her gaze locked into his.

"We're going to be shooting a movie in Berlin this summer. Your mother will be in it."

"Of course," Stephanie said, immediately straightening in her seat. She cast her eyes downward.

The willing young girl was gone; she had been replaced by the ice princess again. "Fascinating," Jordan said.

"What?"

"Never mind. What I'm trying to say is, I'd like you to be in it as well."

She looked up, startled. "Me?"

"It's not a very big part, but it may be a good experience for you, and . . . and you'll earn some spending money." He had planned to say *you'll be with your mother*, but he sensed that Stephanie would not have responded well to that enticement. "Would you like that?"

She was silent for a long time. Finally, she asked, "Will you be there?"

Take it easy, take it easy. He had come to Switzerland to insure his last ride on Mireille's comet; what he'd found was another star, burning in solitude, waiting to be born.

Things were going to be better than he thought. Much, much better.

He smiled slowly, his handsome cat's smile. "I'll see what I can do," he said.

Chapter Sixty-Two

Jim Allerton sat with Mireille twenty-four hours a day.

She never responded to him, but he would read aloud to her, or play records, or just talk. At the beginning, he chatted amiably about their experiences together during the filming of *Field of Glory* and *Josephine*, hoping that reminiscences about the past might trigger some response in her, even though their moments together had been brief and cordially formal. No one ever really got to know Mireille, not with Oliver Jordan's iron grip on her life.

She had never made friends among the other cast members or the crew on her films. Jordan had made sure that she spent every moment away from the camera either locked in her trailer or gainfully employed with publicity appearances. The only time Allerton ever spoke with her, after their first conversation at her wedding, was to discuss changes in the script.

Still, he had watched her, studied her. He had always remembered that first meeting when she had told him, with such longing in her eyes, the story that he had fashioned into *Field of Glory*. Once, he knew, she had loved a man with her whole heart. It had not been the man she married, and it seemed that she would never find that love again. It seemed to burn inside her like an ancient and inextinguishable flame that kept her moving through a life in which she had no real interest.

Since then, Mireille had become one of the biggest stars in the world. She was a dazzling thing, larger than life even to those who worked with her, a special being set apart from ordinary people as if there were nothing human about her. But Mireille's physical presence was all she would give to those around her. Her soul could only be seen in her films.

There were times when Allerton again saw the longing in those green eyes, still felt the presence of the sad, bright fire buried deep in her memory. Even now, lying like a stone goddess in the bed, she seemed to be thinking, remembering, gazing at the distant fire while she waited for death to come to her.

"Where are you?" Allerton asked, wishing desperately that she could take him there.

He had searched for her from the moment he met her, and had never found her, not the real Mireille. But he knew she was somewhere inside that insensate body, waiting, waiting . . . "Don't die, Mireille," he said as he took her face in his hands. "God knows, I'm not the one you're thinking of in there, although I wish I were. Please, Mireille, come back . . ."

He stayed there for a long time. As his eyes were closing with fatigue and his breath came in ragged, harsh gasps, he felt the touch of Mireille's hand on his.

Allerton saw the hand poised, beautiful as a statue's. Her eyes were open.

"Mireille!" He leaped up, rubbing his eyes in disbelief, reaching for a glass of water to give her, trying to walk in two different directions at once.

She smiled at him.

"Oh God, thank God . . ." He knelt beside her.

"You're a good friend, Jim," she whispered.

From that point, Mireille began to heal. She no longer refused to eat, and the intravenous tubes were removed. She dismissed the nurses who had looked after her. She began to walk, first around

Allerton's beautiful old country house, and then along the untrav-
eled roads nearby. In the evenings, she wrote long letters to
Stephanie, careful to omit any mention of the beating.

She and Jim Allerton always dined alone. As it turned out,
Allerton was a marvelous cook who welcomed the opportunity to
show off his skills. Mireille gained weight, and the color returned
to her face. By October, she was as beautiful as ever.

"You don't have to leave," he said shyly after Mireille made a
plane reservation for Geneva.

"Of course I do. I haven't seen my daughter in months."

"Did you ever tell her about what happened in New York?"

"No. It would only have upset her."

"You never tell anyone, do you?"

"What do you mean?"

"I mean you're all alone, Mireille. You always have been, as
long as I've known you, anyway. And I don't think you like it."

She smiled and shrugged. "I haven't thought about it, really."

"Yes, you have."

She was silent for a long time. Finally, she said, "You have a
writer's imagination."

"You can't be in love with Oliver, despite what the papers say."

"Oliver?" She laughed. "God, no. I loathe Oliver."

"Is it still the guy you told me about on your wedding day?"

The green eyes were suddenly filled with pain. "I'm sorry," he
said. "I didn't mean to pry."

She made a move to leave, but he caught her arm. "Look, I
don't want to hurt you. I'd rather die than see you suffer. That's
why I've got to say this. I've watched you hurting for close to eight
years, and it keeps getting worse."

"Jim, don't—"

"You've carried that torch for too long, Mireille. The Resistance
fighter you loved is dead. You've got to let someone else into your

life. All right, maybe I'm not the one you want, but somewhere, sometime—"

"He's not dead," she said.

Allerton frowned, bewildered. "He's not?"

"No. But I am." She looked up at his puzzled face. "Oh, Jim, I wish I could explain it to you. You've been wonderful, but don't waste your time with me. I'm not worth it, believe me."

"Mireille—"

"If I could have helped myself, I would have done it a long time ago. Don't you see? I chose the life I have," she said bitterly.

"People can change." Allerton's voice was kind. "Our lives can change, if we want them to. Please stay, Mireille. For a while, at least, until you get things sorted out with yourself."

"Anyone home?"

They both started at the voice. A screen door banged shut, and footsteps clicked across the wooden floors. A moment later, Oliver Jordan filled the arched entranceway to the room.

"Hope I'm not disturbing anything," he said genially. "You're looking splendid, Mireille."

A low moan escaped from between her lips. Allerton spun around to look at her. She was leaning back in her chair, her eyes panicked, as if she were trying to push through the wooden ladder-back.

"We start shooting in Berlin in three weeks," Jordan said. "I've brought you another copy of the script, in case you left the last one behind." He tossed it on her lap.

She nearly leaped out of her chair at its touch.

"What's going on here?" Allerton asked. He could feel the tension in the air, as if the room had suddenly been charged with electricity.

He need not have spoken. Neither Mireille nor Jordan heard him. Allerton felt the sensation of witnessing some basic, elemental drama being played out in front of him: a hawk swooping down upon a mouse, perhaps; a hunter at the moment before the arrow leaves the bow. The two of them were performing the steps in what seemed to Allerton to be a macabre dance of power and fear that he did not understand.

"Oliver." It was as if he hadn't spoken. "Oliver."

Jordan's head swiveled to face him, like a robot's. "Leave us alone, Jim," he said coldly.

"Mireille?"

She didn't answer.

"Look, I don't know what's happening between you, but—"

"I said leave us!"

Slowly, Mireille held up a hand and nodded. Her face was ghostly pale.

Allerton touched her shoulder, looked over at Jordan once more, then left the room.

Chapter Sixty-Three

"You needn't act as if you expect me to cut your throat," Jordan said, offended by Mireille's frightened reception.

"What do you want?"

"I've told you. We've got to make preparations for the shoot. I've worked everything around you until now. We can't delay any longer."

"I'll never work for you again," Mireille said.

Jordan looked pained. "You're right to hate me." He straightened his tie. "I don't really know what happened. I wasn't myself."

"You almost killed me."

He sat down heavily on the chair next to her. "I love you," he said, his voice quavering. "I've loved you since the first time I saw you. But you never loved me. No matter what I offered, what I gave you . . . Well, there's no point in going into all that again. I made a terrible mistake in trying to force you to accept the things I wanted for you. The career, the fame. Me. Mostly me." He looked down at the floor. "I'm begging you to forgive me, Mireille."

She touched her neck, where the bruises had healed. "Will you release me from my contract?"

"I know that's what you want, and I'd like to do it . . ."

"But you won't."

"I can't, Mireille. *Mozambique* didn't do all that well."

"That's a lie."

"You don't know all the figures. I do, and they're not good. If I don't recoup the loss with *Filigree*, I'll be bankrupt. It's the last film, I promise you. I've promised that in writing."

"You've made promises before."

"I'll keep this one. Please believe me. And it will be enjoyable for you. I've seen to that already."

"Enjoyable?" she asked warily. "How?"

"You'll have Stephanie with you."

Mireille frowned. "Stephanie? What does she have to do with this?"

Jordan shrugged. "I've gotten a special dispensation from the school for her to spend a few weeks in Berlin with you."

She blinked, astonished. "That's a sudden change of heart."

"Yes, it is. And a sincere one." He tried to take her hand, but she pulled away from him. "I've thought at great length about what I could do to make amends to you," Jordan said with a hopeful smile. "Of all the things I've done—with the exception of that last unfortunate incident—perhaps the worst was to keep you from your daughter. We can rectify that now. I know things haven't been good between the two of you, and this time together can help to bridge whatever gap may have opened after . . . after . . ."

The green eyes were blazing at him.

"Please don't distrust me, Mireille. I have nothing to gain from this. It's for you. So that you won't remember me so badly."

"And so I'll do the film."

He rose. "So that it will make it easier for you to do the film. I want you to be happy."

She laughed mirthlessly. "That's why you've been blackmailing me."

"Bring Stephanie along," he said, ignoring her. "If you like, we could even find something for her to do. A small part, perhaps. Do you think she would like that?"

Mireille said nothing.

"Or you could bring someone else along. Your painter friend."

"It's too late for that."

"Pity. I'll see you in Berlin. And perhaps before then."

"I doubt that."

"You never know."

His footsteps retreated. The screen door screeched, then slammed shut. When Jim Allerton came back into the room, Mireille was staring at the space Jordan had occupied.

"What did he want?" Allerton asked.

"I don't know," Mireille said slowly.

What *did* Oliver Jordan want? The declarations of love, the tearful apologies, the promises to change—none of it had been genuine, she knew. Even though Oliver was skillful at feigning sincerity, she wondered if he had ever felt the basic emotions he imitated so well.

But why the charade? He knew that he could force Mireille to make the film. He knew that she had, at last, completely accepted the power he held over her. He had raped her, body and soul, until there was nothing worthwhile left of her. He had taken away her friends, her family, and the only man she had ever loved. He had shown her that he could take her life, if he wanted to. What more did he want of her?

"Will you be doing *Filigree*?" Allerton asked, interrupting her thoughts.

"Yes. It will be my last film."

"In that case, I wish I'd done a better job writing it."

"It doesn't matter."

"Hey, are you sure you're all right about this? I mean, you've been through a lot. Even Oliver Jordan would understand if you weren't up to shooting on location."

"No, he wouldn't." She looked up at him. "You know he wouldn't."

Allerton shook his head. "I don't know what kind of hold this guy's got on you, but I don't think it's healthy."

She smiled bitterly. For a moment it looked as if she were about to cry, but she laughed instead. "Not healthy," she said. She took his hand. "Will you be there?"

"Me? Sure. I'll rewrite the script any way you want."

"It's not the script. I just like it when you're near."

He blushed. "To protect you from the ogre of Continental Studios?"

"Yes."

His face grew serious. "You really are afraid of Oliver, aren't you?" he said.

Mireille's eyes met Allerton's. "If you knew him, you would be, too." She stood up. "I've got to see my daughter."

At La Voisine, Stephanie was distant, as she usually was with her mother, sitting rigid and silent throughout the visit, refusing to make eye contact.

Mireille had written scores of letters and made dozens of phone calls, but the letters were never answered, and Stephanie's side of the telephone conversations consisted of little more than a curt hello and good-bye. It had seemed to Mireille that the strain between them could not possibly get worse, but it had.

"Did you get my letters?" Mireille ventured.

Stephanie nodded.

"Then you know why I wasn't able to come earlier." She had concocted a story about having contracted viral laryngitis and recuperating at the home of a friend in Virginia.

"I said I got the letters. Not that I read them."

Mireille reddened. "Stephanie, why . . . ?" She stopped herself from going on, realizing that they were in the visitors' parlor. "It's been so long since we've talked."

"Has it?"

"You know it has. I wish I could explain—"

"Explain what?" Stephanie asked with feigned innocence. "Why you couldn't clear your schedule to see me for two years? Please don't bother."

"I . . . uh . . . thought we might do something special this evening," she said, determined to be cheerful. "There's a train to Paris. We could have dinner on the way, and spend the weekend in the city."

"I'm busy."

Mireille sighed. "I see," she said. "Then maybe we could go to your room. I'd like to see it."

Stephanie's face was expressionless. "If you like." She stood up and left without a word.

Mireille followed her up the stairs to the upper school dormitory. Stephanie's room was clean and spare. The bed was covered by a plain brown blanket provided by the school. The pretty embroidered bedspread Mireille had sent was nowhere in sight. A single lamp shone on a desk, beside a neat stack of Stephanie's schoolbooks. The walls were bare of any ornamentation. The only artwork in the room was a small framed photograph showing Stefan and Stephanie flanking a snowman in front of the school.

Mireille picked it up. Stefan was still as handsome as he had been at twenty. "When was this taken?" she asked.

Stephanie looked out the window. "Last December. On my birthday. You sent money. Stefan flew here and stayed in a hotel so that he could be with me for the holidays."

"He . . . he's been here?"

"Every month," Stephanie said, her eyes narrowed in spite. "He actually likes being with me." She snatched the picture out of Mireille's hands. "I guess that's something you wouldn't understand."

Mireille stared at her, overwhelmed by her daughter's anger. "I'm glad," she said at last. "I'm glad you're close."

"Isn't that nice," Stephanie said sarcastically. "The two embarrassing family rejects have found each other. Now you don't have to have anything to do with either of us."

"Stephanie, that's not what I meant."

"Why do you even bother pretending? You've never wanted me around, and you got rid of Stefan as soon as it looked as if people might find out about him. So you ran right off to Oliver Jordan. I guess he's cool enough for you."

"Don't talk to me that way," Mireille said.

"Oh. Was I rude? I'm sorry if I can't keep up with your facades. I suppose I don't read the papers often enough."

Mireille closed her eyes. "Why are you doing this?" she asked, her voice low. "I've made mistakes, I know, and I'm sorry for them. I'm sorry I wasn't able to spend more time with you in the past, but that's finally changing. My next film is going to be the last one I ever make."

"Right. I'll start holding my breath now."

"It's true, Stephanie! We'll go to Paris, just the way we've always planned, and live the way we've always wanted to—"

"It's too late for that," Stephanie said savagely. "Don't you see, Mother? I'm not a child anymore. That lonely kid standing by the door with her suitcase is gone." She pushed her hair out of her eyes. "God, sometimes it seems as if I've spent my whole life waiting for the lady in the movies to come to life. Well, she never did. I'm done waiting now."

She stood up and went to her closet. "Too bad I have to cut this delightful visit short, but I've got a date."

"A date? You knew I was coming."

Stephanie laughed as she pulled out a blue dress. "You mean the way I knew you were coming on all those birthdays when you didn't show up? I told you, I'm through waiting."

Mireille sat in silence while her daughter dressed. *I thought I could do everything that needed to be done in time,* she thought. But time, she now knew, had run out. "Who is he?" she asked.

There was a knock at the door. "Stephanie, your visitor is here," one of the nuns announced brightly.

"Thank you," Stephanie answered. She brushed her hair. "Would you like to meet him?"

"I . . . All right," Mireille said.

In the visitors' parlor, she saw Oliver Jordan.

Mireille halted in the doorway, unable to move, unable to speak.

"Why, darling," Jordan said, displaying his most artless grin. "How wonderful to see you again so soon."

Her heart was pounding so hard in her chest that she had to fight for air. "What are you doing here?"

"Oliver has offered me a part in his new film," Stephanie said.

Jordan gave a small shrug.

"You told her?"

"I assumed your answer would be yes," he said innocently.

It was difficult for Mireille to contain her rage. "How dare you go to my daughter behind my back!"

"He wanted to ask me first!" Stephanie shouted so loudly that one of the nuns passing through the parlor turned toward her with a hard stare. "Is that so hard to understand?" Stephanie went on in a harsh whisper. "Can't you even imagine that *my* feelings would count for something?" Her eyes were bright as diamonds. "I knew you wouldn't agree to it. Even if I changed my name, even if you were never seen with me in the film, I knew you couldn't stand to see me share anything that was yours."

She looked up at Oliver. "I'm sorry, Mr. Jordan. I should have told you she would say no. I guess I just didn't want you to go away."

She ran out of the parlor and up the stairs to her room. After a moment, Mireille stood up and walked to the exit. Jordan followed her.

"She's right," he said, lighting a cigarette, a gold-tipped Nat Sherman. "I thought I should broach the subject with her before you did."

"Shut up," Mireille hissed.

"All right, just tell me what you want," Jordan said. "I was only trying to help."

She glared at him.

"Tell me how what I'm proposing would in any way be harmful to you or your daughter," he said, opening his hands. "We're talking about three or four weeks in Germany, the two of you together. You'll have a chance to mend fences, and Stephanie will get to be seen in a major movie. How is that bad for anyone?"

"*You're* bad," Mireille said. "For anyone."

He blew smoke out his nose. "I know how you feel about me. I've apologized. And I'm trying to make things up to you now. I don't know what else to do. If you don't want Stephanie with you in Berlin, fine. At least I tried." He tossed away the cigarette and turned to leave. Mireille watched him go. Perhaps he was right, she thought. A month of structured time together might make it possible for Stephanie to trust her mother again. If things went well, they might yet go to Paris together afterward, to enjoy at least some part of the life she had planned for them for so long.

"Oliver, wait," she called uncertainly.

He turned around, smiling. "Have you come around to seeing reason?"

She didn't answer. She was still thinking, weighing the idea against the man.

"Consider it my way of atoning for the inconvenience your stardom has caused you," Jordan said wryly.

"You probably really see it that way," Mireille sighed. Despite her profound distrust of the man, she couldn't find any fault in his argument. "All right," she said at last. "I'll agree to let her work."

"Darling." He opened his arms to embrace her.

She threw them off. "On one condition," she said. "You won't be around either of us. Ever."

Jordan was taken aback. He laughed mildly. "You're joking, of course."

"No, I'm not. You said you wanted me to be happy. That could only happen if I never saw you."

"I'm the producer of the film, Mireille. I'll have to—"

"I don't care what you have to do. I don't want to see you, and I don't want my daughter to see you."

He inhaled slowly, his eyes half-closed against the smoke. "How gracious. I'll keep your request in mind," he said.

"Good. Also keep in mind that I've been through a terrible ordeal. Don't try to tell me you haven't told every Hollywood insider the story that I let myself be picked up and beaten by a stranger."

Jordan's jaw tightened. He had, of course, protected himself against the truth when it looked as if Mireille might die. "Meaning what?"

"Meaning that I may not be well enough to work the schedule you've set up. You may lose a few weeks in production time."

"If I don't stay away," he finished for her.

"Yes. That's right."

"How much can you cost me, Mireille?" he asked, half-amused.

"I don't know. Shall we find out?"

He narrowed his eyes. "I always said we were alike."

"Is it a deal?"

"Your cooperation for my absence?" He shook his head. "I can't leave Berlin. You know that."

"Just stay away from the set."

He looked away. "If I agree, there'll be no trouble from you?"

"And none from you."

"Done," Jordan said. He kissed two of his fingers, then pressed them on Mireille's forehead. "I'll miss you, Mireille."

She watched him walk to his car. He waved at her as he drove away. Mireille closed her eyes with relief.

After Jordan was gone, she sneaked past the nuns to Stephanie's room and knocked softly.

Stephanie opened it wearing a bathrobe. Her long hair hung over her shoulders. "Yes?" she asked coldly.

"We'll do the film together," Mireille said. "If you still want to."

The look of disbelief on Stephanie's face gave way to pure joy. "Really?" She looked up at her mother, her arms rising as if to throw them around Mireille's neck. Then she caught herself and gripped the back of a chair instead. "I guess that'd be okay."

"There's still time for us," Mireille said. "You'll see. We'll find it."

Chapter Sixty-Four

Jim Allerton met Mireille and Stephanie at Tempelhof Airport and drove them to the house on the outskirts of the city where they would be staying during the six weeks of location shooting.

It was a fairy-tale cottage, all whitewashed stucco and wooden shutters. There were overhanging eaves, boxes of geraniums beneath the windows, and bushes sheared into gumdrop shapes at the foundation. The door was a wooden arch with a carved heart at eye level.

"Who lived here before us, Hansel and Gretel?" Stephanie asked.

As if in answer, the door opened and a plump, smiling woman with white braids looped on top of her head curtsied to them.

"*Guten Morgen,*" the rotund confection of a woman said. "I am Frau Wolfe. I will come in once a day for cleaning. Also, I do speak English, if there is anything you like, *ja*?" She grabbed all their suitcases and hoisted them inside. "I will unpack your things," she called from halfway up the stairs.

"Thank you," Mireille said.

Allerton looked around the comfortable room. It was filled with overstuffed furniture, doilies, and cut flowers. "This beats a location trailer," he said.

"It's lovely."

"What's that?" Stephanie said, pointing through the lace curtains of the windows toward a series of Romanesque towers.

Allerton cleared his throat. "That's where I'm staying."

Stephanie whistled. "Cool."

"I'm sharing quarters with Adam Wells."

He and Mireille exchanged a look, and then both burst out laughing. "In that case, I'm not envious," she said.

Stephanie was still staring at the enormous building. "Is it a castle?"

"Pretty much. A *Schloss*. It was built during the fourteenth century. It's really miraculous that so much of it survived the war. All but one wing is still standing, and the owner has put a lot of money into restoring it." He shivered. "The exterior, anyway. From my shower this morning, I'd say it still has the original plumbing. This is its guesthouse."

"How marvelous," Mireille said. "I'd love to walk through it."

"I . . . uh, don't think so," Allerton said, looking uncomfortable. "It's been redone. In a rather unusual style."

"Oh?"

His eyes slid over toward Stephanie. "It belongs to a friend of Oliver's. The Comte de Vevray." The smile left Mireille's face.

"I think he uses it for . . . well, parties."

"I think I understand. Stephanie, you might like to see your room."

Stephanie smiled at the two of them. "Sure," she said. She paused before the staircase. "So the Count's a pervert, right?"

"Stephanie!"

She ran upstairs.

Mireille waited for a few moments before she spoke. "Was it Oliver's idea that I stay here?"

"It's a beautiful place, Mireille. And except for the city scenes, the location shots will be right on the grounds. They're even going to use the castle. There isn't anything comparable within miles."

"All right." She shook her head. "Forgive me, Jim. I'm just edgy."

"About Oliver?" He smiled. "He's set up headquarters in the city. He's been banished from his own production, remember?"

"Do you think he'll stay away?"

Allerton realized that there was genuine fear in her eyes. "What the hell did he do to you, anyway?"

She almost told him. For a brief instant, she almost blurted out that Jordan had been the one who had beaten her senseless, that he had been blackmailing her into working on his films, that he had destroyed almost everything of value in her life, and that she'd gone along with it all out of a sense of shame so profound that she feared it had replaced her very soul.

"Tell me what he's done," Allerton persisted.

How can I? she thought. She'd become so twisted that again and again she'd chosen Oliver Jordan while she'd pushed decent people like Allerton away. Shame and secrecy had become habits so ingrained that they seemed impossible to break. She wished she could break them, wished she could take this kind man into her confidence, but she knew she couldn't. Not anymore.

"Oliver's done nothing," she said blandly. "We just don't get along."

Allerton said good-bye and then walked toward the dark, turreted Schloss. There was no cheerful maid to meet him there; any servants would arrive with the rest of the cast and crew. The studio had to spend money to keep a star comfortable; writers and producers' assistants had to take whatever they could get.

Inside, the heavy, expensive furnishings were still covered with sheets. Cobwebs hung from the corners. The velvet maroon draperies were closed. Allerton sighed. His first trip to Germany, and he had to end up in Castle Dracula. He lit a candle. Lord, there weren't even electric lights. Picking up the suitcase in his one hand, the flickering candle in his other, he made his way up the curving, dusty stone stairs to his room.

"Adam, it's me," he called as he passed the second-story landing. There was no answer, and when Allerton peeked into Adam's room, it was empty.

Wells had taken what he called the "king's chamber," a huge bedroom with a grotesquely carved four-poster and a ceiling painted with nude figures. The oaken window seats were carved with satyrs sporting huge phalluses or fantastic animals in the act of copulation. The moldings along the doorways were also erotic in nature, as were the painstakingly restored ceilings in all the main rooms. Even the doorknobs were shaped in the form of female breasts.

The Schloss was probably the largest single-family residence in Berlin. In a city bordered by barbed wire and bare-earth trenches, where space was a luxury nobody could afford, the Count's property remained intact, no doubt because neither the British nor the French nor the Americans wanted to be responsible for destroying such a rare, if bizarre, building.

Allerton's room was on the top floor. Of the twenty-three bedrooms in the castle, the drafty attic room was the only one that offered enough light to write by, but it was a long hike. By the third landing, he had to pause to catch his breath.

Suddenly, he stopped. Down the hall was a light behind a door. "Adam?" Allerton called.

When there was no answer, he went to the room and opened the door. It fell open with a creak. In it, behind a big carved desk, sat Oliver Jordan.

"Well, are our two princesses properly installed?" he asked, picking up a decanter of scotch.

"What are you doing here?" Allerton asked.

"Just keeping an eye on my investment."

"But wasn't . . . I mean, I heard . . ."

"I've got some calls to make, Jim."

Allerton wanted to hit the man. Another broken promise, another loss for Mireille. But the man was Oliver Jordan, and Allerton would no more strike him than run his fist through a brick wall.

"Well?" Jordan asked as he picked up the telephone. "Why are you still standing there?"

"Mireille's afraid of you," Allerton blurted.

A smile spread across Jordan's face. "Silly girl," he said.

Despite Allerton's fears, Jordan was somewhat true to his word. He did not appear on any of the location sites, and was not even present during the shots taken in and around the Schloss.

Filming went smoothly. The weather was agreeable, the complex government machinery of Berlin had kept its fingers out of the movie, and Mireille's performance was consistently flawless.

Part of her radiance, Allerton guessed, was the fact that Stephanie was with her. Mireille let it be known from the outset that the girl was her daughter—a fact that amazed most of the cast and crew, who had never guessed at Stephanie's existence.

Stephanie was accepted immediately and did well in the small part she was given. She made friends easily and was eager to learn anything she could about how movies were made. Even her relationship with her mother had eased.

During principal photography, when Mireille was called to be on the set alone, Stephanie explored the city with another young actress on the film, who was teaching her how to drive. And when Mireille and Stephanie worked together, they got along with the ease of old friends.

Mireille never minded when Stephanie spent the evenings with the other young people on the project. With Jordan absent, *Filigree* had taken on a tone unlike any of the other films put out by Continental. Instead of the lavish parties thrown by Oliver Jordan, at which each guest was expected to behave in accordance with his relative value and social standing, the cast members and the crew mingled freely during off hours, traveling in a herd to the restaurants and night spots around Berlin.

It reminded Mireille of the days at Cinecittà with Barbara. She did not want to relive those days herself, and declined the invitations to go along. She was used to her privacy. Besides, this was Stephanie's time, and she did not want to steal it from her.

"Daydreaming?" Jim Allerton asked while Mireille sat on the stone wall of a bridge across the Spree River. Traffic had been rerouted for the morning, so the usually noisy bridge was a peaceful and quiet place.

She smiled and nodded. "I like how things have been going."

Allerton laughed. "Making movies doesn't have to be torture," he said. "How much longer is shooting scheduled?"

"Another four or five weeks, I think." She closed her eyes. "I'm almost free, Jim."

"You aren't serious about that alleged retirement of yours, are you?" he asked with a smile.

"Oh, I am," she said. She picked a pebble from the wall and tossed it into the water. "I've made so many mistakes in my life . . ." She broke off.

"You can get away from him, you know," he said, almost reading her thoughts. "The life you live isn't Hollywood. It's Oliver Jordan. When was the last time you had a lover? No, excuse that. When was the last time you had a friend?"

She remembered Barbara, lying blue and still on the slab in the morgue. "You're the last," she said.

"Well, that puts a lot of responsibility on me, then. As the only person besides Jordan's slithery assistant who's ever been allowed to talk to you—and incidentally, how do you think it makes me feel, to be considered as safe as Adam Wells—I nevertheless feel I have to offer you some advice."

"Let me guess. I should tell Oliver to jump in a lake."

"That's a polite way of putting it." He made a face. "Why don't you, Mireille? You're a big girl now. The *Pygmalion* thing was charming for the first year or two, but these days, no one can figure it out. A lot of people think you're just plain dumb."

She laughed. "That I am, Jim," she said. "That I surely am." She stood up, wrapped her trench coat around her, and went to do her scene.

When she was finished, Allerton was still sitting on the wall, looking careworn.

"How did I do?" she asked.

"What? Oh, fine. You're always wonderful, you know that. Are you through?"

"One more scene, as soon as the cameras are set up." She peered into his eyes. "Do you have something to tell me?"

Allerton blushed. "It'll wait."

"You're not going to propose marriage, are you?" she teased.

"No, I've given up on that. Although I could be made to change my mind."

"That's quite all right. Now, out with it. Go ahead. As you said, I'm a big girl."

"Well, it's just . . . Actually, it doesn't matter, but . . ."

"For heaven's sake, Jim!"

"All right." He made a face, as if he hated passing along the information. "Oliver's staying at the Schloss."

"*What?*"

"I didn't mention it because he hasn't shown up on the set. That was your deal, wasn't it? He wasn't to be on the set. Well, he's not, only . . ."

"Only what?" Mireille asked, her face white.

He swallowed. "God, I hate doing this."

"Tell me!" she shouted. The director looked over at them. "Go on," she whispered.

"Okay. Now, there's probably nothing to this, understand, but . . . well, when the gang was heading to a biergarten last night, I saw Stephanie get into a car. A red Ferrari." His lips tightened into a thin line. "It was him, Mireille. Oliver."

Her color drained completely.

"There's more," he said, looking at the street. "This morning, when I came over here, I saw the car again."

"Where?"

"In . . . in your driveway."

She squeezed her eyes shut.

"Mireille, I'm sorry."

"The *bastard*." She stood up, wrapping the trench coat tightly around her, and ran toward her car.

"What did you say to her?" the director barked at Allerton.

Adam Wells trotted off after Mireille, but she passed him with a screech of rubber and a cloud of blue exhaust.

Chapter Sixty-Five

The red Ferrari was still in her driveway.

Furious, Mireille slammed open the door to the cottage. Stephanie jumped from the sofa, startled. Beside her, Oliver Jordan sat calmly, sipping a cup of tea. "Maman," Stephanie said.

Mireille was breathing hard, glowering at Jordan. "Get out."

"We were just having tea," Stephanie protested.

Jordan put a steadying hand on Stephanie's arm. Mireille watched the gesture with distaste, then stepped forward and slapped his hand away from her daughter. "Don't you touch her," she seethed. "I said get out of this house."

Jordan shrugged eloquently and set down his cup and saucer. "As you wish, madame," he said. With a small nod to both ladies, he left. A moment later, the Ferrari's engine roared to life. Mireille and Stephanie watched in silence as the car sped out of the driveway.

"You just can't stop meddling, can you," Stephanie said when all was quiet again. She spoke in a monotone, staring out the window.

"Stephanie, you don't know Oliver."

"Oh, yes, I do!" she said, eyes blazing. "I know he gave you your start. He helped you win two Academy Awards. He bought you your house. He flew you to Geneva when I was sick."

"You're only hearing what he wants you to hear, Stephanie."

"He gave you everything," Stephanie shouted. "He was your lover, and now you're getting rid of him the same way you got rid of my father!"

"Don't you dare compare that man with—"

"Well, he doesn't need your abuse anymore," Stephanie snapped. "He's got me now!"

Mireille's face went blank. The two women faced each other. "What are you saying?" Mireille said at last.

"Oliver came to talk to me. *Me*, Maman, not you. He doesn't care if you never make another film for him." She tossed her dark hair over her shoulder. "You're too old, anyway."

"And you're going to replace me, is that the tack he's taking? That he'll make you a star? Stephanie, you're seventeen years old. Listen to me," she pleaded. "You can't defend yourself against him."

"I don't need to defend myself." Stephanie looked at her mother hatefully. "You just can't stand to see me have anything, can you? Not a home, not my father, not a friend. Certainly not a career, not if it might take the spotlight off you. That's what you're really afraid of, isn't it? That I might actually succeed at something?"

"Oh, listen to yourself, Stephanie."

"That's just what I'm doing! For once, I'm listening to myself instead of you. And I'll tell you something. I'm going to see Oliver Jordan, whether you like it or not. If I can't see him here, I'll go somewhere else. And I'm going to give him everything he wanted from you but never got. A little decency, maybe. A little kindness."

"He's lying to you. He always lies. Oliver can't accept decency. He doesn't know what it is."

"And you do?" She opened the door. "Don't make me laugh." With a toss of her head, she stormed out.

Mireille ran after her and took hold of the girl's shoulders, but Stephanie shoved her away, then ran off into the wooded hillside, toward the towers of the ancient castle.

When Mireille reached the Schloss, Jordan was standing beside the car, his arms crossed in front of him. Stephanie stood defiantly beside him.

"I'll have you arrested," Mireille threatened.

"There's hardly any need," Jordan said smoothly. "As you see, I haven't even entered the place with the virginal Stephanie, and I have no intention of doing so."

Stephanie turned on him. "Don't give in to her! I want to be with you."

He gave an eloquent shrug and turned back to her mother. "You can drag her away kicking and screaming, I suppose. Or you can talk to me."

"Our agreement was that you would stay away from me and my daughter."

"On the set, dear." He looked around. "Do you see a camera anywhere?"

"I'll walk out."

Jordan laughed. "You know perfectly well you won't. Now, the question is, should we talk privately, or right here? I assure you, I don't care."

Mireille looked fleetingly at Stephanie. "No. Not here."

"Whatever you like." He smiled at Stephanie. "Sweetheart, go along, would you? Your mother and I have things to discuss."

As Stephanie trudged obediently away, Jordan gestured toward the Schloss. "Care for a brandy?"

"I'll meet you in a public place," Mireille said.

"Ah, ever suspicious. How can I convince you that I'm a changed man, Mireille? I'm truly sorry for what happened in New York. I've tried to prove in every way I can that it won't happen again, but you—"

"Where would you like to meet me?" she said stonily.

He sighed. "How about the Café Kranzler, on Kurfürsten-damm?"

"Fine. I'll follow you." She got into her own car and waited. With a shrug directed at Stephanie, who gave him a look of help-less adoration, Jordan got into the Ferrari and drove off.

In the shadow of Kaiser Wilhelm Church, left in ruins after the war, grew the neon blossoms of West Berlin. Elegant shops crowded together with adult movie theaters and crumbling old buildings that seemed to burst out of the bombed-out ground. A band of self-proclaimed anarchists jeered at Jordan's and Mireille's auto-mobiles as they drove past, hooting *"Kapitalistische Schwein!"* and bobbing placards protesting American influence in the city.

Inside the café, ladies in stylish hats sipped drinks with atten-tive young men. An enclave of beatniks occupied a dark corner of the place, smoking intently. A pair of identical middle-aged male twins tipped their hats to Mireille in perfect unison as she followed the maître d' to a table.

This was Berlin, Mireille reminded herself. Despite the recent wall that cut the city in half and isolated the western sector from the rest of West Germany, Berlin had lost none of the sense of European decadence for which it had always been famous.

Oliver, who was seated across from her, seemed to fit in per-fectly. He ordered *Berliner Weisse mit Schuss*, a mixture of white beer and raspberry syrup, for them both. While closing her eyes against the taste of it, Mireille's ears rang with the sounds of muf-fled laughter and the garbled beginnings and endings of a dozen different conversations.

Suddenly, her breath caught. For a moment the sounds of the café took her back to Champs de Blé, to the house where, across the way, the German soldiers sang their songs. Where old Valois had brought them French wine and French girls.

"You're trembling," Jordan said.

"It's . . . it's nothing." Mireille rubbed her arms.

He leaned toward her. "You're still the most beautiful woman I've ever seen," he said.

"Don't bother, Oliver. We both know you too well."

Jordan slapped the table in annoyance. "All right, then. What do you want from me now?"

"I want you to stay away from my daughter."

"Oh, come now. Do you really think I would take advantage of a teenage girl?"

"Yes. You would take advantage of anyone."

He winced. "Mireille . . ."

"I don't want you near her, do you understand?"

He glanced around the room. "Don't get hysterical. There are photographers at the window."

She turned around in panic. A flashbulb went off.

Jordan crossed his arms over his chest. "You were the one who insisted on a public meeting."

She balled her hands into fists, trying to compose herself. "All right," she whispered. "I'm not staying. But I want you to know that if you even attempt to speak with Stephanie again, I'll call the authorities. You won't like that kind of publicity, Oliver."

Jordan looked genuinely amused. "Darling, I thought I was supposed to be the blackmailer."

"Just try me. The Hays Office will see to it that your films are never shown in the United States again. And if you think I won't do it for fear of your dredging up my past to the press, think again."

They faced each other for a long moment before Jordan finally broke. "Mother love," he said. "You'd really sacrifice it all, wouldn't you?"

"I'd kill you with my bare hands if I could," she said.

A woman at the next table turned her head slowly toward Mireille.

"And I'd watch what I said if I were you," Jordan said quietly. "A lot of people in Berlin speak English."

Mireille rose. "Good-bye, Oliver."

He stood up, took her hand, and kissed it. *"Auf Wiedersehen,"* he said. "Until we meet again."

"We won't."

"No? Pity." He shrugged. "No matter. I can wait."

A frisson of fear shot down her back. "Wait? For what?"

He leaned close to her and whispered in her ear, "For Stephanie to come of age."

All at once the room seemed to tilt around her. "Goddamn you!" She jumped at him, clawing at his face.

Heads turned at every table in the place. The waiters stopped in their tracks. The flashbulbs at the windows went off, bathing the room in white light.

Jordan pushed her away from him. The marks from Mireille's fingernails on his cheek were oozing blood. Photographers were shoving their way through the crowd for the photo opportunity of a lifetime.

"No, no, no," the manager of the place said, shaking his head emphatically as he lumbered toward the American movie star. *"Nicht hierein!* Not in my place!"

Some of the onlookers were laughing and cheering. Others left indignantly. Most of them, recognizing Mireille, rushed to surround her. Some tried to tear off pieces of her clothing. Others calmly offered napkins and scraps of paper, requesting her autograph. Reporters shouted questions. The photographers shot everything.

While Mireille tried to extricate herself from the mob, Jordan left quietly, handing the café's manager a thousand deutsche marks for his trouble.

When he got back to the Schloss, Stephanie was waiting for him outside, her eyes concerned and adoring.

Oh my, he thought. *I might not have to wait, after all.* He flung his head back and laughed. Revenge was so sweet.

Chapter Sixty-Six

"Oliver! You're hurt." Stephanie opened the Ferrari's door with an expression of exquisite sympathy. "There's blood all over you."

Jordan lolled his head back on the headrest and allowed his eyes to roll back weakly. "Help me," he moaned. "Please." He let himself out of the car and leaned on the girl for support. "The key's in my pocket," he said breathlessly. "My pants pocket."

As she reached her fumbling short-nailed fingers into his trousers, he felt an unmistakable rise in his own anatomy. How he had changed from the boy he had been, he marveled. The idea of perfect, sculpted, womanly women, now that he'd had the epitome of them in Mireille for so many years, no longer filled him with desire.

But this, this tender meat, this young thing still with the remnants of baby-fat wrinkles along the inside of her elbows, this colt with her taut skin and dewy eyes, with her unpresuming hands— *oh, child!* This was going to be more of a pleasure than he'd thought.

She helped him into the house. "Up the stairs, please," he said weakly. "I'd like to lie down." He directed her to the Comte's bedroom, a vast, sinister cavern draped in black satin and gold embroidery.

Stephanie looked around the room with a brief look of horror. The ornate ceiling was covered in a mosaic of mirrors. The wallpaper was a reddish-tinged Indian mural depicting two-dimensional characters engaged in various aspects of sexual activity.

He dropped onto the big bed, causing the satin to ripple invitingly.

"I'll get a doctor," she said.

He held her hand. "I don't need one. But the blood . . ." There wasn't much of it, but Jordan manipulated his facial muscles until the scratches from Mireille's fingernails yielded enough blood to crust around the lines of his mouth. He hoped it looked worse than it was. Aside from a slight headache—a remnant of the hangover with which he'd started the morning—he felt nothing more pernicious than an erection.

"Then I'll wash your wounds," Stephanie said tenderly.

"You're too kind, darling." It was every young girl's dream, he knew, to care for a handsome, injured older man.

While Stephanie was in the washroom, Jordan sat up to check his reflection in the mirror. Yes, his face looked properly ghastly. He wiggled his forehead up and down a few times to stimulate the flow of blood, then hung his head over the side of the bed.

"Oliver!" she called, running to him in alarm when she saw him.

"It's all right . . . Just a moment of dizziness." He smiled up at her. Gently, she touched the damp cloth to the cuts on his cheek and washed the streaked blood from his face. "Thank you, Stephanie," he said, touching her hand.

"Were you in an accident?"

"No." He shuddered dramatically. "Your mother hit me."

"My . . . mother?" She looked down at the bloody washcloth. "That bitch!"

"With a bottle," he added weakly.

"How could she! Oh, you're bleeding again." She touched the cloth again to his forehead. "Why did she do it, Oliver?"

He shrugged. "I asked her to give you a chance," he said. "I think you could be a star, Stephanie. But Mireille won't hear of it. She won't have her own daughter as competition, I suppose."

She sat down on the bed beside him. "I'll show her," she said. "I'll run away. I'll—"

"Shhh," Jordan said. He touched her long black hair. "There is time. There is time for everything." He pulled one of the shining tresses to his face and sniffed it. "You smell like spring," he said quietly. "You *are* spring."

She smiled, blushing.

"Kindness becomes you, Stephanie." He sat up and took one of her hands, brushing it against his lips. "If only I were younger, much younger . . ."

"I don't want a young man, Oliver. I want . . ." She lowered her eyes, and Jordan could almost feel the sweet moisture gathering in those spanking-white cotton panties.

Inexorably, as if yielding to fate, their two faces met, his lips barely grazing hers.

"I want you," she said, and their kiss deepened.

Yes, oh, yes. You needn't wait any longer, Ollie. Here she is on a silver platter.

How sweet she was, this morsel, this child-woman. He touched her firm, swelling breasts through her blouse. Their nipples hardened beneath his fingers as she shuddered, her cheeks burning. Then slowly, languidly, his arms encircled her and he pulled her beside him on the black satin bed.

"My Angel," he whispered.

Mireille drove back to the cottage, her hands still shaking violently. The police had come to the café. With her raincoat wrapped protectively around her, she had answered a thousand questions while the attendant crowd grew more noisy and curious.

What had she done? they wanted to know. She had cut open a man's face, someone offered. It was her lover, another added. Their pictures had been in all the magazines. She was drunk. They were both drunk. Or on drugs. These spoiled American women didn't know their place. She's the one who hates publicity, isn't she? *Ja*, a princess or something. A *Französin*. She didn't act like she hated publicity. Of course, the whole thing was staged.

"Did you get a shot of her tits?" one photographer asked another.

In the end, since Jordan was not available to press charges against her and the restaurant's owner had already been compensated for any damage, the police left.

She arrived at the house feeling as if her heart had been ripped from her. The fracas at the café had momentarily diffused her despair, turning it for once into anger. But now it was back. She had allowed Oliver Jordan to take her life from her, and now he planned to take Stephanie's, too.

It was the lies—a lifetime of lies, twisted in upon each other—that had strangled them all. When should they have stopped? When Jordan had tried to kill her? When she found Stefan? When Barbara died? When Stephanie left school? Or even before then, before Hollywood, before she had ever met Oliver Jordan?

She couldn't sort it out anymore. When she closed her eyes, all she saw was the recurring image of a woman she had scarcely known: Ankha, frail and ephemeral as a flower, hanging from a light fixture in a rented room. She had died there, just as Barbara had died in another rented room, because, in the end, there had been nowhere else to go for either of them. In the Life, there were no exits.

Her hands shaking violently, Mireille picked up the telephone and dialed La Voisine in Geneva. "Please prepare Stephanie's room," she told the nun in charge of the upper school dormitory. "She'll be arriving back at school within twenty-four hours."

Jordan touched Stephanie's neck with his lips while he unbuttoned her blouse. She responded to him like a young animal, arching her back to meet his fingers. He took one small breast out of its sensible cotton bra, itself now perversely exciting, and rolled his tongue around the pale-pink aureole.

Stephanie moaned. It sounded oddly false, as if it were a noise she believed she was expected to make. Jordan found it all rather endearing. "Am I the first?" he whispered.

Blushing, she nodded. "Will it . . . will it hurt? I heard it would."

"Sometimes it hurts," he said. "Does that excite you?"

"No!" She looked embarrassed. "Well, maybe a little."

"You're trying to think of the right thing to say."

She hid her face in a pillow, a shy child.

"You want to please me, don't you?" he teased as he slowly pulled down her underpants. "Now, don't be tense." He stroked the soft skin of her thighs. Then—so gently—he inserted the tip of one finger into her wetness. "Has anyone ever done this before?" he asked silkily.

Her face still buried in the pillow, she shook her head.

"Never?" He squeezed his hand between her thighs and touched her juicy bud. "One of the girls at school, perhaps?"

She turned around to show her face to him. Her mouth was slack and red and wet. "You're the first, Uncle . . . I mean, Oliver."

"Uncle Oliver. I think I like that. Yes, I do. Spread your legs for me, Angel." Without waiting, he pushed her thighs apart and slid his finger deep into her opening. "God, you're tight. It's going to be good. Very good."

She squirmed. "Please stop for a while," she whispered.

He felt his body responding in anticipation as he took her hand and placed it against his erection. "Open the zipper and touch me," he said.

"I'm . . . I'm scared."

"Don't be." He kissed her.

"No." She snatched her hand away. "I don't want to."

He touched her breasts. A wildness unlike anything he had ever felt was taking hold of him now, as he manipulated her tender nipples to hardness. "You like this, Angel. You like this very much." He pinched them until Stephanie cried out. "Tell me, did that hurt?"

She slid up to the top of the bed. "Please stop. Please."

He shook his head. "You're being a naughty girl, Angel."

"Stop calling me that!" Her voice cracked with fear.

"Shhh. All right. Be quiet, darling. It's just a game."

She got up off the bed. "I don't like this game," she said, gathering the shreds of her youthful dignity around her as she straightened her clothes. "I'm not Angel. I'm Stephanie, and I'm going home."

Jordan watched her, his eyes dancing with amusement. "Now, you know you don't really want to go," he said. He rose slowly off the bed, graceful as a cobra. "Come on. Come to Uncle Oliver." From behind, he clasped his hands around her slender wrists. She struggled against them.

He held her more tightly. "Don't be coy, Stephanie. Let yourself enjoy it."

"This isn't the way I thought it would be," she said, trying to sound defiant. "It isn't romantic or anything. It's just . . . gross."

He ignored her, running his hands along her arms. She prickled in gooseflesh at his touch. "You ought to inject some excitement into those virginal dreams of yours," he said. He caressed her breasts, feeling the adolescent flesh harden again. "Shall I show you?"

"I . . ." She sighed.

This time Jordan knew that the sound was not a fake.

She really did want it, whatever she felt she had to say. "Tell me you like what I'm doing."

"I *don't!*" Stephanie made a halfhearted attempt to get away from him, but Jordan knew what she really wanted. What they all wanted, and shied from, and felt shamed by every time they touched themselves.

"How that hurts me," he said with exaggerated sorrow. "Won't you please me, Angel? Just for a little while?"

"I told you, I'm not—"

He ran his tongue along the rim of her ear, and she shivered. "Angel," he whispered. "Close your eyes. I have a surprise for you."

He held one hand over her eyes, while with the other he opened the drawer of the nightstand beside the bed.

Something cold touched Stephanie's belly, then snaked its way up between her breasts, up the length of her throat, coming to rest beneath her chin.

A hard thing, metal. A finger of steel. When she opened her eyes, she saw that Jordan was holding a revolver.

She gasped.

"Your fear is what makes it special," he said thickly. "Your fear of the cock." He pressed the barrel of the gun deeper into her flesh. "Hard, like this."

"No! No . . ."

He felt her trembling. "I can smell your fear, cutting through that baby-powder girl-smell." He inhaled her fragrance. "Now I can fuck you." He kissed the nape of her neck.

"No," she breathed. "Please don't."

He pulled her long hair slowly, dragging her down to the floor. "You want it," he said. "You all want it."

She screamed.

Mireille's head jerked toward the window.

"Mireille?"

Jim Allerton walked in. "Good God," he said. "Are you all right?"

"You startled me." She looked past him, toward the Schloss over the hill. She thought she had heard a scream. "It must have been the door."

"The police came by the shoot. I thought Adam was going to have a seizure."

"Quiet." She cocked her head toward the trees. "Did you hear something?"

"Like what?"

Mireille held up her hand for silence. There was nothing. Her guilt was making her hear things, she decided. Her desire, after ruining her own life and her daughter's, to hear some atavistic maternal alarm from her daughter.

But Stephanie would not come to her for help, not anymore. If she was with Oliver Jordan, she was there of her own free will. "Come with me to the Schloss," she said with a sigh. "I think Stephanie's there."

"Sure," Allerton said gently. The two of them headed off on foot toward the woods.

Then they both heard a scream.

Jordan clapped his hands over Stephanie's mouth. The girl's terror excited him. He had taken young girls before, but they had been willing. He had lost interest after the first thrust. It had only been with Mireille, pleading for mercy in the hotel room in New York, that Jordan had known true sexual release.

And now this. Mireille's child. There could be nothing beyond this, and he wanted to savor every moment of it. "So you've never been fucked before?" he whispered into her ear. "This will be special, then." He tossed the gun aside, then pinned Stephanie's arms over her head on the floor. "It's going to be good, little girl. You're going to love it."

"Maman!" she cried.

"Calling for Mother, are we? There's an idea. Maybe she'll join us. She's a very good fuck, you know. Juicy. She was known as the best whore in Paris. The Angel of Night, the first Angel . . ."

"What?" Stephanie whispered. "What are you saying?"

"Oh, didn't you know? I suppose not. It was the 'big secret.' Mama's soiled laundry." He licked the salty skin of her neck. "Yes, the Angel fucked for us all. When she spread those long white legs—"

"Stop it!" Stephanie shouted, her lips trembling. "I don't want to hear any more!"

"I believe she was around your age when she started," he went on serenely. "In fact, you're undoubtedly the product of one of those meaningful unions." He shoved his hand up roughly beneath her skirt. "Let's see how you stack up against her, shall we? Breeding does tell."

Stephanie screamed once more as he mounted her. His flesh touched hers, prodding at the tight young orifice, electrified by her shrieks of terror. Jordan felt the sweat beading on his forehead, felt his forearms trembling in anticipation. His eyes rolled up into his head. *Yes. Yes, Angel, you've come back to me, just the way I like you best.*

"Get away from her."

Suddenly, Jordan felt as if his scalp were being torn from his skull. Fingernails were clawing at him from behind. Stephanie gasped. Then another pair of hands picked him up by his loosened belt and flung him off the warm body of the girl.

He spun around, dazed. All he saw were a pair of green eyes that filled the room with their hatred.

Jordan got up slowly, his hands making a halting sign. "Now, let's not be bad-tempered about this," he said, managing what he hoped was a charming smile as he zipped up his trousers. "It wasn't going to go any further—"

"Get away!" Mireille screamed. She sounded as if she were on fire.

Jordan backed up toward the doorway. Jim Allerton stopped him. "Should I call the police?" Allerton asked.

Mireille didn't hear him. She stood like a statue, staring into her past. The man who had lain on the floor with her daughter was old Valois, and the girl lying helpless and exposed was herself. Eighteen years had disappeared in an instant. Her stepfather was lying on top of her, and she was sobbing on the kitchen floor with a piece of broken glass in her hand.

"It was a moment of weakness for both of us," Jordan said, looking like a naughty but lovable little boy.

Allerton bunched Jordan's collar into his fist. Jordan gagged but went on babbling his plea to Mireille as if he were oblivious to the man who held him in a chokehold. "Darling, I'm horribly embarrassed by all this, but there's really no need for the police, is there? Arrangements can be made. Whatever you want. The originals of the press clippings from Paris. Would you like that? You'd be free, Mireille—"

"Stephanie, no!" Allerton shouted.

All eyes turned toward the girl. Backed up against the corner, her hair a disheveled tangle around her face, hanging open, she held the gun in both shaking hands, pointing it at Jordan.

"Stephanie," Mireille said gently, moving toward her.

The girl wheeled around to face her mother. "Don't come near me," she said. "Just tell me, were they true? Those things he said about you, were they true?"

Mireille raised her arms in silent supplication, then slowly dropped them again.

She had lived her whole life in fear of this moment. She had discarded everything she treasured to avoid it. She had given up her dreams, her self-respect, and the love of her daughter in order to pass by this one instant of time. And yet it had come.

"It's true," she said. "It's all true."

"You see?" Jordan spoke up excitedly. "I'm not the liar I've been made out to—"

"Shut up!" Stephanie turned the gun back on Jordan and began to move toward him. "Does this excite you, *Uncle Oliver*?" she whispered hoarsely. Her mouth twisted into an ugly grin.

"Now . . . now, darling . . ."

"My name is Stephanie!" She took a step closer to him. "Not 'darling,' not 'sweetheart.' Not 'Angel.'"

"No, of course not. Stephanie, Stephanie, my . . . my friend. Please put the gun down, Stephanie. It's very disconcerting."

She moved closer.

"Stephanie, I'm begging you. See? Begging." He clasped his hands together in front of his face.

One step at a time, the gun at arm's length.

"For God's sake, let go of me," Jordan hissed over his shoulder. Allerton had been so caught up that he seemed to have forgotten all about the man he held dangling by his collar. He opened his hands.

Jordan rubbed his throat. "Ah, much better." He held out his hand. "Now, give me the gun, Stephanie." Stephanie stopped in her tracks. "Yes. That's right. You don't really want to kill me, do you? Because you know I love you. I do, Stephanie." His eyes were filled with hurt and longing. "I think I've always loved you, from the moment I first saw you."

Mireille's eyes flooded with the memory of promises made and forgotten, of all the lies that had made up the outlines of her life.

"I'll do wonderful things for you," Jordan said in the bedroom voice he had used with Mireille for so many years. "Things beyond your wildest imaginings. I can do it, believe me. I can give you everything you want."

Stephanie lowered the gun.

"Good," Jordan said, nodding reassuringly. "That's right, Stephanie. Give me the gun." He moved toward her slowly. "You're going to have a wonderful future. Wonderful."

"No," she said calmly. In an instant the gun was raised to Jordan's face. "Nothing's going to be wonderful anymore."

"Darling—"

She pulled the trigger.

Jordan's eye exploded. Blood and matter from the back of his head spattered against the wall and rebounded in a spray back into Stephanie's face. She fired again as he fell. And again. And again. When Mireille and Allerton grabbed her and wrestled her to the floor, she shot a fifth round into the wall.

"Stephanie! Stephanie," Mireille cried, shaking her.

She dropped the gun. "Oh, Maman," she said. It sounded like the howl of a trapped wolf. Then she buried her face in her mother's bosom.

Mireille held her, rocking her, stroking her hair.

"Maman . . ."

"It's all right," Mireille said gently. "It's going to be all right." She looked over to Allerton, who was standing ashen-faced over the bloody body. "Get her to Geneva right away," she said.

"Mireille, we can't—"

"Just do it!" she snapped. "And don't tell anyone about this, do you understand? Not anyone, no matter what happens."

She grasped Stephanie around her shoulders. "Now listen to me," she said, forcing the girl to meet her eyes. "You're going to go back to school. You mustn't say anything about what happened. Will you promise me that?"

"But, Maman—"

"Promise me!"

Miserably, the girl nodded her agreement. Mireille helped her off the floor and led her to Allerton.

"What are you going to do?" he asked.

"I'm going to take care of this," she said. "Go. Hurry." Stephanie shuffled out, sobbing.

It's just like when I left, Mireille thought. The journey that had begun when she walked out of that bloody kitchen in Champs de Blé had finally come full circle, and the path would now be taken again by another young girl.

Fortune's child.

"No, it won't," she said to the silent room.

She picked up the gun and examined it. One bullet remained in its chamber. Carefully, she wiped the gun clean on her dress. Then, slowly, she walked over to Jordan's body. His arms and legs were sprawled crazily in a lake of blood; his face was a pulpy, unrecognizable mass except for one pale eye that stared skyward, lifeless as a marble.

Mireille raised the revolver to his chest. "This will be our last dirty secret, Oliver," she said. Then she pulled the trigger and the final bullet thudded into his heart.

The report from the gun was deafening in the still room, but Mireille never flinched. She watched as the body bucked with the impact of the bullet, a jerky, obscene dance. Then she pulled the trigger again.

The barrel was empty. There was no sound except for the empty click of the trigger.

Click.

Sweat rolled down her face into her eyes.

Click.

She could taste it in the corners of her mouth. It was salty, like blood.

Click. Click.

At last her eyelids fluttered and closed. She sank down at his side. His blood oozed up the hem of her dress.

"I'll see you in hell, Oliver Jordan," she said. "Where we both belong."

She was still kneeling beside the corpse when the police arrived.

Chapter Sixty-Seven

The press was ecstatic. Ever since the Reuters news agency broke the story, the details of the grisly shooting in Berlin had made daily headlines around the world.

Mireille had not spoken a word since her arrest. She had not requested an attorney. She had not explained the circumstances of the murder to anyone. She had not mentioned Stephanie's presence. Still, the newspapers were constantly fueled by stories from Oliver Jordan's past—the new Zanuck of Hollywood, they called him. Journalists had always loved his wit and manner, his maverick lifestyle, his lavish tastes. And the stormy relationship he shared with Mireille, the nobody he had turned into a legend, had given them all nearly a decade of sensational news to draw from.

Not much, though, had been found about Mireille herself. The "baroness" from an obscure French province, the youthful riding champion, the former fiancée of the Comte de Vevray . . . She had turned out to be none of those things.

But who was the real Mireille? The actress who had been famous for her mystery was more mysterious than anyone had thought. Her background could be traced to her marriage to Victor Mohl, and to a small part she'd played in a B Western filmed in Italy, but before that, nothing. No one knew a thing about her.

And then an enterprising young reporter for the *Los Angeles Times* who spoke fluent French talked the editor in chief into sending her to Paris to research old issues of French newspapers, and she got a scoop that reverberated through every inch of Hollywood. The old photographs that had appeared in *L'Etoile* twelve years before now reappeared in almost every news publication in the world.

MIREILLE WAS A HOOKER screamed the *New York Daily News*.

ACCUSED ACTRESS'S PAST REVEALED read the more stately *New York Times*.

MURDEROUS MIREILLE—ANGEL OF DEATH? appeared in *Variety*.

A ROLE MODEL FOR OUR YOUNG PEOPLE? was the headline for an editorial in the *Christian Science Monitor*.

By the time Mireille was scheduled for arraignment, the throng of reporters in Berlin was nearly a thousand strong, all of them demanding to hear her explanation of innocence.

She offered none. Mireille said nothing.

The West German district attorney, suddenly a famous man, was on the television news every night with more gory insights into Mireille's sordid past.

"I will leave it to the *Richter*, the judge, and his associates to decide whether or not she is guilty of murder," he said importantly on the steps of the courthouse. "But what we do know, for a fact, is that the woman has led a life of unbelievable debauchery. Is she capable of murder?" His shrug was eloquent. "My guess is yes."

Former call girls from Madame Renée's now-defunct stable came forward, aging beauties anxious to be in the spotlight once more.

"Of course we knew about Mireille," one of them confided to *Newsweek*. "She called herself l'Ange then, 'the Angel.' She was perfect. Madame Renée once said that she was the greatest courtesan since Madame de Pompadour. Some of us thought we'd become movie stars, too. But there was only one Angel."

Madame Renée herself was flushed out of retirement by a horde of journalists. "I'll write a book one day," she promised. "Then I'll tell everything."

"What about Mireille?" someone shouted. "Will you write about her?"

"Read it and find out," she said with a wink.

Within days the madam was signed to write her autobiography with the help of a ghostwriter for an advance of a quarter million dollars.

Victor Mohl, now working as a talent agent, spoke bitterly about how his wife had left him for Oliver Jordan. "She was an extra when I picked her up," he said on a late-night radio talk show. "I gave her a home. She wouldn't have had the clothes on her back if it hadn't been for me. But as soon as I introduced her to Oliver, she was gone. And I never worked as a director again."

Mireille said nothing.

A reporter from the *Berliner Morgenpost* sought out the Comte de Vevray in a nightclub in Cannes. "Oh, my dear," he said with a laugh, "of course she was a *poule*. The most lush, expensive, accommodating prostitute in Paris. A work of art. I was her first patron, you know. Or so she said. But then, l'Ange could make one believe anything. That's how Oliver managed to convince everyone she was a baroness or some such thing. It was all great fun." He sighed and shook his head. "Pity she had to shoot the fellow. He gave marvelous parties."

"She was the most unhappy woman I'd ever met," said Sam Hope, who had won the Academy Award for directing Mireille in *Field of Glory*. "No point in lying about it—Oliver Jordan made her live the life of a puppet on a string. Mireille could have worked for any studio, but she stayed with Jordan. Maybe it was love," he added with a shrug. "Or just Hollywood."

"I have no idea how she will structure her defense," the district attorney said, striking a pose behind his desk. "From all appearances, she does not seem to believe this case is even going to trial. She has not hired a lawyer. A court-appointed *Pflichtverteidiger*—what you would call a public defender—has been assigned to her, but she refuses to speak with him. Perhaps she feels that Americans do not need to obey the laws in our country." He looked indignant as he straightened his tie. "I assure you that if that is the case, she is gravely mistaken."

From the Motion Picture Producers and Directors Association:

> *We urge all motion picture theaters and distributors of theatrical-length feature films to withdraw from circulation the film* Mozambique. *We also recommend that theaters, theater chains, and distributors refrain from showing* Filigree, *or any part thereof, if and when it is released in the United States.*

Mireille said nothing.

Adam Wells refused to comment, having immediately found work as a personal assistant to the chief executive of another major studio. In later years, Wells would become known as "the man who kept every secret in Hollywood."

Without ever having held a position above that of administrative assistant, he eventually retired a multimillionaire.

Anne Rutledge Jordan was not present at her ex-husband's funeral. When questioned about the death of Oliver Jordan, a source close to the New York–based socialite said, "Of course he was having an affair with that actress. Everyone knew that. It was why the Jordans' marriage dissolved. The woman involved was a constant embarrassment to Anne."

Anne sailed for Southampton the following week.

BERLIN (Reuters) — A West German woman claims to have heard international film star Mireille threaten Oliver Jordan just hours before the Hollywood producer was shot dead in his Berlin residence.

Elsa Bonn, who sat at the table next to Mireille and Jordan at a café on Kurfürstendamm, says she overheard the actress during a heated argument.

"She said she would kill him with her bare hands," Mrs. Bonn told reporters yesterday.

A television commentator on NBC reported:

The arraignment for Mireille is scheduled to take place in Berlin tomorrow. The actress is accused of murdering Continental Studios head Oliver Jordan. To the consternation of her millions of fans, she has refused to speak in her own defense. She was found by police with a spent revolver beside Jordan's body, but through all of the astonishing revelations of the four days since, Mireille has adamantly refused to cooperate with authorities in any way.

"For God's sake, Mireille, tell the truth," Jim Allerton pleaded in the small visiting area in the *Landgericht* where she had been jailed since her arrest. "They won't convict Stephanie. It was clearly self-defense."

Mireille plucked at the wrinkled cloth belt of her prisoner's uniform. "I don't know what you're talking about," she said blandly.

He slapped his forehead with the heel of his hand. "Jesus, it's like talking to a wall. Listen to me. You don't have to go through this! I hired a good lawyer for you."

"I dismissed him."

"I know. Why, Mireille?"

"You promised me your silence."

"Not if it means sending you to jail for the rest of your life."

"You told the lawyer I didn't kill Oliver."

"You didn't," he said evenly. "I saw it happen, remember?"

The green eyes gazed at him coldly. "You must be mistaken."

Allerton sighed. "Look, I know you're trying to protect your daughter—"

"Keep her out of this," she warned.

"But her testimony would free you! No one's going to believe me without corroborating evidence. You need her."

"Leave her alone."

"Damn it, Mireille—"

"Guard!" She rose abruptly.

Allerton buried his face in his hands. "Why are you doing this?" he asked miserably. "You're throwing your life away."

She smiled gently. "None of it was real, anyway," she said.

The guard led her away.

"I can summarize this case in three sentences," the district attorney said. "We are going to trial. We are going to get a conviction. And we are going to ask for the maximum penalty allowed under West German law." He shot a steely gaze in the direction of the cameras. "Equality may not exist in the United States, but here even the wealthy and privileged are subject to justice."

The next morning, Mireille stood in the courtroom before the *Richter* and two associate judges. The district attorney had prepared a lengthy *Protokoll*, a report giving the State's reasons for its conclusion about Mireille's guilt.

Reporters packed the courthouse as they never had before, spilling out onto the steps. The arraignment, they knew, was just a formality, but with Mireille as the defendant, it was still news.

"How does the defendant plead?" the *Richter* asked.

The public defender cleared his throat to speak, but Mireille stopped him. "Guilty," she said.

Within a minute, a wall of noise rose up from the throng of press people outside the courtroom. Reporters streamed from the building, searching for telephones to notify their papers. TV cameras rolled.

The district attorney raised his eyebrows and crossed his arms as she left. He had been deprived of the biggest scene of his life.

As for Mireille, she left quietly, passing through the reporters as if they were mist. She had spoken only one word.

Chapter Sixty-Eight

The CBS correspondent gazed into the camera, looking concerned about the news item she was reporting on:

"Mireille's surprising plea of guilty to charges of murdering her producer and lover, Oliver Jordan, has brought the shocking revelations of the past five days to a peak.

"Now, with the necessity for a long and expensive trial eliminated, all that remains to be seen is how West Germany will sentence the prostitute-turned-actress. The question of the moment seems to be: Will Mireille receive the same treatment as anyone else who had openly murdered a man in cold blood? Or will the West German judge grant leniency to the woman because she happens to be an internationally famous movie star?"

Stefan turned off the set. "Damn you."

He put his head in his hands. Outside, the rain was falling, slapping against the window. It was a cold autumn rain, with the wind whipping through the tall buildings, making sounds like the tortured souls in hell.

How far we've come from Champs de Blé, he thought. He closed his eyes and remembered the days he'd spent with Mireille so long ago. Mireille, with her bloody feet and hands, her back studded with slivers of broken glass; Mireille tramping up the wild hills in her shapeless black hand-me-down dress, or running like a colt, naked and laughing; Mireille lying among flowers, her face so beautiful that he had felt compelled to draw it.

He had called her "fortune's child," and he had known even then that it was true. The golden-haired girl was destined for a life beyond his ken. But what sort of life had she chosen—Mireille, who could have been anything? And what had driven her to kill again, as she had killed Valois that night so many years ago?

He picked up the telephone and called Stephanie's school in Geneva.

"I'll try to get her," one of the nuns said with a sigh. "But you may have to wait a while. She's been refusing to take any calls. As you know," she added for emphasis.

He had tried to reach Stephanie ever since he'd first heard about Mireille's arrest, but she would not come to the phone. Nor had she answered the three telegrams he'd sent.

"I'm sorry, Mr. Giroux." The nun sounded exasperated. "She just won't come out of her room. We've tried everything we know, but we can't persuade her to go to class, or even come to meals. She's quite upset."

"Has she seen the news stories?"

"I don't know how she could have. She arrived back at the school before any of us heard anything about the incident. But she hasn't left her room since. Isn't that odd?"

Stefan thanked her for her trouble and hung up. The wind was rattling the glass in the windows. He stood alone in the empty room, hearing the Sister's words again and again:

She arrived back at the school before any of us heard anything . . .

She just won't come out of her room . . .

She's quite upset . . .

Stephanie had been in Germany shooting a movie with Mireille. Then suddenly—from the accounts he'd heard, even before filming was complete—she was back at school, refusing to speak to anyone.

Before the news about the murder broke.

Stephanie knew something. Something that was scaring her almost to death.

He threw some things into a bag and ran out into the rain to hail a cab. "Airport," he told the driver.

If ever his daughter needed someone, it was now.

Come with me, she called.

Nora was falling, her hair blowing around her face, a small smile of contentment on her lips, falling endlessly toward the stone courtyard below.

Come with me.

"I'm afraid," Stephanie whispered.

Dying's easy, the falling girl said. She picked a Gauloises cigarette out of the swirling air and stuck it into her mouth. *It's living that's a bitch.*

She laughed, and the schoolgirl uniform she was wearing was replaced by a long white gown. Her arms were outstretched now, her body forming a cross, and the windblown hair above it was red as flame.

"Barbara? But you were—"

What difference does it make what our faces look like? We're both dead, remember? You killed us.

Stephanie gasped. "I didn't! You killed yourselves, both of you—"

You let Nora go to the roof. The falling figure sucked on her cigarette, its end glowing. *You knew it was dangerous, the roof.*

"Yes, yes . . . Sister Bernadette told me . . ."

And you couldn't keep me alive, either. Ingrate. I stopped you from biting the big one in the sanitarium. You could have returned the favor.

"I didn't want you to die, Barbara."

Then why didn't you stop me?

I couldn't find you.

Oliver Jordan did. Smoke streamed from between her painted lips. *You can imagine what he did with me.*

"Yes," Stephanie said. "I can imagine."

Are you glad you killed him?

Tears came involuntarily to Stephanie's eyes and spilled down her cheeks. "No." She shook her head. "I didn't want to kill anyone."

You'll burn in hell, you know. Barbara took another drag from the cigarette. When the smoke cleared, her face had become Sister Bernadette's, but with bright-orange lips. *Just like your mother. She was a whore, after all. The best in Paris.*

She cackled. The cigarette dangled from between the nun's lips. Her voluminous habit billowed as she fell. *The whore and the killer. Breeding tells. It's your blood, Stephanie. Bad blood. Bad, bad blood . . .*

Stephanie threw herself against the door of her room. Her breath was ragged. Sweat poured down her face. "Get away from me," she panted. "Oh God, make them go away."

Take it easy, kid. Like I said, life's a bitch.

Stephanie reached behind her for the doorknob. To her surprise, it opened. She tumbled out into the dormitory corridor like an animal running from an unseen predator.

No light. No light anywhere. No air. She lunged blindly for the double doors leading to the stairway.

Got to get away somehow. Got to breathe.

Stephanie . . .

"No!" she screamed, scrambling up the stairs on her hands and knees until she reached the roof.

Falling through the heavy door, she hit the pebbled surface with a solid whack. Behind her, an alarm bell sounded, but when the door closed, the shrill noise was muffled by the howling of the wind.

Air. Rain fell on her cheek, cooling it. She looked up. The sky was dark.

"No stars," she said aloud. There had been stars on the night Nora died.

Slowly, she stood up, wiping the rain out of her eyes.

Stephanie . . .

It was no more than the merest whisper, a catch in the wind. Gone now. She rubbed the gooseflesh on her arms. It was cold.

I love the cold, Nora had said.

Come up here with me.

It's almost like flying.

Like I said, kid, life's . . .

Stephanie slammed her hands over her ears.

. . . a bitch.

There was a long moment of silence. The wind died down. The rain stopped. Above, a few stars escaped the clouds and twinkled in the night.

Come to me, Stephanie. The voice was so smooth, so seductive.

Oliver Jordan smiled at her from the brick ledge surrounding the roof. His arms were outstretched. *I'll do wonderful things for you,* he said with a wink.

Slowly, she walked over to him.

That's a good girl. Now climb up here with me. That's right. Look at the stars.

She craned her neck. "They're out again."

You can come with me now, Nora said. *It's almost like flying.*

"I'm afraid . . ."

Dying's easy, Barbara laughed.

"But . . ."

Come to Uncle Oliver, Angel. You are my Angel now, aren't you? Just like Mama.

Stephanie teetered on the parapet.

She thinks she can help you by taking the blame for killing me, Jordan said, still smiling. *See how much good that's done. You're still one of us, Stephanie.*

"Maman!" she sobbed.

Still one of the dead.

The wind sighed, a song of despair that transformed slowly into the shrill ringing of the alarm as the heavy doors burst open, loud and intrusive and real. There were voices everywhere, not the still, certain voices of the dead, but chaotic shouts pitched high with confusion as all sorts of people poured onto the roof.

Their faces melted together in a blur as a man stepped out from among them to come to her. Stefan, the lines in his face etched deep with worry, was there. Stefan was always there. He scooped her up like a doll, hugging her fiercely.

"Listen to me," she said to him quickly, before the voices broke her resolve. "Maman didn't kill Oliver Jordan."

He held her at arm's length and looked into her eyes. "What did you say?"

"She didn't kill him." Stephanie's voice quavered. "I did." She felt his grip falter. "It's true. He tried to rape me. He had a gun. I took it and shot him with it." She turned away. "And I let Maman take the blame."

He moved away from her, studying her face. "Stephanie, are you—?"

"There was a witness. Maman made him promise to keep quiet to protect me."

"Oh my God." She heard Stefan's breath catch. "Oh my God."

She wiped her face with unsteady hands. The truth was urgent now, pressing against the burden of secrecy she had carried until it had almost destroyed her. The truth was waiting to meet the air and the light. "I need to see my mother."

Stefan took her hand, and a look of purest love passed from his eyes to hers. "We'll go to Berlin right away."

As they hurried toward the fire door leading inside the dormitory, she stopped suddenly. "Father?" she asked.

He turned his face to her. His expression was surprised at first, before it softened into understanding.

"That's me," he said.

"Do you . . . do you still love her?"

His eyes misted. "Yes," he said. "None of the rest matters a damn."

On the day Mireille was to be sentenced, she climbed up the courthouse steps, surrounded by a police escort. She had never spoken to the public defender assigned to her, never looked at the mail addressed to her, never accepted the phone calls and telegrams from anxious friends and acquaintances offering help. The procedure was of no consequence to her; whatever the judge decided, her life was over.

But Stephanie was safe. This time, she thought, maybe this time God would look down favorably. Maybe, through her own silence, her daughter would be spared the life her mother had led.

Reporters tried to thrust microphones through the police guard. Some people had come to jeer; they shouted obscenities in German near the entrance to the building, and bobbed placards reading "Murderer" and "Whore." And still there were the fans, weeping and screaming their undying adoration, as if she were Christ walking toward Calvary.

Go away! she wanted to shout at them. *You've followed me around too long. I never wanted you. I never wanted any of it.*

She regretted that West Germany had no death penalty. It would have spared her the trouble of killing herself.

"Mireille."

One voice stood out from the others. It was a soft voice, but at its sound, something stirred within her.

It was Jim Allerton. He was holding a bunch of flowers.

"Stop, please," Mireille said to the police guard. She smiled at Allerton.

He gave her the bouquet. They were wildflowers, lavender and heather and black-eyed Susans, flowers like those that had grown in a field long ago, where she had once loved a man with her whole heart.

"Mireille, please reconsider." His words choked in his throat.

"It will be all right, Jim," she said. "Thank you." She began to move away once more, but he caught her sleeve.

"I've always loved you," he blurted out.

"Yes, I know." She kissed him lightly on his cheek.

Flashbulbs popped. In the press of people around her as she walked into the building, the police had to take out clubs to ward off the crowd.

When they finally dispersed, Allerton saw the flowers lying crushed on the steps.

Mireille saw her daughter and Stefan as soon as she entered the courtroom. The state-appointed attorney stood nervously between them, his eyes glancing frequently at the door through which the judge was to enter.

"Oh my God, no," she gasped.

The guards, believing she feared the sentence, pushed her forward. Stefan caught her before she fell.

"Why have you come?" she asked him accusingly.

"I've told him," Stephanie said. "I'm going to tell everyone."

Mireille's face collapsed. "You don't know what you're doing!" Her voice broke.

"Yes, I do." Her daughter looked at her calmly. "I'm going to stop the lies, Maman. Yours and mine. I'm going to give us back our lives."

"Stephanie, I beg you—"

The judge entered. Those present in the courtroom inclined their heads in salute. Before Mireille was called forward to receive sentencing, the public defender rushed to the judge and asked him to meet with Stephanie in chambers.

"Don't listen to her!" Mireille pleaded.

The judge looked at her, then at Stephanie, before turning back to the young attorney. He nodded once, curtly.

Mireille collapsed on a chair and sobbed.

Chapter Sixty-Nine

Six weeks later, Stephanie and Mireille emerged together from the courthouse doors. Photographers blocked their way. Reporters shouted questions at them.

Mireille had heard them all a thousand times before. They had nothing to do with the matter of her innocence in Jordan's death, or of Stephanie's startling testimony. That news had died after a few days. What the reporters wanted were more details about Mireille's unsavory past.

"Did you really sleep with the president of France?"

"Who is Stephanie's father?"

"Is it true Oliver Jordan discovered you in a bordello?"

The questions still made the hair at the back of her neck prickle. But she had made progress. Not long ago, she thought, she would have paid any price, even her life, to keep her daughter from hearing them.

But Stephanie had changed everything. Stephanie, who had used the truth to fight her demons and conquer them, who had wrestled Mireille's life back for her and given her a peace she had never known before.

My daughter, she thought with pride.

She cast a quick glance at her now as they marched deftly through the crowd of newspeople. Stephanie was beautiful, a confident girl, comfortable with herself and leagues above the cruel questions these strangers hurled at them like stones.

This is truly fortune's child, Mireille thought. This girl would never allow fear to twist her life into a caricature of happiness. This girl would make her own destiny.

As if reading her thoughts, Stephanie turned toward her and smiled. "Come on," she said gently. "I want to take you somewhere."

She led her mother to the train station, where two locomotives headed in different directions shuddered to life. A throng of people jostled around them, hurrying to board.

"Why are we here?" Mireille shouted to be heard over the noise.

"It's a surprise." Stephanie looked around. "And here it comes."

At the far end of the platform walked a man carrying a small suitcase. He moved with an awkward sort of grace, the gait of a man who had lost a leg, yet no longer noticed the loss.

"Stefan," Mireille whispered.

He slowed to a stop.

"Go ahead, Maman," Stephanie prodded.

Mireille started toward him hesitantly. So much had happened. So much loss, so many regrets. The girl who had loved him in Champs de Blé was gone forever; the movie star who had found him in New York had been exposed for the liar she was.

Who was she now? A woman approaching middle age; her career over, tainted by disgrace; publicly ridiculed and gossiped about behind her back.

She had not been surprised when Stefan flew back to New York after his brief testimony to the judge. He had shown her the greatest kindness by accompanying Stephanie to Berlin. He had helped Mireille even though she had never asked for his help. He had helped her despite the fact that she had repaid his love and faithfulness with unpardonable betrayal when she left him for Oliver Jordan without explanation. Stefan had helped her solely because she had needed help. If afterward he left as soon as he could get away, she understood. He deserved a better life than she could give him. Mireille was grateful for all he had done, and she had not expected more.

Now she wanted to turn away, to get lost in the crowd, to take her daughter and leave this place before he could offer her his pity. She looked over her shoulder at Stephanie. The girl smiled at her reassuringly. Stephanie had walked through fire. She would not be afraid of facing the truth, no matter how bitter.

Mireille set her shoulders. *All right, then,* she thought. She would not run from Stefan. She would not run from anything again.

"Hello, Mireille," he said in his gentle way.

She swallowed. "Thank you for everything, Stefan. Stephanie's been acquitted."

"I know. I got back to Berlin yesterday."

"Oh." She blushed. She could think of nothing more to say.

So this is how it ends, she thought. With the polite smiles strangers give one another.

She started to back away. "Well, I think I ought to—"

"I had to go back to New York to quit my job," he said.

For a moment she could only stare at him. "You did?" she asked at last. "What are you going to do now?"

He smiled. "I thought I'd visit Paris for a while."

"Paris . . ." How many times had she promised Stephanie a trip to Paris? Like so many other things, it had never come to pass.

"Will you come with me?" he asked quietly.

She blinked. "Me?"

"And Stephanie. A delayed family vacation."

She laughed nervously. "Delayed by eighteen years," she said.

"Is it too late?"

She had to think. Why was he asking her such questions? "I don't know," she said honestly.

"Are you afraid to find out?"

She looked into his eyes for a long moment, then shook her head. "No, I'm not afraid."

He grinned. "In that case, I've got something for you."

He took out the engagement ring he had bought years before, when they had shared an apartment in New York with Stephanie. When they had been a family. "I've been waiting a long time to give this to you."

Tears filled Mireille's eyes.

"Don't take it if you don't want it," he said. "It won't change how I feel. Nothing ever has."

"Stefan . . ." She faltered. "How can you still love me?"

His eyes met hers, just as they had so long ago, before the world had frightened them out of their souls. "How can I not?"

He took her hand and placed the ring on her finger. "This is our beginning." He kissed her softly, and she drew her arms around him.

"I love you," she said.

A whistle blew. Stephanie stood at the train doors, beckoning them frantically.

Stefan grabbed her hand. "We'd better run if we're going to make the train." He broke into a trot. Mireille kept pace with him, weaving her way between the press of bodies.

"Hurry," Stephanie yelled.

"We'll get there," Mireille shouted back.

And they would, she knew. All three of them, the lovers and the child born of their love.

Mireille ran, laughing, into the future, her eyes so blinded by tears of joy that the milling crowd of people around them seemed no longer to exist. They were flowers in a field, and the new day was young.

Epilogue

1993

Jim Allerton got out of the rented car and shielded his eyes against the sun.

"Look for the funny house," the locals had told him.

A funny house. Great. At this point, after driving all night from Paris on unmarked country roads, everything looked pretty funny.

Still, the building behind the wall of shrubbery did look funnier than most. Which was to say it was a modern structure in an area of France where most of the buildings measured their age in centuries.

As he walked closer, he recognized it at once. This particular house had never been photographed, but its style was unmistakably that of Stefan Giroux. He had designed fewer than twenty buildings during his career, yet each of them was considered an architectural masterpiece. This was, too, even though the house was somewhat incongruously surrounded by a white fence and sported a red door.

Said to be somewhat of a recluse, Giroux rarely gave interviews. The one exception was for *Portfolio* magazine, which featured an article about his daughter. Stephanie, whose paintings now commanded astronomical prices, was rapidly becoming a grande dame in European art circles.

Allerton smiled to himself as he opened the trunk of the car. Who would ever have guessed that their lives would turn out the way they had? Allerton himself was a respected novelist whose screenwriting past was rarely mentioned in the reviews that compared him with Kafka and Pynchon. *Field of Glory* was known only to film buffs; the master print of *Josephine* had been destroyed in a fire; the unedited footage for *Filigree*, never completed, was lost in a warehouse somewhere. Its decomposition by now would be too severe to repair.

Gone. All those years, gone forever.

The painting in the trunk of the car had been wrapped in specially treated paper inside a wooden box for the journey. Carefully, Allerton loosened the screws of the box and unfolded the paper wrapping. The first thing he saw was the title, scrawled across the bottom: *Fortune's Child.*

Even though he had seen it before, his breath still caught at the sight of the sleeping white-haired girl.

He had bought it at an auction near Richmond for next to nothing. The auctioneer had not mentioned that it was a portrait of Mireille. Perhaps he hadn't known. More likely, though, it wouldn't have mattered if he had.

No one remembered her. She had made seven films in eight years, and all of them had been banned from release in any medium after her arrest. The ban was eventually lifted, but by then the adoring public had shifted its interest to other faces, other names. Mireille had been a shooting star, a comet that illuminated the sky with its brilliance one moment and was gone the next.

But he could see her still. For nearly thirty years Allerton had carried the image of his last sight of her on the courthouse steps in Berlin. He had given her a bunch of flowers that had scattered in the wind. He had watched the legend die.

For her, he had come four thousand miles, unannounced, with a painting from her youth.

Delicately, he lifted the framed watercolor out of its box and walked with it toward the house. A woman wearing a wide-brimmed straw hat was kneeling in a flower bed, plowing industriously into the black earth with a hand trowel.

How she's changed, Allerton thought. She was sixty-four years old now. Still lovely, of course—nothing could make that face anything but beautiful—but no one who knew Mireille would recognize this woman as the screen goddess who had set every man's heart afire.

He was about to call to her, then stopped when he saw an old man limping across the lawn. When the man reached Mireille, he placed his hands lovingly on her shoulders. The woman looked up at him and smiled. Even with the distance between then, Allerton could see the love in that smile.

No, he realized, the movie star wasn't Mireille. This woman was. And it would be very rude of him indeed to disturb this woman's happy life.

Slowly, he walked back to the car and placed the painting back inside the box.

Mireille didn't need it. She had everything she'd ever wanted.

Acknowledgments

Many thanks to Rechtsanwalt Johann Wurm of Berlin for his invaluable information about German law; to Eva Lohnas for helping me with German translations; to Sean Dwyer, for assistance with the French language; to my fabulous agent and stalwart friend Laurence Kirshbaum, who has always been on my side, and whose ideas, attention, and care have made this book immeasurably better; to David Downing for his superb, sensitive editing; to Elizabeth Johnson, for giving my manuscript the best copyedit I've ever seen; to Terry Goodman, who took a chance on this book, even though he didn't need to take any more chances; and to Megan Murphy, for remembering something important that I should never have forgotten.

About the Author

Molly Cochran is the author of more than twenty novels and nonfiction books, including the *New York Times* bestseller *Grandmaster*, *The Forever King*, *The Broken Sword*, and *The Temple Dogs*, all cowritten with Warren Murphy. She is also the author of *The Third Magic*, and she cowrote the nonfiction bestseller *Dressing Thin* with Dale Goday. Cochran has received numerous awards, including the Mystery Writers of America's Edgar Award, the Romance Writers of America's "Best Thriller" award, and an "Outstanding" classification by the New York Public Library. Recently, she published a series of young-adult novels, *Legacy*, *Poison*, and *Seduction*, and two novellas, *Wishes* and *Revels*. *Legacy* won a 2013 Westchester Fiction Award.

Visit her at mollycochran.com.